EVIE MITCHELL

Thor's Shipbuilding Series

Volume 1 Box Set

First published by Thunder Thighs Publishing 2021

Copyright © 2021 by Evie Mitchell

First edition

ISBN: 978-1-922561-01-5

Proofreading by Geeky Girl Author Services
Editing by Nicole Wilson, Evermore Editing
Cover art by Tash Drake, Outlined with Love Designs

This book was professionally typeset on Reedsy.
Find out more at reedsy.com

Contents

II Clean Sweep

III The X-List

IV   Reality Check

V   The Christmas Contract

Books by Evie Mitchell

Capricorn Cove Series
Thunder Thighs
Double the D
Muffin Top
The Mrs. Clause
New Year Knew You
The Shake-Up
Double Breasted
As You Wish
Beach Party
You Sleigh Me
Resolution Revolution
Meat Load
Trunk Junk

Archer Series
Just Joshing
He wants Candy
Leave Me Bea
Pride and Joy
Tom and Jeremey

Thor's Shipbuilding Series
Clean Sweep

The X-list
Reality Check
The Christmas Contract

Nameless Souls MC Series
Runner
Wrath
Ghost

Elliot Security Series
Rough Edge
Bleeding Edge
Knife Edge

Other books
Reign Anthology - The Marriage Contract
Puppy Love
Pier Pressure
Bad English

Connect with Evie Mitchell

Website
www.EvieMitchell.com

Newsletter
https://www.subscribepage.com/z2p2x3

Amazon
https://www.amazon.com/author/eviemitchell

Bookbub, Instagram and Facebook
@EvieMitchellAuthor

Facebook Group
Evie Mitchell's Greedy Reader Book Club

Dedication

To my husband,
2020 was batshit crazy and yet here we are.
Together. Happy. Still in love.
There wasn't even a threat of divorce!
I'd say we're #CoupleGoals.
Love you!

I

Thunder Thighs

Thunder Thighs

Ella

I'd always been told I had thunder thighs. Chunky, thick, beautiful—I embraced my curves, just waiting for the right Thunder God to come along and rock my world. Then Gunnar Larsson strode his tall, blonde Viking butt through my bar doors. My thighs were awaiting his plunder.

Gunnar

Walking into Ella Bronze's bar was the best decision I'd made all year. Fuck, all decade. The gorgeous bombshell had curves for days—the kind that made me drool. There was no way this seductive siren was escaping. Looked like it was time to do what my ancestors did best—take what I wanted.

Warning: This over-the-top piece of fluff is inspired by big thighs, sexy Vikings, and a desire to have your pussy plundered. Get thee a Viking and settle in—this instalove story will blow you right off course.

Chapter One

Gunnar

I stepped through the door of the first bar I'd found in this pokey seaside town, thunder crackling behind me. A surprisingly classy sign identified it as the Bronze Horseman; the words hung above the door in a flourish of steel and light. The overpowering smell of meat had drawn me inside. The scent of smoked meat was entirely too tempting when my damn stomach was already eating itself.

The heavy wood door slammed closed behind me, shutting out the sounds of the approaching storm. I paused, taking in the surroundings. The bar was busy but not crushed. A glance showed locals and tourists filled the booths and tables, chatting quietly or listening to the band on the far stage.

I'd docked late, babying my ship to the closest port. A storm had come on fast, and the rough waves had fucked with the engine. It'd shit itself just as I'd docked. An hour of playing with it had revealed a blown gasket. I'd have to seek parts in the morning.

I'd rinsed off the grease and grit and gone in search of food.

It was after ten. I'd assumed my chances in a small town like Capricorn Cove wouldn't be good—but it was tourist season, and this sleepy little town looked to be hopping.

Maybe my luck had turned.

I made my way to the bar, noting the tasteful décor. Rich wood, leather, and bronze, all offset by navy blue and hunter green highlights. The place had had some money pumped into it.

Two men were sitting at the far end of the bar, heads bent together as they shared a meal. I slid onto a stool at the other end, snatching a menu from the closest stack. The menu informed me they served food till twelve. Perfect.

"What can I get you, Viking?"

The words were delivered in the huskiest, sexiest voice I'd ever heard. My cock immediately hardened, and I hadn't even seen the face that delivered that sucker punch.

I looked up. Thick pouty lips, long lashes ringing satin brown eyes, soft, full cheeks, and big cascading brunette curls. My dick, already impossibly hard, pressed insistently against my fly.

Mine.

My gaze dropped, taking in the overly generous cleavage playing peek-a-boo with the v of her shirt.

Fuck.

She tilted her head, nodding at the menu. "See anything you like?"

"You." The word slipped free before I could think.

She laughed, sending that mass of hair shimmering. "I'm not normally on the menu." She leaned forward, her shirt shifting down, giving me a tantalizing glimpse of her lacy bra. "But for you? I may make an exception," she winked, and I felt that deep in my gut.

Who'd have thought I'd be thanking the sea Gods for a busted engine?

"I'm Ella Bronze." She absently brushed a thick chunk of hair back.

"And you are?"

"Gunnar Larsson."

Her cheeks pinkened. "Oh, I was right. You really are a Viking."

I grunted, shifting in my seat. "What do you recommend?" I asked, trying to distract my cock. At this rate, I'd be coming from one fucking smile.

She leaned back over the bar, her tits pressing against the wood as she reached out, tapping one of the menu items.

"Get the fully loaded burger. It's my favorite," she slid off the bar, turning her back to me and bending over to pull a bottle from the back fridge.

Her ass was fucking perfection. Big, curvy, framed by thick thighs that I wanted clasped around my head while I licked her sweet cunt until she creamed on my tongue.

I am a sick fuck.

"Here," she popped the cap, sliding the beer across the bar. "On the house."

I took a sip, eyes on her.

"Good?" she asked.

"Fucking perfect," I growled.

A wickedly seductive smile decorated her perfect lips. We both knew I hadn't been talking about the beer. A man down the far end called her name, interrupting our moment.

"Be right back," she promised.

I watched her sashay away, taking another long drag of

the cool beer. If I played my cards right, I'd be leaving here with more than one hunger satisfied.

Don't you dare fuck this up.

I lifted the beer again, drinking deep.

Chapter Two

Ella

He's here.

I stood in the cooler for a moment, patting my flushed cheeks. For years my family had made comments about my big thighs. Thunder thighs, they'd called them. Big, bold, and ready to crush the first man that dared to get between them.

Years ago, I decided to say fuck it. I'd played them at their own game, owning that narrative. I'd laughed at their criticism, claiming I had thighs so big no mere mortal could lie between them. My thighs could call down the God of Thunder. My thighs were magic.

I owned thighs only a Viking God could plunder.

He's here.

No man had been between them. Maybe I'd bought into my daydream a little too much. Maybe I'd been so caught up in the fantasy that I'd lost sight of reality.

But damn. He was here. He had finally arrived. And on a rumble of thunder, no less. If that wasn't a sign, I didn't know what was.

My nipples were tight, my breasts heavy. Warm desire pooled in my belly, my pussy wet with want.

He's here.

I took a deep breath, smoothing damp palms down my skirt.

"You got this, Ella. You're hot as fuck. You're sexy. You own this damn bar and have made it successful. You are confident, brilliant, funny. If he doesn't want you, then it's his loss."

I remembered the way he looked at me, his dark eyes practically eating me up as we chatted. I had a feeling he wouldn't say no. I had a feeling he'd be taking me to bed tonight.

Or maybe he'll just throw you over the bar.

A shiver of anticipation raced down my spine. I snatched at the small container of pre-cut lemons, returning to the bar.

"Foods up," my chef, Anika, called.

"Got it," I shifted the container under one arm, lifting the warm plate with my free hand.

"Saw him," Anika wiggled her eyebrows, a grin stretching her mouth.

"You gonna take a chance on this one?" she asked. I sent her a wink in reply.

She threw back her head, laughing. "You go, girl!"

I dropped the lemons on the back of the bar, heading toward the hottie at the end. He was nursing his beer, gaze on me. I added a little sway to my walk, feeling that crackling awareness spark between us once more.

"Here you go," I slid the plate in front of him.

"Eat up, big boy." He glanced down at the plate, his

eyebrows lifting.

"This is—"

"Delicious," I promised.

The burger was three types of smoked meat, topped with melted cheese, pickles, onions, and delicious house mustard and ketchup. Anika and I had worked hard to develop the perfect menu.

He took a bite, and I watched as surprise decorated his face.

"Fuck," he muttered. "This is good." He took another bite.

I grinned, deriving an unexpected pleasure from his enjoyment. One of my barmaids caught my attention, and I left him, returning to work. I tried to calm the thrum of anticipation that pulsed through my veins.

I mixed drinks, took orders, and counted down each agonizing minute to close, praying Gunnar would stay.

Please stay.

He did, nursing a second beer, watching me with a dark, thoughtful expression.

An hour before close, Anika came out, dusting her hands on her apron.

"Still here?" she whispered, leaning on the bar beside me. I kept wiping the sticky surface, trying not to glance at him for the millionth time tonight.

"Yes," my voice sounded breathy, light.

"How about you head off? I can close up tonight." Anika nodded at the mostly empty room. "Go have fun."

She tilted her head down to where Drake Andrews and Dane Butler sat, finishing their meals. "I'm hoping to talk them into making me the meat in that deliciously built sandwich."

I rolled my eyes. "You know they're into Blue McKenney."

"Doesn't mean I can't try to change their mind." She reached out, spanking me on the butt. "Go! Get out of here, woman!"

I laughed, jumping away from her. "Thanks, see you tomorrow."

I grabbed my purse from storage and sashayed my way out from behind the bar. Gunnar's dark eyes tracked me as I approached, and I shivered with awareness.

"Hey," I slid onto a barstool beside him, trying to calm my nerves. "You want some company?"

He smiled, lazy and slow. "If that company is you, then always."

That spark crackled between us again; the attraction undeniable. I looked away, nodding at Anika, who sat a beer before me with a wink.

"Your friend?" Gunnar asked, nodding at Anika's retreating back.

"And business partner." I tipped the bottle toward the kitchen. "I had the capital and property; she had the restaurant experience."

"Well, I can safely say this is one of the nicest bars I've ever stumbled into."

I chuckled. He leaned toward me, easily bridging the gap between us. His scent teased my nose, salt, sweat, and a little musk. I looked my fill, taking in the broad cut of his shoulders, the barrel of his chest, his trunk-like legs. A mountain of a man, he made me feel dainty and small—a not so easy feat.

I'd been born curvy. My body was built big and beautiful—and no amount of exercise or dieting was going to change my shape. I'd long since learned to love my curves, accentuating them and finding pleasure in the way my body moved. I'd grown up in Capricorn Cove, compared constantly to the sun-bleached blondes with slim limbs and tanned skin. I hadn't minded. I'd been different, unique. But my body wasn't in fashion, which meant the crossover between boys who wanted me and my attraction to them was minuscule.

I had a feeling that this God of a man before me, that he'd embrace my curves, showing them the love and appreciation I'd always held out for.

"Do you stumble into a lot of bars?" I asked, genuinely curious about this man.

"No." He grinned, slow and easy. "My brother and I co-own a boat building company. Inherited it from our dad after he retired. It keeps me busy."

I tilted my head, frowning. "I've never seen you in town before."

"I'm on holiday. Decided to take a trip around the coast. Saw the storm coming in and had to find a port to wait it out. Engine crapped itself just as I docked. Expect I'll be here for a while waiting for her to blow over and for some replacement parts to arrive." He leaned in, his hand shifting to rest beside mine on the bar. He ran a finger lightly over my pinkie. That single touch sent all my nerves firing, delicious pleasure settling low in my abdomen.

"Maybe the God of thunder was looking out for me."

A blush heated my cheeks. "Why do you say that?"

He closed the distance between us, his big hand cupping my cheek. He eased in, pausing a half hair from my mouth.

"Because I'm looking at an honest to God Valkyrie. And

I'm praying she's here to take me to Valhalla." His lips covered mine.

The kiss started out chaste. Just a pressing of skin to skin, his hand warm against my cheek. But it quickly escalated, his lips seducing mine, tilting my head this way and that for better access. His tongue teased mine, wet, hot, and achingly demanding. I fell into a cloud of desire, asking for more, wanting more, desperate for him to take all that I had to give.

He eased back; his eyes molten. "You wanna go to my yacht or your place?"

"Mine's closer," I answered without hesitation. I slipped from the barstool, leading him through the bar to the door.

The heavens had finally opened, rain poured down, thunder and lightning crackling around us, electrifying the air.

"Come on," I snatched his hand, pulling him into the downpour. We ran, him following me, around the back of the bar to the small cottage at the far end of the property. We stomped up the cottage steps, pausing on the stoop so I could unlock the door. I pushed through, spilling into the small entry, laughter filling the silent room.

We dripped on the wood floorboards.

"Lights?" he asked.

I reached out, flicking the switch. Nothing happened. I frowned, trying again.

"Damn, power must be out," I muttered, kicking off my shoes.

"Was fine in the bar."

"We have our own generator." I headed to the kitchen, pulling out the drawer I'd dedicated for just this kind of situation. "Here," I handed him a torch. "Hold that while I

13

light the candles."

I walked around the living and dining areas, lighting the multiple candles already sitting in hurricane glasses.

"You get power outages often?" Gunnar asked, switching off the torch as the warm candle glow lit the room.

"Often enough to be prepared."

"But you don't have a generator?"

"No, the bar came first. I'll get one, eventually." I blew out the flame on the long match stick, discarding it to the side.

"There," I dusted my hands on my wet skirt. "We should probably get out of these clothes." I pulled my top away from my body with a grimace.

"You got anything I can wear?" he asked.

I quirked a smile. "I may have a dress or two."

He followed me to the linen cupboard.

"Here," I handed him a towel. "Shower is through there." I nodded at the door across the hall.

He headed over, pausing in the doorway. "You coming?"

My breath caught.

You coming?

So easy. As if everything before this moment hadn't already been a life-changing event.

"Y-you want me to—?" I gestured to the bathroom.

"Oh, yeah." He turned to lean against the doorjamb. My gaze flicked down, noting the giant bulge at his crotch. His wet clothes did nothing to conceal it from me. A crack of lightning outside briefly lit the interior of the house. Smashing thunder followed, so loud it rattled the frames on my wall.

Well, you heard the God.

I tried to inject careless confidence into my movement,

brazening my way through this moment. This was unchartered waters for me. Kissing I could do. Getting naked? Not so much.

He shifted, allowing me to pass by, our bodies brushing. That spark crackled between us, the awareness filling the space.

"Take it off," he ordered, crossing his arms, watching me.

I hesitated for only a moment before my hands dropped to my waist, pulling the shirt free of my skirt. I lifted it, peeling the wet material from my body, and tossing it aside, leaving me in a black bra.

Gunnar huffed out a groan. "Now, the skirt."

My body trembled as my hands fumbled with the zipper. I drew it down, pushing the material over my hips, wiggling to get the saturated material free.

My panties, black cotton boy-shorts, were all that kept him from seeing me.

He moved, ripping his shirt free, his hands immediately jerking down his fly to push off his jeans. The material clung to his body, slowing his actions.

He wasn't wearing underwear.

Gunnar wasn't wearing underwear.

Omg. He wasn't wearing underwear!

I choked, aware I was staring as his cock bounced free. The massive member suited his body shape. Large, thick, and completely in proportion with the rest of him. It jutted out proudly, and I was suddenly aware of the differences between us. He was carved stone, beautiful and rough. I was pillowy abundance, curvy and soft. Even our skins contrasted, mine startlingly pale against his deep tan.

"Bra," Gunnar barked, kicking free of his clothes. "Leave

the underwear."

I blinked, tearing my gaze away from his cock. "Leave the—"

"You want me to fuck you in the shower or on the bed?"

Heat pooled in my belly, desire sending sparks straight down to that hidden part of me.

"Bed," I whispered.

"Then you better leave them on, Ella."

My heart thumped in my chest, my body feeling both heavy and alert as uncertainty, anticipation, and desire warred for supremacy.

Gunnar reached into the small shower stall, turning on the water. He tested the temperature, adjusting before being satisfied with the setting. He gestured for me to enter. I stepped past him, immediately sighing as the warm water cascaded over my skin, chasing the slight chill away. He crowded in behind me, dwarfing the space, his naked chest pressing against my back.

"I need a taste," his guttural groan sent shivers down my spine. I moved to turn, but his hands fell to my hips, pinning me in place.

"No," he barked. "Hands on the wall."

I complied, pressing my palms against the tiles, shifting to spread my legs.

"Good girl," he whispered, one hand trailing down my spine. He adjusted the spray, so it fell down my back.

"Gunnar?" I whispered, feeling myself tremble. "I haven't done this before."

His hands, moving in soothing slow circles up and down my back, paused. "Shower sex?"

"Any of this," I admitted, closing my eyes. "I'm a virgin."

He stayed silent and still for a long moment.

I opened my eyes, staring at the tile, heat flushing my cheeks. "Say something," I whispered.

"You want this?"

"Yes."

"You want me to take your hot little snatch?"

I shivered at his dirty words. "Yes."

His hands shifted down, gripping my hips, pulling me back against him. "Don't worry, baby." One hand came up, tilting my chin so I could look at him. "I'll make this good for you."

He kissed me, rough, hard, hot. Tongues tangled, wet and wanting as he took from me, giving me no escape, no option but to surrender to his lips.

I loved it.

He broke the kiss, immediately pressing hot lips to my neck, my shoulder. Fingers trailed down my sides, one hand shifted to my bottom, his hand gripping the cheek of my ass.

I mewed, begging for something, anything, more.

"Shhh," he whispered, gently nipping at my shoulder. "I'll give it to you."

His hands slid over the lace, rounding my side to dip into the underwear at the front. His finger, his clever, clever fingers slipped down, tracing my outer lips.

"You've been a bad girl, Ella." His hot mouth brushed against my ear, shudders wracking my body from the pleasure. "You do this," he pressed fingers against my naked pussy, "for someone?"

"The B-Brazilian?" I stuttered, eyes closed, my body arching as I pressed back into him.

"Mm." He traced my lips again with light, teasing fingers.

"N-n-no." I stuttered, lost in the pleasure. "For me."

"Good answer."

I gasped as his fingers parted me, touching me in a way no one ever had. His fingers dipped into my slickness, dancing across my clit, pulling curses and praises in equal measure from my lips.

"More," I begged, pressing myself into his fingers. "Please, Gunnar."

He chuckled, "I've got you, baby."

He removed his hand from my hip, sliding it up to play with my erect nipple. The other remained at my core, fingers teased my clit, tantalizing me, dipping, dragging, corrupting me until I couldn't stand the spiraling tension.

"Please!"

He pressed hard against my clit, circling once, twice, a third time as I shattered under him, my cries filling the small stall as my body bowed, the orgasm sending me spiraling. I collapsed against the tile, legs unsteady, body shaking in the aftermath.

"Shhh," Gunnar soothed, his rough voice reassuring. "I've got you, baby."

I pressed my cheek against the cool tile, struggling to find my way back to reality—my new reality. The reality that a man had pulled from me with skillful fingers and little effort, something I had only ever done for myself.

The water turned off, leaving us standing in the shower.

"Come on," Gunnar helped me out. He had me stand still while he quickly ran a towel over himself, wrapping it low around his hips before he turned back to me. He ran the fluffy fabric over my skin, pausing to catch every drop of water. He wrapped my hair, long, thick, and heavy with water, in another towel.

18

I allowed him to look after me, letting him move my body in whatever way he required. I'd never had anyone look after me like this before.

He pulled back, taking my hand. "Come on, let's go to—"

My stomach rumbled, interrupting his comment. I blushed.

"Hungry?" Gunnar asked, his lips twitching.

"I skipped dinner tonight," I admitted.

"Go get dressed. I'll see what I can rummage up for you." He pulled me close, my breasts pressing against his chest as he pressed a soft kiss to my lips. "Let's get you fed."

Chapter Three

Gunnar

I heard Ella moving about in her bedroom while I dug through her pantry and fridge. The towel sat low on my hips, my cock tenting the front. I readjusted, trying to calm the beast that raged within me. The candles positioned around the house filled the space with warm, flickering light. Outside, the storm continued to rage, thunder and lightning battling for supremacy.

Ella's pantry was surprisingly well stocked. I pulled my ingredients out, laying them on her kitchen island. I whisked eggs, cinnamon, vanilla, milk, and a pinch of sugar together, pouring it into a flat pan. Putting aside the mix, I sliced thick pieces of sourdough, dipping them, then laying them flat on a heated pan.

"That smells good," Ella said as she entered the room. I paused mid-flip, my mouth immediately watering as I watched her move toward me. She'd dried her hair, letting it fall freely around her face in a messy tangle. She wore a printed kimono, which she'd left untied at the front. Her body was encased in a black slip, the lace and satin clinging provocatively to every dip and curve. I wanted to peel it off and taste every inch of her.

"What?" she glanced down, hands hovering above her stomach. "Do I have something on here? I had to pull it out of storage. I'm not normally a lingerie sort of girl, so it may have some dust—"

I pulled her into me, my mouth descending on hers. She fell into the kiss, letting me take, willingly following me down any path I chose to lead. This level of trust, of blind innocence, it was a heady, powerful thing.

And so goddamned terrifying. I wanted this to be good for her. Wanted her to enjoy every moment. I needed to make this perfect.

I'd never believed in love at first sight. Hell, I hadn't even been convinced that love really existed. But this pull between us was undeniable. The longer I spent with her, the more I became convinced that this was more than just lust or infatuation. Ella made me consider things I hadn't ever turned my mind to before. Things like, maybe these feelings between us weren't simply sexual. Maybe I'd found my soul mate. The fact was, I'd known this woman less than four hours, and here I stood in her kitchen considering the possibility of settling down, of making a life here with her.

My family would laugh themselves silly if they could see me right now. I wasn't exactly known as Mister Love. Decisive, sure. Stoic, of course. The kind to fall head-over-heels for a woman I'd just met? Definitely not.

I broke the kiss, turning back to the stove just in time to rescue the toast.

"What are you making?" Ella asked, coming up beside me.

"French toast with maple bananas."

"Can I help?"

"Sure, can you slice the banana?"

She turned away, moving to the kitchen island. We worked in companionable silence for a few minutes, me cooking the toast, her slicing and transferring the bananas to the waiting pan.

"One minute each side," I explained, flipping the slices. "Then we'll coat with a generous glug of maple and done."

"Glug, huh?" She leaned on the counter beside me, grin in place. "Is that an official measurement?"

I winked. "Just you wait." I held up the maple bottle, tipping it over the pan. An air bubble formed in the neck and bubbled up, making a glug sound as the liquid squeezed past.

"No way!" Ella exclaimed. "I have honestly never noticed that."

"It's a Viking trade secret," I told her solemnly, holding the spatula to my chest. "We only divulge it to the most beautiful of Valkyries."

She laughed, her beautiful eyes dancing with mirth. "I swear to take it to my grave then."

I divided up the food, decorating the toast with maple and banana pieces. We took a seat at her breakfast bar, digging into the syrupy mess.

"Oh, God," Ella groaned, closing her eyes. "This is divine. I should totally add it to our menu."

I grinned, enjoying her pleasure. We ate, talking about nothing in particular.

"Columbia, I got my business degree, then got the hell out," I told her. "I fucking hated college. Hated studying. I'm better with the practical. You?"

"Community college. It's about an hour from here. Hospitality and business," she grinned. "I always knew I wanted to make a go of it here. People are searching for the quaint, quiet spots they remember from their childhoods—but with all the amenities they expect as an adult. I inherited this property from my grandmother. We built the restaurant, and it's doing really well." She leaned forward, her slip dipping just enough to reveal the shadow of her nipples. "And I love this town. The ocean, the people. I can't really see myself living elsewhere. Even a few years away from here would have been too many."

"I feel you," I replied, ignoring my cock that now tented the towel once more. "I'd get home every chance I got. I grew up on boats and beaches. It felt like a part of me was missing while living on campus."

"The Hudson didn't do it for you?" she teased, her hand reaching out to squeeze my knee.

I captured her fingers, entwining them with mine. "I doubt anyone would think the Hudson was a substitute for a great beach." I rested our hands on the towel covering my thigh. "So, what's next for you? Expansion?"

"Actually, the property is so large that this year we've been doing brunch in the yard. It's taken off enough to justify opening for lunch and breakfast next year in addition to the evening hours. We've seen more competition this year with new joints opening. Still, we're a tried and true local with a stellar reputation and the local connections to get all the best produce," she laughed. "I'm also toying with the idea of buying a few more properties. There are three along the cliff road—all outdated and needing repairs—but their owners are getting on and thinking of selling. They have amazing views, which would be a real seller. I was considering maybe snapping up a few and doing them up as holiday homes. Offer them with a package catering deal for weddings."

"Well, shit. That's not a business, that's an empire you're building." I pressed a kiss to the back of her hand. "I'm loving that you're as ambitious as me."

She flushed but didn't look away. We gazed at each other, caught in the connection.

"Baby," I whispered after a long moment.

"Mmm?"

"Get on the counter."

Her eyebrows rose in surprise. "Excuse me?"

"Hop up on the counter."

"But," she tilted her head. "Why?"

I slid off the stool, pulling my towel free. My cock sprang up, ready and rearing to go. "Because I want to eat that pussy."

Her gaze dropped to my cock. Her lips parted, her eyes glazing over.

Fuck yes. This is one hell of a woman.

I was about to lose my patience and lift her up myself when she sank to her knees.

"Ella, what are you—?" I started worried I'd misread this.

"I wanna taste," she muttered, reaching a hand out to my cock. She hesitated, looking up at me. "Is this okay?"

"Fuck yes, baby." It took all my goddamned willpower to keep still. "You take what you want."

I had to admit, I didn't get BJ's as often as I'd like. The fact is, I'm a big guy. I'd once had a woman tell me I was what she referred to as a Mountain of Man. Rough, big, and

24

broad, I intimidated people. I'd had women take one look at me and run the other way. Coupled with a few weeks of hair growth and some less than stellar interpersonal skills, I wasn't exactly the first pick for most people.

Sure, I'd gotten lucky more than a few times. When a size queen wanted to see if my cock matched the rest of me, or I'd spent a while pursuing someone, they may take me to bed. But most took one look at my cock, how thick it was, how long, and completely dismissed the possibility of sucking it.

But Ella hadn't balked. She'd taken one look at me and liked what she'd seen.

I watched as she settled on her knees, her hand wrapping around the base of my cock as she considered me. She licked her lips, a slight frown in place.

Okay, baby?" I asked, my body tense.

"Yeah, just—working it out," she muttered.

"Working—" I broke off, a mangled groan bursting from my throat as she leaned forward, taking hold of me in one quick slide. The heat of her mouth, the drag of her tongue, the warmth enveloping my cock.

Valhalla. Heaven. Nirvana.

I didn't care what name you assigned this pleasure. All I knew was that I never wanted this to end.

Ella drew back, one hand reaching up to brush hair from her face.

"Let me," I grunted, wrangling the movement from my body. I reached down, fisting her hair, pulling it back from her face. She moaned a little as my fingers delved into the thick mass, massaging her scalp.

"You like that?" I whispered, testing the waters a little.

"So much," she panted.

I pulled back on the hair in my fist, just enough to add a small bite of tension.

She groaned, enthusiastically surging forward against my pull, mouth desperately sucking me back in.

It seemed as if my girl liked a little pain with her pleasure. *Fuck, I love that. Perfect for me.*

She sucked and swallowed, her hand stroking the base of my cock while her lips and tongue drove me crazy. She pulled back, tonguing my crown, finding that sensitive spot on the underside.

"Fuck," I panted, holding her head still as my hips jerked, my cock thrusting in and out of her willing mouth. "Gonna come, baby. Tap my leg if you want me to pull out."

She didn't. She kept up her pace, hungry, wanton sounds escaping her throat.

"Fuck!" I exploded into her mouth, cum hitting the back of her throat. She swallowed it down with a small hum of pleasure.

"Jesus Christ," I collapsed back on the stool, hand stroking her hair. "Fuck."

Ella giggled, rising to her feet. She swayed for a second, my hands immediately shooting out to steady her.

"That was—" she bit her lip, searching for the words. "Beautiful."

"Yeah," I grinned, pulling her in close, nuzzling her cheek. "I have to agree. You looked pretty fucking gorgeous with my cock down your throat."

I felt the blush heat her cheek. "Gunnar!"

"What?" I pulled back, one hand slipping down from her hip to slide over her abdomen and down to the seam of her pussy. I slipped a hand under her lingerie, finding her naked and soaked. My fingers slipped through her wet, the musky smell of her desire driving me crazy. My finger found her clit, running in lazy circles. Her nails dug into my forearm, her body arching as she gasped. "You ever do that for anyone else?"

She shook her head, her pants coming faster. Arrogant satisfaction settled in my gut. I would be her first everything. Her final too, if I had my way.

"I think that effort deserves a reward, baby," I murmured, my fingers rubbing a little harder. Her hips rocked against me; her mouth parted as tiny mews escaped.

I kept her like that, imprisoned between my thighs, one hand pressing her to me, the other delivering pleasure.

"Ready?" I whispered; my lips pressed to the shell of her ear.

She nodded, frantic. I leaned down, pulling down her slip dress, her breasts spilling free. I moved in, pressing a hot kiss to her nipple. My fingers moved a fraction up and to the right, finding that spot I'd discovered earlier that night.

Ella exploded under me, her screams filling the house, her body trembling as she coated my fingers in her cream.

"Fuck," I muttered, letting her ride out her orgasm. My cock hardened against my thigh, letting me know he was ready for round two. I'd never had a quicker recovery time. Fucking never.

She trembled against me, her breath short and sharp.

"Shhh, baby," I whispered, brushing comforting hands along her back. I pulled the slip back up, hiding her glorious tit from my view. "Just breathe."

"I've never—that was—" She shuddered.

"I know," I pressed a kiss to her forehead, her cheek, tilting her head up to reach her lips. "Just breathe."

We settled in for a long moment, both of us feeling this connection between us. At least, I assumed we both did. Cause fucking hell if I was the only one feeling this way. At this point, I'd be ready to raze this town to the ground for her.

"Bed?" I whispered when she'd calmed.

"Please."

Chapter Four

Ella

I led Gunnar to my bedroom, having each snagged a hurricane glass candle to light our way. I theoretically knew I should be nervous or perhaps concerned with the way this interaction was turning out. But I felt none of those emotions. Perhaps I was overly naïve or blinded by a flood of endorphins. Either way, this felt right. Leading Gunnar down the hall to my small bedroom gave me just enough time to think about things rationally. Despite all we'd done, I was still a virgin. At this point, I could probably ask him to put his clothes on and send him on his way. I just didn't want to.

The man knew how to kiss. He could play me like a dream. He pulled reactions and feelings from me I hadn't even known were possible. And believe me, I'd spent years and thousands of dollars cultivating a vibrator collection worthy of its own museum. It wasn't like I hadn't had offers over the years. A few guys had asked me out, fewer still had made it to a date. Only one had ever interested me enough to make it to date two. Any attraction between us had died immediately when he'd suggested that perhaps I shouldn't get dessert.

Bitch, please. I'm fabulous and don't need any man telling me I needed to lose weight. I was curvaceous, beautiful, and I didn't need anyone to convince me otherwise. Especially not a man I was considering letting into my life.

I pulled Gunnar into the room, shuffling to a halt before the bed. I set the hurricane glass I was carrying down, the candlelight sending a warm flickering glow across the bed. Outside, the rage of the storm had passed, leaving only the sound of much needed rain pouring down. Thunder continued to rumble in the far distance, but it sounded comforting rather than electrified.

Gunnar placed the other candle holder on the bedside table, glancing about the room. I tried to see it through his eyes. The room was done all in white and soft pastels. I'd gone for a feminine, beach, boho feel. Wood and glass mixed with soft furnishings, plants, and meaningful knickknacks to make the room both comfortable and cozy. In contrast, Gunnar dominated the space. His raw masculinity clashing with the feminine energy.

"You a designer?" he asked, looking about.

"No, I just like pretty things."

He turned back to me, grinning. "Looks real nice."

My heart skipped just a little, pleased by his praise. "It's not very big. But I try to make sure every room has a personality. A different feel."

"And this one is a warm hug?" he asked, walking around, fingers brushing the scarves beside the window.

I laughed, "I guess that's as good a description as any."

He pulled one long scarf free, running the silk across his

palm. He turned to me, a thoughtful expression on his face. "You ever think about how you wanted your first time to go?"

My breath caught in my throat, my pulse jumping.

Only a million times.

As a young girl, I'd imagined a wedding followed by a night of sweet kisses. Disney doesn't generally reveal what happens after the clock strikes twelve. As a teen, I'd imagined hot kisses leading to a rose-covered bed, or a clashing of mouths so passionate we'd only make it as far as the backseat of a car. As an adult, I'd thought about one-night stands and men with whom I'd form immediate connections. They'd whisk me away to their hotel room, showering me with passion. Once, I'd even considered attending a sex club in the city, of offering myself up to whoever wanted me. I'd be blindfolded, letting myself be taken by the person I'd imagine, rather than being forced to be disappointed by reality.

"Yes," I finally whispered, my heart thumping loudly in my ears.

"And?" Gunnar asked, pulling the silk across his palm again. His movements were almost hypnotic. Slow, deliberate. His naked body glowed in the candlelight, shadows dancing lovingly across the planes of his chest. "What did you imagine?"

I shivered, hugging one arm to my body. "A hundred different things," I admitted.

"Which one was your favorite?" The silk dragged lazily again.

"I never thought I'd get to be with a man I actually wanted," I admitted softly. "My favorite was being tied up , and blindfolded. I never knew who he was, just that he wanted me, wanted to take me."

Gunnar gripped the silk in his fist. "He tied you up?" His voice was guttural, raw.

I shivered, my pussy clenching. "And blindfolded me. He gave me pleasure then took my virginity," I whispered my deepest fantasy to him, watching his cock jump, his eyes darken with my words.

"You want that?"

I hesitated. Did I still want that? Was my fantasy of being taken by a faceless man, one only focused on my pleasure, still what I wanted?

No.

I shook my head slowly. "No, not tonight."

He raised an eyebrow in question.

"I want *you* to give me pleasure." I reached up, shedding the kimono. "I'm okay with you tying me up." I slipped one strap off my shoulder. "But I want to watch your face. I want to see your enjoyment." I slipped the other off, pulling the dress over my head and discarding it to the side.

I stood before him, naked. Trembling with anticipation, desire, and a little fear. Not fear of him, never fear of him. No, this was fear of rejection.

He made a sound unlike any I'd ever heard. "Get on the bed."

I dipped my head, fighting a smile. I turned to the bed, climbing on, settling on my back amidst the throw pillows in the middle of the bed.

"Hands up," he barked, stalking toward the bed.

I slowly raised my hands, running them up over the soft skin of my thighs, dragging fingers across the curves of my stomach, up to briefly cup my breasts. I rolled my thumbs over my nipples, pleasure sparking at both the tease of my fingers and his look of barely controlled desire.

"Up. Now," he ordered, reaching for my hand.

I complied, lifting my hands and holding them above my head. He placed a knee on the bed, leaning over me to wrap the scarf around my wrists.

"You say no, I'll stop," he promised, threading the scarf. "You pull on this," he placed an end in the palm of my left hand. "The knot will fall apart. The first rule is to trust you are always safe." He pressed a kiss to my wrist. "You feel safe, baby?"

I nodded, my heart in my throat, unable to answer.

"Good." He stepped back from the bed, watching me. His heavy cock hung large and beautiful, bouncing as he moved. "Spread your thighs."

I slowly dragged them open, watching as Gunnar's expression changed. The naked desire there shifted, growing hungrier, needier.

"Like this?" I let my legs fall open, revealing myself to him.

"Fuck," the word tore from him. "Stay there."

He advanced on the bed, dropping to his knees. Reaching across, he hooked arms under my knees and hauled me down the bed. I let out a squeal as his head dropped to my crotch, his lips and tongue playing cross my seam.

"Oh, God." I arched against his mouth as his tongue dipped, sweeping across my clit. The scarf pulled against my wrists, reminding me of my bindings as I shifted.

"Shh," he murmured, pulling back slightly to press a kiss to my thigh. "I got you, Ella."

His mouth returned, and he played me like an expert

musician. A slow set of circles, a slight suction, a finger pressed just so. I sighed in pleasure, moaning, eyelids drifting shut as he built me up, again and again, never letting me tip over the edge.

"Please," I begged finally, my body writhing under his mouth. "Gunnar—"

He chuckled against me, the vibrations hitting my core. He shifted forward, one finger pressing against my entrance as his tongue flicked against my clit in a pattern made to drive me crazy.

"Gunnar!" I gasped his name, hips pistoning as my orgasm crashed through my body. I fell apart, my body shuddering and quaking with spent need.

Gunnar shifted, resting his chin on my abdomen. I loved the smile that pulled at his lips, the contentment that settled in the lines of his face. He looked—satisfied. Happy.

"Hey," he murmured. "You good?"

"Joyfully perfect." I stretched, the scarf pulling at my wrists. "Oh," I looked up at them, remembering the binding. "I'm still—"

"I got you." Gunnar pushed up, crawling slowly up my body, kisses dragging across the dips and planes of my body. "You ready for more?"

I shivered, bumps rising across my skin. "More?"

"Mmm," he reached down, fingers slipping between my legs. "You feel ready."

I whimpered, pleasure shimmering up my spine.

"You ready for me to be inside you, baby?" He nipped at my collar bone as one of his hands cupped my breast, thumb grazing across my nipple.

"Yes," I breathed the word, arching into his touch. "Yes."

34

He chuckled. "You sure, baby? You ready for me to fill this virgin hole?" His fingers pressed deeper, making me feel an exquisite stretch.

I squirmed, reaching down to grasp his cock in my hand. He grunted, eyes hovering at half-mast.

"In me. Now," I demanded, pulling him toward me, careful not to displace the condom that my lust-filled brain hadn't even registered him pulling on.

Gunnar followed my lead, allowing me to guide him to my core.

"Ready, Ella?" he asked, positioning himself just so.

"Yes."

He pushed forward, stretching me in a way that simultaneously hurt and felt strangely beautiful. He continued in, slowly letting me adjust.

"Okay?" Gunnar asked, his breath whispering against my cheek.

"Oh, yes," I muttered, closing my eyes. "It feels—"

Painful. Wonderful.

"Full."

He laughed, groaning a little when I moved under him. "Steady, or this will be over before it even begins."

He pressed kisses to my cheeks, my lips, sucking gently at my neck before shifting down to trace a path to my breasts. He laved one, then the other, drawing them into his mouth and sucking on my overly sensitive nipples.

I shifted, my lips reaching up to press hot, wet kisses to any part of him within reach. My hands looped over his neck, clinging as best they could while bound. He nestled between my thighs as if he belonged there. These wonderful, thick thunder thighs that had summoned this beautiful god-like

Viking of a man to my bed.

He began to move, thrusting slowly into me, moving with certainty. My body had adjusted to his size and shape, accommodating him, welcoming him in with a heated grasp.

"Feel so fucking good, baby," he murmured against my shoulder. "Amazing. Tight. Hot. So fucking good. So good."

"Your cock is—" I didn't know how to describe it.

He quickened his pace, shifting slightly to change the angle.

"Ohmigod," I bowed off the bed, eyes rolling into the back of my head as he hit a perfect spot. "Again," I demanded. He obliged, his thrusts steady and sure, quickening at my gasped begging.

"Please, please, please—"

He grunted, shifting to move a hand between us. His fingers delved, searching for—

"Fuck!" I screamed, my body shattering into a million pieces as he pressed hard, urgent circles across my clit. "Gunnar!"

He swore, continuing to thrust into me with the same urgency and purpose. Even as I broke apart, this orgasm ruining me for any battery-powered assistance in the future, Gunnar powered through, his face serious as he concentrated on me. All his focus trained solely on me.

It was a heady feeling.

I pulled the thread, unraveling the scarf from my hands so I could knit my fingers in his hair, pulling his head down to mine. Our lips locked, our mouths hungrily devouring each other as he continued to thrust into me, the glide of his thick cock perfect.

"Gunnar," I panted between kisses. "Come for me."

His pace kicked up, his grunts and praises coming faster as his control shattered. He drove into me, bottoming out, my bed thumping rhythmically against the wall while outside the thunder rolled in the distance.

Mine. My Thunder God. My man. Mine.

I moaned under him, another orgasm building.

"Gunnar—"

"Come for me," he demanded harshly. "Come on my cock, Ella."

I broke, crying out as my body tightened, clenched, and spasmed. He muttered filthy, dirty words as I drifted away, lost in the sensations.

"Fuck!" Gunnar shuddered, his cock jerking in me as he came. "Ella—"

He slumped onto me, pulling me close. We breathed together, our bodies calming even as my heart continued to race.

"Okay?" Gunnar asked softly.

"Oh, yes," I whispered, offering him a small smile.

He raised up on one elbow, his eyes warm and affectionate. "Let's get you cleaned up, then I'll try again."

I raised an eyebrow, a smile playing at the corners of my mouth. "Again?"

"Baby, you're no longer a virgin. But missionary is only one position." He pressed a kiss to the tip of my breast. "There's a whole universe of positions to explore."

"Mmm?" I let my eyelids drop to half-mast, my legs falling open. I slid a hand down my body, letting my fingers trail through the wet at the juncture of my thighs. "I do have one or two I've thought about before?"

Gunnar's head dropped, his gaze narrowing to focus on

my fingers. "Yeah?"

"Mmm—" I slid a finger up, dancing around my over-sensitized clit. "Doggy, for one."

"We can try that." His voice was a husky whisper.

"Girl on top."

"Definitely."

"Against a wall—"

He shoved my fingers out of the way with a growl. "Cock tease."

Giddy delight settled in my belly and spilled out of me in giggles as he dropped to his back, hauling me over him. He tore the first condom free, quickly disposing of it before rolling another down his cock. I watched in rapt interest before my gaze snapped up when he issued a harsh demand.

"Ride my cock."

Oh, but I was more than happy to oblige.

I shuffled up, settling over him. He guided his cock to my core, one hand on his member, the other on my hip.

"Slow, baby," he murmured as I sank down.

I whimpered, eyes shutting at the feel of him.

"Shhh," his hands crept up, soothing my sides. "Easy, baby. Easy. No rush. Take your—"

He bit off his words, losing them in a strangled groan as I slammed down onto his cock. My thick thighs framed his body, pressing into his sides. He ran a hand down, resting on my left thigh.

"Baby," he grunted. "You feel so fucking good. You keep this up, and I'm gonna come."

I rolled my hips, enjoying this position. He didn't act like I was too heavy or big. He looked at me with desire, his hands caressing inches of skin I never thought a man would touch.

"Am I—"

"You're perfect," he interrupted. "You feel fucking amazing. You look like a goddess riding my cock." He squeezed my thighs with his hands. "You just keep going, baby. Keep making us both feel good."

I closed my eyes, giving in to the rhythm of my body. My hands drifted from where they rested on his chest, dragging lazily up my body to cup my breasts, thumbs darting out to tease my nipples.

"Fuck yeah," Gunnar grunted, his hands circling my hips. "Tease your beautiful nipples. Pull them a little. That's it. Good girl."

I clenched around him, a low moan slipping free.

"You like that?" he asked, shifting under me. His pelvis pressed up, taking over. He fucked me with deliberate strokes, his cock hitting me deep and steady. "You want more of me? You want more of this? You wanna cum, my good girl?"

Once, twice, we both came in a flash of skin and soft cries. I slumped down, my breasts pressing against his chest as we fought for breath.

His arms came up, fingers dragging down my back over and over.

"Wow," I muttered.

"I second that," he replied, pressing soft kisses to my shoulder.

We lay there for long moments, our breathing evening out.

"You sleep, baby. I'm just gonna get rid of these condoms." Gunnar slipped from the bed. He returned with a warm washcloth, leaving again to allow me time to clean up. I heard him moving around my house. The sound of him blowing out candles and checking locks was surprisingly reassuring. I cleaned the traces of blood from my body, surprisingly okay with the night's events.

I went to the bathroom, brushing my teeth, and slipping into a comfy sleep shirt. I returned to the bed, waiting for Gunnar to settle. I heard him check the laundry, turning the dryer on for another cycle before returning to the bedroom and slipping back into bed.

"All good?" I whispered.

"Clothes are still wet but should be fine by tomorrow," he replied softly, pulling me into him. I'd never spooned with a man before. It felt both overwhelmingly claustrophobic and beautifully comforting.

"Okay?" he asked.

"Maybe," I answer, shifting. My ass settled against his crotch while his hand shifted to my side rather than my stomach. His fingers glided against my skin, drawing soft patterns. I relaxed, lulled by the hypnotic pattern and the heat of him at my back.

Okay, *this* I could live with.

Chapter Five

Ella

I woke to a tangle of sheets and an empty bed. I strained, listening for movement in my house, hearing nothing but the sea in the distance and the call of seagulls outside. Sunlight streamed through the crack in my curtains, the room already feeling hot and sticky thanks to the increased humidity the storm had left behind.

For a moment, I wondered if I'd dreamed Gunnar. If last night had been a beautiful figment of my imagination. Then I moved and felt the uncomfortable stretch between my legs. It wasn't that he'd hurt me, rather I felt well used. And I definitely didn't feel like a virgin anymore.

I quickly walked around my house, double checking each room. My initial sense was correct—Gunnar was gone.

Suppressing the disappointment, trying valiantly to look on the bright side of the last few hours, I showered, washing away his scent and the slight smear of blood on my thighs.

I threw on a summer dress, pulling my hair back into a messy bun. I looked at the woman in the mirror. Her lips were swollen, and dark smudges colored the skin under her eyes. My cheeks were tinted red—from residual pleasure or beard burn, I wasn't sure.

"No regrets," I whispered. "No matter what happens, you gave yourself freely and without restraint. And Gunnar enjoyed you. He worshipped your body, and you rocked his world. Don't dwell. You're gorgeous, fierce, and a complete badass. If he doesn't realize that, then that's his loss. But don't you regret a moment of this." I gave myself a firm nod, mentally dressing in my Wonder Woman costume. "Now, get to work."

I wasn't due back at the bar until early afternoon, but an owner's work was never done. I pulled out my laptop, setting it up on the kitchen island. I stood in the doorway of my pantry, contemplating breakfast options, when I heard my front door open.

My heart skipped, hope rising.

"Gunnar?" I called, stepping away from the pantry.

"Hey." He rounded the corner, carrying a large takeout bag and two coffee cups. "Sorry it took me so long. Anika wanted to make you something special. Said something about—" he continued to speak while placing the items on the counter beside my laptop.

He'd changed. The damp clothes that I'd thrown in the dryer last night were gone, replaced with a shirt and dark board shorts. He smelled fresh, a mix of soap, salt, and him. I watched as he pulled a backpack off one shoulder, dumping it on the floor.

"Hope you don't mind. I brought an overnight bag. No big deal if you're not comfortable—"

My body reacted before my mind caught up. I launched myself at him, clinging to him like a koala. I pulled his head down, pressing frantic, open-mouthed kisses to every part of his skin I could reach.

His hands slipped down, palming my ass before boosting me up. My legs wrapped around his hips as we kissed, our tongues tangling in a desperate, gasping slide. He twisted, shifting, so I sat on the island counter, his cock now perfectly level with my pussy.

My bare pussy.

I pulled back, urgently tugging at the drawstring of his shorts, pulling then pushing them down so I could grasp his cock. It landed in my hand, hot, hard, already pulsing with need for me.

Me.

I groaned, shifting so I could guide it into me.

"Stop. Condom," Gunnar groaned out as I rubbed the head of his cock against my clit. My wetness coated his cock, both of us throwing our heads back in a simultaneous moan. "I'm clean, but pregnancy chances and—" he trailed off.

"Pill," I panted, unwilling and unable to halt the desire pulsing through my bloodstream. "I'm on the pill. Please, can you just—" I pulled him to my entrance, tilting my pelvis toward him. "Please—"

Gunnar slammed home, our bodies locking.

"Fuck," Gunnar bit out, thrusting again. "So good. So. Fucking. Good."

He pounded me on my breakfast bar, ripping my top down, so my dress fell below my breasts. He cupped them, lifting them to his hungry mouth, sucking each nipple, laving them with attention.

"I'm gonna—" my breath caught, my body tensing as I danced on the edge of an orgasm.

"Now," Gunnar ordered, thrusting hard. "Come for me, Ella." He dropped a hand, pressing a finger against my clit.

I screamed, falling into the orgasm, dying a million little deaths as pleasure overrode all other senses. The waves of clutching, delicious tension flowed through my body as I milked his cock. Distantly, I felt him cum, his heat adding to my enjoyment.

He held me tight, one hand lazily stroking my back as I returned to myself.

After a long moment, I pulled back a little, looking up into his smiling face.

"Good morning." His voice sounded husky. Satisfaction etched itself across every inch of his body.

I took one look at his beautiful face and burst into tears. I'd been so convinced he'd left me that this connection had been one-sided. Horrified by my reaction, I ducked my head, shifting to try to escape him.

"Hey, hey. Shhh—" He lifted my chin, pressing a kiss to my forehead. "What's all this? Did I hurt you?"

"I thought you'd gone," I whispered, watching confusion cross his face. "You didn't leave a note."

He blinked, his arms tightening around me. "After last night, you thought I'd just—leave?"

I shrugged, feeling suddenly vulnerable. I shifted backward, pulling the straps of my dress up, covering my breasts. "I don't really know you, Gunnar. You could have been the type to wham, bam, thank you ma'am."

He sighed, rubbing a hand across his face. "True, we've been moving fast. Can't say I'm sorry, though." He stepped back, reaching one hand out to cup my cheek. "Ella, you're amazing. This thing between us—it's—special. Unique. I'm not leaving you. And if I was, I'd make damn sure to let you know where I was going." He pulled me into his chest, holding me close. "I'm sorry I upset you."

I didn't say anything for a long moment, instead, fighting to bring my emotions under control.

"Sorry," I scrubbed at my face, giving him a watery smile. "I just—you're right. What we have is different. I've never had this reaction to someone before."

"I know, baby." We stayed together for another few moments. I reveled in the feel of his strong arms holding me tight.

"Come on," he whispered. "Let's eat."

Chapter Six

Gunnar

The days blurred while I remained in Ella's town. I didn't spend all my time with her, despite my best efforts. I ordered parts for the yacht and did general maintenance. I checked out the town, impressed by the number of tourists I saw floating about while remaining confused by the lack of local attractions available to take their money.

Capricorn Cove was a weird mix of local creative stores selling their small goods and hardened fishermen salty as the sea. Sandwiched between two bigger cities, the town sat smack dab in the middle of some of the prettiest coast I'd ever seen. Considering the proximity to the cities, and the increasing tourist dollars, Ella's idea of expanding her offerings wasn't a bad one.

And neither was the idea I was considering as I watched another tourist try, unsuccessfully, to hire a boat.

"Hey," Ella waved from the dock. She held up a paper bag. "I brought lunch."

I wiped my hands on a rag, grinning at her. "Get that gorgeous ass over here."

She laughed, sashaying down the dock to my mooring. "Permission to come aboard, Captain?"

"Only if you pay the charge."

She giggled, springing across the small gap to the deck, immediately raising on tip-toe as I pulled her close, my mouth descending on hers.

"Hi," she whispered, pulling back from the kiss, her cheeks flushed.

"Hey baby," I pressed my forehead to hers, palming her full ass. Fuck, I loved her curves. Everything about her was full and lush and perfectly decadent. From the taste of her lips to the cream of her cunt, anytime she was around, I wanted to lick her from top to bottom, making her squeal and sigh in equal measure. "Good day?"

"Better now." Her grin slipped, a small frown marking her forehead. She pulled away, busying herself with the lunch.

I knew my Ella well enough by now to understand she wanted to ask something but feared the answer. And I knew exactly what question she was avoiding asking—it was the same one I'd avoided answering for the last week.

As if hearing my thoughts, my cell rang, my brother's ringtone carrying over the gentle breeze.

Ella laughed. "You better answer that."

I gave a long-suffering huff, pulling the phone free and sliding my finger across the screen to answer. "Brother."

"When are you coming home?" Erik sounded annoyed.

Never. I am home.

"Soon," I replied, my answer as vague as it had been every other time he'd asked.

"Gunnar, I need a date. Shit has to be finished. We've got clients waiting for orders and guys pulling overtime to cover your ass. Not to mention we need that yacht back here at some point. You were meant to be back two weeks ago."

"I got held up. That part—"

"Arrived last week. I know because I just paid the fucking invoice. What the hell is going on?"

I watched Ella from across the deck. She'd settled on one of the chairs I'd set up just for moments like this. She'd tipped her face to the sun, her eyes closed, a small smile playing at the corner of her mouth.

"Ella," I finally admitted. "It's Ella."

"The girl you met?"

"Mmm," I turned away, keeping my voice low. "And this town."

"And this—what the fuck ?"

"I'll come back. I'll be back on Monday. But we need to organize an exit plan." I glanced over my shoulder, offering Ella a smile. "I'm gonna set up another shop down here. My girl lives here, her work is here, and the tourist traffic is off the hook. I've already scoped locations for a store and—"

"Are you shitting me right now?" My brother interrupted. "You've known this girl all of—what? Two weeks and you're talking about moving and setting up workshops and—" he trailed off. I could practically feel the waves of displeasure rolling down the phone lines.

"Fuck it, I'll drive down this weekend and meet her."

I blinked. "What?"

"You love this girl?"

"Yeah," I grunted gruffly. I hadn't told her yet, was planning some perfect moment when I revealed all—my plans to stay here, my love for her, the fact I'd already scoped out a private property just outside town. It had its own beach, acres of land, and a three-bedroom two-bath house just waiting for an overhaul.

"Then I'll drive down Friday. We can spend the weekend and work out if you're being blinded by good pussy or if this town will work for our business."

I ignored the pussy comment. "It's that easy?"

Erik chuckled, "Brother, it's never *that* easy. But we've been talking about expanding for a while. We've got the capital and enough clients down that way to warrant at least exploring it as an option."

"Shit." I ran a hand through my hair. "Thought you'd be harder to convince."

"Gunnar, I've never known you to go gaga over a woman. This girl must be pretty fucking special for you to not only extend your vacation, but be contemplating moving down there. I may be your business partner, but I'm also your brother. Family comes first. You want this girl, you want to make it work, I'll go balls to the wall to help you however I can. You know that."

I did. My family was the best part of my life. And I knew they'd love Ella.

"Let me check with Ella. Normally I'd say book your own hotel, but I have a feeling she'll want to put you up."

"As long as I don't hear you doing the nasty, I'll stay where I'm put."

I thought back to last night's activities. I'd tied Ella up, binding her hands and wrapping rope around her body in intricate knots, drawing out her orgasm, teasing her until she screamed through her release.

The Japanese called it Shibari; I called it spank bank material.

"Bring earplugs," I told him, not even caring when he groaned complaints down the line.

"Fine. I'll see your ugly mug Friday." He hung up.

I tucked the phone into my back pocket, turning slowly back to Ella. She'd pulled a big floppy hat from her bag, shading her delicate skin from the sun.

"All good?" she asked.

"Yeah, babe." I parked my ass in the chair across from her, enjoying the view. "My brother, Erik, he's gonna come down this weekend. You cool with that?"

Her body tensed, but she kept her voice casual. "Oh. Is he coming to help you with the boat?"

I hesitated. "The yacht's fixed," I finally admitted.

Erik hadn't been wrong. The part had come in last week, and it had taken me less than a day to fix it. I'd picked this cruiser up from its owner and had been sailing it back to our shop so we could do a complete gut job on it. We designed boats, but we also restored, renovated, and repaired for a price. The owner's request had coincided with my vacation, and I'd figured I'd kill two birds with one stone by sailing her back. I just hadn't expected to meet Ella.

"Oh." She played with the skirt of her dress. "Does that mean you're heading home?"

Baby, I am home.

"Not yet," I reached across, linking our fingers together. It was time I laid it all out there. "We've got a great thing going here. I want to stick around and see where we can take this."

Her cheeks colored. "I—I do too."

I grinned. "Good. My brother's gonna come down and stay for the weekend. I'll need to head back next week to close out my work and pack up my house. Not sure how long that will take," I tipped my head, giving her an easy grin. "Way I see it, we got three options. Option one, I move into your cottage—but, fair warning—I got a ton of shit that'll need storage."

Her free hand reached up, shakily removing her sunglasses to stare at me.

"Option two, I rent a place. Not real fond of that as it implies I'll be sleeping elsewhere when we both know I'll be by your side every single night. But I'll do it if you need me to."

She blinked slowly, looking stunned.

"Option three is my preference. We move into your cottage temporarily, but we look at buying a house down here. I already went looking and made a shortlist of the ones I think'll be perfect for us. I give you the list, you pick out the one you love, and we'll move in there."

I leaned in, pinning her with a look. "Ella, you gotta know. This isn't temporary for me. I'm planning on moving here. Living here. I want to marry you."

She sucked in a breath, looking overwhelmed. "But—" she trailed off, blinking frantically. "What about your business?"

I grinned. "So, you know how I've been hanging out with the locals the last week?"

She nodded slowly.

"Turns out a few guys agree with me that y'all aren't capitalizing on the tourist market." I gestured at the marina. "Spoke to Rick. He wants to sell the marina. Wants to move up to Rhode Island, where his grandkids live. I've put in an offer."

Ella's beautiful big eyes widened. "You what?"

I grinned. "It's a smart investment. You got regulars

51

and tourists. Give this place an overhaul, a few upgrades, introduce a boat builder which," I placed a hand on my chest. "I happen to know."

"You'd move your business?"

"No."

Her face dropped at my statement.

I rushed to reassure her, "Erik and I have been talking about expanding. Maybe franchising out, adding a shop."

"And you could do that here?"

"I've spent the last few days scoping potential workshop spaces. The old fish market storehouse would be perfect once renovated."

I watched a million emotions play across her face. "So, what do you think?"

"You'd do all this? For me?" She looked overwhelmed, confused, disbelieving.

"Baby," I slipped off the chair, moving to crouch between her thick thighs, my hands running up her silky skin beneath the skirt of her dress. "I'd move the earth if you asked."

She bit her lip, her hips tilting slightly toward me even as she continued to look apprehensive. "You're changing your entire life for me. Maybe you should wait to do anything until you're back home and have time to consider all the—"

My hands stopped their leisurely glide. "Excuse me?"

She bent forward, cupping my cheeks. "I'm just saying, you don't owe me anything. If you get home and this turns out to be—to be—" she swallowed. "To be a summer fling, then that's okay."

Oh, no. No fucking way was I letting her think this wasn't anything more than summer fling.

"Obviously, I need to step up my game." I surged to

standing, pulling her up with me. I tugged her behind me, leading her to the cabin and assisting her down the stairs. She followed, a lamb innocent to coming sexual onslaught.

The yacht was dated and in need of a major overhaul both in terms of décor and machinery, but the owner had picked it up for a song and was willing to pay for the work.

It had a full kitchen, bathroom, seating area, and a bedroom tacked onto the back. That's where I took her, pulling Ella through the small cabin and into the tiny room. I crowded her onto the bed, immediately tossing her skirts up and diving for her underwear.

"Gunnar!" she gasped, trying to squirm away. "Wait."

"No," I grunted, hooking two fingers into her underwear and tearing them down her legs. "I need to taste you, baby. Need to show you, you're mine."

She gave in, letting me pull her clothes off, then spread her thighs. I kissed my way up the soft skin of her legs, placing delicate kisses on the inside of each knee.

"You're mine, Ella." I hovered over her core, watching the blush of desire tint her skin with pink.

"You're my home. If that means packing up my life to merge it with yours, that's fine. I want to be where you are. I can no longer imagine living a life that doesn't involve waking up with you, breathing your scent, kissing your lips, laughing with you. And when I leave this earth, I'll find you, Valkyrie. I'll search all of Valhalla for you."

I dropped my head, tongue flicking out to taste her cream. She blossomed under me, opening. I felt her body shudder, her gasps and moans eagerly encouraging my efforts.

"Say you're mine, Ella," I demanded, hooking one finger into her, pressing against her g-spot. Her body bowed up, lifting off the bed as she cried out in pleasure.

"Gunnar!"

"Say it," I demanded roughly, my finger pressing in.

"I'm y-yours," she gasped out, begging for more, begging for release.

"Again," I barked, barely able to constrain my need.

"I'm yours, Gunnar. I'm yours. You own me."

I pulled my finger free and surged forward, pulling her against my cock, impaling her with my hot length. We both gasped, our rhythm uneven, hurried, each straining for dominance.

It was hot, heavy, and unpracticed. It was some of the dirtiest, filthiest sex I'd ever had. I drove into her, growling filthy words as she panted my name over and over, my cock turning her into a mass of squirming, heaving need. Her breasts bounced with reckless abandon, and I reached a hand up, brutally cupping one while my mouth descended to suck on the other. She exploded around me, her hips thrusting against me, her pussy a tight vice of clenching pleasure milking my cock.

"Fuck," I roared, hips pistoning. Once, twice, I exploded, cum filling her insides, coating her with my scent.

I didn't fucking care we hadn't used a condom. I wanted her bred. Wanted to plant a baby in this beautiful woman so we could start our future now.

I collapsed on top of her but pulled her close, rolling us both, so I was on my back, Ella draped across my front. She cuddled on my chest, our breaths equally rapid as we tried to calm.

"That was—" she made a small purring sound.

I grinned, pressing a kiss to her head. "Fuck yeah, it was."

We stayed snuggled together for a long while. The boat bopped gently under our bodies, lulling us into a meditative state.

"Are you sure?" she whispered into the quiet.

"Positive," I told her, not even needing to clarify.

She drew in a shuddering breath. "I want to take this plunge with you."

My arms flexed, holding her tighter.

"I'm just scared. No one has wanted me like you do."

"Their loss." I tilted her chin up, waiting for her to look me in the eye. I needed Ella to see how deadly serious I was. "You're beautiful, Ella. Every part of you. Your body, your soul. You treat everyone with sass and good humor. You strut your sexy ass around your home, and I go weak. I want nothing more than to see that smile on your face and kiss your lips. I don't have any doubts, baby. I haven't since the moment you guessed my beer. You're it for me."

Tears shimmered on her lashes. "I love you, Gunnar."

"I love you too, baby." I pressed a soft kiss to her lips. "Now, which option we gonna choose?"

She sniffed, brushing a hand across her eyelids. "My head says option one—living with me."

"But your heart?" She looked up at me, her gorgeous mahogany eyes shimmering.

"My heart says, option three."

I grinned, not even fucking caring if I looked like the cat that got the cream. "Then, option three it is. Start looking for houses, baby. I don't want to wait another minute."

I rolled over intending to kiss her again. It was the last thing I remembered before darkness enveloped me.

Chapter Seven

Ella

I clutched at Gunnar's hand as the paramedics rolled him down the corridor into the hospital.

"I'm fine," he grumbled. "This is nothing but an overreaction. Give me some painkillers and send me home."

"You got hit by a metal shelf. Your skull is cracked open and you passed out for twenty-minutes, Gunnar. I'm not letting you leave here until you get an x-ray and stitches."

Out of the corner of my eye I saw the paramedics exchange an amused glance.

"You should listen to your girlfriend," one of them advised. "She's right. Head injuries need to be taken seriously."

"I'd take it more seriously if I wasn't naked," Gunnar muttered, squinting against the bright lights in the hall.

After wiggling myself free of his unconscious body weight, I'd realized Gunnar was bleeding profusely and been terrified to move him. First aid training had kicked in, helping me to stay calm in what I could only describe as a truly horrible situation.

The bed rolled to a stop as one of the paramedics broke

off, moving towards the nurses station.

"Won't be long," the other told us cheerfully. "Jim's just checking you in. They'll get you settled in a room in a moment."

I continued to grip Gunnar's hand, my heart shaky as we waited.

"Ella?"

I turned, an automatic smile lifting my lips. "Blue! How are you?"

The woman I'd gone to high school with chuckled, waving a hand towards Gunnar. "Better than you at the moment. Let's get your man to a room."

She took charge of the bed, easily steering it as the paramedics briefed her in on Gunnar's condition. In the small curtained space they transferred him from the stretcher to a bed, wishing us luck before they left.

"Now," Blue tucked a stray chunk of her dark hair behind her head. "Tell me what happened."

Blushing, I gave her the cliff notes version.

"We were on Gunnar's yacht when a shelf came loose and fell on him. The metal cracked the back of his head and he passed out. It was half-attached to the wall so when it swung I think the corner sliced his head as it hit."

Blue nodded, checking Gunnar's vitals. "Any dizziness or vomiting?"

"He passed out for twenty minutes. Lots of blood but seems in decent condition now."

"I'm right here. I can speak for myself you know," Gunnar muttered, as Blue shone a light in his squinting eyes. "It's just a headache and a tiny cut."

She snorted. "The doctor will confirm but it's looking like

a concussion. You don't want to end up like someone I know who thought it was 'just a tiny bump' and ended up with a horrible concussion for three months."

"That was Drake, wasn't it?"

Blue's eyes widened in surprise. "You remember that?"

I chuckled, running my thumb over the back of Gunnar's hand in a reassuring pattern. "of course. He had to take all that time off school. You and Dane seemed like lost little lambs for a while there."

She blushed, looking down, her hair falling forward to cover her expression. "That was a long time ago."

"Your brothers?" Gunnar asked.

Blue shook her head.

"No, they were foster kids my parents looked after until they aged out of the system. They're in the Marines now."

"I always thought the three of you were tight," I mused, remembering the heated glances that I'd seen exchanged between them.

"Yeah, we were." Blue's tone sounded wistful

"Well," Gunnar shifted, grimacing slightly at the movement. "Be sure to thank them for their service next time you see them."

She nodded but I caught a flash of something that looked like regret cross Blue's face.

"You know, I saw them at—"

The curtain snapped open interrupting me. An older woman wearing a funky shirt and capri pants number entered the little space.

"I'm Doctor Peg. Let's see what we're working with."

She took the chart from Blue, listening intently as Blue explained Gunnar's situation.

She briskly checked him over, then unwrapped the bandage from around his head, making a little tutting sound when she looked at the sliced skin. "Let's run an MRI just to be sure there's no internal bleeding. I suspect not but I want to be sure before we send you home." She stepped back, beginning to remove her gloves. " Blue, can you please organize a tetnus shot, painkillers—I'll make a note on his chart on the dosage—and clean the wound area. I'll staple it after the MRI."

Dr. Peg offered us a reassuring smile. " If the MRI comes back fine then we'll send you home soon."

"And if it doesn't?" I asked, my gut twisting.

"Then we'll deal with that if it happens. Likely overnight observations at the very least but we'll see what the scans come back with."

I nodded, Gunnar's hand squeezing mine.

"We'll be right back with the shot." They both exited, drawing the curtain closed behind them.

"Hey," Gunnar said softly, drawing my attention to him. His eyes were still narrowed and his brow pinched as if he were trying to avoid the light. "I'm fine. It'll all be okay."

I drew in a shuddering breath. "I'm meant to be reassuring you."

"Yeah well, you can make it up to me with a sponge bath later."

I chuckled, reaching out to brush fingers across his brow. "I should call your family."

He groaned, his eyes closing. "How about we wait for the MRI results first?"

"Gunnar... what happens if you go into a coma? I don't know all your medical history."

59

He sighed dramatically. "Fine. But don't call Liv. She's a freaking nut and will freak out."

Gunnar had four younger siblings—Erik, Liv, Astrid, and Rune. While Eric shared the running of the shipbuilding business with Gunnar, the other siblings had branched out into their own careers. Liv was a television producer, Astrid was at college finishing a masters in Architeture, while Rune ran a bookstore.

"I'll call your Mom. What's her number?"

He rattled it off as I pressed the digits into my cell.

"Hello?"

"Mrs. Larsson?"

"Yes?"

I swallowed, feeling strangely nervous. "This is Ella. I'm here with Gunnar who's—"

"Oh, Ella! Hello! Please, call me Jemma. I've been dying to talk with you. How is my boy? Treating you well, I hope?"

I swallowed, making big eyes at Gunnar who rolled his then grimaced.

"Um, yeah he is. Only he's had an accident. He's a wake and function, just a laceration on the back of his head that will require staples, and a suspected concussion. They're doing an MRI to double check there's nothing they've missed but they're positive at the moment."

A beat of silence followed.

"Ella?"

"Yes?"

"Put Gunnar on."

I glanced at him. "Um, sure." I held the phone out to him. "Your Mom wants a word."

He sighed heavily, accepting the cell phone. "Hi Ma."

I could hear the shrieks from where I sat. Gunnar winced, pulling the phone away from his ear.

"Ma, calm down. It was a shelf. Not a big deal. No, I wasn't being an idiot. It fell. No, I wouldn't have died if Ella wasn't there. Yes, I understand that you want grandchildren. Yes, she's very nice. Yes, I love her. Yes, I've told her. No, I don't need you to come here. No, I'm fine. Ma, put Dad on."

My body warmed, a happy little fire crackling in my gut as his admission of loving me.

"Dad? Yeah, I'm fine. A bump to the head and a cut. Yep, couple of staples because of the location. Nah, we're fine. Ella's good." He shot me a smile. "Yep. Keep you posted. Thanks."

There was a pause then another eyeroll followed by an immediate grimace. "Love you too. Here's Ella."

He handed the phone back to me.

"Hello?"

"Ella, it's Sune. Thanks for taking care of our boy."

"Oh, no problem. He's easy to care for."

Gunnar smiled, reaching out to intwine our fingers.

"Keep us posted. If you need anything let us know. He's got a thick head so I expect they'll send him home where he'll act like a man-child for a few days. Don't let him fool you with the poor-little-me act."

I grinned, already liking his parents. "I'll keep that in mind."

"Call us once you know more."

"Will do. Bye."

"Bye."

I hung up, sliding the phone back into my pocket.

"Thanks. Sorry, they're nutty."

I lifted one shoulder in a half-shrug. "I don't know, they seem pretty normal to me."

He raised an eyebrow. "Normal? Shit, what do I have to expect from your family?"

"Oh, Viking." I raised up, leaning over the bed to press a kiss to his forehead. "I have four brother's. You can expect *all* the crazy."

Chapter Eight

Gunnar

I woke to a headache, a dry mouth, and arms that were empty of Ella.

Unacceptable.

With a groan I swung my legs over the bed, rubbing a hand across my face, grimacing as the late afternoon sun hit me right in the eyes.

"—and then he threw up. All over his date. It was spectacular."

My brother's voice floated down the hall, Ella's laughter tubmbling after it.

What the....

I pushed up, staggering a little as I attempted to shake off the afternoon nap.

I'd been discharged from the hospital two days before, but the pain killers had a tendency to knock me out.

I reached down, adjusting my cock. The bastard had gotten used to a little afternoon delight after our naps. Waking up to Ella sucking me off had to be a highlight of my life.

I stumbled down the hall, my brain still a little foggy.

"So tell me about Gunnar at—"

"No," I interrupted, leaning against the door jamb. "I think Erik's told you quite enough already."

Ella and Erik twisted, their expressions mirrors of amusement.

"Welcome back to the world of the living." Erik moved across the room, coming to embrace me in a one armed thumping hug. "You scared us."

My brother stood only a few millimeters shorter, but I liked to think it was enough for me to retain the title of being the older, wiser and taller brother (that's if we both ignored Rune who, even as the baby of the family, towered over all of us).

"Did Ma come with you?"

He laughed, stepping back and giving me a gentle punch to the arm. "Nah. I managed to talk her down. She expects a phone call and proof of life shot, but you're safe from an invasion for at least another day."

I clapped him on the shoulder then moved past him, headed for my girl.

"Hey Valkyrie." I leaned down, capturing her lips with mine.

She sighed, her body melting into mine, her weight a warm embrace against my aching muscles.

"feeling better?" She asked, reaching a hand up to brush fingers against my forehead.

"kiss me again and I'll tell you."

Behind us, Erik made a choking, gagging sound.

"Ignore him. He doesn't appreciate romance or love."

"More like I don't appreciate cheap one-lines."

64

He reached between us, snagging Ella's hand, pulling her away from me. "You picked the wrong brother. I'm much smoother."

"Yeah he is." I agreed, reaching out to flick his ear. "He waxes. Smooth as a baby all over."

Ella giggled, her eyes dancing as she looked from Erik to me and back. "You two are crazy."

"Only about five percent of the time." Erik gave me a look. "You seem okay."

"I am." I ran a hand over the back of my head, gratified that the site of my injury seemed less tender. "Just a bump. No biggie."

Erik nodded, considering me. "Should we go check this marina out then?"

I raised an eyebrow. "Now?"

"Sure." He hip checked Ella. "We can get dinner at this little lady's bar after."

"You're paying," I warned him even as Ella waved me off.

"Family doesn't pay."

"Of course they do." I argued, turning on my heel to head back to the bedroom to find a shirt. "Gotta support small businesses."

"Don't worry, you don't have to pay." I heard Ella reassure Erik.

"Yes he does!"

The argument continued until we got to the marina where, as the sun hung low in the sky, we walked every inch.

"I mean, it's pretty horrible." Erik said as he poked at a rotted banister. "Every single part of this will need to be replace. I can't imagine the store fronts are much better."

We all looked up to the row of stores that lined either side of the marina. They were included in the price and, apart from a few selling bait or gear, most stood empty.

"Gonna be a lot of work." I cocked my hip, leaning against a post. It groaned in protest but stood steady.

"Mm." Erik muttered, squinting out at the boats lining the harbour.

"And expensive," Ella pointed out, biting her lip.

"And—"

"Fine," Erik tossed up his hands. "You've convinced me. We'll take it." He waggled a finger in my face. "But this is gonna be your baby. Don't come crying to me if this doesn't work out."

I grinned, holding out my hand for him to shake. "Promise."

Chapter Nine

Gunnar

"Jesus Christ, slow the fuck down," Erik demanded from the passenger seat of the truck. "The last thing we need is to fucking roll this thing."

I glanced at the dash, easing my foot off the gas as I registered my speed.

"It's been a month," I muttered. Erik sighed heavily beside me.

"Ah, young love." He shook his head. "Look, Ella's awesome, but you went decades without her. Surely you can live another twenty minutes."

Barely.

I didn't dignify him with a response. He'd get it one day.

I'd spent the last month closing out my responsibilities. I'd put my house up for sale, packed all my shit in a truck, and put a down payment on a house in Capricorn Cove.

Our house.

Ella hadn't been wrong about the older generation looking for a move. We'd been inundated with house offers when word had got around that she was looking to buy. She'd sent me pictures of one with two words—our home. I'd put a deposit on it that day.

I didn't care that it needed work or that we'd probably need to add additions on at some point—the house sat up on a protected little block with views out to the ocean. The front of the massive block was flat with plenty of space for a yard, entertainment, and even a shed. The back was a mess of trees and brush, but a sloping stair path led down to a private beach—complete with a small pier perfect for docking a little fishing boat.

We'd picked it up for a song and would be moving in this weekend. I had plans to fuck Ella in every room of the house. And that beach? Perfect for a little afternoon delight.

Beside me, Erik opened the manila folder, interrupting my daydream.

"We're gonna need to renegotiate this," he muttered for the umpteenth time since this trip started. "The terms are good, but I think we can do better."

I ignored my brother, focusing on navigating the tight turns that took us around the coastal road to home. We were in the final stage of negotiations to buy the marina—including the old fish market that would eventually become our new workshop.

"If we took that old yacht club and overhauled it, got Ella in to run it, we could make some serious buck with weddings and what-not," Erik muttered, making notes in the margin of a page.

My heart lifted as we turned the last corner, coming into sight of the sign welcoming us to Capricorn Cove.

Home.

Ella.

I forced myself to slow the truck, abiding by the speed limit as I navigated to Ella's small cottage. We'd be picking up the keys to our new home tomorrow. Tonight was for reclaiming.

Down the street from Ella's house, I pulled in at a motel.

"You know, maybe you should let me run this past Ella tonight. I think we could really—"

"Get the fuck out," I grunted, ignoring my brother's protests.

He sighed dramatically. "You really can't keep that girl to yourself. That's selfish."

I can today. Just watch me.

He slammed the door shut, calling through the window, "don't be late tomorrow. We need to—"

I drove off, bumping down the road, ignoring his yell. I hadn't held Ella in a month. A truly unacceptable occurrence.

I pulled the truck into her drive, noting with approval that her car sat ready—packed to the gills with stuff jammed into the backseat. Boxes sat ready on her porch, waiting to be loaded.

My truck skidded to a halt, gravel flying under the wheels as it protested. I parked, throwing open the door and quickly locking it, fumbling with the keys in my haste. I jumped the stairs to her porch, pausing to snatch the pinned note off the door.

I'm inside. Come find me.

My cock, already harder than a rock, gave a jerk. I could cut a fucking diamond with this thing. I pushed through, throwing it shut behind me, and stalked down to her bedroom. Boxes lined each room as I passed, her

69

frames and knickknacks, candles, and frills all packed away in preparation for the move. Only boxes and furniture too big to wrap remained, ready for tomorrow.

I found her in the bedroom. The room had been stripped, empty except for the bed. No boxes, no comforts, just a bed still dressed in lavish pillows and white bedclothes. On it, in only a scrap of lace and a smile, lay my beautiful woman.

"Ella," I breathed her name as if it were air.

"Viking," she greeted, a naughty smile on her lips.

I stalked to the bed, hands coming to the hem of my shirt, jerking it over my head and tossing it heedlessly to the side. I paused at the foot, shoving down my pants and underwear, cock springing free as I closed the final distance to her.

My hands grazed her skin, her scent filling my nostrils as my mouth descended.

"Ella," I whispered as my lips touched hers. Our mouths met, hungry and desperate. Wet, hot, and hard, our tongues danced as we kissed, tasting that which we'd missed.

"Baby," I groaned, hands skimming down her sides. "I can't wait."

"Then don't," she replied, nipping playfully at my jaw.

I let out a feral growl. "Fuck."

I scooped her into my arms, searing my lips to hers. Delicious heat spread rapidly throughout my body, pooling in my aching cock. She tasted like home.

I pulled back, looking down at her exquisite body. "I like lace bras, but god damn if I'm gonna let you keep this one on."

I snatched her close, and once again, our tongues clashed, and lips grasped as my hands roamed her skin, touching and caressing, driving her passion higher. I suckled at her neck

70

while edging the material down, revealing skin, tracing the curve of her breast through the lace.

I flicked her nipples with my thumbs, grinning as she gasped her pleasure.

"Oh!"

I watched Ella fight for control, her eyes glazed with passion, her lips plump and already swollen from our kisses. Ultimately, she gave up, surrendering to my pull as I easily unlatched her bra and drew it from her. I tossed it across the room, heedless of where it landed.

My mouth descended to suckle first one nipple, then the other while her hands gripped my head and her mouth panted words of encouragement.

"Please, Gunnar, please. Oh, please. Yes, like that! Please!"

I drew back to kiss her. "Take your panties off."

She helped me, lifting her ass to wretch them off, throwing the silky material away. Once gone, she pulled me closer, hands reaching out to grasp my cock. She took me in hand, jerking slowly up and back, teasing my member.

"Jesus Christ, fuck. Fucking fuck, fuck," I groaned, fighting the urge to pump into her hands. "I've missed you, baby. Missed you so fucking much. Love you, Ella. Love you so fucking much."

I pressed kisses to her mouth, praising her, worshipping her as she jerked my cock, her hand perfectly fitting to my cock.

"Can't wait," I panted. For the first time in my life, I was gonna lose control. "Need to be in you."

"Thank God." She dropped my cock, squirming to get into position. "I've been dying for you."

I found her core, sliding fingers through her slick heat,

finding her wet and ready.

"Baby," I groaned. "You're so fucking wet for me."

"I've been wet all day," she admitted, red flushing her cheeks. "It's been so hard not to—"

I surged in, both of us gasping as I filled her. Her tight pussy clenched around me like a vice, tight, hot, wet—fucking perfect.

I reached down, lifting her legs, encouraging her to wrap her thighs around me. I needed to be surrounded by her; I needed to glory in her.

We crashed together, two parts of one whole, our bodies meeting again and again in a brutal, glorious ritual.

"I love you!" she screamed as her body clenched, every part of her thrashing as she tipped over, falling into the chasm of ecstasy. I followed, emptying myself inside her body.

We collapsed, our bodies intertwined, our skin pressed tightly together.

"Don't ever leave again," she whispered, her legs and arms wrapped tightly around me.

"Never," I promised.

Our bodies cooled; the desire only slightly more controlled.

"Where's Erik?" she finally asked, pulling away slightly.

"At the motel. I didn't want him interrupting."

She giggled, her beautiful face lighting up. I pressed kisses to it, ignoring her squeals, enjoying the taste of happiness on her skin.

This is home.

Later, after more lovemaking and a failed attempt at showering that ended with the need for another shower, we headed to the Bronze Horseman in search of food.

In a booth, curled into one another, we ate slowly, discussing the next steps on our journey together.

"I don't expect it to take long," I told her, referring to the meeting Erik and I had to go over the final marina contract tomorrow.

"Well, the council is all for it. I've already been fielding calls from local builders eager to get their piece of any new construction." She chewed absently on a chip, a small frown furrowing her brows. "Actually, that's one thing you've never told me."

"'What's that?" I asked, tracing swirls across the delicate skin of her inner wrist.

"What your company is called."

"I haven't?" She shook her head.

"Huh. I thought you knew. It's Thor's Shipbuilding."

She jerked, a strangled sound coming from her throat. She coughed twice, the blockage immediately clearing. I handed her a glass of water—urging her to breathe.

"You okay?" I asked, briefly wondering if I'd need to perform a Heimlich maneuver.

"Yo-you-your company is called Thor's Shipbuilding?" Her voice sounded strangled.

I rubbed a hand over her back, frowning. "Yeah. Are you sure you don't need—"

She threw her head back, roaring with laughter. Heads swung our way, tourists and locals alike gaping at Ella as she lost all control. Tears ran down her face as she bellowed laughter.

"You-you-you're," she gasped around new fits of laughter. "An ac-act-actual Viking!"

I shrugged, now seeing the humor in the situation. "I

mean, I wouldn't say yes but—"

"Oh my god. I can't," she continued to giggle, brushing away tears, and beaming at me.

"Is this funny?"

"All my life, I've asked for a god to come and tame these thunder thighs." She slapped her beautiful legs, beaming at me. "And you arrived. This glorious Viking of a man, ready and willing to plunder my pussy. And best of all? You're a god of thunder. Thor's fucking Shipbuilding, if that isn't a sign, I don't know what is." She started laughing again, her joy contagious.

"Baby, you can call me whatever you want," I told her, pulling her close, one hand slipping under the table to cup her center in the dark. She froze, laughter dissipating as desire took over. "Just as long as you call me yours."

She rolled her eyes, groaning. "That's so corny."

"But true," I withdrew a hand, slipping it into my back pocket, pulling the small pouch free. "I love you, Ella. I know we're just starting our lives together, but I want to do this right."

I handed her the velvet pouch, watching as she pulled the drawstrings open. She held out a hand, tipping the pouch. A ring tumbled out, landing in her palm. Princess cut white diamond surrounded a band decorated in Celtic knots with sapphires. She looked up at me, her eyes wide.

"Marry me."

Her beautiful eyes filled with tears even as her lips moved to deliver the answer I'd hoped for.

"Yes."

We kissed, me sliding the ring on her finger, her sobbing tears of joy.

"I'm so glad it was here," she whispered against my lips.

"This is the only place it could be. It's the first place I saw you." I nodded over at the bar. "I fell in love with a Valkyrie right there."

"And I, my Viking," she sniffed, grinning. "I love you, Gunnar."

"I love you, baby."

She tilted her face up, and I obliged her, willingly drowning in her kisses.

She called me her God of Thunder, but she was the one who'd summoned me—changing my world.

Chapter Ten

Gunnar

"Oh look, it's Dane and Drake."

I glanced up from the cereal box I'd been perusing to see Ella pointing down the end of the aisle.

The men in question were tall, and muscular. One broad, the other lean. Both had a look about them that said ex-military.

"Who are they?"

Ella rolled her eyes. "You remember, Blue's boys."

I wracked my brain trying to remember why that name sounded familiar. "The nurse who looked after me when I hit my head? The brunette?"

Ella nodded. "Yeah. She's sweet on them."

I eyed the men. "Both of them?"

"Uh-huh." Ella plucked the cereal from my hands, tossing it in our cart. "They're together but I think they want Blue to be with them too."

I pushed the cart, following Ella down the aisle. "And your town would be cool with that?"

She gave me a look. "I'm sorry, you're not?"

"Not what I meant." I raised one shoulder in a half-shrug. "Love is love, babe. I just meant this is a small town. Don't expect that people will be exactly welcoming of a polyamorouos relationship."

Ella chuckled. "Then you haven't lived here long enough. For a while back in the sixties there was a commune out in the mountains by Lovers Lake. Honestly, this town is all about love."

I reached over pulling her into me, pressing a kiss to her a temple. "Mm, well it's certainly been that way for me."

She laughed, shoving me away, her engagement ring catching the light from the fluorescent bulbs above us.

A possessive kind of love warmed my blood.

"When we get home we should—"

Ella cut me off, a hand flying to my mouth as she forced me back a step.

"What are you doing?" I asked against her palm.

"Shh! Blue's hugging Dane!"

I peered around the end of the aisle, catching sight of Blue hugging one of the two men.

"And?" I asked, completely baffled by my fiance's behaviour. "Are you suddenly best friends with Blue?"

Ella tilted her head back, a small grin lighting her eyes. "No. But I want everyone in the world to be as happy as you and I are."

Well damn.

I leaned down, my arm hooking around her to pull her body against mine, our lips meeting in a hungry kiss.

I'm not sure how long we stood like that, our lips devouring each other, our hands roaming each others body.

"Ahem," came a cough behind us.

We both twisted, an older gentleman with a cane and basket grinning at us.

"Sorry, kids." He nodded at the shelf behind us. "Normally I'd leave you alone but I'm in desperate need of pasta sauce."

Ella blushed as we moved out of his way.

"You too have a good day." He winked, moving off towards the registers.

Ella's head landed on my chest, her hair falling over her flushed cheeks. "That wasn't at all embarrassing."

"Lovers lake commune, remember?"

She huffed out a laugh. "Shudda up. Let's get this done then you can take me home and ravish me."

With pleasure.

Epilogue One

Gunnar

Five years later

"I now declare the Capricorn Cove marina open for business!"

Ella beamed up at me as together we snipped through the ribbon, officially opening the updated marina. Around us, the towns people I now called friends cheered. This town had adopted me, opening their arms and embracing my efforts to bring in more jobs, more tourists, and more opportunities.

The band struck up a tune as the crowd surged ahead, strolling down the new board walk, checking out all the now filled storefronts where café's and businesses hawked their ware.

While the majority of changes had happened gradually over the last five years—things like repairing the boardwalk and attracting businesses to the area—the major renovation had taken three years to complete.

Now, we were here. Finally.

Ella's arm wrapped around my waist as we chatted with friends and tourists.

"Shall we?" I asked as the crowd thinned, the majority of people finding food and places to stop and listen to the band.

"Let's."

Hand in hand, we walked the wooden length reminiscing about the various trial, tribuations, and triumphs that had accompanied us over the past five years.

We walked down one of the docks to where my large yacht was berthed. I helped Ella onto the deck, taking a moment to enjoy the weight of her in my arms.

My wife is freaking gorgeous.

I couldn't help but relish the reality of her. Every day I fell more in love with this brilliant woman. Her generosity, her openness, her love. Every single day had been an absolute joy.

Ella took a seat on one of the chairs I'd placed specifically for her, repositioning it slightly to stay in the shade. I sat beside her, our hands intwining as we faced the marina, watching the crowds meander along the boardwalk.

"Do you regret it?" Ella asked quietly.

'Regret what?"

She gestured at the marina. "Do you ever wish you hadn't stayed?"

I burst out laughing, doubling over, the hilarity of her question striking deep.

"Let me say this once and once only—Fuck. No."

She grinned, pleasure dancing in her eyes. "I didn't think so but you just never quite know."

"Do you?"

She shook her head. "Never, Viking. Not once."

I relaxed marginally. "Then why ask?"

She shrugged. "You wanted a challenge. I guess I wondered if the marina being done would mean you'd move on now."

"Never. The marina being done just means I can take five minutes to breathe before digging into the next challenge."

She cocked an eyebrow. "And what is the next challenge, Mr. Larsson?"

I shrugged. "Maybe expanding Thor's Shipbuilding. Now that the economy is back on track, we're seeing an uplift in business. I wouldn't mind branching us out down here into separate commercial and recreational arms."

"It'd mean taking on more workers."

"Mm."

"And less time at home."

"We could balance it."

She tapped a finger to her cheek. "Look, I'm supportive so long as you agree to take weekends off. VJ is going to need you to take him to soccer practice."

I froze. "VJ?"

"Viking Junior."

I turned move fully towards my wife. "Ella, what are you saying?"

She moved out joined hands, shifting until my palm could press against her belly. "Congratulations, Viking."

Joy pure and fear warred within me, fighting for dominance.

"Are you happy?" Ella asked, her gaze searching my face.

"I...." Words failed me as visions of little cherub faces danced in front of my eyes. Adorable girls with my hair and her eyes, laughing with delight as I taught them how to handle a yacht. Young boys with their mother's smile, eating at her restaurant or running along the boardwalk, school bags in tow.

"Gunnar?"

I jolted, finding Ella's expression had shifted, the happiness now replaced with anxiety.

"There are no words for the joy you've brought to my life." I cleared my throat. "I love you. If I could, I'd marry you all over again."

Tears shimmered on her lashes. "Love the sentiment but let's put that money towards baby's college tuition."

I chuckled, tugging her up and across, settling her on my lap. Her arms wrapped around my neck, her head resting on my shoulder.

And just like that, I held my whole world in my arms.

Epilogue Two

Ella

Ten years later

I didn't normally work nights in the bar anymore. Not since the kids had come along, and we'd opened the three other restaurants and the two event centers. Between the marina, Gunnar's workshop, our numerous hospitality ventures, and the kids (not to mention one very naughty puppy), I just didn't have the time or desire to work night shifts.

Gunnar had made good on his next challenge, growing the business until it could split into commercial and recreational shipping arms. And as he'd promised, he attended every game, every dance recital, every PTA meeting. The man loved being a dad.

I finished wiping down a table, contemplating if it was worth closing early tonight. We'd been shorthanded thanks to a gastro bug that was floating around, so I'd pulled on my big girl panties, farmed the kids out to their friends for a sleepover, and headed in to work. My gorgeous husband had been forced to leave us yesterday to deliver a trawler—his normal delivery guy had been struck down by the same illness.

"Ella," Anika came waddling out of the kitchen, a hand on her pregnant belly. "I'm gonna head off. This storm has chased everyone away and this one—" she patted her stomach. "Is ready to play for the US Olympic soccer team. I need his Daddy to settle him down."

I glanced around the room, letting out a sigh. Mid-season was normally our busiest time, but tonight's storm had kept even our most foolhardy and dedicated patrons indoors. The windows of the bar shook as thunder crashed outside.

"Go take off," I told her with a head jerk towards the door. "I'll close up."

She grinned, offering me a wave. "I'll catch you tomorrow."

I locked the door behind her, moving about the bar. I needed to restock a few small things, mop the floor, cash out the till, then I could finally head home.

Gunnar wasn't due back until tomorrow. Ten years on, and we still hated to be separated even for one night.

I was nearly finished when the front doors jingled, opening.

A man stepped through, thunder rumbling loudly overhead as he paused in the doorway, the doors slapping closed behind him. Windblown, water dripping off his clothes and onto the clean floor, he was still the most attractive man I'd ever seen. His eyes caught mine, a small smile pulling at one side of his mouth. He turned, locking the door, then strode across the floor to take a seat at my bar.

I met his gaze, letting the naked desire in his eyes heat my blood. I sashayed over to the bar, my green dress doing nothing to hide the curves of my body. I leaned against the counter, purposefully letting him catch a glimpse down my top.

"What can I get you, Viking?" I asked in a husky whisper.

"The same thing I wanted ten years ago," Gunnar rasped out. "You."

I slowly rounded the bar, coming to stand in the gap between his legs. His hands reached out, settling on my hips.

"Missed you, baby."

I sighed, letting my body fall against his. Our lips met, our tongues tangling in a hot mess of wet want.

"Gotta taste you," he grunted, slipping from the bar and hauling me across to one of the long wooden tables. He lifted me up, laying me out on the wood like I was the feast, and he, the hungry Viking.

He pushed the skirt of my dress up, making a sound in his throat when he realized I wasn't wearing panties.

"Naughty girl," he dropped his head, his tongue finding my wetness, seeking my clit with purposeful, talented priority.

"Gunnar!" I grasped his hair in my hands, pressing him closer to me as he devoured my core. His lips, tongue, and fingers drove me wild as they danced across my sensitive flesh, pushing me higher.

"Please!" I begged when he withdrew. "I need you."

He stood, his hands dropping to his fly. "You miss me, baby?"

"So much," I admitted, watching hungrily as he teased me, drawing down his zipper with agonizing speed.

"Good." He shoved his pants down only far enough to reveal his cock. Big, thick, and wonderfully hard, he stroked it while watching my chest heave with need.

"You want this?" He gave a slow tug from base to crown, pre-cum glistening in the dim light.

"Yes," I breathed the word, entranced by his actions.

"Where?"

"Cunt now, mouth later," I told him; my need too great to consider waiting any longer.

"Good girl," his praise hit me right in my crotch, wet slicking down my thighs. He brought his cock to my entrance, teasing me for just a moment.

"Please Gun—" I strangled the rest of his name as he surged forward, bottoming out. His cock hit me, full and to the root.

"Fuck!" he roared as thunder crackled outside. We writhed together, our bodies shaking with a desperate, clawing need. He surged in, again and again, his cock thrusting and gliding along overly sensitive skin until finally, finally, finally, I tripped over the edge, falling into a spiral of outrageous pleasure.

"Gunnar!"

"Ella!" He pressed a nipping kiss to my collarbone even as he continued to thrust. "Ella, Ella, Ella—" he chanted my name, his thrusts lost their rhythm, becoming choppy, rough, and hard. His need drove him until finally, he thrust into me, his cum painting my insides.

Gunnar collapsed on top of me, his body heaving as he struggled to come back to himself.

I loved it. I loved this man. I loved our passion. I loved our life together.

"I love you, Viking," I whispered, threading fingers through his damp hair.

"Love you, Valkyrie. Thanks for summoning me home."

My thunder thighs would always be ready to summon this

sex God.

II

Clean Sweep

Clean Sweep

Erik

Nappies, poop and so many sleepless nights I was pretty sure in some countries this would be considered torture and my kids could be tried for war crimes.

Yep, I was now a dad. A dad who had no clue what he was doing. A dad who somehow ended up with two kids who weren't his but I fuc- er, I mean - gosh-darn I loved them.

Only... I needed help. A LOT of help. My house was a wreck and I needed sleep. Badly.

Enter Laura — the Queen of Clean.

She had to be an apparition caused by my sleep-deprived mind. Cause god knew she was exactly what I'd always wanted in a woman, and one glance at her curves and pretty smile had me reconsidering the need for sleep.

Laura

Being offered my own TV show was a dream come true. As the Queen of Clean I had an opportunity to educate people about the importance of cleanliness.

Only one look at my latest project and all I could think of was dirty, sweaty, filthy things.

Erik Larsson is tempting me with sweet murmurings, beautiful babies and a helpless need for a spotless kitchen. The man knows my weaknesses... the only problem?

I'm meant to be leaving for my next assignment at the end of the month.

The Queen of Clean doesn't stick around... right?

Warning: This hilarious read involves cute babies, gorgeously helpless men, and an appreciation for a clean house that goes over oh so well. Settle in greedy reader, you might need gloves for this delicious mess.

Prologue

Erik

Having a soon-to-be sister-in-law who owned a bar was fucking awesome. The holiday period might be Ella's busy season at the bar, but the upside was having free reign of the place for Christmas.

When my brother, Gunnar, had invited us down to stay in Capricorn Cove for the holidays, I'd been worried that we'd scare the girl off. Back home our family wasn't known as the local vikings for nothing - loud and large, there wasn't one subtle thing about us.

But I shouldn't have worried. My brother had chosen well, Ella came from hardy stock. She'd embraced us with open arms, tapping a keg, serving platters of roasted vegetables, slow cooked meats, and delicious sides. I'd even heard rumors there were multiple desserts still to come.

If she'd been worried about meeting the family, she didn't show it, nor should she have fretted. We'd welcomed her with a rowdy embrace and - now having experienced her bar, the food and the free beer - I was pretty sure we'd be picking her over Gunnar.

As I watched Ella and my brother interact across the table, teasing and laughing, sharing secret smiles and lingering touches, an ache settling in my chest.

I'd never admit it, but I wanted what he had. Love. A good woman. Hope for a family in his future.

God, you're a sap. Get over yourself.

"Should I bring the desserts out?" Ella asked Gunnar.

I perked up, shaking off my pity party.

Gunnar glanced at the table, chuckling as he surveyed the ravaged remains. "Yeah, and I should probably tap another keg."

She pushed up, Gunnar following. I reached for plates and platters, my siblings and parents doing the same. There was a flurry of movement as we began to pile plates and walk them into the kitchen.

"Oh, please don't!" Ella cried, fluttering her hands at us. "We've got this."

"Many hands make light work, sis," my youngest sister, Astrid, called. She brushed past me on her way to the kitchen, her arms full with a platter of decimated turkey bones.

We piled dishes into the industrial sink then Ella shooed us out of the kitchen, telling us to put on some music and help ourselves to more beer. I caught Gunnar's expression, sending an amused glance at Liv who rolled her eyes as we trickled out leaving them alone.

"He's gonna fuck her," Liv whispered.

I made a face, "Jesus Liv, did you have to say it? God, pass me the mind bleach please."

She punched my arm, chuckling. "She's awesome. And he deserves happiness."

"Yeah."

In the dining room my youngest sibling, Rune, stood at the jukebox, perusing the titles.

"If he chooses anything but a Christmas song Ma's gonna flip," Astrid said, flicking her long blonde hair back from her face.

The door to the restaurant jingled and I frowned, exchanging a glance with Liv. She shrugged.

"Maybe a lost customer?"

The door jingled again, this time more urgently followed by a knock.

"Gunnar? Ella? You in there? It's Sheriff Rodriguez."

I headed over, opening the door to two men, each holding a baby in one arm.

"Hey, I'm Erik, Gunnar's brother." I stepped back, gesturing them in. "Come in outta the cold. Gunnar and Ella are just out back."

The police entered, both looking at me with grim expressions. The babies were cradled gently, their little bodies held close and tight.

I shut the door, nodding at the little ones. "Bit late for them to be out, isn't it?"

The police exchanged a look as my Ma and Pa came over. One of the babies began to cry, the other joining in a moment later.

"Oh you sweet little angels. Here," Ma reached out, offering to take a baby. "The little one likely just needs a cuddle."

The Sheriff handed over the baby then turned, considering me with tired eyes.

"Erik Larsson?"

"Yep," I smiled, but a feeling of unease slipped down my

back.

"Right," the Sheriff raised a hand, scratching his forehead. "There's no easy way to say this but um…." He gestured at the babies. "They're yours."

Around me, everyone froze.

"Excuse me?" I blinked.

"The boys. They're yours. At least they are, according to the letter we received when the mother dropped them off." Ma handed the baby to Rune, coming to stand beside me. "Erik, what is he talking about?" My father came to my other side. "Erik? Are these children yours?"

"I…." Words failed me.

"Erik?"

"Son?"

"Sune, be calm." My mother told my father, but she looked worried. "I'm sure there's a perfectly reasonable explanation."

"Jemma, the police have turned up with babies. *Babies*.What possible fucking explanation could there be that would be reasonable right now?"

"There's a note," the Sheriff said, handing it over to me. "It explains, well, not everything but a little."

I opened it, running a hand through my hair as I read the words printed in neat black ink. Around me, my family, the police, they all faded into the background as the second officer handed a crying baby to Astrid, then came to stand beside the Sheriff, his hands making pacifying movements as if to try and calm us down.

Dear Erik,

You probably don't remember me, three years ago I filled in for your mother for two weeks while she was ill. You were kind to me then and I hope you'll be kind to my boys now.

I'm unable to care for them. Their father isn't in the picture, a one night stand who ghosted me with a fake number. I don't have the money or resources or, to be honest, inclination to be a mother.

I had an adoption set up but the parents found out they were pregnant with a miracle baby and dropped out. I'm stuck and desperate.

I went to your warehouse, hoping you'd help me. They said you were in Capricorn Cove, so here I am.

I know you're a good man. In those two weeks I saw more kindness from you, more genuine love for your family and your employees than I have ever experienced in my life.

I'm hoping you'll take on my boys. Well, your boys - if you'll have them. I put you as the father on their birth certificates.

They're yours. I've made it so. Their names are Ulf and Leif but you can rename them if you wish.

I know this all seems selfish, but truthfully, I just want them to have the kind of life they deserve. The kind you can give them - one filled with goodness and love.

Don't try to find me. I'm not interested in being a mother and I expect it'll be hard to find me since I used a fake name and ID on the birth certificate.

If you don't want to keep them, that's okay. But I hope you'll do right and find them a good home. Please give them the love and kindness I can't.

Thank you.

Abruptly, the noise cut through the buzzing in my head, overwhelming me as my family shouted questions, the babies screamed, and the police tried to calm everyone down.

"What the fuck is going on here!?" Gunnar bellowed, cutting through the commotion. Even the two babies quietened.

"Sorry to be the bearer of bad news, Gunnar." Sheriff Rodriguez held up his hands in a helpless gesture. "We had these two kids dropped at the station today. No one saw the mother, she left them in the lobby then took off. Left a note though." he nodded at me. "The mother signed over responsibility to your brother."

"Excuse me?" Gunnar asked, setting down the giant pie and bowl of cream he'd been carrying. He walked across the room, the babies resuming their crying.

Not babies, my sons.

I didn't know how to describe what I was feeling in that moment. Joy, anger, frustration, a fuckload of terror. All of it coiling in me as I struggled to process how my life was about to shift.

Has shifted. Fuck.

I watched as Gunnar took Ella's pie and ice cream from her and handed them off to Dad, immediately plucking one of the babies from Astrid and putting it to Ella's shoulder. She rubbed soft circles across its little back as Gunnar walked to me, both of them staring at me with worried eyes.

I cleared my throat, handing the letter to my brother.

"It… it seems like one of our former employees has bequeathed her children to me."

"Who?" Dad demanded, his accent thick with emotion. "Who did this?"

I found myself once again lost for words.

"It doesn't say." Gunnar answered for me. "Just says she worked with us for a while and always remembered Erik's kindness towards her. She'd gone to the other store but got told he was here. She arrived today and left the babies, knowing Erik would be able to take care of them. She's signed them over, said she won't be back for her boys."

"Dear lord," Ella breathed, pressing the little body closer to her, her face pale.

"I'm sorry to do this to you, Erik. Particularly on Christmas." the Sheriff said, looking mighty uncomfortable. "I can take them home with me, or we can call Child Services. Will need to do that anyway. But I figured what with you being named…" He trailed off, looking uncomfortable. "Is there any chance you're the father?"

All eyes came to me and I found myself suddenly frozen.

Was there a chance?

"Oh, Erik…" Ma sounded heartbroken. "How could you?"

"I…" I paused, frowning, shaking my head, clearing the shock. "Actually, I can't be. I haven't been in a relationship since…" I hesitated. "Since, she-who-must-not-be-named. And that was nearly two years ago."

There was a pause as the room processed my words.

"So, what do we do now?" Astrid asked, the second baby cradled in her arms.

Good question.

I blinked, my mind feeling as if I were walking through quicksand, every decision slow and difficult. I looked from one baby to the other, trying to decide what the best option would be.

"I guess we try to find their mother." I finally said, worry sitting deep in my gut.

What if she doesn't mean it? What if she just needs help? I could help her. We all could.

"And if that falls through?" Gunnar asked.

I rubbed a hand over my face, knowing in my gut I couldn't abandon them. "I'll organize the adoption."

Pandemonium broke out once again, Sheriff Tristan trying to bring about calm as my parents and Astrid shouted over each other. Rune and Liv went to the bar for another drink, while Gunnar plucked the other baby from Astrid, moving to stand with Ella. I sighed, turning to deal with the cops.

I had no peace to consider my decision until hours later. The babies were tucked into a temporary crib the motel had managed to find, my family had all gone to bed or were back at the bar, drinking heavily.

I looked down at the two little boys, both of them finally sleeping. Bottles and diapers, formula and a changes of clothes had appeared as if by magic thanks to the Sheriff.

"What am I getting myself into?" I whispered into the quiet. "I'm not cut out for this."

One of the babies shifted. He blinked opening his little eyes then closing them, his hand stretching out.

I hesitated, unsure of what he might need. He squirmed, his little body moving. Terror, pure terror splintered down my spine, freezing my insides.

God, please don't wake up.

I reached down, placing my finger in his palm. His little hand curled around my index finger, barely making the width, his skin ridiculously soft. He settled, his eyes once again blinking at me before closing.

Beside him, his brother wiggled making a slight whimpering sound. I laid a hand on his stomach. He stilled, settling back into sleep.

"Your momma didn't tell me which of you is which." I

whispered, wishing she'd thought to include some more information.

They were quiet, both peacefully sleeping. So little, so vulnerable. My heart skipped, swelling as I watched them.

"You, my little one, will be Ulf," I whispered to the first baby, running my thumb over the fingers that gripped my index.

"And you're Leif," I told the second one, feeling his little chest rise under my hand.

I hesitated, then breathed life into the words that were etching their truth on my heart.

"And I'm Erik. Your dad."

* * *

"So, they're mine?" I watched Sheriff Tristan Rodriguez nod from across the table.

"They're yours," he confirmed, and I felt a weight lift from my chest even as another settled on my shoulders – responsibility.

"It appears that she named you on the birth certificate. Even though the paternity test proves they're not yours by blood, Child Services has cleared you for full adoption." He stood, holding out a hand. I grasped it, blinking as he pumped it twice, a smile breaking across his face. "Congratulations, Daddy."

"Th-thanks," I stuttered, feeling suddenly disconnected from this situation.

"Good luck," he said, clasping a hand to my shoulder and giving a squeeze.

"Umm, yeah," I muttered, sinking back down to the chair in his office as reality set in.

Shit, I'm a dad. Like an actual fucking dad. Fuck. What the fuck do I know about being a parent? Fuck!

Beside me, my sons slept curled tightly around each other, their little hands clasped together. A week ago, on Christmas, these babies had been handed over to me. Their mother, a woman I vaguely remembered employing for a temporary period, had bequeathed them to me. I didn't really remember her beyond a fuzzy outline of a woman who answered our phones while my mother was on sick leave.

But she'd remembered me. Remembered me enough to give me this responsibility. Her letter said she wanted me to be the man to raise her babies. To help them grow into good men. To give them the life and love she couldn't.

"Fuck," I whispered.

A hand slapped the back of my head, pitching me forward. "Ma!"

"Language!" My mother admonished, settling into the chair beside mine and nodding at the babies. "You're not a bachelor any more, Erik. You can't be saying things like that around little ears."

God, another reason I am woefully unprepared for this responsibility.

I turned, panicked, to my mother. "Ma, I can't do this."

"Yes, you can," she corrected, leaning over and straightening the blanket covering my sons' legs. "You're just having jitters."

"No Ma, I really can't." I stood abruptly, tugging at the tie around my neck, loosening it and the top two buttons

102

of my dress shirt. I only ever wore a suit for three reasons – business, funerals, or weddings. Apparently, I could add becoming a parent to that list.

"What do I know about kids? And two? Twins? How the fu—I mean, how am I meant to know what to do?"

"You aren't. Welcome to parenthood." Ma stood, straightening to her full height, reaching out to wrap me in her arms. "Erik, you're a good man. You care, you try hard, and you'll learn. Your father, your siblings and I are all here to help you. You're not doing this alone."

I sighed, letting my mother reassure me.

Call me weak, call me a pussy, I didn't care. I was a fucking momma's boy and proud of it. Hand me the shirt, cancel my man card 'cause I would die for this woman.

"You're going to be a wonderful father." She sniffled, pulling back and then dusting my jacket as if lint had somehow appeared in the last two seconds. "Now, pull yourself together and let's get these babies settled."

I sighed, rubbing a hand over my face. "Thanks, Ma."

"Congratulations, Erik." She stretched on tiptoes and I bent, letting her press a kiss to my cheek. "I'm proud of you... Daddy."

I blew out a breath. "Okay," I turned, looking down at the twins still peacefully sleeping. My heart felt full, a helpless loving warmth suffusing every cell in my body.

"Let's get my sons home."

Chapter One

Erik

"Astrid," I juggled the phone on one shoulder, desperately bopping up and down as Leif screamed in my ear. "Please, I'm begging you. I have the buyer meeting me in less than thirty minutes. The nanny has bailed for the third day in a row, and Ma is in Capricorn Cove, wedding dress shopping with Ella." My eldest brother, Gunnar, was getting married to an amazing woman. I liked Ella, loved my brother, but today? I cursed them both. This wedding had damned inconvenient timing.

I closed my eyes as Ulf started fussing. "Please, Astrid. Please, my favorite sister. Please. I'm begging you, help."

"Shi – I mean, shoot." I muttered registering the date. I'd forgotten to change the month... twice. "When did you start back?"

"Last week," she replied, and I heard laughter in the background. "Remember? I stayed with you for spring break. I told you I was going back early to get that project done?"

I blinked then sighed as Ulf joined his brother in an effort to break the sound barrier. A familiar smell floated up to me as Leif's butt bubbled under my arm.

"Fuc- er, fudge," I muttered, shifting Leif around.

"What about Liv?" Astrid asked, referring to our sister.

"She's in New York filming."

Panic clawed up my throat.

"Dad?" Astrid asked, sounding just as desperate.

"With Ma."

"Rune?" She asked, referring to our youngest brother.

Desperate times, desperate measures.

"I'll call him." I promised, praying for help. "Sorry to bother you."

"Any time. Good luck. Oh, and if you need, tell Rune you're calling in my favor."

"Favor for what?" I asked, juggling my son onto the changing table positioned in my office.

"Don't worry about it, just call it in.'"

"Will do, thanks Sis."

"Anytime."

I hung up, dropping the phone to the side and immediately focusing on my son. "Right, let's get you cleaned up then call Uncle Rune."

I pulled his onesie free, then gagged as I opened his diaper, finding a poo-ocalypse.

"God damn it, Leif. You're three months old. How is this possible? *How?*"

He gurgled at me, no longer screaming now his diaper was off. This one was my nudist. Even at three months he hated clothing. I knew he'd be ripping clothes off as soon as he gained some motor function.

I cleaned him up as best I could, attempting to keep myself

as clean as possible when shit was literally getting real.

"I'm coming Ulf," I called, hearing him fussing. I finished dressing Leif, then lifted him up and set him on my shoulder. Leif gurgled happily against me, his little legs kicking as I moved to the crib and set him down, placing him beside his brother. Ulf, not one to enjoy being left alone, immediately ceased crying. He reached out, his little hand finding his brother. They both kicked their legs in unison, gurgling happily for a moment as they reconnected.

"You guys are lucky you're cute," I told my sons, rubbing an arm across my forehead. "It makes up for last night's lack of sleep."

I blew out a breath glancing at the clock.

"Fu- er, fudge." I muttered, reaching for my phone and dialing my brother.

"What?" He answered in his usually gruff manner.

"I need a favor."

"Nope."

"Rune, just listen. Astrid said to remind you that you owe her and that I'm calling it in on her behalf."

"Fuck," my brother muttered. "Fine, where are you?"

Relief loosened my shoulders. "Work. The kids are changed and will need a bottle in about twenty. Once done they'll sleep but—"

"Yeah, yeah. I got it," Rune hung up and I breathed a sigh.

My brother was anti-social with a capital anti, but he loved his nephews. He also owned his own business, The Literary Academy, a bookstore slash café which specialized in new and used books as well as kickass coffee and meals. He'd inherited the failing store from my grandmother when she'd finally decided to retire, and within two years had turned it into a profitable venture.

Everything taken care of (for the moment) I went to the bathroom to freshen up, catching a glimpse of myself in the mirror.

Fuck.

Dark circles rimmed under blood-shot eyes. My hair looked disheveled and in need of a cut, while a thick layer of unkempt scruff decorated my cheeks.

Shit. I am the living embodiment of parenthood.

The twins were sleeping more now – thank God. But they were on alternating sleep cycles – fuck you, Satan. Which meant when one was sleeping, the other seemed determined to keep me busy.

I pulled open the medicine cabinet, reaching for shaving cream, a shitty disposable razor, some eye drops and a brush.

As I cleaned up, I praised my ma for her foresight. In addition to being my receptionist and office manager, she stocked our workshop with all sorts of useful items for times exactly like today.

Within five minutes I looked if not presentable then at least alive.

"Good enough," I muttered, tossing the razor and stowing the other items.

Back in my office, the kids were watching the cell of little long ships, Vikings and Valkyries, and, for some reason, a dragon, dance and twinkle above their heads, their little legs kicking and arms flailing as they babbled happily.

Yep, definitely my sons.

I let them gargle away, listening with half an ear while I quickly packed a bag for Rune and mentally rehearsed my sales pitch.

This new client was a heavy hitter with cash to spend. Wanted something sleek and expensive for his wife's birthday. I'd met Nick when he'd flown me out to London just before Christmas and my life went nuclear. The guy had heard about us opening a second shop in Capricorn Cove and was prepared to sign on the dotted line – hopefully. Turns out his wife was from there – strange considering less than six months ago I'd never even heard of the place.

I wanted this sale. Bad. It'd be our first commission for the new workshop, and a great start to our expansion.

At Thor's Shipbuilding we prided ourselves on our attention to detail. Our products, be it a custom wood kayak or an extravagant fifty-foot catamaran were the finest quality available.

I had a team of twenty who worked on our projects. In addition, I had trusted contractors who I'd bring in to do custom work. This business model allowed for flexibility and financial security. If a contractor couldn't deliver to the quality I wanted, that was their issue. If the market fluctuated, I didn't have to let my core team go.

Only, these days the core team was missing two. Gunnar was in Capricorn Cove setting up our second workshop and he'd taken our foreman, Mac, with him. I was pleased our business was expanding, god knew we had more projects on the books than we'd been able to keep up with. But the loss was hitting me hard.

I'd trusted Mac to run the shop and keep shit going while Gunnar took care of the financials as well as working on the builds. I designed and built, but my role had shifted to handling clients over the last few years.

Fact was, since Dad had semi-retired, Gunnar and I had

grown the business. We now sold to exclusive clientele who wanted bespoke luxury. We'd increased our reputation and built a sustainable business that allowed us to expand even while we enjoyed the finer things in life.

Without Gunnar and Mac, much of the responsibility had fallen to me while I tried to find replacements. Yet another thing to add to my to-do list, it could go right after finding a new, more reliable nanny, open college funds for the boys, and pick up more formula.

"Yo," Rune greeted as he entered my office. He stomped directly to the kids, leaning down to place a hand on Ulf's stomach. "They ready?"

I picked up their bag, handing it over with a grateful, "Yep."

"Cool." My brother was six foot eight and built like a brick house. He looked like a mountain, sounded like a bear, and walked with the subtlety of a pack of stampeding buffalo. Unless he was trying to be sneaky, then the fucker was quiet as a whisper. He'd scared the fucking beejebus out of me more times than I cared to admit.

"There's formula in the bag and—"

"We're good," Rune muttered, lifting Leif and putting him in the double stroller. Ulf came next and I watched him settle my son with gentle hands as he started to fuss. "We'll catch you at home." *Shit.*

"Can't you take them to your place?"

Rune lifted a brow. "No."

"Look, just... they've had a rough few days, and the nanny is obviously fired. Or maybe she's just run away screaming."

Can I join her?

"Anyway, I haven't had a chance to clean anything up yet."

Rune shrugged, pushing the stroller through the door.

109

"Later."

"Fudge," I muttered with a sigh knowing exactly how bad my house was. Disaster zone? Nope. More like hazardous waste dump. "Ma's gonna hear about this."

"Boss?" Ian poked his head around the door. "Guy in a fancy ass car just pulled up."

I straightened, reaching for my suit jacket and shrugging it on. "Thanks. I'm on it."

He flashed me a thumbs-up then headed out.

Right. If you get through this, get the orders sorted, post an ad for a new foreman shipwright, then get the boys fed, washed and in bed, you can have half a beer.

I blew out a breath, running a hand through my hair. "Let's hope this guy is worth it."

An hour and a half later I waved the client off, a signed contract in my hand and a weight off my shoulders. Ian came over, clapping a hand on my shoulder.

"He signed?"

"He signed." I confirmed. "Looks like you guys have a job for at least a few more months."

Ian grinned, his teeth standing out against the red of his beard. "Speaking of jobs, not to add to yer load but ye sister called."

I froze, asking hopefully, "Astrid?"

"Nah, the harpy."

I shuddered, closing my eyes.

Liv.

"Did she say what she wanted?"

He shook his head, sawdust puffing out from his hair at the movement. "She don't talk to the likes of me."

That's because she's got a crush on you.

110

I wasn't one for meddling and he'd figure it out, soon enough.

"Better call her then."

"Aye," he muttered, a little of his native Scot slipping free.

I pulled my cell free, dialing my sister. She picked up on the first ring.

"Just listen, don't speak," Liv barked.

I braced. Experience had taught me to expect the worst when it came to Liv.

Please not an elopement. I don't want to have to bury your body.

"Rune called. Your house is a pigsty. That's fine. I get it. You're a single dad, co-owner of a business, you got nanny problems. Erik, I. Get. It."

I opened my mouth to speak but she cut me off.

"But here's the deal. You can't live like that. And, I can't have my nephews living like that. So, here's what I'm gonna do for you."

I closed my eyes, pinching the bridge of my nose and sucking in a deep breath, knowing I was about to hate whatever came out of her mouth.

"My new show is taking off and we've just been renewed for a second season. The test audiences love it. *Love it,* Erik. I have a free month come Friday. Instead of taking off to Fiji like I planned, I'm gonna pack up my girl and bring her and my team to you. We'll spend the month doing our thing and get you all sorted."

Liv paused for effect. "You can thank me now."

I counted to three slowly before responding. "Liv, you know I love you –"

"Oh, I know."

"—but," I continued. "I'm fine. The boys are fine. We're fine. It's just been a busy week."

"Uh, no. Rune found a dead rat in their nursery."

I shot straight. "What?"

"Check family chat."

I pulled the phone away from my ear, fingers rapidly navigating to our family group chat. Sure enough, after a bunch of responses, including one from my mother threatening to immediately come home, there was the picture. A dead rat next to Mr. Snuggles.

I gagged, then bit out a curse. "Fuck."

"Yeah," Liv agreed. "Now, I have the solution."

"Tell me."

"The Queen of Clean." I frowned. "Huh?"

"It's the show I was telling you about at Christmas, remember?"

Nope.

"Vaguely," I lied. Liv made an annoyed sound. To be fair, Christmas day was when the twins were handed over to me – meaning everything else from that time until right this second was a bit of a blur.

"I found Laura on Instagram. She was posting a bunch of cleaning videos for her family's business. She's a fourth generation cleaner and they do everything. As in crime scenes, domestic houses, commercial, you think it, they clean it. The videos are addictive. She even made me want to clean."

Well that's a goddamn miracle.

My sister wasn't exactly known as a domestic goddess.

"So, I reached out and found this amazing personality on the other end. Bro, she's awesome. Like crazy pretty,

112

hilarious, smart and never, not once, shames people for their cleaning practices. She just comes in and wants to help. It's like… if Mary Poppins and Tina Fey had a baby."

What?

"Uh-huh," I muttered, running a hand through my hair. "So, you're gonna bring her here?"

"And get your house ship-shape. You need a hand; Laura is the person to do it."

"I don't know," I muttered, thinking of the piles of dirty onesies and my never-ending laundry basket. Not to mention the dirty dishes and bottles that took up just about every surface in the kitchen…

"Erik, there was a rat in your house."

Shit. Time to swallow your pride, man.

"Fine, when can she start?"

"Friday," Liv confirmed. "We'll arrive Thursday morning, get sorted then start filming Friday." That gave me just two days to clean before they arrived.

"Oh, and you're staying with the parents until Friday."

"I'm what?"

"A rat, Erik. Where there's one, there may be more. The boys could get the plague. Or have their faces eaten off in their sleep. Is that what you want, Erik? A faceless child?"

I shuddered at the image, fear and shame settling in my stomach. I needed to call Rune, get my kids outta there.

"I gotta go."

"Rune's at Ma's. And don't worry, I already let everyone know I'm on it."

"Thanks," I muttered, knowing Ma would still be losing her shit.

Better add a call to ma to my to-do list.

113

"See you Friday, brother of mine."

"Love you."

"Love you and the boys." She hung up, leaving me to dwell in my self-pitying anger.

My boys deserve better. Fuck.

My phone rang and I looked down at the caller id.

"You're the reason I'm in this mess," I told my brother in greeting.

"A rat?" Gunnar asked. "Seriously?"

"I don't know how it got there," I groaned.

"Well, it looked pretty wet, nice and freshly dead, if that's any consolation."

"It's not."

Gunnar cleared his throat, "You know, if it's too much with the kids, and me moving here... well, Ella and I discussed it and we—"

"Stop, no." I interrupted. "Don't even go there."

I ran a hand through my hair. "It's just been a rough few days. The twins had a little stomach upset, they're out of sync with their sleep cycle, the nanny is AWOL, and I was more focused on landing the Del Laurentis account than cleaning."

"Promise?"

"Swear."

There was a pause. I could feel Gunnar weighing whether to push it. Finally, he let it go and I breathed a silent sigh of relief.

"So," he asked. "Did we get it?"

"Dude, you doubt my ability to close a deal? Of course I got it."

He chuckled, "I should have known better."

"You wound me," I said, mockingly. "For that, baby-sitting duties next time you're in town. A whole weekend."

"Fine," Gunner grumbled. I heard him suck in a breath, like he was startled.

"You okay?"

"Um, nothing. I... I gotta go."

I rolled my eyes. "You saw Ella."

"Yeah."

"Is she naked?"

"New swimsuit."

I sighed. "Go. Leave me to do the work of three men while you plunder and pillage."

"Thanks, owe you."

He hung up, and I looked out at the water, breathing in the salt, listening to the familiar soundtrack of my workshop. Taking one last calming breath, I turned to the workshop, calling,

"Ian? You got a minute? We need to talk schedules for this month."

The Queen of Clean better be worth it.

Chapter Two

Laura

The Uber pulled up to the house as I glanced at the address on my phone for the third time confirming that, yes, we were in the right place.

Wow.

The modern beach house stood at two stories with a beautiful balcony at the front, and lots of windows. Painted a gorgeous, navy blue with white highlights, the house stood amongst a cute little garden brimming with flowers, and even had a little white picket fence. I half expected a Labrador to come tearing out, tail wagging ready to greet me.

"Looks like a postcard, don't it?" The driver remarked.

"Indeed," I agreed, reaching for my bag. "Thanks for the ride."

"Any time, let me help you with your bags." He got out, helping to unload my three suitcases, two boxes of cleaning products, and tools from the trunk.

"You want me to bring these up to the house?" he asked, pulling my hand truck free and loading it with my baggage.

Yep, I was the kind of woman who owned and travelled with her own moving equipment.

"No, thank you. I've got it from here." I smiled. "Thank you so much."

"Have a good day, Ms. Sweep." He got in the car and pulled away while I took in the picture-perfect house once more.

Gorgeous didn't even come close to the beauty of this place. It felt... serene. Peaceful. Like a sanctuary.

Like home...

I shook off the thought, gripped the handles of the truck and swung the little gate open, pushing my things along the cobbled walkway up to the porch. Wisteria vines wrapped around a small entry arbor, a beautiful, whimsical way to welcome you into the yard.

Note to self, the garden needs a weeding and good tidy.

As beautiful as the entry was, I couldn't help but catalogue the few minor issues I'd already noticed. Weeds sprang from fertile soil, the flowers and bushes were beginning to become overgrown, and the grass looked a little long, as if it had needed a cut a week or two ago.

The porch itself felt abandoned, cobwebs hung from corners and I noted the layer of sand and dust that coated the porch swing. I could smell the sea and thought I could hear the waves lapping, though I wasn't quite sure how far I was from actual water.

I raised a hand to knock on the door and heard an almighty crash follow my brisk tap. There was silence for a moment then what sounded like a male cursing. The unmistakable wailing of a baby followed.

I hesitated, wondering if I should come back.

Footsteps sounded on the other side with a deep voice

calling, "Coming, Liv."

"Oh," I called, "I'm not—" The door was wrenched open as I finished saying, "—Liv."

I blinked, staring at the wealth of skin before me, my mind uncharacteristically blanking.

Skin. Man. Hot. Dirty. Skin. Filthy. Man.

The chest was broad with a smattering of hair and some muscle. Not six-pack chiseled but defined enough to make me appreciate that this was someone who did manual labor…. Or went to the gym. He was covered in flour and some kind of sticky coating.

Was that… chocolate?

"Shit, you're not Liv," the person who owned the magnificent chest muttered.

I was dimly aware that he was speaking, but all I saw was a filthy dirty man.

And I wanted to ride him like a pogo stick. After I cleaned him. Preferably with my tongue.

Whoa. Down girl. Abort! Abort!

With conscious effort I pulled myself together, managing to look up and into the face of this demi-god.

"You must be The Queen of Clean," the guy said, a small smile playing at the corners of his mouth.

"Laura Sweep," I confirmed, holding out my own hand to shake. He clasped it and I about died. His hand engulfed mine, making my large one feel small and dainty. His palm was calloused but warm and strong as he gently squeezed.

I wanted that hand on me. Everywhere. Now.

Pull it together, Laura!

"Sweep?"

"Family name," I said absently. "We own the Clean Sweep

118

Company." My gaze dropped and I nearly swallowed my tongue.

He's wearing grey sweatpants. Please Lord, I need some help right now. Forgive me for these less than pure thoughts. Satan is tempting your girl something fierce today, Lord.

My lady parts tingled for the first time in... well, a long damn time. And I was more than happy to have stumbled across this hunk of a man.

"Come on in," he invited. "I'll just be a second. Gotta get the baby."

He turned, hurrying down the hall and disappearing. I entered, immediately assessing the situation even as I tried to shake off my attraction to my client.

The only time I ever lost control like this was when... actually, I never lost control like this. This was legitimately the first time I'd ever had my brain lock into a sexual frenzy.

Unsurprising. I mean, did you see that guy?

I forcibly refocused on the house. It was... well, describing it as a disaster zone would be kind. Baby clothes, toys, books, blankets and what looked like a plate with a crusty piece of half-eaten toast decorated the entry. A quick peek into the first room showed a sitting area that had been reconfigured as a playroom. It too was a mess.

How many kids does this couple have?

Liv had been pretty vague when she'd explained this project.

"An opportunity has come up. The house is a mess and they need an urgent intervention. Can you be in Cape Hardgrave by Friday?"

I'd immediately said yes, expecting to treat this like any other job. I'd live with the family, work out their ebb and flow, try and figure out what their triggers were, then teach them a few tips and tricks to get their house organized and improve their cleanliness.

No problem.

Only, there was a problem. A very large, very shirtless, very attractive problem. And my lady parts were totally onboard with this particular problem.

"Sorry," the guy returned, walking back down the hall towards me. In his arms were two babies and I blinked as he carried them, sending me a sheepish look.

"Leif and Ulf are only here while I tried to grab some clothing but I guess I should have just waited till tomorrow, yeah?"

I blinked, taking in the hot guy who just became even hotter as he carried the babies.

"Sorry, I… I need a minute." I told him, placing a hand to my chest. "What's your name?"

He frowned, "Liv didn't tell you?"

"No," I murmured, watching as one of the babies snuggled closer into the guy's chest.

"I'm Erik, Liv's brother." He hefted the babies up slightly. "And these are my sons, Leif, and this big man is Ulf."

"Well," I blinked, staring at the adorable babies. "Twins. You and your wife must be busy."

"Actually, it's just me."

"Just—" I looked at the chaos with new eyes. "You're a single dad?"

"Yeah, long story but I adopted these two." He pressed a kiss to Ulf's head. "Worth every minute of crazy."

Adopted. He'd adopted twins. Be still my heart, this man deserved a blow job followed by a beer.

"Wow," was all I could manage. "You're brave."

He chuckled. "Or stupid. Verdict is still out."

His place wasn't dirty or unorganized out of neglect, it was chaos because this poor guy was living with two babies and little sleep every day on his own.

I reached across, laying a hand on Ulf's back. "Can I help you with one?"

The guy looked unreasonably grateful. "Actually, could you take both for a minute? I was just trying to get a load of washing on but knocked over the detergent. It's everywhere."

"Oh, why don't you look after them and I'll get it sorted?" I asked, glancing down the hall. "Which way is the laundry?"

"It's through the kitchen but—"

I didn't let him finish, immediately setting off. Cleaning was not only in my name, my blood or my job title, it was a part of me.

Some people hated cleaning. I knew that. But my earliest memories were going along with my family to jobs. Mom or Dad would hand me my own spray bottle and rag and they'd let me clean a window or dust a table. We'd listen to music and they'd press kisses to my cheeks, exclaiming over my efforts and how wonderfully spotless everything looked.

As I got older, the need to clean, to give people that ah… moment that came when entering a beautifully clean house, grew. When Instagram took off, I started posting videos showing us cleaning various filthy things. People seemed to enjoy the videos so I kept posting and people kept watching and then it got kind of crazy.

Someone had shared a video I did of cleaning dried blood off a blouse. A local news station picked it up and ran the story on their morning show. I'd been invited to discuss cleaning and they'd loved me and asked me to be part of a regular segment. Liv had seen it and contacted me about recording a series where I helped families who needed a spring clean. Next thing I knew, I had eight episodes recorded and the network wanted another season – this time twelve episodes.

Cleaning was addictive viewing, apparently. Go figure.

The kitchen was equally as filthy as the rest of the house. Food crusted across surfaces, the kitchen sink overflowing. Flour and chocolate sauce were splattered across the floor and up some cupboards.

"I knocked it over looking for the spare can of baby formula," Erik said with a laugh as we passed. "Then did the same in the laundry trying to clean my chocolate coated shirt."

I flicked him a smile over my shoulder as I bypassed the mess. "Don't worry, I know exactly what to do to get chocolate stains out."

I found the laundry and laughed. Two giant piles of dirty washing sat on a counter. This room was just as beautiful as the rest of the house – if you overlooked the current mess.

I found the broom closet and pulled out a dustpan and brush, quickly cleaning the spilled detergent and making a mental note to add child-proof locks to my list of things to talk to Erik about. His kids were still little but they'd be crawling soon, and a quick look in the under-sink cabinet showed a few things that could definitely hurt their little bodies.

"Thank you," Erik said from behind me as I finished cleaning the spill and began to sort the clothing.

"Don't worry about it," I offered him a grin, "I actually love cleaning."

"Well, you'd be the first in this house." He had one baby on his arm now, a bottle in hand. The other baby was on his back, expertly held there by a woven wrap.

He should have looked ridiculous, or at least a little less attractive. Instead, his hot factor increased and I found myself doing a scrupulous rub of the corners of my mouth to ensure I wasn't drooling.

"I just needed some decent clothes before tomorrow," he continued, adjusting the bottle for the little one to drink. "We're staying at the parentals' while they're visiting my brother and his fiancé. This house is ready to be condemned, so I may as well go fu- er, mess up theirs."

I hid a grin as I began to sort the piles of dirty laundry. "I wouldn't go that far. It's just a little mess, nothing that can't be fixed."

"You say that now but just wait." Erik warned.

He shifted slightly, his big body brushing against the broom and knocking it over. It fell, smacking the ground and startling the babies. They both began to cry.

"Fuc- er, fudge!" He barked. He began to bop on his toes, up and down, trying to soothe the babies.

"Still having trouble self-censoring?" I asked, enjoying watching this man navigate chaos.

He barked out a laugh. "Who knew I swore as much as I do? Never realized I had such a filthy mouth."

Oh, honey. I know exactly what you can do with that filthy mouth.

I chided myself, picking up a pile of sorted colors and placing them in the machine.

I added detergent and switched it on, glancing out the external laundry door, my body immediately locking.

"What?" Erik asked, immediately coming to my side. "Is it another rat?"

"Another- no!" I laughed. "And ew. Really? A rat?"

He sighed. "It was only a little one but still…."

I shook my head. "No, it's the water. I haven't seen the ocean in…. forever."

He shifted the feeding baby and tilted his head toward the door. "You wanna see?"

I nodded eagerly.

He led me outside. The laundry sat off to the end of his house. Outside, there was a large outdoor covered entertaining area, complete with outdoor grill, kitchen and firepit. There were some old growth trees, a large stretch of backyard, then a fence blocking the grass from the jetty.

"We're in the lagoon. If you take the boat down that way," he jerked his head to the left, "in about two miles you'll be in the ocean."

"Wow," I whispered, watching the water gently lap. "This is incredible. Your boys are so lucky to be growing up in such an incredible house."

"Less than two months ago I lived in a little apartment over my workshop."

I raised an eyebrow. "Workshop?"

"Did Liv tell you anything about me?"

I shook my head, turning back to watch the water. "Just that you needed my help."

"Typical," he muttered. "Well, I'm co-owner with my brother, Gunnar, of Thor's Shipbuilding. We inherited the business from my dad on his retirement, who inherited it

124

from his dad and so on and so forth. We build boats. Yachts, kayaks, luxury or business, you name it we build it. We're well known, got a good client base, got excellent products. We're popular, and we've just expanded this year to a new workshop down in Capricorn Cove, you know it?"

"Can't say I do."

He shrugged. "Neither did I till my brother ended up there after a dodgy engine and fell into the lap of the love of his life. But the town is well-placed and we're now owners of the local marina. Expanding, diversifying our interests. You know?"

I nodded; it was what my family had done as well. People always needed cleaners, but some were in more demand than others when an economy tanked.

"Anyways, I lived at the workshop, stockpiled my money and had a chunk of change sitting there for when I got married and wanted to settle down." He looked down at his son. "Turns out, the cart came before the horse but I'm not complaining." He sent me a rueful grin. "Wanted to buy a fixer-upper but with these two keeping me busy, Ma talked me into a move-in-ready and next thing I knew I was buying this place."

"It's perfect," I shot him a teasing grin, "if not a little messy."

He barked out a laugh. "Yeah, well it's more work than anything else at the moment with just me. Normally Ma or my sisters help but they've been living their own lives and I'm swamped at work. It's our busy season, everyone wants to buy a boat for summer. Too bad I have to break the news that our boats take longer than a week to make."

I looked back out at the water, a contented sigh slipping free. "It may be more work now, but as they grow this is going to be a forever kind of home. Your boys will have cookouts back here, swim in the lagoon, and build a treehouse, and you'll probably get a dog at some point."

"Hush your mouth," he barked, pretending to turn away from me, covering one of Leif's ears. "Don't give them ideas."

I laughed. "You've done the right thing, Erik. Your boys will thank you for it."

He made a non-committal sound in reply.

We stood outside, the sound of the water, the rustle of a slight breeze in the leaves, the smell of salt and sea, and the gurgles of babies our accompaniment.

I tilted my head to the sun, closing my eyes enjoying the warmth of the beautiful Spring day. A deliciously selfish thought crossed my mind.

I could get used to this.

A hot man, beautiful babies and a gorgeous house. Who couldn't?

Don't even go there. Ignore the pull. You know single dads are your kryptonite. Abort! Abort!

But I couldn't help the tiny kernel of… something that unfurled in me. It wasn't hope or lust or anything so simple. This was deep and earthy, grounding and solid. It felt complex and distinct.

"Can I take you to lunch?" Erik's question snapped me out of my revelry.

"Lunch?" I repeated, as if the word were foreign.

"Yeah, there's a bunch of great cafes just down from here. Can I tempt you?"

"Of course," I replied, watching him grin in response. For a moment his gaze dropped, brushing across my breasts and down my body. I saw the flash of approval in his eyes before

126

he snapped back to attention.

"Let me just have a quick shower then we can go."

"Sure."

He walked away, and I shamelessly ogled his ass. Tight and gorgeous. Zero regrets.

Oh yes, this man was very dangerous.

Chapter Three

Erik

I lay in bed that night, replaying the day's events in my head, all of which seemed to focus intensely on Laura.

Laura Sweep, a woman with curves, smiles and a wicked sense of humor. She loved kids, animals, and cleaning. She'd delighted in my house, loved our town, and jumped into helping me with the twins throughout the day.

If I had words to describe Laura, I'd say cheerfully capable. And for a single dad struggling, that was hot as fuck. The fact she was also a walking wet dream? Bonus.

God, what do I need to do to get her stay?

My cock ached. It'd been over two years since my last relationship and god knew by the time that had ended, she'd killed whatever had been left of my mojo.

Let's just say, if Dolores Umbridge had been a super-hot woman of twenty-eight, that would have been my ex.

I pushed away all thoughts of that soul-destroying woman and concentrated back on Laura. Her curves, her smile, the way she cooed to Ulf when she'd held him while I fed Leif over lunch. We'd returned and she'd helped me get the boys settled, clear out the guest room where she was temporarily staying, and then we'd sat outside watching the sunset while I'd grilled some burgers and we'd enjoyed the unusually warm Spring night.

She'd arrived a day early thanks to Liv's hapless assistant mixing up their flights.

Thank you, God.

I slipped a hand down, fisting my cock and biting back a groan as I imagined Laura walking into this room, a cotton dress swishing about her knees, a knowing grin on her face.

If she were here, I'd order her to strip, watching as her beautiful breasts bounced free. I'd get her to crawl up the bed, then drag my lips down her body, tasting and teasing until she was a rosy, flushed squirming mess of desire.

I fisted harder, knowing I was close as I tilted my head back, imaging her taste, imagining her whimpers, hot with need for a woman I'd only met hours before.

A fractured cry stopped my desire with the power of a car crash. I swore, immediately throwing back my bed sheets and rolling to my feet as Leif's cries filtered through the baby monitor.

I hiked up my sweatpants, grimacing as I readjusted my hard as a rock cock. It ached in protest.

I know buddy. I get it. Cockblocked. Again. Fudge.

I made my way to my kids' room, trying to think of things like poopy diapers and baby vomit to get the monster hard-on to ease. It helped. Just.

Leif lay in his bed, his little hands clenched, his screams loud and angry.

"I know, little man, I'm here." I cooed, picking him up and pulling him to my chest. "The world is an angry and terrible place. Tell Daddy all about it."

I did the familiar parent bounce, trying to comfort my crying son as I figured out what was wrong.

Diaper is fine. Temperature feels good. He ate an hour ago so he should be good. Gas?

I laid a hand on his little back, rubbing gently as he continued to protest.

"Is he okay?" the sleepy voice asked quietly from the door.

I turned, and immediately regretted looking. My hard-on roared back to life. Two-and-a-bit years of sex deprivation had regressed my libido to fourteen-year-old Erik.

Hubba hubba.

If this were a cartoon, my eyes would have bulged out of my head, my tongue rolling right to the floor. Laura was stunning.

She wore tiny sleep pants and a long shirt. Her breasts were free under the material and I could just see the outline of her nipples.

Jesus man, you're a father now. Get your mind out of the gutter.

But I couldn't. I really, really fucking couldn't. I wanted to kiss up her curvy legs, wanted to fuck those tits and cum all over her body. I wanted to taste between her legs until she shattered, then do it all over again.

I must have given myself away as awareness spiked in the room. Her gorgeous nipples hardened under my gaze, a delicious blush coloring her cheeks.

"D-did you want a hand?" She asked, crossing both arms over her ample chest and blocking my view.

Yes please.

I mentally chastised myself for the barrage of mental

images of exactly where I wanted Laura's hand to go.

"I think we're good," I said, regretfully. "Thanks though."

Just as I said it, Murphy's Law kicked in and Ulf began to stir breaking the tension.

"Shi—shoot," I sighed. "Actually, I would love a hand. Can you take Ulf? He normally only wants a cuddle."

"Aww," Laura walked over to the crib, lifting Ulf and pulling him close. "Are you a little snuggler?" She asked, settling in the rocking chair beside his crib.

I continued to pace, knowing Leif would eventually settle. His hiccupped cries already starting to slow.

"For some reason you expect twins to be the same. Same looks, same little mannerisms. And this young, you don't expect them to have personalities. Like, they're too little to be anything but a sleepy little ball of cuteness. But that's really not the case. Leif is my loud kid. Always wailing his desires, letting the world know he's here and he wants everything now. Ulf is quieter. He loves to cuddle, will just relax in your arms and let you hold him without protest for hours." I smiled down at my boy. "Can't wait for them to start talking."

Laura's chuckle was soft and pleasing, my dick jerking his approval.

"Be careful what you wish for," she said, pushing off with one foot and setting the chair to a gentle rock. "My sister's kids are nuts. From the time Arabella could speak she hasn't shut up. And she's sassy. I babysat her and her brother a few months back. Her brother had a fall while I wasn't watching and she immediately told me she wouldn't nark if I gave them candy." She chuckled again. "Little scammer."

I found myself smiling, the bone-aching tiredness I'd lived

with for months briefly fading. "I expect life will be crazy, but I'm looking forward to it."

Laura bit her lip, tilting her head to one side as she considered me.

"You want to know why I took them on."

She huffed out a laugh. "That obvious?"

"Nah, it's just the same question everyone asks."

I pulled Leif closer, breathing in his baby smell. His little hand reached out, brushing the side of my face as he watched me with big, sleepy eyes. "When they were handed to me my first thought was no fuc- I mean, fudging way."

Laura dipped her head, but not before I caught a glimpse of her amused smile.

"But then, I don't know. I read the note their momma left me, and I saw their tiny bodies. It had snowed, and I remember thinking, how can I toss them out into the cold?"

I shook my head, shooting her a grin. "They wouldn't have been in the actual cold. The Sheriff was there, and I'm sure they would have called Child Services or something." I looked back down at Leif. "But it was Christmas. And they were screaming and there were no toys for them and I just thought, wow, I need to do something."

"And you did."

I nodded, looking back at Laura. Her eyes were warm with approval, her face tinged with a little pink. In her arms, she held my son, his sweet little body turned into her. "Yeah, best decision of my life." I admitted, shifting Leif slightly. "Hardest too. And loudest. And messiest. But the best." "Well," Laura stood, taking Ulf over to his crib and gently laying him down. "I can't help with the loud, but I can definitely help with the messy."

Can you help with the hard too? My cock asked.

Fuck, I'm a bastard.

She grinned at me, a sparkle in her eye. "I spoke to Liv tonight, she told me the name of the episode."

I braced.

"Daddy I'd like to Clean." She chuckled as I sighed, rolling my eyes.

"Liv is a nut."

"I love her," Laura declared, coming to me and holding her hands out for Leif. I let him go and she took him to the rocking chair, settling back down. "She's making my dreams come true."

"You dreamed of being a reality TV star?" I asked, eyebrows raising in surprise.

"Nah," she set the chair to rocking, tucking Leif's body close to her. My squirmy kid immediately settled, blinking up at her in surprise.

Oh, so you'll do it for her but not for me. Traitor.

Not that I blamed him. I wouldn't mind being snuggled up to those breasts right now either.

Down, boy.

"My real dream is to branch out on my own. My family all have their place at the company. But I was an unexpected surprise. Baby number five. The odd addition. No one really knew what to do with me, and I needed to find my own place." She shrugged. "Turns out, this is what I'm good at. Helping people."

"Does it stick?" I asked, watching her with an almost trance-like obsession.

"Does what stick?"

"The cleaning tips. The families you help?"

"Oh," she chuckled. "Sometimes, yes. I have a private group where they all send me questions and share cleaning tips. One family immediately reverted back to their former ways – but they had bigger issues than I could help with. But others take it on. They just never got taught how to do things or thought that cleaning products were too expensive or a million other myths."

"Do you enjoy it?"

"Love it," she said, flashing me a smile. "There's nothing more satisfying than helping people. And a clean environment, an organized environment, it helps people be creative, restore balance. It gives them the space to reconnect. Your environment is so—" she cut herself off with a laugh. "I'm preaching, sorry."

"It's fine," I tried unsuccessfully to hide a yawn. "I'm seriously interested but it's late and I've barely scraped together three hours of sleep over the last two days."

"Go," Laura lifted a hand making a shooing movement. "I've got these two. Go sleep."

I blinked. "I couldn't do that."

But God is it tempting.

"Sure, you can. I have stellar babysitting references, a great smile and know how to change a diaper." She jerked her head at the door. "Go. If I need anything, I'll call you."

My feet led the way, the temptation of sleep too much. "If you're sure…."

"Go!" she called, laughing. "I got this."

I went back to bed, face planting on the mattress and letting out a long, satisfied sigh.

"He's a good daddy," I heard Laura murmur through the baby monitor. "You're very lucky to have him."

134

Leif gurgled and she laughed quietly. "Oh yes, you are. So, so lucky, aren't you?"

I smiled, eyes closed, listening to Laura's calming voice and my kid's soft sounds as I drifted off to sleep.

Chapter Four

Erik

Whose idea was this?

I silently berated myself as my sister, my own flesh and blood, gleefully led a camera team around my house, pointing in horror at new hygiene issues to film.

"I found mold!" Someone yelled excitedly from my downstairs bathroom.

"I've got dust," another called from the living room. "Layers of it."

A grown man shouldn't sound that excited by dust.

Laura stood in my kitchen, her hair and makeup being touched up as we waited for Liv to get her shots.

This was day two of what I assumed would be a never-ending filming cycle. Yesterday hadn't been this bad.

I'd woken from the best sleep I'd had in months to find Laura had fed, changed and moved the twins downstairs, Mozart playing as she'd dangled soft toys for them to grab. She'd made me breakfast, smiled at my sleepy questioning, then directed me to shower.

I'd planned on taking her and the boys out for a quick

walk but Liv had arrived, entourage in tow. We'd spent the day doing posed pictures and filming shots of me with the boys. Laura had explored the house while I'd been otherwise occupied.

I gritted my teeth, going in search of my sister.

"Liv," I called, tracking her down in the twins' room. "We need to talk."

She made a dismissive gesture, directing the cameraman to film something in the boys' toy chest. Of all the rooms in the house this one was the cleanest. I made sure of that.

"Liv," I barked, finally losing my patience. "Now!"

She sighed, straightening and moving to me. "Didn't figure you for a diva."

"Liv," I sucked in a breath, forcing calm into tone. "Here's the thing. You can't do anything that could put me at risk of losing the boys, or bring my business into disrepute."

She frowned. "Why on earth would you assume I'd allow that to happen?"

I blew out a breath, crossing my arms over my chest. "This is overwhelming, Liv. I legitimately don't know if I should be grateful or shitting myself. There are people everywhere, you hired someone to nanny my kids, there's a woman currently picking through my junk drawer." I shook my head. "Everyone has dirty laundry, mine's now gonna be on TV."

"Yeah," Liv replied, getting close and laying a hand on my arm. "But only in a way that makes it seem like you're overwhelmed."

Which I am.

"Which you are," she said, giving my arm a slight squeeze. "And that's okay. The narrative we're pushing is: great dad, loves his kids, successful businessman, just overwhelmed by the changes in his life and needs a little help." She smiled. "I got this, bro. You're safe. The boys are safe. I'm not going to do anything to jeopardize your life."

I let out the breath I'd been unwittingly holding. "Right, of course. Thanks."

Liv chuckled. "You've got nerves. You're fine, Erik. Just breathe. We're all only here to help."

I nodded, still not entirely convinced but willing to try.

"Great, gotta get back to it. Go find Laura in the kitchen, she'll fill you in on her first suggested change and we'll get that filmed in an hour once the kids go down." With that, Liv turned back, directing the camera guy to take a sweeping shot of the room.

Dismissed and only slightly less anxious, I left, heading for the kitchen. Laura stood at my island counter, a clear laundry tub filled with soapy water on one side, a pile of dirty bottles on the other.

"You ready?" I came around, standing beside her. The production crew shuffled around everyone getting into place.

"I mean," I nodded at the people avidly watching us. "Sure?"

She chuckled. "Just concentrate on me. It gets easier, promise."

Oh, baby. I'll concentrate on you every day.

I shoved the thought aside, subtly shifting. Turns out Laura was a magnet for my dick.

"Okay," Liv called, settling in beside the camera guy. "Let's get this started." She looked at us. "Quiet guys, and action!"

Laura smiled straight at the camera. "If you're not a parent who breastfeeds, then today we're going to be talking about one of the most important cleaning actions a parent can do in the kitchen when they have young ones, sterilizing bottles."

She proceeded to explain the importance of good sterilization and the reason behind it – stopping bacteria. I listened, interested and at the same time a little aroused by how good she was at this. Laura... sparkled. She gave off this energy and warmth that said, I'm not here to preach, I'm here to help.

And I lapped it up. I watched her dip the bottle into the soapy water, explaining where people should pay particular attention when cleaning.

"These days, most bottles are dishwasher safe, but it's worth us knowing what to look for when we pull them out. Dishwashers do a great job, and save a lot of time, but they're not perfect." She then turned to me, "Erik, can you assist?"

The cameras and lights followed me as I dipped my hands into the hot water and followed her instructions.

"Very good," she praised, holding up my cleaned nipple and bottle. "Now, we're going to talk about how to store this in an easy to organize way. As Erik knows, the worst thing is trying to find a bottle and lid during early morning feedings, am I right?"

I chuckled. "Try telling a three-month-old to wait for his food. You wanna know what hell looks like? My kid can definitely tell you."

We both laughed.

"Cut!" Liv yelled, immediately coming to stand beside us. "That was amazing you guys. You're absolutely sparking together. The chemistry is," she raised a fist to her lips, pretending to blow on a burn. "Sizzling."

I rolled my eyes. "Thanks, I think."

"We're resetting for the pantry so that gives you five. Grab a drink or whatever and we'll get set up." Liv strolled away, disappearing back into the chaos.

"Gonna admit, never thought I'd find learning how to clean interesting."

Laura laughed. "No one ever does."

"Do you want to have dinner with me?" The words flowed out of my mouth before I could rethink the proposition.

Laura froze, her mouth forming a small 'o'. "Really?"

"Shit, sorry," I ran a hand through my hair. "Fuck, that was bad right? Sorry."

"No, I mean," she cleared her throat. "I'd love to."

I perked up. "Serious?"

"Yeah." A warm grin split her lips. "Seriously."

Yes. Don't you fuck this up.

I cleared my throat. "Great, I'll organize a sitter. Next weekend work?"

"Sounds perfect." We grinned at each other for a protracted moment.

"Laura, can you come here a minute?" My sister called from the living room, breaking the awareness between us.

"No rest for the wicked," Laura sighed, rolling her eyes good-naturedly.

I watched her move through the room, unashamedly watching her ass, my cock throbbing his approval.

You're not fourteen anymore, dickhead. Pull it together.

I did, but God it was hard.

Pun intended.

Chapter Five

Laura

"Erik," I said, exasperated with the man. "What on earth are you doing?"

He looked up from where he was seated in his massive garage, piles of junk haphazardly scattered around him.

"Sorting." He lifted a yearbook he was currently perusing. "Gotta check if it sparks joy, right?"

I sucked in a calming breath then slowly blew it out, incredibly aware of the cameras capturing every moment.

"I left you here three hours ago. Three hours. What have you done during that time?"

He gestured to a shoebox. "Figured what I want to get rid of."

I heard a strangled laugh from the crew behind me.

Calm, Laura. Stay calm.

Erik, it turns out, may have moved from a tiny apartment to this giant house, but it hadn't stopped him from hoarding things in a storage container. A very large, very expensive storage container.

I'd never seen Liv more excited than when we'd cracked

141

that baby open and a box had immediately tumbled out, spilling its contents on the concrete entry. The contents being, wait for it, empty used tissue boxes.

I still twitched thinking about it.

"Magnificent television," Liv had declared, practically dancing with delight. "My brother is a hoarder!"

Erik had protested, but even I had to admit he seemed to have difficulty letting things go. I mean, used tissue boxes?

Erik had explained that he used the cardboard when creating lettering for different painting projects. But I wasn't so sure. It had taken a full day, but we'd cleared all the junk and brought it back to his house, unloading it in his garage.

I tasked him with getting down to the bare minimum. In three hours, he'd only managed a shoebox. A freaking shoebox?

Breathe Laura. Even perfect men have their issues.

I crouched in the garage, reaching for the box and rummaging inside. There were three receipts, a stray button, two bent paper clips and a chocolate wrapper inside.

"Erik," I said slowly, clearly. "Please don't tell me this is it."

He tilted his head to the side, giving me an eyebrow lift. "Are you disappointed?"

Calm!

"I'm not disappointed, just… surprised." I said finally. "There's a lot still to get through if this is it."

"It took me a while to double check the button wasn't from one of my existing shirts."

I blinked once. Then again. My vision clouding with grey as Erik watched me. For a beat he looked utterly genuine then his lip twitched, his eyes brightening right before he burst out laughing, slapping a hand on his knee.

Behind me, I heard the crew laugh.

"You goddamned liar," I said, picking up a stuffed animal and throwing it at him. "You're already done!"

He caught it easily.

"Mostly," he agreed, still chuckling. Erik tossed the toy from hand to hand. "Gotcha."

"Totally," I agreed, reaching for the yearbook. "Now show me your photo."

He groaned, then flicked through presenting me with an image I wasn't expecting.

"Glasses and braces." I laughed. "You were head of the drama club."

"Four years," he agreed. "Never did land an actual role, turns out I'm not very good. But I was enthusiastic."

I patted him on the shoulder. "I'm sure that helped."

He laughed. "Not even once."

I looked around at the space. "So, getting back to this mess. What can go?"

Erik gestured at a pile of furniture and boxes. "That's for the house." He twisted, nodding at another rough pile. "That's for donations, and that," he pointed to the last rough pile. "Is junk and can be tossed."

I eyed the second largest pile. "And exactly where in your house are these things going?"

Erik hesitated.

"You were going to say the attic, weren't you?"

He huffed out a laugh, shrugging. "They're things the boys will use when they get older."

I pushed up, crossing to the pile and began to sort through it. "Okay, the desk can go in your office—you need one. This," I held up a ratty jersey. "You really want to keep this?"

143

"Hey," Erik snatched it away from me, hugging it to his chest. "This is a prized possession."

I quirked an eyebrow, skeptical.

"This, my friend, is a St Louis Blues jersey. A jersey that I wore every single day of the 2018-19 season. The season, Laura, where they started as the lowest team in the entire competition. Fifty-four years without a Stanley Cup. Everyone gave them zero chance of a change. They lost a coach before the season, and had a rookie goalie. No one but the fans believed in them. Then they won eleven games in a row. They made it to the Western Conference finals. Then the Stanley Cup finals. Then they won the whole thing. The whole damned thing, Laura." He lifted the jersey. "It took me all season but I got every single signature." He gave me a serious look. "And I didn't even touch on the babies, puppy or Bob and Layla."

Bob?

"Are we talking about St. Louis, Missouri?" I asked. "You don't live anywhere near there."

"But my ma is born and raised, and my grandparents bleed blue all year long."

"Well, hand it over then." I gestured at him. He hesitated then gave me the jersey, watching suspiciously as I smoothed it out then held it up to the light, examining the fabric and noting the placement of the signatures.

"What are you going to do with it?" He asked, watching me like a hawk.

"You'll see." I tossed it over my shoulder, gesturing towards the internal door. "Now, would you like to see your newly improved kitchen?"

"Lead on." The crew followed us; a second crew already

set up to capture Erik's reaction. He didn't disappoint.

His mouth dropped open, his eyes bugging out of his head as he looked around. "I have white tiles."

I laughed, nodding. "Yeah, turns out they just had years of grime build up. A deep scrub and soak and that backsplash looks like new."

"Damn," he muttered, running a hand over the kitchen countertop. "I haven't seen this since before I moved in."

He wasn't wrong. The kitchen had been particularly heinous.

I opened his pantry, gesturing for him to come see.

"Holy... wow," he remarked, surprised at the orderliness. "I can actually see what I own."

"Actually..."

Erik laughed, moving to the fridge, opening it, then laughing again. "You did."

I shrugged. "Got to do a thorough clean."

I guided him through the kitchen, explaining how we'd change a few cupboards to drawers, and showing him how to use the new kid safety locks we'd placed on them. I showed him where I'd stored his various items, and guided him through the new process I'd put in place to make his life easier by food prepping.

"Seriously, Laura. I can't thank you enough." Erik said, looking overwhelmed. "It may not seem like a lot to you, or to others. I mean, it's just some drawers and some cleaning. But this is gonna save me. I haven't had time to do anything but eat, sleep, feed babies and work since the twins came. And even the sleep is in pretty short supply." He quirked a smile my way. "Seriously, thank you. This is huge, I feel like a weight has been lifted off me."

"You're welcome." I finally said, emotion welling up. "Now, should we get started on your living room?"

He laughed. "No rest for the wicked?"

"No rest when there's mess," I corrected with a cheeky smile.

"Then lead on, Queen of Clean."

"And cut," Liv called. I snapped back to, suddenly reminded of the camera crew.

"That was great guys, let's reposition in the living room. You've got five for a break while we get sorted."

Erik reached out, capturing my hand before I could walk away. "Queenie, seriously. Thank you."

I made a dismissive gesture with my hand. "Anyone can do this."

"But you did it for me. And for my boys. And that means something."

I tried to reply but found myself at a loss for words. Erik's expression was deadly serious, his gratitude palpable.

"Any time," I finally said. He squeezed my hand and then let it go. "Guess we're in the living room?"

"Uh, yeah." I replied. "Just give me a minute."

I made my way to the bathroom, splashing a little water on my flushed face.

Damn, that man is trouble. And yet, I didn't want to stay away.

Silly girl.

Chapter Six

Laura

On Friday, after a little over a week of constant filming, the camera guys left, leaving Erik and I with an empty house for the weekend.

"Pizza tonight?" He asked, shutting the door on the last crew member.

"Perfect," I answered, reaching down to scoop up a rag someone had left behind.

Erik's house was slowly coming together. We'd cleaned the kitchen from top to bottom, reorganized his cabinets, and worked at streamlining his functionality in the kitchen. He'd already seen the benefit after a fairly hectic night with the twins, who'd both picked up a mild bug.

"God." He scrubbed a hand over his face. "I'm wrecked."

"Why don't you have a—" the screaming of a baby interrupted my suggestion.

He sighed, straightening and moving to the stairs.

"Coming buddy," he yelled, taking them two at a time.

I hesitated, there was only Ulf's cry this time and I decided not to go up and offer assistance. Instead I went to the laundry room and took care of the piles of clothing, making a mental note to focus here next.

Many didn't know it, but a well-organized laundry could save people hours out of their week. Also, pro-tip, buy wrinkle free clothing. Unless you were going to a business interview or needed to wear a suit week-on-week, investing in wrinkle free clothing freed you from a life of ironing. Best. Tip. Ever.

I transferred the first load to the dryer, and set the next load to clean. Ordinarily I liked to line dry, but with two babies in the house, clothing was a constant need.

I picked up a folded load and went to the twins' room, finding it empty. I put away their tiny clothes then went in search of Erik and the boys.

I found them in Erik's room.

I'm gonna have to clean the bedroom, cause I'm pretty sure my ovaries just exploded.

Erik was passed out on the bed, the twins nuzzled into either side of him, all of them sleeping peacefully.

DILF. The man is a DILF. I am in sooo much trouble.

I stood there, just taking in the quiet peace of this beautiful man and his two sons. I couldn't deny the chemistry between us. Liv, the crew, even the nanny had commented on it. We revolved around each other, joking and laughing to such an extent Liv had asked if we wanted to co-host a show.

Erik had declined, but I couldn't help but wish he'd said yes.

And that's terrifying.

My life was in New York. My family lived there; my core business was there.

But you could work from anywhere...

148

I shook off the tempting thought. My career was just beginning, my world expanding in a way that I'd never imagined.

Not to mention you've only just met the guy and he has two other pretty big priorities. Hell, you haven't even kissed him yet.

Yeah, I really needed to get my head on straight and my mojo locked down. Travelling for a potential four months of the year wasn't exactly conducive to a stable family life.

On silent feet, I backed out of the room, leaving the sleeping boys and their incredibly yummy daddy to their nap. I headed back to the laundry but startled as I entered the kitchen, finding Liv seated at the island.

"Jesus," I said, hand pressed to my heart. "Warn a girl next time."

Liv chuckled, holding up an open bottle of white wine, eyebrow raised in question.

"Please," I said as I passed her. "Let me just get this last load of laundry going and I'll be right back."

I swapped out the wet clothes with dirty, setting it on the spin cycle and loading the dryer before returning.

Liv held her glass in one hand, twirling it absently, her head cradled in the palm of her other hand.

"You okay?" I asked, sliding onto the stool beside her and reaching for my glass.

"Mm," she murmured, her eyes glued to the wine.

I let her have silence, both of us decompressing after a long week.

"You know, I'm conflicted," Liv finally said, breaking the companionable silence. "I have this friend, she's talented, a hard worker, hilarious, and oh so wonderful. She's also the host of my most popular show," she tossed me a grin but it faded a moment later, her eyes locked with mine. "And she's the first woman my beautiful, generous, loving brother has shown interest in for years. She sparkles when he speaks to her, he lights up when she enters the room."

Liv paused, considering me.

I swallowed past the lump in my throat. "And your dilemma?"

"Do I encourage this because I know these two people would be perfect together, or do I discourage them knowing it's just as likely there will be heartbreak?"

I opened my mouth, words failing me.

"Hey, anyone home?" This came from the entry, the sound of a door slamming followed the voice. Upstairs, I heard a piercing cry, the noise waking the babies.

Liv sighed, her lip pressing into a thin line.

"Drink your wine, Laura. We're gonna need it."

"Sorry!" The voice called cheerfully from the entry. I heard the sound of boots clomping down the hall then a head poked around the kitchen doorway.

Furry. Red. Sasquatch.

The yeti-come-man was the furriest person I'd ever seen.

"Ah, I see the harpy is here," the man-beast said with glee, pulling off his cap and slapping it against his thigh. Dust poofed out at the action, gently floating to the floor.

My eye twitched but I ignored the compulsion to get a dustpan and broom.

"Ye must be Laura," the man bounded over, his actions like that of an oversized baby bear. "I'm Ian." His paw of a hand swallowed mine as he shook it enthusiastically.

Unlike his cap, the rest of him was clean.

"Nice to meet you," I said politely, shifting in my seat to

150

make a move. "You want a beer?"

"Don't fash yeself, I got it." He walked to the cupboard, removing a glass then reached for the wine.

I saw Liv's eyebrows rise before she wiped her face clear. I ducked my head, hiding a smile.

Ian took a sip then grinned, "I see ye bought the good stuff. Nice taste."

I nodded at Liv. "Actually, Liv bought it."

He considered her with renewed interest over the rim of his glass, swirling it gently.

She ignored him, purposefully looking at me. "So, what are we doing for dinner?"

"Pizza," Erik said, entering the kitchen, a baby on each arm. "Already ordered. And yes—" he said before Ian or Liv could comment. "—I ordered no pineapple."

They glanced at each other, then immediately looked away, both taking a long drink of their wine.

"You want me to take one?" I asked Erik, holding out my arms for one of the babies. He handed me Leif then went to the fridge, snagging a beer.

"Thanks for letting me sleep." He rubbed an arm over his face. "God, I needed that."

I grinned, then looked down at Leif who pulled at my top, his hand firmly fixed. "Did you have a good sleep, little man? Hmm?"

He blinked up at me, giving me a big smile.

"Such a handsome boy," I cooed, swaying around the kitchen. "You want some dinner?"

Ian moved, placing his glass on the island and pulling the cupboard open, calling, "I'll get ye some yummies. Let's see." He pulled a can of formula, holding it up triumphantly.

151

"Gourmet baby milk? Delicious!" He danced around the kitchen, surprisingly agile for a man of his size, humming *Be Our Guest* from *Beauty and the Beast*.

Liv appeared unable to process Ian's antics, instead pouring herself an overly generous second glass.

After the babies were fed, we settled them in the living room, soft toys on their chests to distract them while we devoured the pizza.

The evening was enlightening. I learned that Erik was an absolute sweetheart to everyone in his broader orbit – as evidenced by his and Ian's close relationship. Liv dropped the occasional embarrassing story, and he constantly checked in on his boys.

Apart from being a bit of a mess, the guy is near perfect.

"I got this," Liv muttered, getting off the sofa and clearing the remains of our dinner. "Besides, I better hit the road."

"Big weekend?" I asked, perfectly content to continue tickling Ulf's feet, his chubby legs kicking out at me as he gurgled his delight.

"Something like that," she muttered.

"I better be going too," Ian said, stretching. "Yer Pa asked me to help get the duplex sorted for the new apprentice."

"This is the girl Gunnar recommended?" Erik asked from his position beside me on the floor. He was holding a set of dangling soft scarves for Leif to grab. "What was her name? Gabby?"

"Yeah, that's the one. Gotta install the extra safety and accessibility supports tomorrow for her."

"You need a hand?"

"Nah, mate. Rune's gonna help but we should be good. Thanks," he leaned down, jiggling each baby's leg gently.

"Farewell boy-o's. Ye be good for yer daddy-o." He stood, throwing me a smile. "Night, Laura. Thanks for helping out our main man."

"Any time," I said, pushing to my feet.

We waved Liv and Ian off, both of them bickering as they walked down the path to their cars.

"Not sure how I feel about that," Erik muttered, watching them from the window in the sitting room.

"That they're attracted to each other?"

"Mm," he shook his head. "Wish they'd just sleep together and get it over with. I'm sick of the bickering."

I chuckled, watching Leif yawn. "Your sister is great, except for the fact she's the most sexually repressed woman I've ever met."

Erik made a gagging sound. "TMI, woman!"

I rolled my eyes. "Why do brothers have such an issue with talking about sex?"

"Uh-huh, nope. The only person's sex life I'm interested in is yours."

We both froze.

"I meant mine, sorry, mine." Erik corrected in a hurry, swearing under his breath. "Fuck, I mean, fuck, fudge, fu-ah, hell." He shut up.

I tilted my head to one side, "Erik, have you been thinking about what sleeping with me would be like?" I tried not to grin as I teased the poor man.

"Fuck it," Erik muttered. He threw back his shoulders, looking me straight in the eye. "Yeah, I have. How do you feel about that?"

Instead of answering I closed the distance between us, raised up on my tiptoes and kissed him.

153

He allowed it for a beat, then took over.

Holy shitstacks. Who the fuck let this guy kiss? He needs to come with a warning label.

Erik didn't kiss, he devoured. He let my lips caress his for only a moment before he took over, plundering my mouth in a way that felt oh so good.

His hands came to my waist, pulling me closer, one hand stayed there while the other trailed up my back, fisting into the hair at the back of my neck.

Holy shit. Ho-ly sheeeeeeeiiiit.

The words rolled around in my head on repeat as he kissed me, over and over and over again. His mouth trailed from my lips dipping to taste my neck.

"Delicious," he muttered against me, his teeth grazing against the sensitive skin. "So soft."

I pushed his mouth to my skin, groaning when he took the hint and began kissing and sucking. He felt amazing, my body coming alive under his hands, his mouth, his tongue.

Erik backed me to the couch and I dropped onto it, my legs finally giving out. He followed, dropping to his knees before me.

"Need to taste you," he grunted, his hands falling to my pants. "Get these off."

Together we pushed and pulled them down my legs, my underwear coming along for the ride. He fell on my pussy, his lips tasting and teasing, his tongue stroking. There was no other word for it, the man *worshipped* me.

A gurgled sound had us both freezing. Our heads whipped to the floor where Ulf and Leif were both sleepily settled on their little mat.

"Crap," Erik whispered. "Do you think they saw?"

A hysterical giggle burst from my lips, "I don't know. How far can a three-month-old see?"

"God, I'm gonna have to take them to therapy."

I lost it, my head tipping back as I roared with laughter. It took Erik a beat but he joined me, his head resting on the inside of my thigh.

As we calmed, I found that I couldn't stop stroking my fingers through his hair.

"Guess we better call it a night," Erik sighed.

"Yeah," I agreed, the needy desire dissipating. Amusement and an aching sense of missed opportunity filled the void. "But just FYI, you can go down on me anytime."

Erik winked, rising to his feet and hauling me off the couch. "Let me put the boys down, then Netflix and actual chill?"

I blew out an exaggerated sigh. "Fine. I'll take your scraps."

Erik pulled me into his side, dropping a kiss on my head as he laughed.

"Queenie, my scraps are worthy of a gourmet meal."

"Promises, promises."

Chapter Seven

Erik

"I get it, I owe you." I handed over Ulf to Rune. "I'll be back tomorrow. There's formula and bottles in the cooler bag, their blankets in the –"

"I got it," Rune rumbled, lifting Ulf a little higher. "Go." I hesitated. My brother had looked after my boys a few times but it didn't make leaving them any easier. I suspected it would be like this no matter their ages, be they three months or thirty years.

Rune shut the door in my face, and I sighed. My brother, for all his gruffness loved our family, and particularly his nephews, fiercely. I just wished he'd find a partner and settle down; god knew a little time between the sheets might improve his attitude a little.

Speaking of...

I made my way back to the car; Laura was on her phone with her agent. Something about an endorsement deal for an environmentally friendly product she loved.

She saw me, flashing a bright smile and a wave as she continued to chat on the phone. I slid in the driver's side, setting us off as she wrapped up her call.

"Thanks, Merry. Yeah, I'll read over the terms but if you think it's good then I'm sure it is." She paused then laughed. "No, but thanks for the vote of confidence. I'll chat with you later. Bye."

She hung up, dropping the phone in her clutch. "Sorry about that. Turns out this was a bigger offer than we were expecting and Merry wanted to chat through the changes."

"Endorsement deal, right?"

"Yeah. It'll be my first major sponsorship. But part of the terms is that they give a percentage of sales for a particular product to a clean water charity."

"Clean water charity?"

"Oh gosh, yes." Laura nodded enthusiastically. "Did you know that one in ten people don't have access to clean water?" And then she was off, discussing the intricacies of the issue, passionately advocating for why this was a cause close to her heart, and describing all the ways she was working to make clean water a reality for every person.

I pulled into the restaurant parking lot, finding a vacant spot near the entrance.

"Sorry," Laura finally said with a self-conscious laugh I immediately detested. "I get carried away when I talk about something I'm passionate about."

I unclipped my seat belt, and reached across to wrap my hand around the back of her neck and gently squeeze.

"Queenie, don't ever apologize for something you're enthusiastic about. You obviously love what you do, and you're passionate about this charity. The fact you can do both is exciting." I squeezed again. "Let's go celebrate. You can tell me more over dinner. I'm proud of you."

157

She blinked twice, a grin bursting across her pretty face, lighting her up.

"Sounds great."

The restaurant was a family run bistro down towards the main pier in town. I'd been going there since I was young enough to remember. The food was seasonal and always delicious, the service warm and genuine.

And the view? Well, it had gotten me laid more than once.

Laura's intake of breath as we entered and upon seeing the beauty of the water stretched out for miles before us, had my cock twitching.

We're gonna get lucky tonight.

I mentally slapped myself.

Laura was dressed in a flattering black dress and wedge heels. Her hair was up in a little bun thing that had stray hairs dancing down her cheeks and neck. She looked soft and inviting. Until you looked at her chest and then it was pure siren.

The neck of the dress had little crisscross straps above the curve of her breasts, in addition to a deep v that emphasized her abundance.

Every time I looked at her, I wanted to lick the curves of her breasts. I wanted to free them and suck her nipples, I wanted to fuck her against a wall while her tits bounced free in time to the thrusting of my cock.

I'd had a hard-on since before we'd left the house, and no amount of thinking about things like taxes and baseball stats was budging it.

We were seated at a table close to the windows, Laura sighing happily as she propped her face on her palm and gazed out.

"You really love the water," I remarked, enjoying watching her across the table.

"It's always been my dream to live close to it. I love the smell and the sounds and just... everything, you know?"

I chuckled. "Yeah."

She sighed, pushing back and opening the menu. "Wow, this looks fantastic."

"You really can't go wrong with anything here." We settled on a chef's sampler, six courses with three samples of dessert. The night stretched on, us sharing and remarking on the food, Laura sharing about her life, me sharing mine.

This woman is incredible.

I couldn't shake my attraction to her. Fact was, she was amazing, and the more I spoke to her the more I wanted her in my life, my kids' lives, and my bed.

You're a lost cause.

Yep, and I didn't regret it for one moment. I suddenly understood how my brother could decide to move to a strange town, shack up with a woman, and decide to get married in less than six months.

I'd known Laura less than two weeks and I already wanted her to be the mother of my boys and any future kids we had.

Crazy? Probably.

Taking on not only me but two kids would be asking a lot of anyone. But Laura didn't seem phased by the masters of mess.

The bill arrived and I was more than ready to take this home. We'd been flirting outrageously all night, the awareness building between us as our fingers lingered, our eyes met and held, the smiles and innuendo becoming just that fraction more knowing.

159

"Home?" I asked quietly.

"Sounds perfect," Laura replied, rising from the table.

We exited the restaurant, Laura tucked under my arm, one of her arms wrapped around my middle, the other pressed to my stomach, our bodies brushing as we moved, laughing and chatting on the way out to the car.

"Erik?" A familiar voice threw an icy bucket of water over my mood.

I froze, Laura stiffening as she registered my reaction.

I turned us slowly, reluctantly, seeing Claire and her husband standing by their car. She smiled, looking over at Laura then back to me.

"Erik, I thought that was you," she stepped away from her car, coming towards us, her arms out as if she were about to hug me. "It's so great to run into you."

Laura disengaged, allowing Claire to wrap her arms around me. I remained frozen, like a stone, my emotions in lockdown as she squeezed.

She still wears Chanel.

Her perfume clung to me, overwhelming my senses. She stepped back, smiling brightly at Laura.

"Hi, I'm Claire. I'm sure Erik has told you all about me."

Laura took her hand, a fake smile pasted on her face. "Yes, of course," she lied.

"We're in town for Connor's sister's wedding." Claire grinned at her husband. "Thought we'd take advantage of staying with family and get a night out and away from the baby."

They have a baby.

She looked back at me, her smile still on her face. "It's so lovely to see you, Erik. Have a good night."

She turned, walking back to her car and sliding in. Laura slipped an arm back around my waist and we watched silently as they pulled out and drove away.

"She's the one who broke your heart?" Laura asked quietly.

My chest deconstructed, air suddenly rushing out as the ice in my veins melted at her straightforwardness. "Yeah."

"Seems like a bitch."

A startled laugh burst from my lips. "What?"

Laura shrugged. "Introduces herself but doesn't ask about me. Talks about herself, drops how happy they are with the baby thing, then leaves. Doesn't once ask how you are or what our relationship is."

"Well... fuck." I muttered. "You got her number."

Laura gestured at the pier. "Wanna talk about it?"

I looked down at the beautiful woman beside me. "Actually, yeah."

"Let me get my coat from the car and we can go for a walk."

"Okay."

Chapter Eight

Laura

I snuggled into my coat as we walked the length of the pier. It was a beautiful Spring night, if not a little chilly. But the moon was high, the breeze soft, and the stars bright. The waves crashed comfortingly as we strolled. At the pier, there was a set of stairs which took you down to the beach.

I led, kicking off my shoes at the bottom and sighing in pleasure as the sand wedged between my toes.

We strolled in companionable silence, sitting down under the pier, sheltered from the breeze and curious eyes.

"It's not a long story," Erik finally said, his hip and leg pressed against mine as we settled in the sand. "Just a sucky one."

I glided fingers through the sand, head tilted his way, listening.

"We'd been together for three years. I'd thought she was the one. She'd refused to move into the little apartment I owned above the shop and said she had no room for me in her one bedroom. So, I'd been looking for a new place. An agent had just finished showing me a two-bedroom condo when she'd walked out of the apartment across the breezeway. I got to see her make out with him while I just stood there watching. That was a fun experience."

He looked at me, a wry smile on his lips. "Then she married him."

"Damn," I muttered, pulling my legs up to my chin and resting my head on them. "That is sucky."

"We broke up, obviously. But it fucked me up, you know? She said she hadn't seen a future with me, but she hadn't known how to break up with me either."

"I'm sorry," I reached out a hand, giving him a squeeze.

He lifted one shoulder. "You know, seeing her tonight, it was actually kind of cathartic, if you can believe it."

"Mm?"

Erik looked at the ocean for a long moment then turned to me. "Makes me realize we were never meant to be. I always thought I'd feel something if I ran into her. Like anger or regret maybe? Tonight, I was shocked, sure. But now I've seen her, and I've processed, honestly, I feel nothing but relief. It was shitty what she did, sure. But maybe it was right."

"Right?" I asked softly, not following.

"Mm, we weren't meant to be. But you and I?" He raised my hand pressing a kiss to my knuckles. "Tell me there's something here. Tell me I'm not the only one feeling this."

I stared into his dark eyes, seeing the hunger and hope, knowing mine reflected the same.

I opened my mouth to deny it but the words eluded me. "There's something," I admitted. "It's a hell of a big something."

"But?"

I swallowed, laying myself bare. "But I want this career I've started. I want to travel and help people. I want to be Laura Sweep, the Queen of Clean. I want to make a difference."

"And you think you can't if we take this further?"

"I don't know. You have kids. How would you feel about me travelling so much?"

"Babe," Erik leaned in, his face serious. "I'd never ask you to give up your career or who you are. You can't love someone for who you want them to be. You love someone for who they are. You're Laura, Queen of Clean. You're genuine and open, and if you have to travel to do that, then fine. We'll make it work. That's what people do."

That's what people do.

Was it really this simple? Was it really as easy as saying yes to him?

We haven't even slept together yet.

My body and heart said it would be amazing, but my brain was crying out for some rational thought. There was no logic in how we were feeling, no explanation for how rapidly this relationship was progressing.

Do it. Take a leap of faith.

"Okay," I whispered, then repeated it louder and with more conviction. "Okay. Let's do this. Let's work out what this is between us, let's explore it and build it and... and..." I paused, overwhelmed. "Let's be us."

Erik surged to his feet, hauling me up with him. "Come on," he ordered, pulling me along. I laughed, the wind whipping my hair as we sprinted through the sand.

"Where are we going?" I asked, laughing at his determined expression.

"The workshop, it's closer than home and there's a bed."

We hurried over the sand, stopping to kiss and touch, laughing as we tumbled and fumbled our way along the beach towards the marina.

Erik pulled a key from his pocket opening the door at the back of a large warehouse. I pressed against him, biting playfully at his shoulder as he pushed it open. He laughed, pulling me inside and kicking the door shut. His body pressed to mine, warm, hard and smelling of salt, sand and man.

I tasted laughter and need on his lips, opening to let him taste me in return.

We stripped in the doorway and on the stairs leading up to the apartment. A trail of clothing marked our path.

Perhaps I should have felt self-conscious or anxious, especially as I'd just seen Erik's ex and she was beautiful.

But I didn't. I felt nothing but desire. Desire for this man, desire for connection, desire for the things we were doing and about to do. In large part, that was thanks to Erik. He murmured deliciously filthy requests as he stripped my clothes from my body. His touch reverent but commanding. He kissed me and looked at me and touched me like I was the only thing in his universe that he wanted.

He lay me on the bed, immediately pulling at the last of my clothes. He discarded my underwear and dropped to his knees.

"Been dreaming of this." He leaned in, hovering for one protracted second, anticipation spiking before he closed his mouth over my pussy.

"Yes," I breathed, eyes closing, hands gripping the headboard above me. "God yes."

Erik licked me with an attention I couldn't help but

commend. His talented tongue and lips set my hips wiggling. I groaned encouragement as he worshipped me.

If I were the sacrifice and he the priest, this was an altar on which I would gladly die.

I came in a crescendo of feeling. Every cell in my body exploding with the joy that came with a satisfying orgasm delivered by someone you love.

Love?!

I didn't have time to get stuck on that, Erik commanded all my attention as he surged up the bed. Gloriously naked, I had only a moment to appreciate three things – he was beautifully made, gorgeously proportioned, and he had a huge dick.

Yay me!

My body lit up as he pressed down, his mouth falling to my breasts. He kissed them, pulling first one nipple, then the other into his mouth. He laved them with attention, stroked them, his mouth branding my body, wrecking me one tantalizing touch at a time.

"My turn," I finally told him, flipping us over. I sat up, legs straddling him as I ran fingers down his delectable chest.

Erik grinned up at me, tucking one hand behind his head, his bicep flexing in the most wonderful way. A chunk of hair fell over his forehead, while under me his body relaxed.

"Your wish is my command."

Mm, yes it is.

It was my turn to drive him mad. I tasted my way down his body. With agonizing slowness, I revealed his secrets. Erik had sensitive nipples. There was a spot by his hip that made goose pimples break out across his skin. He had a tattoo over his heart with the names of his boys hidden within.

I loved on his body, enjoying his uneven breathing, loving the grunts and groans as I explored. As I moved lower those groans changed to whispered orders. And like any good girl I completely ignored him.

I lowered my mouth to Erik's cock, positioning myself just so. I looked at him, his eyes darkly intense as he glowered at me hungrily.

"Ready?" I asked, purposefully breathy, knowing the heat of my mouth would heighten his anticipation.

"God help me if you don't—"

I swallowed him, his cock hitting the back of my throat as he broke off with a strangled curse.

"Fuck, Queenie. Laura, suck me. More!" The orders flew thick and fast and I found that unlike before, now I was powerless to ignore him. I needed to please, needed to give him what he wanted.

I swallowed his cock, my tongue teasing the head, my mouth hot and needy as I tasted, teased and choked on his length.

A dark part of me liked that.

My body hummed with need, my thighs slick with wetness when Erik finally broke. His hands hooked under my arms and hauled me up his body. He took a bare second to position me, his gaze meeting mine as he thrust up and in.

A scream ripped from my throat, his cock filling me in the most perfect of ways.

"Fuck," he grunted, thrusting again.

"Tight, hot, perfect."

He pinned me in place above him, my tits bouncing as his cock plundered my body. One hand dropped, his thumb finding my clit.

He circled, once, twice, and then I broke. Body arching, hair tumbling, my pussy milked his cock as I came, his name tearing from my lips. Erik followed a moment later, groaning as he emptied inside me.

I collapsed on his chest, and his arms immediately held me tight as we breathed through the aftermath.

"Erik?"

"Mm?"

"I think you broke me."

He chuckled, his body moving mine. "Ditto."

We fell silent. His hands trailed soft strokes up and down my back.

"This is real, isn't it?" I looked up, finding his eyes at half-mast, a satisfied smile on his face.

"Oh, yeah." He pressed a kiss to my forehead, his arms tightening around me. "You got a problem with that?"

"No," I admitted, unable to conjure a single protest. "But that could be the sex talking."

He chuckled again, rolling us so he loomed over me. "Then I better keep you sexually satisfied."

He lowered his head kissing me again, and I had to admit, the man certainly knew how to satisfy.

Chapter Nine

Laura

I'd woken Erik up with a blow job, he'd reciprocated by licking me until I came. Twice.

A girl could get used to this.

We'd spent the rest of Sunday hanging out with his sons, making out while they napped, and generally relaxing and getting to know each other. When we'd picked them up, Rune had silently handed me three books. Two were parenting guides geared towards step-parents, the last a novel I'd been wanting to read but hadn't had time to pick up.

Erik had explained this was Rune's way of showing approval. His super power was knowing the exact book you wanted, and he showed approval by giving it to you.

He'd never gifted a book to Erik's ex, and I couldn't help but feel slightly smug about that.

Monday dawned far too early, with the crew arriving for the final week of filming.

It took less than ten minutes for Liv to realize the dynamic between Erik and I had changed. She pulled me aside, crossing her arms over her chest, her eyebrows raised in question.

"What?" I asked, trying not to grin.

"Don't what me, missy. Spill."

I zipped my smiling lips, pretending to throw away the key. "Hussy," Liv rolled her eyes, zero heat in her words. "Fine, just promise me you'll be gentle with him."

"I promise."

She sighed. "Guess it was too good to be true. Are you going to at least see this season out?"

I tilted my head to one side. "Liv, why would you think I'd be quitting?"

She blinked. "You're not?" "No," I scoffed. "And Erik would kill me if I did. We talked about it. We're gonna make it work. It'll mean that we'll have to restructure the show. I don't want to do more than two weeks away from the boys at a time, but I think we could make it work."

Liv blinked at me rapidly. "Laura."

"Mm?"

"My brother is an idiot if he doesn't marry you."

I laughed; tension I hadn't realized I was carrying easing from my shoulders.

* * *

The rest of the week was a flurry of activity as we wrapped up filming. In between takes, Erik had done his best to manage his business, meet our filming requirements, and juggle his daddy responsibilities.

I found myself falling more in love with the man who

seemed bound and determined not to let anyone down.

Love.

That was a word that hadn't passed through either of our lips yet. But it hovered on the tip of my tongue like a secret waiting to be shared.

Maybe today.

I'd woken up early, finding the house strangely quiet. Yesterday had been our final day of filming. After I'd returned home to pack up my life, I'd be returning in a few weeks for the recap and to move in with Erik.

A terrifying thought.

I couldn't wait.

I'd slipped out of the bedroom, leaving Erik passed out on the bed. He'd immediately shifted, pulling my pillow into him and burrowing deep. The man was a shameless snuggler.

I took a cup of coffee out to the jetty, dangling my feet over the side of the dock, sipping coffee as I watched the rising sun twinkle across the water.

"Last day today," Erik remarked, settling down beside me some time later. He handed me a fresh cup of coffee; a donut balanced on the lid.

I grinned, taking a bite.

He placed his own cup and donut beside him, pulling the baby monitor from his sweatpants pocket and setting it down behind us.

We sat in companionable silence, enjoying the morning light.

"Once upon a time," Erik said. "I dreamed of something like this. Kids in bed, sleeping peacefully. Sharing an early morning with my woman." He glanced at me, his heart stopping grin in place. "This is better than any dream."

I sighed, relaxing into him. "I didn't see you coming, Erik Larsson."

"Is that a bad thing?"

I chuckled. "No, definitely not."

"I love you, Laura."

The words registered and my heart expanded, warmth washing over me as his declaration settled in my soul.

"I love you, too."

We sealed our declaration with a kiss then pressed our heads together, grinning.

Applause interrupted our moment. Heads still pressed together, we turned, finding Erik's family – his entire family – as well as the crew watching us.

Correction, filming us.

Erik sighed. "Sure you want to join this madhouse? There's still time to bail out."

With all the love in my heart I answered, "Nope, you're stuck with me now."

"Thank fuc- er, fudge."

And with that Erik kissed me.

Epilogue One

Laura

Three months later

"It's live!" Liv yelled from the living room. Her announcement was followed by a stampede as all the Larssons ran to get in place.

I exchanged a glance with Ella, Erik's newly minted sister-in-law. She rolled her eyes, letting out a little laugh.

"Welcome to the family," she picked up a massive bowl of popcorn. "get used to the crazy marauders. It doesn't get any less loud."

I grabbed two giant bags of chips and followed her into the living room. Gunnar, seated in the armchair, had grabbed his wife and was lifting her onto his lap, pressing kisses to her neck as she giggled and wiggled, trying to keep the popcorn upright.

I looked to Erik, finding him grinning at his brother.

"You wanna keep the PDA to a minimum?" He asked, reaching over and removing the bowl from Ella's hands.

"Nah, I'm good," Gunnar replied, immediately taking advantage of Ella's free hands to pull her into him and kiss her.

I laughed, tossing the chips on the table and making a leap for Erik. "Come on, I think we can take them in the obnoxiously adorable couple stakes."

He pulled me in, murmuring, "I'm up to the challenge."

I peppered his face with kisses then squealed when he fell onto the couch, pulling me down and across him.

"Boys!" Jemma, Erik's mother, snapped. "Leave the girls alone. I want to watch this before the children wake."

I laughed, rolling off Erik and settling in beside him. He draped an arm around my shoulders, immediately pulling me into him. Ella made a move but Gunnar kept her tight against him keeping her on his lap.

It's almost like they're related.

I hid my amused smile, waiting for Liv, Astrid, and Rune to find their seats. Sune, Erik's dad, handed me a beer.

"You ready for this?" He asked, settling beside me on the couch.

"Definitely."

"I'm not," Erik grumbled. "You sure we have to do this?"

"Yes!" came the resounding answer from around the room.

I chuckled, patting Erik's leg. "Sorry, Babe. Looks like you're outnumbered."

He sighed heavily. "Fine. Get on with it then."

Sune hit play, and the episode started.

"Oh, Erik," Jemma whispered when they showed the mold in his bathroom. "Really?"

"Sorry, Ma. It's gone now."

She shook her head, shoving a mouthful of popcorn in her mouth. Sune leaned over. "She's been singing your praises to the extended family."

"She has nothing to thank me for," I replied as the footage moved to us cleaning Erik's kitchen. "He did all the hard work."

The episode continued with his family ribbing him when they showed the storage container footage, and sorting through his mess. It showed me educating him on stain removal for the boys, and discussing the fifteen minute a night rule for cleaning – the one I used so I didn't let mess pile up and waste my weekend.

The footage rolled, showing the final day of filming before I left. It was me talking about my experience and what I hoped for Erik and his twins.

"I hope that he finds a little bit of peace in what I've taught him. It's not easy being a single parent, and I have nothing but love and admiration for him."

The final footage showed me hanging the St Louis jersey I'd had framed in his office before leaving.

"Why don't you do something like that for me?" Sune asked Jemma.

"Because you support the Bruins." She returned, not even offering him a glance.

I sniggered.

"Is that it?" Astrid asked as the screen went dark. She leaned forward, snatching the final handful of popcorn from the bowl.

"No, there's the recap where Laura returns a few weeks later for a visit," Liv replied, rubbing her hands together. "It's always the part where people cry."

I glanced at Erik, raising an eyebrow in question. He shook his head, rolling his eyes.

"Don't get your hopes up."

I laughed, snuggling into his side.

The footage began and I frowned, glancing up at Erik. "This isn't the recap."

"Isn't it?" He asked, giving me a surprised look. "It's what I remember filming."

"Hey, I'm Erik," said the image of Erik on the TV. "And I'm a recovering mess-a-holic."

I laughed, delighted.

"Thanks for watching this episode where the Queen of Clean comes in and bails out my dorky daddy butt. Laura, you've changed my life. Completely."

The footage cut to a montage of him and his boys with… me. The images and video were taken from the weeks we'd cleaned his house, and ended with Erik and I kissing on the deck, the morning sun behind us.

"Erik," I whispered looking up.

He grinned but nodded at the screen. "Keep watching, Queenie."

"Just to be perfectly transparent, Laura's moved herself in." Screen Erik said. "And thank god for that because I love her."

There was a photo of us, holding the boys, laughing over hamburgers the night I'd moved in.

It cut back to Erik.

"Laura, you may have cleaned out my house, but you've filled my heart." Screen Erik got down on one knee. "Will you marry me?"

I looked up, finding Erik watching me. "Are you serious?"

"Completely." He pulled a ring out of the gap between the sofa seat cushion and arm, holding it up. "Laura Sweep, Queen of Clean, my Queenie. Will you marry me?"

I may have stuttered the word. Or maybe I shouted it. Or maybe I didn't say anything. I couldn't remember. Just like the day we'd first met, my mind went blank and all I could see, taste, smell, feel was him.

Erik. *My* Erik.

He slid the ring on my finger as he kissed me, tasting just as wonderful today as the first time we'd kissed. Tears of joy ran down my cheeks as his family squealed and leapt about, showering us with congratulations and slowly pulling us apart.

Someone retrieved the twins, and they were passed around, making their way to Erik and me as his mother squished us together for a photo.

I held Leif, Erik holding Ulf as we gazed at each other, happiness in our every line.

"You're stuck with us now." He told me, pulling me close to press a kiss to my forehead.

"Guess you better get used to a clean house then."

"Queenie, nothing turns me on more than watching you clean my pipes."

"Overshare!" Gunnar yelled, making a face. "Jesus brother!"

We laughed as his mother took the picture. It was the image I'd use on Instagram to announce our engagement. The image that the papers would publish and the fans would gush over.

And it was the image that would hang in our bedroom beside our wedding photo.

Epilogue Two

Erik

Three years later

"Want Momma!" Leif yelled, stamping his little foot in protest.

"Buddy, I've already told you, Momma's on an airplane, remember?"

"Swoosh!" Ulf said from beside me, his arms shooting straight out as he swayed from side to side.

"Got it in one, Bud," I praised. I lifted the shirt once more, prepared to bargain with my stubborn son.

"Come on, Leif. If you put your shirt on, I'll let you have some chocolate milk with breakfast. Just don't tell your mom, deal?" He considered the deal, eyeing the shirt with suspicion. "Ulf too?"

"Sure," I promised, desperate to seal the deal.

"O-tay," he thrust his arms up in the air, waiting for me to slip it on.

I sighed in relief, wrestling the shirt into place. Finally dressed, we then shared breakfast—the naughty chocolate milk treat, greedily devoured – then grabbed our pre-packed bags to head to Grandma's.

"Okay boys," I yelled, shoving them through the door at my mom. "Have fun!"

"Erik, you don't want to come in for a –"

"No time!" I yelled, frantic. "Gotta go, love you Ma!"

I heard my dad laughing from inside as Ma stood in the doorway, a frown in place as she watched me practically sprint for my car.

Call me a terrible parent, but I'd lied to my kids. And I felt zero shame.

Momma wasn't still on an airplane. Momma's plane had already landed and she was in a cab on her way home right now.

And she had been sexting Daddy for over three days. The woman was about to be punished.

I, barely, managed to stay within the speed limit as I drove home, managing to pull into the driveway just as the cab pulled up to the curb.

I parked, throwing open the door and slamming it shut, clicking the lock as I headed for my woman.

She stepped from the cab, her handbag over one shoulder, looking daisy fresh and entirely fuckable in a beautiful summer dress that hugged every curve.

"Hey stranger," she called, a smile lighting her face.

God, she's stunning.

I thought it every time I saw her. Thought it every time she returned from her trips. I'd thought it the day she'd walked down the aisle to me, flowers in her hair, that gorgeous smile on her lips.

I stalked to her, pulled her close, my lips meeting hers in a hungry kiss.

"Damn honeymooners," the driver muttered, getting out and unloading Laura's bags.

I ignored him, focusing on my wife.

It'd been three years since Laura had entered my mess of a house and set everything to right. She'd made this house a home, loved on my boys, loved on me.

She still had her career, her show winning an Emmy last year. Her social media numbers were through the roof and only increasing, endorsement deals coming her way every day. We made it work because it was worth it. Every single moment we had together made all the stress and juggling and travel worth it.

"Missed you," she murmured against my lips.

"Missed you more," I replied.

We backed up just a little, Laura still in my arms but trying to peer around me.

"Where are my boys?" She asked, frowning.

"Grandma's."

Laura looked up at me, a sexy grin pulling at her lips. "Oh really?"

"Mm," I bent to kiss her again but was interrupted by the driver.

"Sorry," he muttered. "You need anything else?"

"No, thanks."

We waved him off then I picked up her bags and followed her into the house.

"Erik," she said with a delighted laugh. "You didn't."

I dropped the bags in the entry, closing the door behind me and coming to wrap my arms around her middle, resting my head on her shoulder. "It's the one you wanted, right?"

She looked at me, heart in her eyes. "Yeah, and it's perfect."

I'd long ago learned that the way to Laura's heart wasn't through flowers or chocolate – though she liked those as well. Nope, the best gift was a new cleaning instrument.

This time I'd gone big. To be fair, it was the longest she'd been away – three weeks in total. I'd missed her, the boys had missed her, our house missed her.

Don't tell her, but I'd had a cleaning company come in yesterday. She may be the Queen of Clean, but I was certainly still the Master of Mess. And the last thing I'd wanted today was something to distract her.

She pulled away, running her hands over the industrial grade carpet cleaner. "It's gorgeous," she murmured, lifting the hose. "Ooh, lightweight and ergonomic."

Honestly. My wife was the only woman I knew who would want a vacuum more than diamonds. Seriously, the woman had a Pinterest dream board filled with what she called, 'cleaning porn'.

That's my wife.

You can admire it later," I swung her up and over my shoulder, and headed for the stairs.

She squealed, her legs kicking in my fireman hold. "Erik! Put me down! You'll throw your back out!"

I ignored her, zeroing in on the bedroom.

Three weeks of no sex. Three weeks of not seeing her, smelling her, tasting her.

Too fucking long.

I deposited her on the bed, covering her with my body, my lips finding hers.

We came together, a desperate, dirty mess of grasping limbs, gasping breath and glorious release.

After, we lay together, side-by-side on the bed. Both of us

181

panting as we came down off a fucking incredible high.

"Never doing three weeks again," Laura muttered, her eyes closed.

"Thank fudge for that."

She chuckled; eyes still closed. "I brought you a present."

I perked up, finding energy I thought she'd drained. "Present?"

She chuckled, rolling to her side. "It's in my purse."

I went downstairs, finding her discarded purse and carrying it back to the room. When she said purse, she really meant giant-fucking-handbag. Honestly, it was like Mary Poppins had handed over her magic tricks.

We'd once blown two tires and spent over four hours on the side of the road waiting for AAA. The woman had produced food, clean wipes and a miraculous amount of entertainment for our sons from the depths of that thing.

I handed it over. "Is it sexy?" I asked, hopefully.

"Not quite," she tugged a small wrapped gift free, handing it over.

I shook it, listening. "It doesn't jingle. Or bark."

"Nope," she said, smiling.

"Hmm, so it's not a pony?"

"Sadly, no."

"Damn," I ran a finger along the edge of the wrapping paper, ripping it clean through. She watched, biting her lip as I pulled the cloth free. I shook it out, blinking as I registered the tiny onesie. A onesie that read; *My Daddy owns Thor's Shipbuilding.*

I looked from the onesie, down to Laura, back to the onesie then back to Laura.

"Queenie, does this mean...?"

She nodded, a grin bursting across her face. "Turns out I didn't have the stomach flu while in New York."

I fisted the material, dropping to pull her to me. "Are you okay? How do you feel? Shit, do we need to schedule a doctor's appointment? How far along are you?"

She laughed, holding me close.

"Erik, it's gonna be fine. We're only about eight weeks along. I've scheduled a doctor's appointment for tomorrow. I've had a little nausea in the mornings but nothing crazy."

I bent, pressing a kiss to her mouth. "Queenie, I don't know what to say."

"Are you happy?" "Fucking ecstatic," I pressed another kiss to her mouth, then another. Somehow more turned on by the knowledge I'd planted a baby in her. The blood of my ancestors sung through my veins demanding I celebrate by branding this woman.

She. Is. Mine.

This time I paid closer attention to her body, noticing subtle changes. Her breasts were more sensitive. Her body more responsive.

I rolled her so she could ride me, watching her breasts bounce, her body move as she rode us to victorious release.

My Laura, my full-bodied, gloriously talented, wonderfully intelligent, amazing Laura was pregnant.

We both came again, me bellowing her name, Laura on a broken scream. She fell beside me, panting and I couldn't stop myself from leaning down and pressing a kiss to her stomach.

She laughed, swatting at my head.

"Do you think it's a girl or a boy?" I asked, grazing fingers across her stomach.

"I don't mind."

"The boys will be happy."

"Don't I know it. Do you think they'll let up on the puppy idea?"

"Not a chance."

We both laughed.

Laura yawned, rubbing one eye. "The only other downside is the fatigue."

"Stay here, have a nap. There's nothing you need to do. I'll deal with your luggage."

I sailed through the housework, unpacking her stuff, doing the laundry, deciding to throw on a crockpot for dinner that night.

I went back up to the bedroom with a sandwich and a tall glass of water. I'd spent the last hour googling what pregnant women could and couldn't eat, and had already placed an order for home delivery.

Gotta nail this husband of a pregnant wife role.

Laura was still passed out on the bed, gently snoring.

I took a moment just admiring this magnificent woman before I placed the plate and glass quietly on the bedside table.

Then I bent, pressing a soft kiss to her belly murmuring, "Welcome to the family, little Viking."

III

The X-List

The X-List

Rune

What kind of crazy person doesn't read? Apparently my new neighbour. She's loud, sassy, flirty and infuriatingly, annoyingly cheerful.

And a non-reader. The worst kind of human.

So why is that when I dare her to enter the charity read-a-thon, I suddenly find myself carefully curating her list?

And those books… they're definitely not your momma's romance.

Gabby

I'm used to people underestimating me. Normally I can brush it off with a laugh. But Rune? He gets under my skin. So when he make an off-handed comment that a non-reader like me shouldn't bother with the town's charity event, I can't help but accept the challenge.

Only these books are not what I remember from the school book list. Not. Even. Close.

And Rune? Well I'm beginning to see him in a new light. Or, should I say, hear him?

Warning: This sexy little number is inspired by hot books, men who read, and a slight exhibitionist tease. Get thee a man who knows how to handle you between the covers, and settle in — this steamy read will have you begging for more.

Chapter One

Gabby

"We're here," I whispered to myself as I pulled up behind the moving van, parking my car in front of the gorgeous duplex bungalow. A thrill of excitement ratcheted down my spine, sending the butterflies in my stomach fluttering with nervous anticipation.

Gunnar, my boss, came from around the front of the truck, giving me a smile. I exited my car, coming to meet him halfway.

"Welcome to Cape Hardgrave," he gestured at the bungalow. "Not much to look at on the outside, but she'll do for the next six months."

The bungalow was a single level brick and weatherboard home. It looked as if it were an original build, but had been divided up and updated at some point over the last fifty years. Whoever owned it was obviously a fan of yellow since the entire structure was painted the same shade as a sunflower. Only the roof, doors, and trim were different – a striking black.

"The garden isn't pretty right now. But once spring starts

in full, you'll find the house gets a little more palatable."

I threw a smile at my boss. "You mean the greenery tones down the loudness of the yellow?"

He chuckled. "More like the riot of flowers distract the eye. Come on," he began walking up to the house. "Let's see how you like the place."

I'd applied as a carpenter with Thor's Shipbuilding back in Capricorn Cove. Gunnar, the owner, had put me through my paces and liked what he'd seen. He'd offered me a job, asking if I was willing to apprentice as a shipwright. Considering the woodshop where I'd worked for the last two years had gone bust thanks to shitty financial management, I was more than happy to go back to school and get some new skills. The best part was he was still paying me at full wage while I did the bridging course.

I'd left school early, apprenticing in order to set myself up for when the state would throw me out on my ear.

I was a foster kid, bouncing around homes until I'd wound up in Capricorn Cove with the McKenneys. They'd been a nice bunch. Generous with their time and love, sharing their little town with me and the other kids in the home. When I'd said I wanted to become a carpenter, they'd helped me out, ensuring I still got my high school diploma even while I got trade certified. When I'd aged out of the system, they'd helped me out, setting me up with a little apartment, making sure I had food, telling me that I'd always had a place at their table if I ever needed anything.

So, I stayed. Finding work with a local carpenter, designing custom pieces, working on houses, building cheap tables – in a small town like Capricorn Cove you had to be a jack of all trades. I'd enjoyed the work but loved the paycheck more. I'd been saving for a deposit on a home, still living in that first shitty apartment with its flaking walls and damp smell. It'd been cheap and a place to sleep. Nothing special but it worked for me.

Or at least it had until the workshop had gone bust and I'd been forced to dip into my savings to continue covering rent.

When Thor's Shipbuilding had bought the marina, the town had been a flutter of excitement. I hadn't expected to land the job, but Gunnar had liked my work and I wasn't about to look a gift horse in the mouth. Most people took one look at me and made judgments about my ability to perform. I didn't blame them, but it still pissed me off.

Cape Hardgrave was the headquarters of the century old business. I'd done my research, looking into the Larssons' financial situation, what their employees said about them, client lists – the works. Thor's Shipbuilding was world-renowned, highly distinguished but small and boutique. The people who came to them paid top dollar for quality and name.

When Gunnar had said he wanted me to apprentice I'd agreed, willing to suck up the cost of living and moving for the apprenticeship period at the established headquarters. And when he'd said that it would be all-inclusive? Well, I'd practically thrown myself at the opportunity. It was like all my Christmases had come at once.

We walked up to the house; a ramp had been installed on one side of the stairs. I lifted an eyebrow in question.

"Our grandmother lived here before she moved in with my parents. She used a cane for a few years before graduating to a walker last year, though she mostly uses a wheelchair in public these days. The ramp was easier for her to navigate than the stairs."

I nodded, tucking that info away for later. While Gunnar sprang up the stairs, I navigated the ramp, following him up to the entry.

The entry consisted of a wide porch with sweetheart swings on either corner, little picture windows, and two black doors.

"You're in the first apartment." Gunnar turned the key in the lock, opening the door and leading me inside.

Beautiful wood floors, high ceilings, and white blank walls. The place felt empty but warm.

"It's your place," he said, leading me through the space. "Feel free to pop up art or pictures or move stuff around. We don't mind."

Those butterflies morphed into bats as I walked through the hall, grinning as Gunnar began the tour.

"Master bedroom with ensuite to your left. There's a small guest bedroom to your right. Linen closet in the hall," he opened the doors showing me a well-stocked closet. "If you need anything else linen-wise just buy it and hand the receipt to Ma. She'll reimburse you."

He gestured to a door on our right. "Main bathroom and another closet." He opened a door on the left. "Office space," Gunnar threw me a grin. "You'll need it. Erik is rigorous in his testing."

I chuckled, following him into a small living room, complete with comfortable furniture, a tiny dining room with a round table, and a small but completely functional kitchen.

"You can open this up," Gunnar said, showing me how to open the large bifold doors onto the back deck. "Gets a great breeze year-round."

Now I could see why the house had been built backward –
with the bedrooms on the road. The backyard opened onto
a sloping yard with a magnificent view out to the ocean. The
back porch was completely covered and I could see there
were sliding screens to keep the bugs out. The yard itself
was flourishing, beautiful greenery, and budding flowers
ready to bloom in the coming weeks. A slight breeze tickled
the hairs on my cheek; salt and pollen heavy in the air.

"This is beautiful," I told Gunnar, spreading my arms and
sucking in a deep, satisfying breath. "You're sure I'm living
here rent-free?"

He chuckled. "Oh, it's not rent-free. Erik's gonna work
you hard. Don't have any doubts about that."

I laughed, following him back inside. "I look forward to
it."

"Laundry's through here, all your utility access is in there
too." Gunnar gestured at a door off the side of the kitchen.
"Out the side of the house there's a single carport but it's got
a small workshop at the rear. Feel free to use that however
you want."

I nodded, taking in the gloriously retro kitchen.

"If you need anything else just call. Ma's put together a
welcome pack, it should be around here somewhere. There
are groceries in the fridge, and I have no doubt she'll be
around later to visit." He knocked on the wall dividing my
apartment from the one next door. "And my brother Rune
should be done with work later. He's a little quiet, comes
across as testy but he's a good kid."

"Kid?"

Gunnar laughed, "I mean, I guess not but—"

"Hello?" A voice called from the entry, interrupting Gunnar.

"Hey, come on down. We're in the kitchen."

What sounded like a stampede of people thundered down the hall. A woman, her dark brown hair streaked liberally with grey, a man who had to be Gunnar's father, the resemblance was so strong, a woman who looked vaguely familiar held one baby, while a man who I assumed was Gunnar's brother Erik held another. They entered the kitchen in a jumble of limbs, smiles, and chatter.

"Gabby, meet the family. Well, some of them."

The older woman came in, dropping a basket on the kitchen counter and opening her arms. "Hi Gabby, I'm Jemma. Sorry, I'm a hugger!" she wrapped her arms around me, pulling me close.

I sent a deer-in-the-headlights look over her shoulder at the older man. He chuckled.

"Jemma, let the poor girl breathe."

She let me go, stepping back and slapping a hand on the older man's chest. "Ignore him, Gabby. Sune has no manners."

"My mother and father," Gunnar said, gesturing between the two. "And this is my brother, Erik, and his fiancé Laura, and their two boys, Ulf and Leif."

"Hi," I held out a hand and Erik took it, giving it a warm shake.

"Welcome to the Cape," he said, juggling the baby. "Hope you don't mind that we're intruding. Thought we'd pop out to help you move in."

"But first," Jemma pulled a sourdough loaf from the basket. "Lunch."

194

I was quietly but efficiently shuffled out of the kitchen and onto the back deck, a baby somehow ending up in my arms, while Erik, Sune, and Gunnar described the workshop to me.

"Obviously," Erik said, handing me a bottle of soda that had appeared as if by magic, "we're not expecting you until next week. But if you feel like coming and checking us out, let me know. I'll make sure I have some time to show you around."

"That'd be great," I said, dodging a flailing baby arm. "Gunnar said you were upgrading the workshop?"

Erik laughed. "Not the workshop itself, that'll have to wait till next winter when work slows a little. We're upgrading the office at the moment, adding a nursery." He nodded at his boys. "We're a family affair and these two have reminded me of that. We're adding the nursery so no one has to juggle family and work. They can do both happily."

"That's... wonderful," I said, lifting my drink in salute. "And super progressive."

"He just likes Ma's free babysitting," Gunnar said, knocking his shoulder into his brother. They both laughed and I smiled, watching them, already feeling at ease with my decision.

"Besides, with Laura's film schedule, I like to have the back-up."

I froze, drink halfway to my lips. "Film schedule?"

"I'm the Queen of Clean," Laura answered, stepping onto the deck, a platter laden with sandwiches in her hand. Jemma trailed, her hands holding two pitchers of drinks.

"It's a reality TV show where I—"

"Clean people's houses. I've seen some of your social

media clips." I leaned forward, glancing between her and Erik. "Did you meet on the show?"

They both chuckled, nodding.

Jemma sat, gesturing at me to start eating. "Please, we're not formal here."

Around food and drink, I learned more about the workshop, the business, and their family.

There were five children altogether, Gunnar, Erik, Liv, Astrid, and Rune, but only Gunnar and Erik were part of Thor's Shipbuilding. Gunnar was engaged to Ella, who owned a bar back in Capricorn Cove. I'd met her a few times, a lovely bubbly woman, confident and warm. She was the reason Gunnar had bought the marina and moved to the Cove.

Erik and Laura had met on the set of her TV show when she'd been asked by Liv, who was a television producer, to help him out. Having just adopted twins, Erik had been overwhelmed by the responsibility and cleaning and needed some extra help.

I couldn't help but smile at the way they described their relationship, both of them.

Gunnar had driven me up to the Cape but would be heading back to Capricorn Cove later tonight. The way his family teased him; I had the impression that he didn't like being away from his fiancé for long.

In addition to Gunnar, Erik, and Liv, there was Astrid and Rune. Astrid was away at college, completing her masters in architecture.

"And your other son?"

"Rune is—"

Leif let out a screech, his hands kicking angrily as he

demanded to be put down. We laughed, his momma rolling her eyes.

"Let me just go swap out this kid's diaper."

"You want me to do it?" Erik asked, handing Ulf to his mom and moving to stand.

"No, Babe. I got it." She touched his shoulder on the way out, and he captured her hand, pressing a quick kiss to her palm.

I approved of both the intimate, tender gesture and his willingness to take on diaper duty. While I'd loved working with Gunnar, there hadn't been a guarantee that I would like his brother just as much. All that I was observing, from lunch to the way he interacted with his family, boded well.

We chatted some more, settling back as the midday sun warmed the deck. I could just imagine summer days spent here, listening to music, pottering around the garden, the breeze cooling my skin, sticky from the hot sun.

"-and you'll want to go to the Fire Ball which is coming up," Jemma said, interrupting my daydream.

"Fire Ball?"

"Mm, every year the town raises money for the fire department. They often fly out to help some of our neighbors during the season. We make sure our boys and girls have the right equipment for that."

"Sounds good," I said, refilling my glass with the home-made lemonade. "Is there an auction? Or do we just donate or...?"

"There's always an auction. And the business purchases the table for our employees to attend," she fluffed her hair, sending Sune a grin. "It's an excuse for me to buy a new dress and look half-decent for a night."

197

Sune leaned over, pressing a kiss to his wife's lips. "You always look perfect."

She chuckled, waving him off, a slight blush heating her cheeks.

That kind of timeless love was so rare, my heart ached to experience something like that. Looking around at the table, seeing how loving they all were to each other, I ached to experience that kind of family.

One day.

"But aside from the auction and the Ball, there's all sorts of fundraisers in the lead-up. There's a pie drive, the local school holds a fair, and there's a fun run."

"Don't forget the readathon," Erik said, reaching across the table to snag the final chocolate chip cookie. "Rune, my youngest brother, runs it. You can sign up at the Literary Academy." He grinned, "it's a café-slash-bookstore. You'll want to go in the morning, Rune makes a mean cup of coffee."

"I'll check it out."

"Well, we should get you moved in." Erik pushed up from his chair, stretching.

"If you get the spare key, we can pop them down in Rune's place," Laura commented, digging through the diaper bag. "I think I brought a spare baby monitor and it's about time for their nap anyway."

"Don't worry," Erik waved a hand. "Rune has one."

They trooped next door while Sune, Gunnar, and Jemma headed outside with me.

The van was small, I'd only brought the bare essentials. When I'd decided to take up Gunnar's offer, I'd sold all my furniture, adding the proceeds to my dwindled savings. I'd done the figures - it would have cost me more to store my stuff than to sell it and buy new ones once I returned. The only things in that van were a custom cherry wood bed with beautiful matching side tables, a few boxes of clothes and some personal items. Two suitcases, a bike, and my spare prosthetics were in my car.

We moved it all inside in a surprisingly short amount of time, Laura diligently cleaning every item.

"You never know what it's picked up," she told me, brandishing a spray bottle and cloth. "Particularly in moving trucks."

Once my bed was rebuilt, and all the clothes and whatnot stowed away, the family called goodbyes, Erik reminding me to check out the Literary Academy. "Seriously, best coffee in America."

I laughed, waving them off.

In the silence of the house, I straightened a rug, dusted an imaginary piece of lint from the couch as I made my way through the house to the back deck once more.

Stepping into the sunshine, I raised my arms, throwing them out wide, closing my eyes and tilting my head to the sun. Gentle warmth heated my skin, the breeze teasing my hair. I could smell pollen and damp earth as it mixed with the salty bite that came from the ocean in the distance. I heard birds trilling, the soft rustle of leaves as the wind brushed through branches, and, if I concentrated very hard, the very dim crash of waves.

I opened my eyes, dropping my arms and resting them on my hips, grinning out at the view.

"Welcome home."

Chapter Two

Rune

I had to face it; this was going to be a shitty day.

In the grand scheme of things, I guess it wasn't that bad. But right now, I was damn grumpy.

The day had started off well enough. I'd woken, gone for a run, then tried to drive to work only to find I had a flat tire. Ordinarily, this wouldn't be a problem as I carried a spare. Only, I'd loaned the spare to my soon-to-be sister-in-law Laura for some segment she was doing for her social media. I didn't get it, nor did I care that much but it had been mildly annoying now that I needed it.

I'd sucked it up, pulled out my old bike, and ridden into work. Where I'd found a late delivery from last night had been left on the back dock. The back dock which had been impacted by last night's rain. The books were ruined. And all of them had been part of an overdue delivery for eager readers desperate for an author's new release.

I'd quietly dealt with that issue, photographing the damage and writing a curt email to the dispatcher. We may have been a small store, but we punched above our weight in sales.

I knew that the dispatcher had accidentally dropped that little tidbit when he'd last been out. There was no excuse for this nonsense.

By the time I'd opened the store, I'd been mildly inconvenienced. That had changed when the tourists arrived.

A large pack of young twenty-somethings with more money than sense, they'd tumbled through the doors of my store, laughing and disrupting my regulars in for their morning coffees.

"Oh. My. Gawwwwwwd!" one of the girls squeaked, staring glassy-eyed at the book tunnel. "Quick, take my picture! This is so going on the 'gram."

I'd inherited the Literary Academy from my grandmother. The store had been failing before I'd taken over, added the café, bumped out the back, and created book-sculptures to generate interest. It'd taken me about a month of eight-hour days to finish the giant book tunnel that separated the café from the bookstore. Booths lined the tunnel, positioned just so for people to have a coffee or wine, and read an hour away.

In addition to the tunnel, there were themed areas. Like in the kids' section, I'd created a pirate ship out of books that they could play on. In the romance section, there was a sculpture of lovers embracing. In gardening, there were flowers, and so on. I rotated the sculptures every month or so, refreshing some of the smaller ones to create new interest and generate new buzz online.

I'd realized early on that if I was to turn a profit then I needed to reinvigorate my gran's idea of cool. As much as it pissed me off, making a photo-attractive business was generating a fairly decent return.

Even if people didn't buy a book, they at least bought from the café, so the trade was good. And foot traffic and pictures drove more foot traffic and pictures, which was good for the town as well.

Even if I hated it.

I cleared my throat, catching their attention and tapped on the blackboard above my register.

Quiet, please. Don't disturb the other customers.

She flushed, her face taking on a mulish expression.

"And just who are you?" she demanded, hands moving to her hips.

I inwardly sighed. Yep, it was gonna be *that* kind of day.

I tapped the title embroidered on my chest, the one reading Head Librarian.

"The owner," I replied, gesturing at the filled tables around the joint. "You can take your pictures, just keep it down a little."

She sniffed, lifting her head and giving me a side-eye. "One star for service."

Her friends dragged her away, taking her into the bookstore while one of her friends stayed behind ordering them to-go coffees.

"Sorry about Shayna," the girl told me, leaning across the counter, positioning so her shirt gaped open at the neck. "She's still a little wasted from last night."

I shrugged, keeping my eyes on the frothing milk.

"So, you own this place?"

I nodded, quickly pouring the milk into the waiting coffee in the recyclable cups, adding a dash of froth, chocolate, or cinnamon as required.

"You doing anything later?"

I finished with the coffees, sliding them into a tray and across to her.

"Reading."

She laughed, rolling her eyes. "Oh, reading. Well, surely you could put that off and come out dancing with us later."

"No," I replied, moving back to the machine and beginning to make the next order, having just spotted Mrs. Howell hovering outside while her granddaughter diligently parked her tricycle.

The girl looked shocked for a moment then shrugged. "Whatever. Your loss. Weirdo."

She flounced off, coffees in hand, following her friends into the bookstore. I hoped Jill, who was on duty in there today, had clocked them early.

Mrs. Howell, her granddaughter holding the door open, entered, fluttering a hand to her face. "Oh my, it certainly smells good in here."

She made her way through the tables, calling hellos, as Maisy danced about, handing out flowers she'd picked from her grandmother's garden.

The little girl had been living with Mrs. Howell since her mother had gone to jail. Everyone in town knew, but we didn't talk about it. Just like we didn't talk about how Mr. Murphy and Mrs. Scree had been carrying on for years even though in public they pretended to hate each other. And we definitely didn't talk about the fact Mr. Rodney liked more than one glass with his dinner and had to be regularly driven home at closing.

There were more secrets and unspoken bullshit in this town than I'd like, but it was home.

"What would you like today, Maisy?" Mrs. Howell asked,

looking down at the girl.

Maisy rocked on her little heels; her lips pressed together as she considered the menu. Considering she didn't yet read; I had no idea what she thought to garner from her perusal.

I slid the cappuccino, two shots with extra sugar, across the counter to Mrs. Howell, who took it gratefully.

"One muffin and a spwinkle cup." Maisy finally said, missing her r's.

"Coming right up," I replied, turning to the display cabinet and finding the muffin space empty. "Actually, give me a second and I'll see if there's some fresh muffins in the kitchen."

I ducked out the back, finding another tray our chef had left cooling on the counter.

Returning, a woman stood at the counter. Long dark hair that complimented her high cheekbones, and beautifully flawless complexion. Her lips were wide, painted a glorious red, and eased into a fucking gorgeous smile. Around her neck lay a turquoise encrusted choker. It may have been a nod to her heritage, or just a trinket she liked, but it put me in mind of sex. Filthy, sweaty, dirty sex. Long nights spent in bed, my hand wrapped around her neck as I devoured her mouth, my cock buried between her thighs.

I felt like I'd been punched in the gut, such was my reaction to her.

Mine.

I had to attribute this reaction to the werewolf novel I'd been reading last night.

Fated mates aren't a thing, dickhead.

"Hey," the woman lifted a hand in greeting. More turquoise jewelry glinted, thick rings around her index finger and thumb. "You must be Rune."

She looked me up and down, interest warming her gaze even as she laughed. "I feel sorry for your momma. You guys are all massive. Viking stock, right?"

I popped the tray on the counter, nodding. "And you are?"

"Gabby, your new neighbor." She held out a hand and I took it, giving it a quick shake. Her grip was warm and firm, her fingernails painted black and white. Aviators were pushed up onto her head, tangled in her hair.

"You're the apprentice?"

She nodded, dropping my hand, and looking around at the café. "Yeah, just here until October, maybe November depending on how my training goes." She threw me a smile. "Don't worry, I'll try to keep the noise to a dull roar."

I didn't know what to make of this woman. She wasn't at all what I was expecting when Erik had said they needed the other apartment. I guess I'd expected someone younger or less sure of herself. Not this bold woman who wore her body like she knew all the secrets of the world.

"Rune?" Mrs. Howell called. I looked her way, seeing her gesturing at Maisy. "Can you watch her for a moment, dear?"

I nodded, taking a muffin from the tray and placing it on the small plate I kept just for Maisy. Mrs. Howell headed for the restroom while Maisy made her way to the counter. I slid the muffin across to her, watching as she reached up, carefully sliding it off without dropping it.

"Take that to your gran's table and I'll get your drink," I told her.

She nodded, balancing the plate, tongue poking out the side of her mouth as she tried not to drop the treat.

"What can I get you?" I asked Gabby, my hands moving automatically to pour milk and chocolate into a milkshake glass for Maisy.

"Can you do a caramel latte?"

I nodded.

"And I'll take a muffin to go." She frowned at the menu. "Gosh, everything looks good."

"Try the blueberry pancakes," I told her, knowing in my gut she'd like them.

She laughed, the sound delightfully rich and genuine. "I was just thinking about that. You totally read my mind. Let's do it."

"Excuse me." The little voice had us both glancing down as I finished making Maisy's drink.

"Yes, honey?" Gabby asked, a gentle smile on her face.

"What happened to your leg?"

I shifted, subtly glancing over the countertop to see Maisy touching Gabby's prosthetic leg. I tensed, waiting for Gabby to tell her to stop, but instead, she smiled.

"What do you think happened?"

Maisy bit her lip, screwing her face up as she squinted, thinking.

"A shark," she declared. "A weally, weally big one!"

"Nope," Gabby chuckled. "The only sharks I've met have been very friendly."

She leaned against the counter, one hand steadying her as she stuck her leg out. "Sometimes, babies are just born this way. That's what happened to me."

Her shorts cut off mid-thigh, revealing yards of leg. Her left ended just below the knee, a prosthetic making up the lower part of the limb. A bright pink compression sock covered her skin from just above her knee, disappearing into the prosthetic.

Maisy frowned, running her tiny hand up the carbon fiber limb.

"You didn't lose it?"

"No, honey. I never had it to begin with."

Maisy nodded. "It's pretty," she whispered, her fingers tracing the vines and flowers that decorated the leg.

"Do you like it more than my other leg?" Gabby asked, gesturing at the tattoo that decorated her right calf. The black tattoo was intricately detailed, a turtle swimming through the ocean, a map of the world on its back, only small parts of the USA marked by pops of color.

"I like this one better," Maisy declared, patting the prosthetic. "I like pink."

I finished making Gabby's drink as they chatted. Maisy's gran returned, calling her back to the table.

Gabby picked up her drink and packaged muffin, accepting their invitation to sit with them for breakfast.

"Food's up."

I picked up her pancakes, delivering them to the table.

"Oh Rune, you should invite Gabby to join the fundraiser," Mrs. Howell directed, laying a hand on my arm.

"Fundraiser?" Gabby asked, cocking an eyebrow in my direction as she picked up her fork.

"Readathon," I told her gruffly, watching with unholy interest as she sliced a bite of the pancakes, lifting it to her mouth. "Raising money for the fire department."

"Ah, your parents mentioned something about that yesterday." She slid the bite between her lips, her eyes closing as she moaned, slowly chewing.

Fuck. I had to shift, adjusting my stance to avoid anyone catching sight of my rapidly hardening cock. I hadn't been this horny since reading Kati Wilde's Hellfire Rider series. That whole week I'd been hard as a fucking rock.

Ask her out, doofus.

Don't fucking rush me.

I cleared my throat, frowning as I tried to work out how to ask her to dinner.

Been a while.

"This is so good, thanks for the recommendation," Gabby forked another bite.

"Are you interested?" Mrs. Howell asked. "You just need to get some sponsors and for every book you read, they pay for it."

"I'm doing it!" Maisy piped up, playing with her paper straw. "Mr. Jennings said he'd give me a dollar a book!"

"Wow, that's awesome Maisy." Gabby raised a hand, slapping palms with the young girl. "But I'm not a reader. Maybe I can just sponsor our girl, Maisy here?"

My world screeched to a halt.

"Not a… you don't read?" I repeated.

"Uh-huh," she affirmed, licking her fork with a tongue that, only moments ago, I'd contemplated tasting.

I grunted, stepping back from the table. "Enjoy your breakfast."

I returned to the counter and the line of patiently waiting customers.

Sighing, I settled in, making coffee, serving food, and watching, with one disappointed eye as Gabby quietly charmed Mrs. Howell and Maisy. She got up, placing a tip on the table, and calling goodbye as she left, shooting me

208

a smile and a wave.

I stared at the door for a long moment. Feeling eyes on me, I glanced over to find Mrs. Howell watching me, pity written across her face.

"I'm sorry, Rune." She shook her head. "I had high hopes for that one."

So did I.

I turned away, mulling over how I could turn a non-reader into a bookworm.

My bookworm.

Chapter Three

Gabby

I fed the wood through the saw, watching carefully to ensure the wood didn't buckle or slip. Once complete, I shut the saw off, lifting the cut and checking the line.

Perfect.

A flash of movement in the corner of my eye caught my attention. I looked over, pulling my earmuffs down, pushing my safety glasses up, and smiling at my new boss as he headed over.

"Hey, it's after five. The gang is clocking out, you wanna come for a drink?"

"Sure," I shifted the wood, laying it against my shoulder and following him as we walked back into the main construction space.

Capricorn Cove's branch of Thor's Shipbuilding had nothing on the Cape workshop. This was a professional operation from top to bottom. I could see why Gunnar had sent me here to learn – he wanted to replicate the processes and layout back in the Cove. But without seeing it and experiencing the flow and pulse it would be almost impossible to understand.

"How are you finding it?" Erik asked, tucking his hands into dusty jeans.

"Amazing," I told him honestly. "The guys are wonderful; this workshop is just… next level, and the projects are really great."

He laughed, slapping me gently on the back. "We do alright. You'll let me know if you have any issues though?"

Apart from your brother?

"Promise."

We chatted as we walked into the main workshop, pausing so I could lay the cut with the others I'd need next week. Thor's Shipbuilding complex was set-up in a series of three warehouses, each interconnected. The shipyard consisted of the main warehouse where the ships were built and repaired. Within the main warehouse sat offices off to one side, including the lunchroom and the soon-to-be completed nursery. Upstairs was an apartment that had been used by Erik before he'd adopted his twin boys. Now it was empty, but I'd heard rumors they were only keeping it that way until the end of the school year when Astrid graduated.

The two outbuildings contained different workshops and storage. Giant in size, one had been divided into three, built to store wood and steel, with the relevant machines and tools ready to go. The last one was for critical work. A dust-free workshop with set up for painting and fabrication. I'd watched in awe as one of Erik's men, Rafe, had demonstrated how to create a small fiberglass hull in less than an hour.

"You want a lift?" Erik asked when we made it to the locker room.

"Where are we going?"

"Literary Academy. They do beers and wine Friday and Saturday night. Oh, and for book club on Tuesdays – but that's mostly women who attend. And Rune."

Damn.

I hesitated, my hand gripping the leather of my bag as I considered my options.

It was only my second week in the Cape, but I'd already fallen in love with the people, the location, and the work. I wanted to pack up, move here, and settle down.

Or at least, I wanted to except for one big, broad roadblock – Rune.

The man glowered at me, one big, gruff attractive lump of unfriendly mountain man. I'd visited the Literary Academy every morning this week, determined to get my caffeine fix and meet the locals. The morning of my first full day in the Cape I'd assumed Rune had maybe been interested. I'd liked the way he'd looked at me, approving and slightly heated. But day two had proven me wrong. He'd been curt, his jaw clenched and eyes dead as he'd served me. So, I hadn't gone back. Instead, I'd tried the other coffee places around town, quickly discovering that Erik hadn't lied – Rune's was the best in America. Or, in this case at least, the best in town.

So, putting on my big girl panties, I'd returned the following week, determined to ignore Rune's chilly reception. It wasn't easy, but his coffee made the bite a little easier to bear.

"Gabby?"

"Sorry," I pulled my bag free, settling it over my shoulder. "Yeah, I'd love a lift if you can."

"No problem, let's toss your bike in the back. Are you planning on riding home after drinks?"

I hesitated then nodded. "Can you give me a minute to swap my legs?"

"No problem," he grabbed his backpack, swinging it over his shoulder. "I've gotta grab something from the office. Meet you at the truck?"

I nodded.

He left and I pulled out my regular limb, sitting to swap it out.

I owned three different types of prosthetics, each serving a different purpose. My heavy-duty one was for work. It was specifically designed for standing for long periods, and for rough terrain. But it was graded as being suitable for heavy-duty work but didn't have the same flexibility and lightweight design that my every day held. The other two were every day, one really for general use, while the second was good for hiking and bike rides.

Most people only had one, maybe two. But I'd volunteered to be a part of a trial for a new lightweight, low-cost version. The carbon fiber with the pretty painting had been designed specifically for me in exchange for participating in the trial. Once a year for the last three years I took myself off to Chicago to participate in testing and updates. It'd lasted me three years, though I'd had to swap out the socket last year due to some issues with pain. If all continued to go well, the company would be producing these in mass quantities within the next year or two. Affordable, durable, prosthetics. I couldn't wait.

I swapped out my leg, and decided to change my shirt, replacing the battered, filthy plaid with a nice plain black cotton. I washed my face, scrubbing dust from my skin, then ran a brush through my hair. It was only when I found myself looking for a tube of lipstick that I realized what I was doing.

"Stop it," I ordered, shaking a finger at myself in the mirror. "Rune doesn't even like you."

But it didn't stop me from wanting him too. God, he was just my type. Built like his Viking ancestors, the man was massive. Bigger than both his brothers, broad and strikingly blonde. He wore his hair clipped close to his head, and was clean-shaven. I'd heard rumors that he used to have a man-bun and beard – but it'd scared Maisy so he'd cut them off.

A man cutting his hair for a four-year-old, be still my beating heart.

I locked up before walking out to meet Erik at his truck, finding my bike already loaded. He was on the phone, sitting in the cab. I slid in, mouthing sorry as I closed the door. He brushed me off with a dismissive wave, starting the truck up then putting his call on Bluetooth.

"Laura, you're on loudspeaker. Gabby's here with me."

"Hey, Gabby!"

"Hey," I replied, feeling a little awkward.

"I'm just trying to convince my bonehead fiancé to fly to New York for the upcoming long weekend."

He sent me a *kill me now* look.

"Uh, I didn't realize you were in New York."

"I'm not. I'm sitting at a table with the guys at the Literary Academy waiting for him to get here. But I want to book these tickets now."

I blinked, raising an eyebrow at Erik who shrugged, shaking his head.

"Is there… a rush sale or something?"

214

"No, I just want it sorted."

"And I told you, Queenie," Erik replied, indicating to pull out of the shipyard then halting to wait for traffic. "If we're going to New York we're going for longer than a week. I don't want your family thinking I'm rushing off."

Behind us the automatic gates slowly closed, sealing the yard for the weekend.

"And *I* don't want to stay longer than we need to. The boys are finally in a good routine and—"

"Fine, book it. But add two days on." Erik told her, pulling out in the traffic. "I'll work it out with the team."

"Oh, they're here. Let me ask," there was an audible scramble on the other end of the phone.

Erik blew out a sigh, sending me an exasperated look. "Pray your future in-laws aren't crazy. Mine are cleaning freaks. I spilled a little airplane coffee on my pants the first time I met them and seriously, Laura's dad made me take them off so he could deal with it. I met her grandmother in my boxers."

I sniggered, as Laura came back on the phone. "Ian says it's fine as long as you agree to let the boys off at lunch on the Wednesday before Gunnar's wedding so they can drive down early."

"Fine, fine." Erik rolled his eyes. "It's not like I have a business to run."

"See you guys soon!" Laura made a kissing sound then hung up.

Erik blew out a breath, shaking his head once again. "Are you flying or driving back to Capricorn Cove for Gunnar's wedding?"

I blinked. "Um, I didn't think I was invited."

215

Erik waved a dismissive hand. "All employees are invited." He turned down Main, headed for the store. "We're planning on doing a road trip down, though God knows how that'll go with the twins."

I shifted. "Are you sure? I mean, I've only been an employee for a few months and –"

Erik shrugged, turning into the parking lot and finding a space. "I'll check with Gunnar, but I'm pretty sure he's assumed you're coming."

"Is it a fancy wedding?"

Erik laughed, putting the truck in park and switching it off. "Not even close. It's gonna be a ceremony in their backyard, followed by a party. They've organized food trucks, rides, and games. The whole town is invited to see Ella shack up with my bro."

The clutch of anxiety eased. "Ah, so it's more like…" I tried to think. "Like a royal wedding. Where everyone celebrates."

Erik barked out a laugh, shaking a finger at me. "God, don't tell my brother that. He's got a big enough head as it is."

Chuckling, we both exited the truck, heading inside.

I'd only been inside the Literary Academy during the day. At night, it transformed. Soft lighting in the café, old-school reading lamps on tables, a live musician playing softly in the corner. Twinkle lights hung from rafters and guided people down the book tunnel, inviting them to get lost amongst the stacks.

"Wow," I muttered. "Wasn't expecting this."

Erik heard, shooting me a grin. "We used to go to a bar down from the shipyard. But Evan doesn't drink, so we started coming here so he could get a shot of coffee."

We found Laura and the other Thor's employees easily, they were arguing about what to buy Gunnar and Ella for their wedding. At the table sat Ian, our foreman shipwright. He had a touch of Scottish brogue still in his tone, though he'd moved to America in his early years. He was big, broad, and incredibly red. From the top of his head to the tip of his beard, and all the way down to the hair on his toes, the man resembled nothing so much as a hairy red bigfoot. For all his size and hair, Ian was surprisingly refined, having surprised me more than once with his knowledge of wine, literature, and politics.

Beside him sat Jack, the youngest member of our group. He was studying marine architecture at college and had spent the last summer interning with this motley crew. If I'd been even two years younger, I'd have given him more than a passing glance. But the boy still had much to learn, and as I neared my late-twenties, I couldn't find it in me to want to teach him.

Gavin and Rodney were next. They were surprisingly thick as thieves for men who had virtually nothing in common. Where Gavin was all comedy and friendliness, Rodney was prickly as a porcupine. Gavin was a bit of a player, leading the women of the Cape on merry chases, while Rodney had settled down with his high school sweetheart, marrying her the week after graduation. They worked well together and had a wealth of experience that I was more than willing to bask in.

Our final two seats were taken up by Laura, Erik's fiancé, and Evan, who was sipping tea. He looked utterly at ease in the store, a stack of books sitting beside his teacup.

"You got any ideas?" Laura asked Erik, before pressing a

welcoming kiss to his mouth.

"For?" He slid in beside her, wrapping an arm around her chair.

"Your brother's wedding gift."

"Nope. That's why I have you." He gave her a squeeze, shooting her a smile as he reached for her glass, taking a sip.

"Nah-uh," Ian said, shaking his head, his red shaggy mane flying. "She wants to get them a carpet shampooer."

I raised an eyebrow at Gavin in question. He rolled his eyes, tilting his head towards the bar. "You want a drink, Gabby?"

"I'll get it," I glanced at the table. "Anyone need a refill?'"

Ian requested a chardonnay, but everyone else waved me off as Erik and Laura began to argue about why a carpet shampooer was a terrible wedding gift.

"Queenie, they have wood floors."

"But rugs! They'll need to wash the rugs."

I chuckled, finding the drink menu and quickly perusing the options.

A glass of white wine and a mojito landed in front of me. I glanced up; eyebrow raised when I saw Rune watching me. Damn him, He looked good, his work shirt stretched tight over his chest, an apron tied at his waist. His face was blank, but his eyes held… something as he watched me.

Why do you have to be so attractive?

I wouldn't care half so much that he didn't like me if it weren't for the way he looked… and how he'd treated little Maisy that first day. I couldn't shake how gentle he'd been with her.

"For me?" I asked, nodding at the glasses.

"On the house," he said gruffly, moving about the bar to

get another drink made.

"Uh, thanks."

Way to send confusing signals. Make up your mind, dude.

I reached for the mojito, taking a sip, and finding the drink slightly different to what I expected.

"Wow," I muttered, licking my lips. "Is that mango?"

He nodded, his hands moving in a flurry of motion as he tipped, shook, and stirred.

"Nice." I took another sip, considering him.

"Hey Rune," a young woman came up, leaning against the bar. I saw her interest in him, a small nugget of amusement threading through me when I realized he wasn't at all interested in her. Rune's body language shifted his back straightening, his body shifting slightly away from her.

"Florence," he greeted, finishing the pour then lifting delicate glasses filled with a cloudy liquid and placing them on a tray. "What can I get you?"

I sucked another sip, hanging around to watch.

"I'll have a cowboy cocksucker," she said, sending him a wink.

"We don't serve that."

I hid a smile, finding this immensely amusing. Not because I didn't support my fellow thirsty woman – sister, I was there for you. But because Rune looked so incredibly awkward as he tried to give her the brush off.

"Oh," Florence pouted, glancing at the menu then holding it out to him, pressing her breasts to the bar so they were more pronounced. "How about this one?"

Rune took the menu, closing it and placing it back in its holder. He got to work, making her a strawberry daiquiri in record time.

219

He placed it on the bar, taking her money. For a moment, Florence hovered as if waiting for him to take the initiative, but Rune had turned back to me, ignoring her.

"Maisy wants to know if you're still going to sponsor her."

Florence sighed heavily, looking disappointed but flounced off, sending a rueful smile and an eye roll my way. I returned it, laughing as she mouthed *good luck* at me.

"Gabby?"

I turned back to Rune. "I promised her I would," I told him, finishing off my drink.

He took the glass then held up a bottle of rum in question.

"Yeah, another would be great."

As he made it, I considered him, the liquor likely giving me courage I wouldn't ordinarily have.

"Why do you hate me?"

His hands froze mid-motion. His body freezing as his head slowly turned towards me, surprise in every line of his face.

"Hate you?"

I nodded. "It's pretty obvious. You can't even look at me most days and I've only been here a few weeks." I shrugged, trying not to let him see how his reaction hurt. "I guess it'd just be nice to know what I did."

As Rune finished making my drink, a waiter returned to the bar with an empty tray. He picked up Ian's chardonnay handing it to him. "Could you take this to Ian, please?"

The guy nodded, whisking the drink away. I slid onto a bar stool, waiting for him to explain.

He grabbed a cloth, wiping down the bar as he pursed his lips, considering me.

"I don't hate you."

"No?" I raised an eyebrow, circling my paper straw in the glass, swirling the mango syrup. "Sure about that?"

He blew out a breath. "Sorry. I just find it hard to meet new people."

I lifted an eyebrow. "Really? You're gonna Mr. Darcy me?"

He blinked. "You've read Pride and Prejudice?"

"Geez, don't sound so surprised. Just because I don't love to read doesn't mean I'm a complete illiterate."

Not to mention Colin Firth makes me thirsty as fuck.

If the fact he was running the damp cloth over the exact same spot repeatedly was any indication, it looked like I'd surprised Rune.

"Then why won't you join the readathon?"

I rolled my eyes. "I don't know Rune, maybe because I don't enjoy reading? Or maybe because I don't want to."

He frowned. "What was the last book you read?"

I absently sipped the mojito, trying to remember. I had to stop a shiver when Rune's gaze dropped to my lips, his eyes darkening a fraction.

I shrugged. "I don't know. Probably an instruction guide your brother loaned me."

He shook his head, "not non-fiction, fiction. What was the last book?"

"Can't remember."

Rune's face flushed, his lips thinning into one disapproving line. "So, you haven't given books a chance."

I rolled my eyes. "God, I don't know. What's your beef with this?"

"Do the readathon, read, let's say twenty books of my choosing, and I'll sponsor you a thousand dollars."

My eyebrows lifted. "Excuse me?"

221

"Twenty books, a thousand dollars." He crossed his arms, glowering at me.

"Ten."

"Fifteen."

"Done!" I slapped a palm on the bar then held it out to shake. "You can't back outta this one, bucko."

His hand encompassed mine, warm and solid, and ridiculously large. His eyes glinted as he shook my hand, giving it a tiny squeeze. Something sparked between us at the contact, a shiver of awareness racing down my spine.

"You can pick up your first books tomorrow." He held my hand for a beat too long before turning away to serve a new customer. I picked up my glass, taking a long, badly needed drink.

Oh, joy.

Chapter Four

Rune

I woke to music. For the third Saturday in a row, I woke to music streaming through the wall beside my head.

Gabby, I'd learned, didn't know the meaning of quiet. She woke to music and played it through her morning routine. She chattered to the birds and flowers outside as she ate breakfast, she sang in the shower, and yelled at the TV.

And the thin walls of our duplex hid nothing from my ears.

For years I'd lived beside my grandmother, assisting her, ensuring she had what she needed to get by. When that situation became untenable due to needing around the clock assistance, she'd moved in with my parents. That had been two years ago, and I'd grown used to the quiet.

Gabby was an unpleasant, unwelcome shock to the system. *You sure about that bud?* Asked my erection.

I groaned loudly, reached for the spare pillow on my bed, and pulled it over my ears attempting to block the noise.

These days, I had weekends and Friday nights off. When I'd taken over the store, I'd worked around the clock to ensure it was a success. Now that we were financially viable, I'd eased up, hiring more staff to take on the work and allowing me to concentrate on the business side.

But in the last few weeks, a gastro-bug had hit the local elementary school, and most of my day staff were single parents so I'd been forced to fill in. It wouldn't normally be an issue, but it just so happened to coincide in the lead up to finals, which meant my college students were on restricted hours. I'd pulled more hours this month than I had in awhile.

Ordinarily, I didn't mind. But after three weeks in a row with only one day off, I was feeling pretty wrecked.

The music switched from pop to rock then to an acoustic mix.

My eyes drifted close, my breathing evening out as I started to fall back to sleep.

A crash shook the bed, jolting me awake. A startled shriek and more crashing followed.

Gabby!

I scrambled out of bed, dashing to the back deck, and around to Gabby's back entry. The door was open and inside I could see a trail of destruction.

"Gabby!" I bellowed, running inside, head swinging wildly about as I tried to track the scene.

Fuck. Fuck! Where is she? Fuck!

"Help! I'm in the bathroom!"

Her voice was muffled and I had an immediate vision of her hiding from an attacker.

I bolted through the house, down the hall, past the empty main bathroom, and into her room, stumbling to a halt at the door.

Her room was trashed. The trail of destruction began

on her back deck, continued through the living room, and down the hall, and had its grand finale in her bedroom.

Lamps and picture frames lay broken on the floor. A basket full of laundry had been tipped over, the clothing now strewn about the room. A prosthetic leg lay between the bed and the ensuite door, looking as if it had been discarded in a hurry.

The music abruptly cut off as I stared at the giant pelican sitting in the middle of Gabby's bed.

"Ferdinand!" I barked, placing my hands on my hips. "What the fuck man?"

The ensuite door opened a fraction, Gabby's poking her head out. "Wait, you know this beast?" She squeaked, her eyes wide, hair a rioting mess.

"Unfortunately."

Ferdinand raised up, flapping his wings wide, making a low, hoarse, almost barking sound in greeting.

Gabby opened the door a little wider, hopping to lean against the jam as she stared at the monster on her bed.

"My grandmother was a wildlife rescuer. Ferdinand is one of the nestlings she saved." I sighed, looking at the mess. "He normally stays in the garden but might have freaked out when he saw you instead of Nan."

Gabby pressed her lips together as Ferdinand began to groom himself, looking for all the world like he was in for the long haul.

"And your grandmother just let him walk through the house?"

"Sure."

She shook her head. "Can you pass me my crutch? It's in the closet."

I glanced her way, taking in her tiny sleep shorts, and her thin black cotton t-shirt. She was braless, her hair wild, missing a leg as she leaned against the doorway, her expression begrudgingly amused.

Gorgeous.

My erection, or what had remained of it after the Ferdinand intrusion, roared back to life, my cock thickening, and lengthening.

Fuck.

I wore only boxer briefs and a thin sleep shirt, the material hiding precisely nothing from her.

Fuckity fuck a fucking fuck.

I twisted abruptly, heading to the closet, opening the door, and blinking in surprise.

"Oh, yeah. Watch out for the body parts." She sounded amused.

Parts for her prosthetic sat on shelves in the closet. Different types of feet and sockets. Finding the crutch, I pulled it free, carrying it over.

"Thanks." She tucked it under her arm, hopping to readjust her weight. Now comfortable, she finally looked me over, her lips quirking a little as they landed on my raging erection.

"Ignore it," I said, gruffly. "I do."

She tilted her head, her eyelids lower, a warm flush coming to her cheeks. "I didn't realize pelicans were your thing."

I barked out a laugh. "Yeah, that and being woken by screams from my neighbor."

She chuckled, then nodded at the pelican currently making a nest on her bed. "So how do I get rid of him."

I sighed, running a hand over my cheek. "Don't laugh."

She blinked. "Excuse me?"

I mentally girded my loins, knowing this was about to hit a whole new level of strange.

"Just… don't laugh." I turned to the pelican, giving him a stare. "Hey, Ferdinand."

He looked up from his preening, giving me a dark-eyed stare. "Do you have time to sing a goodbye song before you go?"

Behind me, I heard a strangled laugh, and sighed again.

Ferdinand flapped his wings, gargling at me.

"Goodbye, goodbye, Ferdy goodbye. 'Cause now it's time to go, but hey, I say, well that's okay, cause we'll see you very soon I know," I crooned making a gesture at him to get off the bed.

With a happy flap of his wings, he hopped off the bed and began to waddle out to the hall. I continued to serenade him with a bastardized version of the goodbye song from the children's TV show Bear in the Big Blue House as he finally made it outside, Gabby following us.

"The moon, the pelican, and the big yellow house will be waiting for you to come and play. Come and play. To come and play." I gently slid the screen door shut behind him, calling. "Goodbye now, Ferdy."

With a final bark, he flapped his wings then took off, heading back to the water.

Behind me, Gabby snorted, the strangled laughter spilling free. "Oh my god," she leaned on her crutch, clutching it as she bent over slightly, her laughter bellowing out. "Oh my god!"

I blew out a breath, mentally counting to ten.

"You know," I said mildly, gesturing at the mess. "I was

gonna help you tidy up, but now I'm thinking you don't deserve it."

She finally calmed, wiping away tears of laughter. "That was, by far, the weirdest and most enjoyable morning I've had in years."

I cocked an eyebrow and she chuckled.

"I stand by my statement." She tilted her head. "Is your nan still alive? Cause she sounds like a real character."

"Yeah," my heart punched a little. "She's still alive and kicking. But she had a stroke and finds it harder to get around now, not that she'd let us know it. Still just as crazy."

"You'll have to tell her Ferdy came by," she started giggling again. "And that you rescued me from the bathroom with a song."

I sighed. "You're gonna tell my brother about this, aren't you?"

"Oh, yeah."

I crossed my arms in front of my chest, giving her a glare. "Well, just for that I'm gonna make you add the Bible to your reading list."

She laughed, straightening and repositioning the crutch, shifting to move into the kitchen. "I'm sure my sinner butt could probably use some words of wisdom."

"More like forgiveness," I muttered.

"Coffee?" she asked from the kitchen.

I shook my head. "Nah, thanks though. But I've got to get to work." I looked around at the chaos. "Actually, I'll get dressed then come and help you clean. Can't leave it like this."

"You sure?" She lifted the handle of her coffee pot. "Won't take me two minutes to pop a pot on."

228

My lips quirked. "I'm sorry to say but I don't do drip anymore. My tastes are a tad more refined these days."

She rolled her eyes, replacing the pot. "Sorry I don't have an espresso machine for you, Mr. Bourgeois."

"Oh, a fancy burn from the woman who doesn't read." I teased back.

"Hey, just because I don't read doesn't mean I'm not intellectual."

I held my hands out, "point well made." I dropped them, still trying to ignore the throbbing ache in my cock. "If you want a good coffee, I'll bring one over. Unlike you, I do have an espresso machine."

She blinked. "Holy shit. You've been holding out on me, Rune?"

My name on her lips did something to me. Something I liked a whole hell of a lot.

Down boy.

I shrugged. "Give me a few to shower and dress and I'll bring a cup over."

"You do the coffee; I'll bring breakfast."

"Done."

We split, both of us dressing, me having the world's quickest (and coldest) shower. Her music starting back up as I finished dressing, tying off my shoelace. I made us coffee then carried over the cups. As I entered the house, the music switched, the intro song for Bear in the Big Blue House playing.

"I guess you don't want this coffee," I pivoted on my heel but Gabby, sputtering with laughter, called out a protest.

"Don't! I do! I really need some of that sweet, sweet, elixir. I'm sorry... well, not totally. But it was worth it."

I turned back, finding her holding one plate in each hand.

"I made French toast…" she said, holding one plate out to me then the other as if she were trying to entice me over. "Come on, you know you want some."

Yeah, I do.

I came in, placing the mugs on her counter then taking the offered plate. We ate, side-by-side at her breakfast bar, Gabby chatting, me listening and, surprisingly, enjoying her chatter.

After, she popped the dishes in her dishwasher while I took stock of the mess. It wasn't as bad as it had initially appeared. A few broken picture frames, some knocked over ornaments, an upended side table. The main damage was in the bedroom.

"I'll get the dustpan and broom," she said, heading for the laundry.

Together we worked quietly and efficiently, setting the place to rights once more.

In the bedroom, we cleaned the floor then considered the mess of feathers on her duvet, including a small tear.

"Washing machine, then I'll see if I can save it." Gabby decided.

We removed the feathers, stripping the bed, and quickly placing all the linen in her washing machine.

While I waited for her to finish straightening the bedroom, I walked around her living room, taking in the photos and numerous photo albums stacked on the mostly empty bookshelf.

"Nice family," I commented when she came back in.

Gabby paused; a stack of papers Ferdinand had displaced in her hand.

"Thanks, but they're not actually my family," she looked back down at her papers, flicking through them again, sorting them into some semblance of order. "I just collect them."

I frowned. "Collect?"

She lifted one shoulder in a shrug, "You know, some people collect paintings, I collect photographs."

I glanced at the wall again, taking in the posed family snaps, the black and white images from by-gone eras, and the slightly fuzzy candids.

"Where do you get them?"

"Garage sales, antique stores, estate sales. Sometimes I pick them up at Goodwill," she waved a hand at the albums stacked on the bookshelf. "Family pictures are rarely sad. More often, they show joy. But these were discarded. And it feels wrong that something that was created in good times is discarded because of misfortune."

"Whatcha mean?"

She pulled a paper from the stack, setting the others aside as she turned to me. "People don't give away happiness. The reason these photos are now with me isn't because they intentionally decided to discard them. It's because something happened. Either people passed, or they fell on hard times or any number of things. So, I collect them. Good times deserve to be celebrated."

I blinked slowly, staring anew at this woman. A woman I realized I'd fundamentally miscategorized from the moment we'd met.

"What's on your list for today?" she asked as if she hadn't just rocked my world.

To kiss you.

231

I cleared my throat, fighting the sudden ache I had inside me to hold her close, to love her, to build a life with her.

Pull yourself together, dude.

"Work." I gave myself a mental shake. "I should probably be heading there now."

She nodded, biting her lip and tipping her head slightly to the side. "I should come in to get my list, yeah?"

"List?"

She grinned. "Of books?"

A sudden surge of lust hit my gut. An image of Gabby reading a book in bed beside me materialized. She'd be dressed in that thin cotton t-shirt and tiny sleep pants. We'd be reading the same book, a romance I'd picked out for us. We'd read the same scene at the same time, both of us getting hotter as the leads stroked and caressed, speaking filthy, dirty things to each other.

I shifted, attempting to hide the fact my cock was pressing against my zipper. My dick heavy and hard. It seemed to be a new normal around Gabby

"Right," my voice sounded off. Deep and low, a little gravelly, hoarse. "Come in later and I'll work it out."

"Just not the Bible, okay?" she laughed, the sound did nothing to help ease my need.

"We'll see."

Father forgive me because I'm about to sin.

Chapter Five

Gabby

As I rode my bike into town, I found myself distracted by the image of Rune standing in my room. He'd looked like a conquering Viking – if that Viking wore only boxer briefs.

Despite being a woman of the world, a woman used to looking after herself, I couldn't deny that it had been nice to know I had back-up. Granted, the back-up had only been required to serenade a pelican from my room, but the memory of big, wild-eyed Rune bursting into my house to slay the dreaded pelican invader had lit a warm little pool of pleasure in my belly.

Not to mention that erection. Phew! Girl, go get on THAT!

Ah yes, the erection in the room. That tent in his briefs had proved one thing – the man was big *everywhere*.

My body gave a delightful shiver remembering how he'd looked at me. It was as if I were a dollop of cream, he couldn't help but want to taste.

And that in and of itself was a marked moment. It wasn't that men didn't find me attractive; I knew they did. I'd dated on and off over the years so I'd had a lot of experience with men who were happy to date me as long as I didn't show them the real side of my life. The side where I sometimes needed to use a crutch, and where I needed a stool in the shower.

It didn't bother me, but people with no experience of disability often struggled. They didn't have the words or know how to ask the questions. They made assumptions or talked down to me as if my leg missing meant I was somehow less capable of making decisions.

I'd assumed Rune was like that. That he'd taken one look at my prosthetic the first day and decided I wasn't worth the trouble. But today had me reassessing that assumption.

The man had looked at me like he wanted to lay me on the bed and eat me from top to toe. He'd not handled me with overt care, instead just getting me what I needed, ensuring I was okay before getting on with it.

He was fucking with my head and emotions and I just didn't know if I liked it.

But I definitely don't hate it.

I parked my bike out front of the Literary Academy. The café was crazy busy, people spilling onto the chairs and tables outside. The smell of fresh coffee, warm baked goods, and a citrus tang sat heavy in the air, inviting people in.

In the few weeks, I'd lived in the Cape, I'd yet to visit the bookstore. The café, sure, no problem. The books? Not really my jam. Also, if I was honest with myself, I'd felt like a bit of an interloper. Rune hadn't exactly been friendly, and I hadn't exactly made an effort.

Gird thy loins, Gabby. We're going in.

I pushed through the old wood doors, and entered… wonderland. Inside the store was cool and smelled of old books. The kind of smell that reminded me of libraries, old scotch, and a crackling fire, though only the Lord knew why.

The store was larger than it first appeared. The Literary Academy occupied old warehouses. The brick walls were left bare, same with the timber beams that made up the soaring ceilings. The space would have felt large and somewhat sterile, if not for the dividers.

Each section was marked by things hanging from the roof, and towering sculptures made from books or paper. There were lights strung here and there, creating little places to draw the eye. As I walked further into the store, I found myself getting lost in a maze of shelving, stumbling across a lover's nook or a surprising art piece, a reading area, or a pirate ship made from books.

Acoustic music gently played through carefully hidden speakers, and it felt like such a world away from the bright bustle of the café next door. I suddenly understood why Rune had created the book tunnel. Without it connecting the two, gently guiding a person from the bright into the calm it would be a shock, all impact lost.

"Excuse me?" I asked a woman who was seated at a small table in what looked like a replica of an old study. The small nook was complete with a beautiful desk, leather seats, a globe, and an old desk lamp.

"Yes?" she asked, raising an eyebrow.

"Can you tell me how to get to the counter? I'm a bit turned around."

She chuckled. "You've not been here before?"

I shook my head.

She nodded at the shelves. "If you keep the shelves with a white line on their bottom on your right, you'll find the counter."

"Thank you."

I followed the line, backtracking my steps, and winding around until I found the carefully positioned counter. It didn't sit at the front of the store as I'd anticipated, rather it was tucked beside the tunnel, an old school cash register decorating the front of a desk. Books piled on either side and behind the counter was a giant book shelf that stretched up the whole back of the warehouse wall. All the books were black, except those in various russet shades which together made up the words, *The Literary Academy.*

I hovered, waiting my turn as Rune stood behind the counter, serving an old lady.

"I distinctly remember it being a blue cover," the woman said, peering at the book in her hands.

"You said it's a romance and has a character named Greer." He nodded at the book. "That's it."

She shook her head. "No, I don't think so."

He pressed his lips together then nodded. "How about you try this one, Maeve, and if it's not the book you want then I'll try and find it for the next time you're in?"

She frowned. "But I don't want to read this book. I want the book with the blue cover."

"And the person named Greer?" he asked.

She nodded.

He held up a hand for a moment as if thinking. "Okay, give me a moment."

Rune headed out from behind the counter, another staff member immediately taking his place to serve the next customer. A few moments went by before he returned, carting a book with a blue cover.

"I think I might have found it. It's by Sierra Simone. But Maeve, American Queen is racy. As in it's got a little threesome action in it. And it's part of a trilogy. You okay with that?"

Can I get Rune to add that to my list?

She eagerly reached for the book. "That's the one I was thinking of."

"You want the other books in the series?"

She nodded, already opening the novel to the first page.

He left and returned a moment later carrying two more, ringing up the sale. "You want me to add these to your list?"

"Please."

She paid then headed through the round door, which looked slightly like a door from that movie about the Hobbits, then into the tunnel headed for the café.

Rune turned, catching sight of me lurking like a stalker. His lips quirked into a smile.

"Feeling nervous?"

"Puh-lease," I told him with a wave of my hand. "I'm gonna own this challenge."

He grinned, leaning on the old desk. "Okay, tell me three things you like."

"What kind of things?"

"I don't know, movies, music, you tell me."

I thought about it for a moment. "I like period dramas, Sons of Anarchy and Star Wars."

He nodded, that same look he'd given Maeve crossing his face. "Be right back. Ash, can you get Gabby set up on the X-list?"

"Sure thing, boss." The girl had been scanning books into their system. She had bright red hair, a lovely smile, and wore a Literary Academy shirt that read, Geeky Book Girl.

"I like your hair.".

"Thanks! My old job would never have allowed it. It's why I love working here." She pulled a tablet out from under the desk, giving it a quick wipe with an antibacterial cloth before handing it over. "If you could just enter your details, we'll get you all signed up for the readathon."

I read the terms and conditions, checking over the information. I entered my details hit submit then handed it back. While I'd been doing that, she'd been printing out some documents. She handed them over.

"The top sheet is your sponsorship sign up. You'll get this all in an email as well so you can post to social media and get more sign-ups. People can pay just a lump sum or can pay by the book. You list the books you read below, then one of our members will send you three questions about it. If you get them right then we know you've read it."

I raised my eyebrow. "Wait, this involves a quiz? I didn't realize I was back in high school."

She laughed. "Two years ago, we had a member who registered for the readathon. She said she'd read two hundred books in the two months. It only took Rune three minutes to discover she hadn't read even half. So now, to make sure sponsors aren't getting ripped off, we check."

I nodded, looking back down at the sheet. "Why's it called an X-list?"

Ash pointed at a large blackboard on the far side of the door. "Normally we have our recommendations up there. Over summer, we track people's reading tally. The more X's you get, the more money we have coming in. Hence, the X-list."

I nodded, looking at the many marks on the board. "Looks like a decent fundraising effort."

"Oh yeah, it's second only to the street fair. Are you doing the parade this year? Erik always puts on a great float."

"Sorry?"

How does she know where I work?

She laughed, her hair shimmering in the soft light. "This town is pretty tight knit, gossip spreads like wildfire. And Laura attends Tuesday night book club when she's in town." She disappeared behind the big old desk then stood up, handing me a flyer. "You should totally come. It's mostly just women gossiping and drinking wine, but we do share book recommendations as well."

I looked at the flashy flyer. "The Greedy Readers Book Club?" I asked with a laugh.

"Yeah, because we're insatiable."

I grinned, liking her even more. "Tuesdays you say?"

"Uh-huh. Wine, we normally split antipasto platters, and always gossip."

"Count me in then." I tucked the flyer in my back pocket.

"Great!" Ash practically vibrated with excitement. "Are you gonna be on the float?"

I blinked at the sudden change of topic. "Huh?"

"The Thor's Shipbuilding float. For the parade for the fair. Last year they did an under the ocean theme and all the guys dressed up as mermaids. The year before that they did Gilligan's Island. Erik was Ginger."

I laughed, trying to picture it in my head. "Well, no one's mentioned anything yet."

Ash flapped her hand. "Probably 'cause it's not till the end of August. We still got time." She grinned. "But you should casually mention to Erik that we've already designed our theme for this year and it will be epic."

"Don't tell her all our secrets," Rune said, returning to the counter, a pile of books under one arm.

"I'm just saying. We're winning this year; I can feel it." She looked at me. "It's a bone of contention each year as to who places higher – Thor's Shipbuilding or the Literary Academy. The brothers go all out."

"And who won last year?"

"Oh," she cackled while Rune rolled his eyes. "Neither of them ever wins. That always goes to the art school. But we're hopeful about this year." She held up crossed fingers.

A customer waved from between two stacks, calling for assistance.

"I got it," Ash said, turning to help. "See you Tuesday, Gabby."

"See you," I called as she disappeared into the stacks.

"She's nice."

Rune nodded then dropped his gaze to the books he'd placed on the counter. "You ready?"

"As I'll ever be," I sighed, making a face.

He grinned, then picked up the first book on the pile.

"Julia Quinn, The Viscount Who Loved Me." He held the book up. "Second in series but you don't need to read the first, and I think you'll like the humor in this one more." He popped it down, lifting a bright yellow book.

"Educating Caroline, Patricia Cabot. Again, historical, again great humor." He placed that down, reaching for the third book. "Nina Levine's Storm MC. It's about a motorcycle club. Intrigue, suspense, love. You'll enjoy it." He held up another, and I burst out laughing at the cover.

"Is that a blue guy… with *horns?*"

He grinned. "Let me introduce Ruby Dixon's Blue Barbarians. You'll read this one and beg me for the others. They were our top-selling series last year." He placed it on the pile. Then hesitated, his hand hovering. There were three books left.

"You can choose your fifth one – more motorcycle, another historical, or something completely different."

I cocked my eyebrow. "What do you mean by completely different?"

He shook his head. "You just have to decide."

I looked at the covers then reached out, touching the different one. "Okay, I'll give this a go."

He moved to place the book on the pile but I took it, reading aloud.

"Kiss of Steel by Bec McMaster," I flipped it over, scanning the blurb. "Honoria Todd has no choice. Only in the dreaded Whitechapel district can she escape the long reach of the Duke of Vickers. But seeking refuge there will put her straight into the hands of Blade, legendary master of the rookeries. No one would dare cross him, but what price would he demand to keep her safe?"

I looked up, shooting Rune a grin. "Have you given me only romance novels, Mr. Larsson?"

He shrugged. "Romance novels are the best novels."

I laughed. "Is it a historical?"

"Kind of. It's steampunk."

I wracked my brain, trying to remember where I'd heard that term before. "Oh, like Howl's Moving Castle?"

He nodded, looking impressed. "Actually, yeah. Kind of like that."

"Cool," I returned the book to the pile. "So, these five are my starter kit?"

"Mmhmm." He rung them up for me, then asked if I wanted a bag.

"No, it's fine," I pulled off my backpack, handing it over. "I came prepared."

He loaded the books and I paid, wondering if now would be a good time to invite Rune to lunch.

"So," I said, leaning against the counter. "I don't know about you but—"

"Fancy seeing you here!" Erik's big voice boomed in the quiet, interrupting me.

I turned, seeing him and Laura, a bouncing baby strapped to each of their fronts, entering via the Hobbit door. Behind them trailed Jemma and Sune, Sune pushing an older woman in a wheelchair.

"Gabby," Erik greeted. "Have you met Grandmother Larsson?"

I shook my head, moving to greet the older woman. "Mrs. Larsson, it's lovely to meet you. I'm staying in your beautiful home."

The older woman smiled but it was a bit wonky, one side not quite lifting. Rune had mentioned a stroke, and I now understood why she needed to live with her son.

"Call me Nan. Rune said Ferdy paid you a visit this morning." Her words were slightly slurred and a little slow but I understood her perfectly.

"Ah yes, or the winged assassin, as I've started calling him." She laughed delightedly. "Ah, I like that."

"Would you like to join us for lunch?" Laura asked, one hand on baby Leif's back as he snuggled into her. "We're here to drag Rune out for a bite as well."

Rune sighed, gesturing at the shop. "Told you, I gotta work."

"Oh hush," Jemma said with a dismissive flick of her head. "This is your mother's orders. You don't rest enough. We'll only be an hour."

Before my eyes, Rune changed. He shifted from the loose, quiet but amusing man I'd been getting to know, to the near-silent wall of muscle I'd first met.

I frowned, glancing from him to his family.

Rune crossed his arms over his chest. "And what happened last time?"

The family laughed. "So, lunch went for two hours, it's not that big a deal, Rune."

A muscle jumped in his jaw, his face flushing. I saw it. I saw the change, and yet it was as if no one else did. Not his nan, not his parents or brother. Not even Laura.

Only me.

"Do as your mother says," Sune ordered, wheeling Nan around. "We'll find a table. Don't be long, your grandmother is hungry."

I hung back, waiting until his family had left before turning back to Rune. His eyes were on the door, that muscle in his jaw still jumping.

I looked at him, wondering how far to push this.

"Are you okay?"

He blinked as if only just realizing I were still there. "What?"

"Are you okay?" I repeated, gesturing at the door where his family had disappeared. "They completely ran roughshod over you."

243

He blew out a breath, watching me wearily. "And you think I should go to lunch?"

"No, I think you're busy and have a store to run." I gestured at the customers hanging around, the boxes of new books he was obviously processing behind the counter, and the sandwich sitting half-eaten behind the counter.

"I'm gonna assume that's yours?"

He shrugged. "Doesn't matter. Give me a second to call, Ash."

I leaned across the counter, halting him with a hand to his arm. "Rune, you don't have to give in. If you're too busy, tell me. I'll make excuses then keep them so busy and entertained and just utterly dazzled by my sheer brilliance, that they won't even notice you're not there."

His lips didn't move, his expression didn't change. "They won't accept that."

"And you seem to care too much about what they expect versus what you want or, in this case, need to do." I squeezed his arm. "Trust me, Rune. I got this."

He searched my face for a moment looking for… something. Reassurance maybe? Hope?

"Okay," he finally said. "Thanks."

"No problem," I waved a hand, pretending to flick hairs out of my face. "Just call me Lady cause your family is gonna go Gaga for me."

Only the very corners of his mouth lifted. "Good luck."

I turned, carrying my backpack with my hand-picked books, making a mental note to interrogate him more about this later.

He may be large and growly, but Rune obviously hated disappointing his family.

And God that's attractive.

As promised, within a few minutes of sitting down with Rune's family, I had them sufficiently distracted with stories of Capricorn Cove while waiting for our food to arrive.

"Now, Gabby," Nan held her knife and fork at a jaunty angle, giving me the kind of smile I imagined a shark wore right before it ate the sweet little fish it was hunting. "Tell me, are you interested in my grandson?"

I blinked, shooting a look at Erik. "Umm, no? I mean, he's a nice guy but it kind of looks like he has his own family thing going on and I'm really not the kind of girl to get involved in a polygamous relationship – not that there's anything wrong with that but it's not for me."

A beat of silence followed my comment, everyone at the table stared at me.

Nan tutted under her breath. "Not *that* grandson. The single one."

Her comment broke the tension, sending the rest of the table into hysterics. As I'd planned, she dropped her line of questioning, only to start the background profile. I'd watched enough cop shows to know that she had to have been a detective in a previous life.

"And what does your family do?" she asked after I'd told her about my previous job.

"Ah, actually, I don't have family."

The delicate skin on her forehead wrinkled. "You're an orphan?"

I shrugged. "Maybe. Who knows? I've been a ward of the state since I was a few months old."

"But you said your last foster home was pretty good. Do you stay in touch with them?" Erik asked, juggling a fussing

Leif.

I shrugged, trying to ignore how these questions prodded the familiar ache in my middle. "They were my last home, and partially the reason I settled in the Cove. But I came to them at a pretty bad time. The McKenneys were great, don't get me wrong. But Mrs. McKenney got diagnosed with breast cancer a few months after I moved in. They had bigger problems than me."

Nan opened her mouth but Leif, god bless his little soul, let out a high-pitched screech, big fat tears rolling down his red little cheeks.

"He's been very fussy today," Laura told the table as Erik excused himself to take Leif outside. "I think he might be teething."

"A little whisky to the gums," Sune said tapping his lips. "Works every time."

"Don't tell them that!" Jemma slapped his arm, laughing when he turned to her pressing an exuberant kiss to her cheek.

I looked around the table, experiencing a familiar sense of melancholy. Was it possible to miss what you'd never had? Not love, though I'd never had what Sune and Jemma did. No, it was family that made my soul ache. The familiarity that came with years and experience, inside jokes and shared memories. The beautiful family before me had that.

It's not for you, remember?

I'd tried. Many, many times I'd worked hard to entwine myself into a family. I'd been whatever curried the most favor. But eventually, after years of rejections and sudden movements, I'd resigned myself to the fact there was something wrong with me.

I just wasn't family material.

It didn't stop me from wanting it though. Desperately.

Chapter Six

Rune

I'd built a reading nook in the garden a few years back. A pergola with passionfruit vines under which there was a long semi-circular bench seat, wide enough to stretch out and lay on.

Sometimes, like this afternoon, I carried out a low table, complete with a pitcher of lemonade and an antipasto platter. Stretched out, enjoying the afternoon sun while I read was how I unwound from a hectic week at work.

It was here that Gabby found me. Soft piano music playing from the Bluetooth speaker, the afternoon sun warm on my face, and a great book in my hands.

"Hey," she called softly, pulling me gently from the story.

"Hey." I marked my place with a finger. "What's up?"

She held up the yellow book in her hand. "I was just looking for a place to get started."

I grinned, scooting down one side of the long seat to make room. "Sit down, stretch out."

She did, settling in, our feet only inches away from each other.

"Can I have a glass?" She nodded at the lemonade.

"Sure," I pulled a glass free from the stack. Neighbors or family were always stopping by so I'd learned to bring extra.

We sipped and nibbled our way through the afternoon, reading in quiet companionship. Me, a crime thriller, Gabby the historical romance.

"This is good," she murmured at one point, turning the page. "Like, really good. Do you think they've made a movie?"

I made a sound of displeasure. "Even if they had, the movie is rarely as good as the book."

She chuckled, glancing up. "I can't actually remember the last time I read a book and enjoyed it."

"What was the last book you read? And don't say a manual this time."

Gabby's lips lifted in a smile as she tilted her head back, considering my question. "Maybe... maybe something at school? I just remember being fed up with the crap they were assigning us."

I grunted, shaking my head. "Schools need to update their material. The thing that pisses me off the most is you have a whole generation of kids you could be engaging by giving them relevant material. Really good material. Instead, you shove stuff they can't relate to down their throat. Like ninety percent of it is written by CIS white males. Kids need something to inspire them. Something that they feel. Not some adult asking them to describe in a thousand words why a dead guy described the curtains as blue when we all know he probably didn't even pay attention to what color he assigned."

Gabby stared at me for a moment then burst out laughing,

her body shaking with her hilarity.

"What? Am I wrong?"

She shook her head, still laughing.

"Exactly." I pretended to begin reading again, opening my book with a flourish.

"You should've been an English teacher."

I shrugged. "Thought about it, but then Nan got sick and needed help at the store and… well… it just fit."

We were quiet for a while and my eyes strayed to my book, beginning to scoot down the lines of the page, slowly being sucked back in.

"Rune?"

"Mm?" I blinked, looking up.

Gabby hesitated. "How come your family treats you like that? Like what you're doing isn't a real job or something."

I shrugged, grabbing my bookmark and putting the book aside. "It's not that they don't think it's a real job it's more they just forget I'm an adult."

"Huh?"

I laughed; the sound slightly frustrated. "I'm the baby of the family. Six years separate me from Gunnar, and there's only two years between him and Erik. They grew up together. Then there's Liv and Astrid, then me. I was more like a doll for the girls to play with than a little brother to tag along. I've grown up, my family just hasn't realized it yet."

She eyed me, her gaze drifting up my legs, across my chest, and finally up to my face. I tried not to react, liking the way she looked at me far too much.

"It's hard to believe when they see you that they don't immediately realize you're fully grown."

250

My lips quirked. "Have you seen the size of my family?"

She chuckled. "True. Your poor mother."

We returned to reading. In companionable silence, we continued until the night encroached and our stomachs began to rumble.

We split a pizza, staying outside until the mosquitos drove us back to the covered porch.

I sipped my beer, Gabby sitting in one of the chairs, drinking tea. As the hour grew late, Gabby began to squirm. Not a lot, just enough that I noticed, her breath catching, becoming more rapid.

I tried to ignore her, tried to silence the little voice in my head that was wondering which part of the book she was reading. I tried and failed to ignore the question that kept playing over and over in my mind.

Was she getting turned on?

Gabby let out a little moan. Low, barely audible, her breath catching. The sound snapped the little control I had left. My cock jumped, thickening embarrassingly fast in response. My body heated, my focus immediately narrowing in on her till I couldn't take it anymore.

"Gonna head to bed," I muttered, pushing to my feet and walking to the door. "Night."

"Night," she called, her gaze burning into my back as I left.

I headed straight for my bedroom, unzipping my pants, not even bothering to shove my jeans all the way down my legs.

I fisted my cock, roughly jerking my length, my spare hand braced against the wall as I imagine Gabby alone, reading that fucking novel.

As I stroked, I imagined her in bed, the book in one hand,

her other drifting across her breasts, teasing lightly. Down her body it would glide as she devoured the naughty words, imagining it was me doing those things to her.

I groaned, fisting harder, fancying I could hear her through the wall.

"Rune."

I froze, my body solid, straining to hear.

"Oh, Rune…"

Through the wall, through that piss-poor excuse of a wall, I could *hear* her. Her little mews and whimpers then the electric pulsing buzz of what could only be a vibrator.

My heart thumped against my ribs, my body shuddering as I listened to Gabby pleasure herself.

"Fuck," she whimpered. "Oh God."

My hand began to move of its own volition, stroking my cock, my eyes drifting close.

"Please," Gabby begged. "Oh, please."

"Louder," the word exploded from me, guttural and desperate. "Louder, Gabby. I wanna hear it."

Through the wall, I heard the buzz change, as if she had shifted. There was a pause, brief but devastating.

Fuck.

I lifted, getting ready to move, to go apologize for intruding. But the buzz changed again, Gabby moaning in response.

"Rune… keep going."

Chapter Seven

Gabby

I can't believe I'm doing this. What the hell?

I pressed the vibrator closer, hitting the button to change the pulse setting, teasing myself, drawing this out.

Rune's listening.

The book had gotten me hot. The slow build-up, the way the hero was gentle but fierce with the heroine. I'd been sucked into the story, hook, line, and sinker.

But this? Right now?

Amazing.

"Let me hear you, Gabby. I wanna hear your hot little moans."

Rune's voice sounded above my head, filtering through the thin wall. I shuddered, a groan slipping free as I circled my clit.

"Louder," Rune barked, his voice rough and demanding.

Desire spiked through me, lighting my nerve endings on fire. I moaned, writhing on the bed, my body a wanton, desperate creature.

"Rune," my voice sounded unfamiliar. Breathy, low, an

aching need audible.

"You want me to describe what I'd do to you?"

I licked my lips, my free hand pushing up my shirt, reaching under the cup of my bra, fingers finding my nipple.

"Yes," I whispered, then cleared my throat, raising my voice. "Yes, please."

"If I was in there, Gabby, I'd be stripping you naked while I kissed every inch I revealed."

I shuddered, my body tingling at the images his words painted.

"I'd pull those goddamned sleep shorts down your legs, then lick my way up your thighs. I'd taste you, determined to memorize you. Would you be spicy, Gabby? Or sweet? Would you taste of salt and sea? I wanna know, babe. I wanna taste those thighs and then see you wearing those goddamned shorts and remember my lips brushing your skin."

Oh lord.

This man was killing me.

"Turn the fucking vibrator off," he ordered hoarsely.

I hit the button, discarding it easily.

"Fingers," he told me, his voice rough. "Use your fingers."

My hand drifted between my legs, hovering above my curls. "How?" I asked, feeling surprisingly bold.

"Part your lips. Pretend I'm there, pretend I can see everything. Show off for me."

I did as directed, spreading myself with one hand, imagining Rune at the end of my bed, his gaze hard and needy as he stared at me, watching me circle my clit, my body flushed under his gaze.

"Are you wet, Gabby? Tell me."

"So wet," I breathed, circling my clit with firm presses, my fingers sliding easily through my slick arousal. "God this feels good, but…"

My desire overrode my sense of self-preservation.

"But?" he prompted.

"Wish it was you."

I heard his groan full of need and desire, heavy and guttural. I shuddered and increased my pace, driving myself higher.

"Rune!"

"Come, Gabby. Come now. Show me, let me hear."

I arched pretending he was before me, his gaze hot and focused on my fingers, on the way I rubbed myself, on my pretty pink pussy. I spread my legs wider, my body on full display as I finally shattered, my body clenching as I came in a glorious, sweaty, wet mess.

Through the wall, I heard Rune join me, his groaning gasp a maddening tease that flared my arousal once again.

"Rune," I whispered, stretching a hand out to the wall, pressing my palm flat to it. "Come over."

"Fuck yes."

I heard him move, shuffling about then freezing as the sound of his cell's ringtone pierced through the quiet.

"Fuck!"

I heard him answer, then silence as he listened.

"I'll be right there."

More shuffling as I pushed up, quickly setting my clothes to right then heading out to the front porch.

"Rune?"

He came to the door, a backpack on his shoulder, his face grim. "Leif's in the hospital, they think it's just a fever and gastro, but Erik and Laura are freaking out and want me to take Ulf while they stay with Leif. Ma and Dad aren't answering the phone – they're probably out on the boat with Nan, they do that when they can't sleep thanks to the heat. So, I'm the only back-up they got at the moment."

I nodded, reaching out. "You need a hand?"

He paused, eyebrows shooting up. "You wanna come and babysit?"

I bit my lip but nodded. "If you need me."

He seemed torn, wanting me to come but not wanting to burden me.

I smiled. "I'm offering, Rune."

"If you want…"

"Let me grab some stuff and lock up."

Chapter Eight

Gabby

They may still treat Rune like a kid, but they sure as hell trusted him to be an adult when it mattered. We arrived at the small hospital, finding Laura and Erik a frantic mess.

"Here," Erik handed Ulf to Rune, his hair standing on end, his eyes bloodshot and rimmed with dark circles. "If he starts vomiting, diarrhea or any signs of fever—"

"We'll bring him here," Rune said, accepting the diaper bag from Laura.

"We wouldn't ask this but if it's contagious…" Laura reached out, placing a hand on Ulf's back.

"He'll be fine."

Erik caught Laura around the waist, pulling her tight. "If the fever breaks and they can get more liquids into him we should be discharged tomorrow."

"Then you guys can come pick Ulf up tomorrow night. You'll need some sleep." Rune told them, shifting his nephew into the crook of one arm.

I didn't know much about babies but I'd been quickly learning since moving to the Cape. Being around Erik meant being around his family, when they said Thor's Shipbuilding was a family business – they meant it.

"Thank you," Laura whispered, tears glistening on her lashes. "I don't know what we'd do without you."

Rune shrugged, looking uncomfortable. "Go look after Leif. I—we've got this."

Erik and Laura looked my way for the first time since we'd entered the hospital waiting room.

"Thank you," Erik said, giving me a small smile. "You didn't have to come out."

I waved him off. "Go look after your baby."

Laura and Erik turned as one, hurrying back to their son.

"You ready?" Rune asked.

I looked up, about to answer then realized he was speaking to Ulf. Ulf grinned up at his uncle, his chubby little arms flailing.

"Right, let's go."

I reached for the diaper bag but Rune shook his head.

"Nah, I got it."

I'd been surprised to learn that he had two baby seats in the back of his car. When I'd asked why he'd shrugged.

"Just being a good uncle."

My heart had skipped, a warm shimmer gliding down my spine to pool in my belly at his words.

He strapped Ulf in with surprising efficiency then we were headed back to our place.

His place, dummy. Not ours.

This night wasn't exactly going how I planned. Or not planned, in this case. I hadn't expected to get myself off with Rune listening through the wall, giving directions. I also hadn't expected to be looking after a baby less than an hour after one of the hottest experiences of my life.

Shouldn't I be embarrassed about this?

I found I didn't have either the modesty or shame to care that much. I'd loved it, and, I had to admit, I wanted more.

Rune turned on the radio, then switched to a playlist, calming classical music pumping out.

I lifted an eyebrow in his direction.

"It's a baby classical music list. The music is shown to help them feel calmer, happier. I figure, with his brother missing, our little guy needs all the help he can get."

I grinned but turned away before Rune could see exactly how much I liked his efforts.

Be still my ovaries.

This man was dangerous. He looked like a Viking god, was a doting uncle, read romance (hello great sex life), and was a hard worker. There had to be a downside.

"Are you messy?" I asked, genuinely wondering where the downside was.

"Huh?"

"Messy. Laura met Erik while teaching him how to clean. Are you also messy?"

He scoffed, shaking his head as Ulf gurgled from the backseat. "Hell no. My brother is the anomaly."

Hmm.

"Can you cook?"

He nodded, shooting me a questioning glance.

"I'm just trying to figure out your flaws. So far I can't find one."

The grin that stretched his lips was devastating. My heart skipped, butterflies scattering.

"I'm sure there's many but I'm happy to keep you in the

dark."

He pulled into the driveway, parking just by the porch.

We climbed out, Ulf sleepily mumbling a protest as Rune lifted him out of the baby seat.

"Come on, little dude. Bedtime."

I followed, carrying Rune's backpack and the diaper bag. Rune pressed through the door to his apartment and I followed, expecting the mirror image of mine. Instead, I stopped dead, looking around in wonder.

The place was one giant art piece.

The entry hall was a massive mural which stretched up and across the ceiling, incorporating the basketweave lights.

"Is this the inside of a boat?" I whispered, reaching out a hand to touch the wall. The art was so life-like it was jarring to feel plaster instead of the polished wood of a ship.

"A longboat," Rune said, opening the door to his spare room. "Let me put him down."

I followed, my gaze dancing from one unique item to another, shocked by the detail and effort.

The spare room was no different. Rune had turned it into a nursery. Hand-carved cribs sat end to end against one wall. Toys were spread out across the floor, while a heavy shag rug in green covered most of the floorboards. There was a changing table and a rocking chair in one corner. The walls were covered in floating shelves which were filled with books, all for children.

The walls were again murals, this time a kid's version of a Viking scene, complete with a dragon hiding treasure, mermaids, wolves, and even a crow, peeking out from behind a bookshelf. In addition to the Vikings on the longboat – all of which bore a striking resemblance to his family –Valkyries were riding in on flying horses.

"No wings?" I asked, touching a horse as Rune placed Ulf in his crib.

"In Norse mythology, Valkyries rode horses who could fly through air or ocean – but there are no mentions of wings. That appears to be from Greek mythology and doesn't fit the scene."

I threw him a grin, watching as he switched on a small night light, the soft glow pulsing gently through the room.

Ulf was out, his tiny body rising and falling with each breath.

Rune turned on a baby monitor, then picked up the other device, carrying it with him as he gestured for me to follow.

I dropped the bags in the corner of the room, then, with a last look at Ulf, tiptoed out.

The rest of Rune's house was just as stunning. There were burnished bronze art pieces, sculptures made from books or wood, little drawings on walls – some in frames, some hidden amongst the furniture, like a tiny image of Ferdinand that sat above an electrical socket, as if resting on the edge.

And everywhere I looked there were books, I couldn't help but grin.

"This is incredible," I whispered, once again reaching out a hand to touch a wooden piece. It was a coffee table, but the tabletop had been carved into a map of the world, the grooves inlaid with a bronze resin. It glinted in the dull light, shimmering just a little.

"Is this by a local artist?" I asked, running a hand over the beautiful wood. I wanted to create something like this.

"Uh, kind of. You wanna drink?"

I pulled back my hand, turning to see Rune in the kitchen.

"Sure."

He put the kettle on, waiting for it to boil as he busied himself, pulling out mugs and herbal tea.

I reached for the canister, reading it aloud, "Peppermint?"

"Nan got me hooked. It was all she'd drink before bed."

I chuckled, replacing the canister and watching as he went through the age-old ritual of measuring out the tea leaves. It felt comfortable, familiar.

Like home.

I squashed that thought. I was only here for six months. After that, I'd be headed back to the Cove. Rune's place was here, with his family. I could see that. They needed him. And he was a part of the community, his business essential.

And you're not.

I knew it. I was disposable. Always had been, always would be. Years of foster homes and failed promises of adoptions had proved that.

It also doesn't pay to get involved with your bosses' brother.

I took the offered drink, inhaling the sweet scent before taking a sip, mentally resigning myself to this conversation, mentally building my walls.

"Rune, this can't go further."

His face wiped clean. "Excuse me?"

"This," I gestured between us. "Your brothers are my bosses. And I'm leaving. I have to go back to the Cove. It doesn't make sense to take this further."

A muscle in his jaw jumped, a mulish expression settling.

"So, you'd throw away whatever possibility we have, whatever potential may be between us because of distance?"

"It's not just distance. There's my job too. I want this career. This opportunity is important to me. It's going to

262

help me secure my future."

"And you think if we didn't work, I'd jeopardize your career?"

I shrugged. "Wouldn't be the first time a woman has had her career derailed by a spurned man."

"I'm not like that."

"I know," I sighed, staring at my tea. "But I know where I stand. Family is first. They'd pick up on the issues between us and want to show loyalty. They'd never fire me – they're too nice for that. But they might make it so I decide to leave."

"They wouldn't."

"Maybe not intentionally, but it would be the result all the same."

"Gabby—"

Ulf's cry split through the house.

"I'll get him," I said, jumping down from the seat at the counter and heading for the hall.

"Gabby, wait."

I picked up my pace, desperate to put distance between us. Tears burned my eyes, blurring my vision. It was the reason I didn't see the toy on the floor. The bloody toy.

"Fuck!"

I tripped, crashing to the floor.

"Gabby!"

Ulf cried harder at the sound, but Rune came to me, his hands gentle as he searched my body for injury.

"Where are you hurt?"

"My pride?" I muttered, groaning as I rolled over.

Rune's hand paused on my leg. "Damn, it was the toy, wasn't it?"

I nodded, pushing myself to a seat and examining my leg.

Everything looked fine, except for the bruise forming on my knee.

"Damn," I brushed myself off, shifting to begin the slow push to stand. "Give me a second."

"Here," Rune held his hands out, wiggling his fingers invitingly. "I'll pull you up."

I took it, letting him haul me up then sucking in a breath and leaning into his chest as I realized my prosthetic had moved, shooting pain ratcheting up my thigh.

"Can you help me to the chair?" I asked, leaning heavily against him.

I expected him to help me hop over, instead, Rune lifted me, easily carrying me the few steps across the room. He gently set me down, making sure I was okay before stepping back.

"Go get Ulf," I said with a wave. "I just need to adjust it."

The fall must have slipped one of my liners, not a lot, but enough to shift it so when I put weight down it was painful. I pulled my leg off then began the long process of removing liners and socks peeling down to the end of my leg.

"Can I be rude and ask some questions?" Rune asked as he bounced Ulf, soothing the baby.

I looked up, shooting him a grin. "You wanna know what I call her?"

He blinked. "What?"

"My leg. Some people call them a stump but that makes me feel like I'm gonna sprout leaves and roots. I just call her Peggy."

His lips quirked as I patted my leg, his eyebrows raising in a question.

"You know, like a peg leg." I made a pirate arr noise.

264

He grinned but shook his head. "I was actually gonna ask if you get hot in all those layers."

"God yes," I kicked my leg at him, enjoying the air on my overheated skin. "It's not so bad during the day, but I have to wear a shrinker sock to bed. Not because I'm an amputee, but because I get inflammation. It sucks, some people don't have to but I'm not one of them."

"What's it do?"

I patted my leg. "Helps to fit my limb into the prosthetic. Without it, it's painful."

"Huh, I guess I just assumed it'd be fitted for you."

"Oh, it is," I said, starting to pull on the liner. "But even a small amount of water weight or swelling can mess up the fit. So that's why you have these," I held up a sock. "You pad out or reduce depending on what's happening."

"And you do that every morning?"

"Yeah," I rolled on the silicon, checking the fit before feeding the pin into the shaft and locking it into place.

"I didn't realize it was like a pin-lock system."

"Not all of them are. I have three and each is slightly different."

"Hmm."

Rune turned back to the crib, Ulf now sleeping again. As soon as he shifted the baby, Ulf woke, his hands and feet kicking out in protest.

Done with my leg, I stood, making my way over and placing a soothing hand on the baby's back.

"You just miss your brother, don't you little one?" I cooed, subconsciously swaying in time to Rune's movement.

He held Ulf up, giving him a narrowed eyed glare. "You're not sleeping in my bed tonight, bucko. You know that. I already said no to you and your brother last time."

Ulf kicked his legs happily, a small drool bubble forming at the side of his mouth.

Oh, he was so gonna get his way. Lucky kid.

I hid my smile, stepping back as Rune resumed his sway.

We watched each other, our eyes holding.

"You know, I don't date," Rune said finally, his voice low as Ulf snuggled back into his uncle's chest.

"Oh, I realized that when you rejected poor Florence."

He blushed. "She's not interested in me anymore than she is in reading the works of Jane Austen."

I chuckled. "So she wasn't hitting on you?"

"Oh, she was." He hesitated. "But she's more interested in winning the bragging rights."

I cocked an eyebrow. "For a date with you?"

He shook his head. "For sleeping with me."

"What?"

Rune blew out a breath, "I'm a virgin, Gabby."

Chapter Nine

Rune

No one ever believed me when I said I was a virgin. I was a guy, for one. And yeah, it might be cocky but I knew I was attractive – my brothers were so it only stood to reason I was aesthetically pleasing as well.

It wasn't that I'd made a conscious choice to remain sexually abstinent. And God knew I wasn't a saint – I watched porn, read erotica, and fisted my cock regularly.

But I just hadn't met a woman where the timing – and relationship – worked out. In high school, I'd only had to bring my girlfriends home for them to fall in love with Gunnar or Erik. In college, there'd been one or two that might have come close – if not for Nan.

God, how pathetic did it sound blaming my grandmother for my lack of game.

I read. I read a lot. I knew I'd take over the bookstore when I returned to the Cape, so I decided to get a head start on knowing my product. Nan helped with that. She'd send me a new book box every month, packed full of novels for me to devour.

Though she'd include her favorites – the romance ones in particular. Which never bothered me. I liked a good romance. But kids were idiots and the jock fuckwit of a roommate I'd been saddled with had seen them and spread the rumor that I was gay – as if it were a curse or some other ignorant shit.

I hadn't cared, except that women hadn't looked at me after that. When I'd finally come home, Nan had suffered her first bad spell, and I'd moved into the house, converting it into a duplex (a man needed his own space). Then it'd been either work or caring for her. There hadn't been an in-between time.

Well, not until last year. These past twelve months I'd finally been able to let up and breathe. As hard as it was to say, Nan moving in with my parents was a blessing, and while difficult, the best thing for both of us. I loved her, but I no longer needed to be her carer. She got more companionship and support with my retired parents than with me.

So yeah, I was still a virgin. And the shocked look on Gabby's face was nothing new. Any time someone found out they did that same stare, the one that said *'what's wrong with you?'*

Answer, not a goddamned thing.

"I'm… surprised," Gabby said, tucking a stray strand of her dark hair behind her ear. "I wouldn't have thought you were a virgin after… earlier."

I chuckled. Ulf turned his head burrowing deeper into my chest, a little drool wetting my shirt. "I'm a virgin, not an idiot."

She laughed, her teeth flashing in the dim room. "Touché."

We both quietened, a comfortable silence falling over the

room.

"You know, sex would change this," Gabby whispered.

I'm counting on it.

I nodded, peeking down at Ulf.

"It's not that I don't want you, Rune. It's that..."

I waited, wondering if she'd admit it.

You're scared.

She shook her head. "If you're good here, I should go to bed."

I nodded. "Yeah, get some sleep."

She came to us, pressing a little kiss to Ulf's cheek. "Call me if you need anything?"

I nodded; my throat full. She gave me a smile, running her finger gently across Ulf's cheek one last time before leaving.

I listened, hearing her walk out the front and head next door.

"Fuck," I whispered, shaking my head. "She's gonna be harder to win over than I thought."

Ulf gurgled sleepily and I grinned. "Don't worry, buddy. I'm not deterred that easily."

My phone beeped. I pulled it out, the family chat icon blinking.

Erik: Leif's fever broke. They're keeping him overnight just to be sure and top up his fluids. Looking good otherwise.

Liv: THANK GOD!

Gunnar: Call if you need us, Ella and I are on standby.

Astrid: Keep us updated and give little Leif a kiss from me.

I hit reply, awkwardly snapping a picture of Ulf sleeping in my arms.

Rune: [Photo] As you can see, Ulf is *very* worried. Good to hear he's on the mend. No rush to come pick up, we're good.

269

Erik: Thanks bro, appreciate it.

Laura: Tell Gabby thanks too.

"Ah, damn."

Liv: Gabby?

Astrid: !?!? GABBY?? WHO IS GABBY???

Ella: Wait, OUR Gabby?

Gunnar: Fuck. You break her heart and we're keeping her over you.

Erik: ^^What he said. That girl deserves better than this family.

Laura: Hey! What does that mean!?

Ella: Excuse me!?

Liv: Oh, you're in for it now. Rune – should I add her to group chat? Someone text me her number.

Suddenly, I found I didn't mind their ribbing quite so much.

Chapter Ten

Gabby

You're a wimp.

It took me a full three days to get up the courage to see Rune again. Now it was Tuesday evening and I was standing outside The Literary Academy psyching myself up to go in.

"Hey! Gabby! Hey! You came!"

I twisted to see Ash bouncing along the sidewalk towards me.

"Yeah, I finished all my books."

"Ooh! Yay!" She reached for the door, holding it open so I could enter. "You'll still have to pass the test."

She chattered on about the latest book while leading me through the maze to the seating area. About ten women were seated on various couches and loveseats, glasses of wine in hand as Rune walked around, topping up their glasses.

Our eyes met, his immediately dropping to my legs, narrowing in on the bruise on my knee.

"You okay?" he asked, coming to stand next to me.

I nodded, remembering that night. While I'd had only minor bruising on Peggy, my naked knee had smacked the floor pretty hard, leaving a dark blue bruise.

"Hey everyone, this is Gabby," Ash gestured at me, bouncing over to sit beside an older woman. I spotted Laura and made a beeline for the seat beside her. She smiled a greeting, handing me a glass.

"How's Leif?" I asked, gratefully accepting the wine.

"Back to normal. Though God knows Erik and I have more grey in our hair than we did last week."

I chuckled, taking a sip of the rich red wine. "I'm glad."

She considered me over the rim of her glass. "Thanks for helping with Ulf."

I shrugged. "It was all Rune, to be honest. I just tagged along to the hospital to make sure he didn't crash in his haste to get there."

She let that one slip as an older woman called the meeting to order. Turned out, Ash hadn't been kidding – this was a wild, *wild* group. It started off with a male appreciation circle, where we all had to name our favorite male of the week based on their 'talents' if you get what I mean. We then segued to books we'd read and loved, which somehow ended up in a discussion about the best sex toys on the market and the oldest member of the group, Beryl, discussing a thing called *'the dick-tator'*.

I'm telling you – W.I.L.D.

"This is honestly, the craziest night I've had in awhile," I whispered to Laura. Only, my voice came out louder than anticipated, causing the other drunk women to laugh uproariously.

"It's the best," Laura agreed, slightly slurring her words.

The night wound down, partners appearing to pick up their women. Erik waved as he escorted Laura out. I laughed as she kept groping his ass, sending me exaggerated winks over his shoulder.

"You want a lift home?"

I blinked, realizing I was the last person in the store.

"Oh," I rubbed a hand over my face. "No, I should be fine to ride."

I pushed to my feet then immediately reached out, searching for something to steady myself as the world shifted.

"Oops! Maybe not," I giggled.

Rune chuckled, coming over to help me. "Let's get you in the car and I'll lock up."

"Wait!" I pulled back a little, pointing at the X-board. "You haven't asked me the questions. Go!"

Rune's lips quirked. "Which books did you finish."

"All of them."

His eyebrows rose in surprise. "Really?"

"Uh-huh."

"Huh, not bad for a non-reader."

"Psh," I blew a raspberry his way. "I'd say I'm now a reader, thank you very much."

"We'll see." He moved to the board, picking up a piece of chalk and holding it at the ready beside my name. "Okay, first question – Educating Caroline. What was Caroline surprised Brandon read?"

I pursed my lips, trying to remember. "The dictionary!"

He grinned, marking a cross.

"Not three questions?" I asked.

"Not tonight. We need to get you home."

I let it slide.

"Okay, next book. The Viscount Who Loved Me, the siblings played a game, what was it and what was Kate's equipment called?"

I laughed, delighted that he referenced my favorite part of the entire book. "Pall Mall and the mallet of death, of course."

He made another notch on the board. "In Bec McMaster's Kiss of Steel, what does Honoria offer Blade?"

"Speech and etiquette lessons instead of becoming his mistress." As Rune added another cross, the wine loosened my tongue. "But really he only accepted so he could seduce her.

Like I wish you would."

Rune froze but I didn't pay him any mind. "Or maybe you'll declare I'm your mate and just wake me with your mouth on my pussy, like in Ruby Dixon's Blue Barbarian. Or maybe like when Kick pushed Evie up against the wall and fingered her." I brushed hair back from my face. "I'd like that. God, so much." My body practically vibrated with need.

"What about you leaving?"

I tried to clear the fog in my head, instead finding the fog was clearing the lies I'd been telling myself.

"I want you more, I want... us more than I want this job."

Rune swallowed, his voice strained as he asked, "Now?"

I thought over the question. "No, not now. I'm too drunk to appreciate it fully."

"When?"

I tried to piece together my thoughts. "Tomorrow night?"

"Done."

"Wait!" I held out my hand for him to shake. He took it, his big hand engulfing mine. "See?" I said, licking my lips. "It's now a deal."

274

"You'll forget this tomorrow."

"Definitely not," I informed him primly. "My body wants yours too much."

He groaned, dropping my hand to run both of his through his hair. "You're killing me, Gabby."

I laughed, delighted. "Well, maybe I'll let you hear me through the wall again."

His eyes flashed, desire raw and desperate on his face. "Let's get you to the car."

Chapter Eleven

Rune

I saw Gabby through the glass door of the café, my body immediately clenching in response.

Maybe I'll let you hear me through the wall again.

Oh, she'd delivered on that threat. For over an hour last night, I'd listened like a sick fuck as Gabby had pleasured herself through the wall, telling me in graphic, filthy detail exactly what she was doing while I'd fisted my cock, desperate for her taste.

I'd never been this way about a woman before. Never thought about her with such a voracious intensity.

Now she was here, looking no worse for last night, while I felt like ants were squirming under my skin such was my need to touch her.

I suddenly had a new appreciation for Jane Austen's wretched Captain Wentworth as he pined away for Anne.

You pierce my soul. I am half agony, half hope.

"Hey," she said, giving me a knowing little smile. "You look tired."

I moved to the coffee machine, giving her a single raised

eyebrow in response. She had the good grace to blush.

"I'll bring your new books over tonight," I told her, my hands automatically moving to froth the milk. A small smile played at the corners of her mouth.

"Only the books?"

I shrugged. "Did we make other plans?"

My cock felt heavy and hard, my body tight as I waited for her answer.

She took the offered coffee cup, her fingers brushing mine as she took it.

"I thought we had... an appointment."

I leaned over the counter, bending close to her ear. "Say it, babe."

"Your mouth on my pussy."

We both shuddered.

"If you want it, I'm more than willing to give it to you."

Gabby pulled back a fraction, her gaze catching mine, searching my face. "But do you want it?"

"More than you'll ever fucking know."

The gentle pink became a full flush. "Tonight then."

"Tonight."

The waiting was torture. Every moment of the day seemed to drag. I made mistake after mistake, until finally, I called it, leaving work at lunch.

The perks of being the boss.

Back at home, I didn't know what to do. I tried reading but found myself drifting. I went for a run but came home just as agitated. I showered then found myself out on the back deck, charcoal pencil in hand as I began to sketch. From memory, I pulled up the image of Gabby on that first day. The curve of her lips as she smiled, aviators tangled in her hair. Long, graceful lines for her neck, shorter strokes for the turquoise encrusted choker that had wrapped around her throat.

I returned to her cheek, spending an obscene amount of time perfecting the curve of her smiling lips. I moved up, shaping her cheeks with shading, adjusting it just so to capture the beauty of her expressions. The tilt of one eyebrow, the shape of her eyes, the flare of her nose, each line required my full attention to ensure it was perfect. To ensure it was Gabby and not some poor imitation.

"Wow." Gabby's breath on the back of my neck finally broke the spell. "That's… I don't even know what to say to that."

I blinked, trying to refocus. I looked down at the drawing, casting a critical eye over it before looking back at Gabby, studying her.

It wasn't bad. But it didn't capture her spark. It didn't capture the way her eyes twinkled like she had some joke she wanted to share with you. Or the absent brush of hair from her face. It didn't capture how she constantly shifted from one leg to the other, the movement fluid and so subconscious it was like water.

"I should have realized you were an artist. Or should I say, *the* artist." She touched the edge of the heavy paper. "Are all the pieces and paintings in your house yours?"

"Most of them," I admitted, finding my voice was low and gruff as I stared at her, unable to tear my gaze from her beautiful face.

She smiled. "The sculptures at your shop?"

"Mine."

She nodded, her head tilting to one side as she looked at

me. "You're a mystery I enjoy discovering."

I laughed. "I have nothing to hide."

"Hm, maybe mystery isn't the right word." She raised one hand to her lips, tapping a finger against it. "Ah! A present. That's better. You're a present I enjoy unwrapping."

Desire ignited my blood, sparks leaping between us in the early afternoon light.

"Would you like to unwrap it now?" I asked.

Her eyes darkened, cheeks flushing as she nodded.

I put aside my equipment then reached for her hand, leading her to the door before pausing. "My bed or yours?"

"Mine," she whispered.

I nodded, stepping through. I led her to the bedroom, stopping in the middle of the room.

"You prepared for this."

The linen was turned down, the fan above us lazily pushing air through the warm room.

"Of course."

I turned to her, drawing her into me. "Gonna kiss you now, Gabby."

"Please do," she whispered as I cupped her cheek.

Yes.

My soul sighed at the first press of our lips. She was warm and wet, tasting of cream and spice. That first kiss unleashed something within in me, flaming the desperate need I harbored for this woman.

You have bewitched me in body and soul.

"Fuck," I grunted against her lips as my arms crushed her to me. I had no pretty words in me for this moment, desire having burned away all restraint.

Her mouth opened under my lips, her body sinking into

279

me as her tongue teased mine.

Fuck that.

I lifted her into my arms, turning us both before setting her on the bed and covering her with my body. My mouth was possessive and demanding as I took what I wanted, branding myself on her body. Under me Gabby moaned, her body shifting as she let me lead.

I ran my hands over her body, grazing my palms down her sides then back up. Even as my body burned and everything in me roared to possess her, I put the brakes on, slowing it down, taking my time to build us both up. There was no hurry, no clock ticking in the background. There is only Gabby.

She placed a hand on my chest, pushing me back a few inches. Her lips pink and swollen, her eyes slightly glazed, her cheeks flushed.

I groaned, reaching down to kiss her again but she shook her head, stopping me.

"Let me take my leg off first."

I rolled off, propping myself up on the bed, watching as she reached down to begin removing the prosthetic.

"Can you... maybe not stare? Do something else," she said with a laugh. "You're freaking me out."

I grinned, deciding to tease her. "Like this?" I shifted, reaching behind me to strip my shirt off. Her fingers faltered, hovering over her leg as her eyes raked my chest.

"I... haven't seen your chest before."

I'd been wearing a shirt the morning of Ferdinand's invasion.

"Considering we only just had our first kiss, I'm not surprised."

She groaned, hands covering her face, peeking out at me from between her fingers. "How are you a virgin?"

I chuckled, guiding my hands down my chest to rest on my fly. "Luck?"

She rolled her eyes, her hands moving quickly to remove the equipment then peel the socks and sleeves from her leg.

"Seriously, look away, this isn't sexy."

"I don't know about that." I propped one hand behind my head, using the other to shove my jeans low on my hips, pulling my hard cock free. "I find everything about you sexy."

Gabby's eyes widened as she watched me lazily stroke my cock.

"What?" I asked innocently.

She licked her lips, "you're... umm... don't let this go to your head but... very big."

"And you're surprised?"

"Oh no. I mean, you did burst into my house to save me from Ferdinand with that monster."

I grinned. "But?"

"But I just wasn't expecting it to look even *bigger*."

I couldn't deny the awe in her voice was doing fucking amazing things for my confidence.

"Hurry up," I ordered. "I wanna taste you."

She began to move, pulling off the final layers. "You've already tasted me."

"Not where I want to."

She shuddered, tossing the sleeve aside, looking at me.

"Done?" I asked, giving my cock another lazy stroke.

She nodded, licking her lips.

I reached for her, pulling her on top of me, enjoying her

little squeal of surprise as I used her momentum to roll us both over, pressing her into the bed.

"Relax," I told her, enjoying how her breath caught every time I issued an order. "Let me explore."

I hesitated for a moment. "If I do anything you don't like, let me know."

She nodded.

"Do I need to be careful of your leg?"

"No, but just a warning, I can't shave it." She ran a hand over her residual limb. "Ingrown hairs can rub and cause infections. It's probably a little hairy."

I cupped her knee, gliding my hand down to the end of her leg, circling the smooth skin then back up. "Hair isn't a turn-off."

I kept up the gentle touch as Gabby lay back and I started at her mouth, teasing her gently before deepening the kisses until our tongues were a tangle and our lungs gasped desperately for air. When her body arched under me and her hands began to claw at my back, I shifted, drifting my lips across her beautiful face to her ear, biting gently on the lobe before sucking the sting away.

She whimpered but turned her head, allowing me greater access. I kissed and sucked my way down her neck, nibbling along her collarbone.

My hands dropped to the skirt of her summer dress, pausing. "You good if I take this off?"

She nodded, eyelids drifting open to find me watching her. "Please do."

I chuckled, pulling the dress up slowly as I continued to lay kisses along her neckline, my mouth practically watering for a taste of her breasts.

Her dress came off easily, leaving her in a pair of black lace underwear and a lace bra.

"Fuck," I swore, staring down at her. "You're gorgeous, Gabby."

She flushed, then reached for me, pulling me down to press a desperate kiss to my mouth before drawing back.

"Go, taste." She encouraged, pushing me down her body.

Thank Thor for decisive women.

I unclipped her bra, removing it from her body, revealing her breasts. Dark perfect nipples, breasts a generous handful, her body nothing but curves.

"You good there, virgin?" She laughed, watching me intently staring at her breasts.

"Fuck, yes."

Chapter Twelve

Gabby

I shivered – whole body shivered – at Rune's tone. His head dipped, his mouth closing over the nipple of my left breast.

"Oh God," I groaned, fingers burrowing into his hair, holding him to me. "Yes, like that."

He laved my nipple, his tongue decadently delicious against my sensitive body.

"Rune…" I arched under him, thrusting my breasts up as if I were a sacrifice. He made a satisfied noise in the back of his throat, a cross between a growl and a curse, the sound sending a responding quiver straight to my core. He looked up, his eyes flashing, raw desire on every line of his face before lowering his head to my right breast.

He paused, a whisper away from my nipple to grin up at me. I whimpered, then reached down, trying to find his glorious cock.

"Uh-uh. Don't distract me." He lowered his head, his mouth finding my breast.

I squirmed under him, desperate little noises escaping me. His free hand, the one not massaging my left breast, glided slowly up my rib cage, his hand came to rest against my throat.

Yes.

I closed my eyes, all my senses tuned to Rune.

"Fuck it."

My eyes snapped open as Rune abandoned my breasts, dropped to my pussy, shifting my legs wide to bend to my lips. His eyes met mine.

"I can't stand not knowing your taste."

His tongue. His nasty, filthy, gorgeous, beautiful tongue licked into me, continuing upwards, finding my clit.

"Fuck, Gabby. You're so wet, honey. You like this?"

I nodded, words escaping me as he teased my clit, his tongue and lips gentle but demanding. He looked so fucking satisfied as he tasted me. His gaze dark and full of fire, I was unable to look away.

"Come for me."

I moaned, my body shaking as his talented tongue teased every nerve ending.

A little more.

"Harder," I whispered, grateful when he responded, renewing his efforts.

A little—-

"Rune!" My thighs clenched around his head, my body feeling as if it were breaking apart as I cried out, my body bowing with the force of my climax.

He swapped tongue for fingers, moving up the bed to press hot, gasping kisses to my skin even as he continued to play. His lips met mine and I tasted myself on his tongue, somehow finding myself more aroused by that than I'd even been.

285

"You ready?" he asked, guiding himself to me.

I hesitated. "I'm on the pill. And I'm clean."

"I never had a doubt."

I grinned. "Then come on, virgin-boy. Let's pop your cherry."

He kissed me, capturing my mouth fiercely, his teeth nipping at my lips, his tongue dancing against mine. I melted into him, my hips arching up, encouraging him to use me.

Rune surged forward, his thick cock working into me.

"Fuck." I flinched. He was big. Bigger than I'd expected, my disused muscles tight around him.

"Gabby?"

I looked up, giving him a small smile. "I'm good, you're just… rather large. You might need to work into me." I bit my lip. "How's it for you?"

"Valhalla."

I chuckled, my amusement shattering into naked desire as he shifted, gradually working his cock in.

I groaned, hooking my thighs around his waist and pulling him tight to me. Without meaning to, my hips shifted and we both hissed out a breath.

"Fuck, Gabby. Fuck. You're so tight." Perspiration dotted his skin, his body tense above mine. I buried my head in his neck, pressing tiny kisses there, listening to his labored breaths, his pulse fluttered against my lips.

"Rune?"

"Yeah?" His voice sounded tight and strained.

"Fuck me."

He needed no further encouragement. Rune surged forward, this time we met in pleasure, our bodies working in tandem.

"Fuck," he groaned. "I'm close."

"It's okay." I panted. "I wasn't expecting—"

He cut my words off when he started to circle a thumb around my clit.

"Oh god, oh my god. Oh fuck. Oh, fuckity fuck. Rune, Rune, Rune." his name became a chant as he brutally fucked me, plundering my body, drawing from it exactly what he wanted.

My nails dug into his back and with a slight twist of his thumb, he sent me over the edge once more, my body devastated.

Rune thrust twice more then threw his head back, roaring his pleasure. He collapsed on me; his weight heavy but not overly suffocating. We lay panting, our hearts racing, for long minutes.

I tried to make sense of this moment. How I'd ended up here. Where it was going to next.

You can't keep him.

I knew that. I'd planned to only have tonight. But after that, I knew tonight wouldn't be enough.

You're leaving.

I knew that too.

Protect your heart. You're not the family kind of girl.

I closed my eyes, mentally building a wall between us.

He propped himself up on an elbow, a boyish grin on his face. "Please God, tell me that was good for you."

"Nah," I made a dismissive gesture. "Average."

He chuckled, pressing a kiss to my throat. "Liar."

I captured his face in my hands, committing his beautiful face to memory.

"It was perfect, Rune. Absolutely perfect."

"Good," he rolled, taking me with him so I was on top. "Now it's your turn."

I looked down, finding his cock was already hardening under me.

God bless newly ex-virgins. Their recovery time was inspiring.

"Oh, I think I can give you a little something." Even as I leaned down, my lips meeting his in a hungry kiss, I reminded myself that this wasn't for me. I wasn't that lucky. Unlike the romance novels he had me reading, there wouldn't be a happily ever after in my future.

Rune isn't for you. He never was. He never will be. You only have this moment.

And as much as I knew it would hurt, I was determined to wring all the memories from him.

I just hoped he'd forgive me when it came time to leave.

I cupped his jaw, pulling back a fraction, my gaze sliding over every inch of his beautiful face.

"You okay?" he asked quietly.

"Perfect."

He moved back in, pressing urgent hot kisses to my mouth as I filed this moment away, committing every detail to memory.

He's not for you. He never was. He never will be.

A single tear slipped free, falling down my cheek and onto the linen below.

Please remember me, Rune. Please don't hate me when this is over.

And with that wish of my heart, I pushed away all concerns for tomorrow and gave myself over to today.

Chapter Thirteen

Rune

"Rune?"

I wasn't sure who was more insatiable – me or Gabby. We were at the point where we only had to glance at each other before our clothes were disappearing and I had her taste on my tongue. I'd never thought of myself as an exhibitionist, but it was becoming increasingly clear to me that I would take this woman wherever and whenever she desired.

"Rune?"

That included on my fucking desk at work. I was meant to be scanning in a new book shipment, instead, I was staring at the spot where I'd laid her out last night, taking my time as I went down on her, teasing and taunting her hot body until she'd come, screaming my name.

"Rune!"

I snapped to, blinking at Ash. "Hey."

She laughed. "Hey space cadet. We're about to close up. That all good?"

I glanced at my watch, frowning at the time.

Fuck. You've spent an hour daydreaming about Gabby. Get

your head in the game, man!

I nodded. "Yep, let's do it."

It was parade day in Cape Hardgrave. All the businesses in town would be shutting early to head to Main Street for the kick-off of the fair. The parade would lead through the streets to the fairgrounds where the winning float would be announced, followed by the official opening of the fair.

Despite spending every free minute together – in bed and out – Gabby had been surprisingly tight-lipped about Thor's Shipbuilding's float. But then, I hadn't given her any hints about mine either. I'd even gone so far as to stash my costume in the office safe.

We closed up, heading to the storage shed down the block. I unlocked the roller door, revealing the beautiful longboat inside. It'd taken me and the team months of designing, crafting, and decorating but we were finally done.

"We're so winning this year," Ash declared, moving to loop arms with one of my other employees, Steven. The kid looked overwhelmed but not displeased with her attention.

"But does it work?" Natalie, one of the moms, asked. Her kid, Dee, was bobbing up and down, sucking nervously on her thumb as she looked up at the big ship.

"Does it work?" I scoffed, gesturing at them to grab an end. "Pull it into the lot and I'll show you."

We moved it out, revealing the ship's full glory. The mast was perfect, complete with a handcrafted sail, courtesy of Maisy and her grandmother, Mrs. Howell. The oars were positioned just so, and I'd handcrafted the dragon's head stempost myself.

But it was what dwelled at the bottom of the ship that I considered our pièce de résistance. Under the fake water,

I'd installed a little smoke machine and battery pack. When turned on, the dragon's eyes lit, and smoke billowed from his nose and mouth.

I switched it on now, testing it. For a moment nothing happened.

"Damn," Steve muttered.

"Give it a second," I told them, turning up the smoke level slightly. Wisps of white began to curl from the dragon's nostrils and my employees cheered.

"We're totally winning this year!"

Maisy and Mrs. Howell arrived a short time later, Maisy in her little Viking outfit, Mrs. Howell holding a shield for her.

"Thanks for doing this, Rune," she said as Maisy ran to join the other kids who were climbing over the float.

"Don't mention it. She knows most of the kids from Drag Queen story time, it made sense she should join in."

The kids were mostly those of my employees. But a few, like Maisy, attended some of the regular free programs I ran at work.

"We're ready!" Ash called from the stern. "All aboard, Captain!"

We quickly changed into our costumes, my employees chatting excitedly about winning the competition. I hooked the float up to the SUV and Mrs. Howell gave me a wave, letting me know she was good to go.

"Slow and steady," I said to the team. "Ready when you are, Mrs. Howell."

"Roger!" She took off at a snail's pace, the float gliding gently behind. Even at such a slow speed, it took us no time at all to make it to the gathering area.

"Oh God," beside me Ash snorted. "Rune... your family...
"

I looked up from where I'd been breaking up a sword fight between two tiny Vikings to see the Thor's Shipbuilding float.

I shook my head, catching sight of my Nan nestled on the bow. I cupped my hands around my mouth, bellowing, "Nan! You traitor!"

In a buxom pirate wench outfit, complete with fake parrot on her shoulder, she gave me a bright wave. "Your brother asked first!"

Another point of contention – who Nan chose to align with each year.

"Next time you need a trip to the hairdresser, call someone else!"

I could hear her cackle over the bustle of the floats as the parade master assigned us numbers and directed us into position.

Ash sidled up to me, giving me a grin. "I slipped Bruce a fifty to put us in front of your brother."

I held up a hand, offering her a high-five. "This is why you're my favorite."

I hadn't seen Gabby but I could see Erik and Laura at the front of the pirate ship, both with a twin dressed as either a tiny parrot or a monkey strapped to their chest.

My phone vibrated in my pocket.

Gunnar: Rune... I'm sorry but...

I clicked the attached picture and shook my head. Liv, Astrid, Gunnar, and Ella were all dressed as pirates standing at the back of the boat.

Rune: You're a disgrace to our family.

Ella: If it makes you feel better, he's already split his pirate pants.

She sent a picture of the giant tear down the back of Gunnar's pants.

Laura: I hate to take sides but... we're totally winning this year. Sorry, Rune. We have a secret weapon.

I looked up but couldn't see anything unusual. The rest of the team from Thor's Shipbuilding had brought their families and were dressed as pirates. Even Ma and Dad were there, giving me a wave and laughing when they saw the longboat.

Just you wait.

The parade master stood at the front, lifting a megaphone to his mouth.

"Good afternoon everyone! I'm Bruce, the parade master. Welcome to this year's parade. Now, we're gonna take this nice and slow. Two full car lengths between each float. The lead float will set the pace. When we get to the end look for me, I'll be the one in the hi-vis directing you to where to park. There are two awards – best in show and crowd favorite. Voting will take place directly after for an hour. The fairground will be open for food and drink. Once the mayor makes her speech, we'll announce the winners and open the fair, and rides will start. If you need help call the number on your information pack, otherwise see you at the finish line, good luck!"

With a cheer from the crowd, Bruce waved the first float through. It took a little while but we were tenth in line.

"Hit it, Mrs. Howell."

She turned the music on, the soundtrack from the TV Series Vikings pumped out of the loudspeaker I'd installed in the back of the SUV. I bent, switching on our secret weapon, laughing when the smoke began to slowly wisp out of the dragon's nose and all I heard were groans from behind me.

"Never fear! The dreaded Pirate Captain Gabby is here!"

I turned, and immediately knew we'd lost. Gabby stood at the front of the pirate ship dressed as a hot but entirely appropriately attired pirate queen – complete with authentic-looking peg leg. Beside her, stood Ferdinand, flapping his wings and looking ridiculously pleased when she fed him a small fish.

I heard cursing and groans behind me.

I shook my head, narrowing my eyes to give Gabby a death stare. She laughed, sending me a saucy wink before turning to the crowd we were beginning to near.

"Argh! Who be these sailors that we're about to plunder?"

Around me, our Viking kids threw chocolate coins into the crowd as we wound our way slowly down Main Street.

I was mostly preoccupied with making sure the kids didn't stab each other with their fake swords, but occasionally caught glimpses of Gabby, laughing with my family, ribbing the other guys from Thor's Shipbuilding, or balancing against the Mast and pulling off her leg to shake it at the audience.

I couldn't help but appreciate how seamlessly she fit. It was as if she'd always been here. As if she were meant to be a part of our family.

Admit it, you're fucked.

I knew she was still keeping distance between us. Despite my best efforts, I knew she still saw our relationship as a summer fling.

Well, fuck that.

My ancestors demanded more of me than allowing the woman I loved to slip through my fingers.

Brace, Gabby.

Little Miss Pirate Queen was about to get her heart pillaged.

Chapter Fourteen

Gabby

I honestly couldn't remember the last time I'd had this much fun.

Or been this full.

I shoved the remaining ribs away from me, groaning as I patted my stomach. Beside me, Rune took a look at the plate, raising an eyebrow in question.

"Please," I said, shoving it at him. "I'm about to burst."

He took it, starting in on the remaining food.

"Legs like hollow trees, that one." Nan shook her head. "He'd eat us all out of house and home if we let him."

Rune rolled his eyes, but picked up a rib, tearing off a hunk of meat.

Why do I find that so arousing?

There was definitely something wrong with me.

"What do you think, Gabby?" Ella asked, leaning around Gunnar to give me a friendly smile.

"Sorry, about what?"

She gestured at the fair. "Starting something like this up back in the Cove."

"Oh." I swallowed, feeling Rune tense beside me. "I think it's a great idea. It'd not only be good for town morale but will bring in some fundraising for the emergency departments."

Ella nodded. "I figure if we approach Farrah—"

"Farrah?" Liv interrupted.

"The Mayor. She's the sister of my head chef, who also happens to be my best friend." She laughed. "It's nice to have a direct line to the top. Anyways, if we approach her, maybe she'd be willing to help set this up." She turned back to me. "You'd be willing to help too, right?"

I nodded, my stomach clenching at the idea of returning to Capricorn Cove. "Yeah, of course."

"Great."

From my other side, Ian stirred. "Will these women, Anika and Farrah be at your wedding?"

I saw Liv tense, her face wiped clean.

"Anika's my bridesmaid. And considering the whole town is invited, it wouldn't surprise me if the mayor makes an appearance," Ella said.

"They single?" Mac asked from across the table, earning a slap to the back of the head from Gunnar.

"Dude!"

"I said no fraternizing with the guests." He looked around the table. "That goes for the rest of you cretins. I don't wanna have to deal with your bullshit on my wedding day."

Ella rolled her eyes. "Except if you're already together, like Rune and Gabby."

I choked on my drink, shooting a wide-eyed look at Rune. He ignored me, tearing off another rib.

"Um, we're not, that is… it's not quite like… that…?" I

297

stuttered.

The table all looked at me, then Rune.

"Jesus," Astrid cried, shaking her head. "Rune, what did you do?"

"We actually like this one!" Liv said, reaching across the table to snatch at my hand. "She's wonderful."

"I already told you," Erik shook his head. "We've adopted her. You're kicked out of the family, buddy."

I looked around the table to see everyone glaring at Rune. He shot me a look as if to say, *see? And you were worried.*

I pushed up, suddenly overwhelmed.

"I… I have to…" The plastic white chair fell as I danced away from the table, needing to get away.

"Fuck, Rune! What did you do!"

"Go after her, dimwit!"

"Gabby, wait."

I heard Rune follow me, calling my name as I wove through the crowded eating area, desperate to escape.

I couldn't process my feelings right now. Rune was offering his love. His *family* were offering me their love. It was… too much.

I stumbled into the parking lot, tripping, feeling myself start to fall. Rune caught me, pulling me back against his hard chest.

"Gabby."

My name on his lips said in that warm, tender, heart-rendering loving way… it broke me. Tears flowed freely, my fingers an ineffective barrier. Rune growled, turning me around and pulling me back into his arms, tucking my head into his chest, holding me as I cried.

"I don't want to hurt," I sobbed, revealing my biggest fear.

"I don't want to fall and then get discarded like every other time."

"Honey..." his arms were a tight vice around me, like chains binding us together. I knew I should have felt trapped, but instead, it felt as if he were trying to tie me to him, keeping us connected despite the storm engulfing me.

As I calmed, Rune released me a little, just enough to look down at me.

"I'm about to lay some truth on you, Gabby. So, brace."

I tensed, waiting for the inevitable words to emerge from his mouth, my stomach clenching, bracing me for their impact.

"I want to marry you."

I blanched. "What!"

"Not right now. Maybe in a year or so. I know you need time. But I can't see my future without you. At first, I could. I'll be honest, falling in love with a non-reader?" his lips quirked. "It's a huge deal breaker for me."

He brushed a stray tear from my cheek. "But then you kept appearing in my life, making it impossible to see or think of anyone but you. And yeah, I foisted books on you in hopes of you becoming a reader, but I suddenly found I didn't care that much. I found that I liked watching you. I liked your expressions and movement. I liked the way you joked with Maisy and teased my brother. I liked that you weren't afraid of my nephews, and bravely faced off Ferdinand."

I hiccuped a laugh, my heart thumping wildly in my chest.

"I love you, Gabby. It wasn't instantaneous but these past months have been the best of my life. I know you're committed to going back to the Cove, but, if you'll have me, I'll go with you."

"What about your store?"

He shrugged. "A store is cool and all, but it's not home. It's not my heart. You are."

I threw myself at him, wrapping my arms tight around his neck.

"Are you sure?"

"Fuck yeah."

I raised up, kissing him with everything that's in me. He immediately took over, feasting on my mouth before breaking the kiss to press little nibbles to my jaw.

"I love you, Rune. Take me ho—"

"Ahem."

We froze, both of us twisting to look over his shoulder at his family who were simultaneously watching us and attempting to look inconspicuous.

Rune sighed, stepping back slightly to sling an arm around my shoulder. "Make it quick."

Erik turned to me. "I know you're planning on going back to the Cove, but Mac here wants to stay with Gunnar. Which means Ian's about to get promoted and I'm gonna need another hand to help out."

He gave me a grin. "You want the position?"

My heart thumped. "Gunnar?"

"Look, it's gonna be a loss. But I figure what I lose in an employee I'll gain in a sister-in-law."

I looked up at Rune, my heart in my eyes. "And what say you, Sir? Should I stay?"

His grin was slow but brilliant. "Fuck. Yes."

I turned back to Erik. "I guess it's a yes."

At my words, Rune swept me up, throwing me over his shoulder, headed for his truck. His family called out ribald suggestions as he headed out, flipping them the bird over his shoulder.

My phone vibrated in my pocket. I squirmed, pulling it carefully free.

Liv has added Gabby to Larsson Family chat

Astrid: Welcome sis!

Ella: Get ready for the crazy.

Gunnar: Don't tell her that, you'll scare her off.

Erik: She's gotta be prepared. Besides, this is Rune we're talking about. She probably already knows.

Liv: Don't listen to them. We're all perfectly sane.

Laura: I don't know. You remember the rat incident, right?

Ella: or the time Gunnar moved to Capricorn Cove after knowing me less than a month?

Gunnar: Hey! You make it sound like I didn't decide to do that within three seconds of meeting you.

Laughing, I tucked the phone back in my pocket as Rune continued to carry me to his car.

This must be what being in a family feels like.

Chapter Fifteen

Rune

I wasn't gonna make it to the house.

I knew this, my fear of losing Gabby, my relief at her agreement to stay, my overwhelming anger at her for building a wall between us instead of talking to me, it all exploded, searing through my veins, wiping every thought from my head except one – mark her.

I whipped into the parking lot at The Literary Academy, throwing the truck into park then jumping out. I ran around to the other side, throwing open her door and lifting her out once again, tossing her over my shoulder.

"Rune!"

"Quiet," I ordered, charging toward the staff entrance. "I'm this close to fucking you against the brickwall right now. You say one word and that restraint is gonna break."

She was quiet for a moment while I fiddled with the key, cursing when I couldn't find the right one.

"I'm okay with a fuck against the wall... if that's what you need."

The little control I had shattered, splintering reason, and

logic. I set her down, backing her up until her back pressed against the brick of the wall. We were in the alley between The Literary Academy and a furniture store next door. The alley was sheltered from view of the main street, and both stores were closed for the day.

But that didn't mean there wasn't a chance of getting caught.

Mine.

"Turn around," I ordered, my hands dropping to my belt. "Hands against the wall, spread your legs."

Gabby stared at me for a moment then turned, moving far too slowly for my liking, the rage still fizzing through my blood.

I pressed into her back nipping at her neck, sucking her ear lobe. She groaned, arching up, her spine bending back to try and grant me better access to her neck.

"You're never fucking leaving me, Gabby," I told her, unzipping her pants and roughly shoving them down her legs. "Never. You got me?"

She nodded but it wasn't enough for the fear still running through my veins.

"Say it!"

"I'm yours. I'm never leaving."

"Again," I demanded, rising up to rub the head of my cock against her clit.

"I'm yours," she whimpered, her hips jerking as my cock collected her slick, spreading it to better tease her sensitive skin.

"I'm yours, Rune!"

I slammed my cock into her, brutally punishing us both. She cried out, pressing back against me, her body bowing as she tried to take me. I worked into her tight little snatch, marking her, branding her, desperate to fuck this need out of my system.

"You're mine, Gabby. We're a fucking family. You and me, babe. You and fucking me. No more running. No more walls. Nothing but this," I thrust harder, my hands holding her hips in place.

"Yes, oh my god, yes."

I nipped her neck then sucked the sting away, ensuring I left a mark.

"You're gonna come for me, Gabby. You're gonna fucking milk my cock and take my load then you're gonna say thank you and tell me again you love me. Got it?"

She nodded, now incapable of words as her body jerked with the motion of my thrusts.

I reached around, my fingers finding her clit. I found a rhythm I knew would drive her crazy, my fingers knowing just where to press.

"Now," I ordered, tweaking her clit. Her pussy gripped me in a vice, her body bowing, nothing but gasps leaving her lips as she came.

I followed, my cum branding her.

Mine.

She dropped but I caught her, pressing her close, holding her tight, nuzzling her neck gently as we both came down.

"Rune?"

I winced, wondering if I'd taken this too far.

"Yeah?"

She sighed, looking up at me with dreamy eyes. "Let's do that again."

Any leftover tension dissipated, leaving me feeling a little

304

like a wet rag.

"How about we get cleaned up first. Then I'm gonna take you in our bed."

Her lips lifted; the smile so heartbreakingly beautiful that my fingers itched for canvas to capture it.

She reached up, pressing a kiss to my mouth. "I love you Rune, please, take me to our home."

Her every wish would always be my command.

Epilogue One

Gabby

"No."

"But—"

"I said, no. Abso-fucking-lutely not."

I hid a grin, pretending to flip through the bridal magazine that Liv had brought over.

"Look, as Gabby's Maid of Honor –"

"Excuse me?" Astrid interrupted from the kitchen, placing hands on her hips. "Who the fuck decided this?"

I chanced a glance at Rune catching him mid-eye roll.

"Ladies, if we can get back to the issue at hand—"

"I did," Liv answered Astrid. "You get to be mine."

"What if I don't wanna be yours?"

Liv frowned. "Why the ever hell would you not want to be my Maid of Honor?"

Astrid held up a hand, marking off the reasons on her fingers. "One, you're a crazy control freak. Two, you're totally gonna be a bridezilla. Three, you're not even dating let alone engaged. Four—"

"What about the guy from Ella's wedding?" I asked. "I

thought you liked him."

Liv waved us both off. "It didn't work out."

"Probably cause you're too controlling..." Astrid muttered.

Liv ignored her, turning to Rune. "Brother, I get it, you're possessive. But I'm telling you right now, there *will* be strippers."

"No, there won't."

"Yes, there will."

"Do you remember Ella's bachelorette party?" my future husband asked. "Do you remember the police being called? Do you remember Ian having to bail you out of jail?"

Astrid snorted, caught Rune's glare then ducked her head, suddenly very interested in lace samples.

"Look," Liv made a placating gesture at Rune. "We've learned our lesson; I'm not going to allow that to happen again."

"Yes, because there won't *be* any strippers."

Her mouth twisted into a benign smile. "Of course, brother."

He frowned. "I mean it, Liv. If I hear of one goddamned man in a G-string—"

"I said, okay." She turned to me. "Now, dresses."

I shrugged. "I still think a Vegas wedding would be fine."

"It's getting more attractive every day," Rune muttered.

"Absolutely not. Now, do you want white, eggshell white, ivory, champagne, oyster, cream, blush, or..."

Hours later we finally bid farewell to the maids from hell.

"We really should just elope," I told Rune for the hundredth time that day. "We can live stream the ceremony from Vegas."

"Yeah, good luck sneaking that one past Liv. I'm pretty sure Ma gave her authority to place a tracker on our bank accounts. They even get a whiff of us purchasing a ticket they'd be here, stopping our escape." He shot me a grin. "They're determined to welcome you into this family properly."

Too late.

In the year since Rune and I had been together, his family had been nothing but wonderful. His sisters had welcomed me with open arms, slowly changing every photo on my wall from those of strangers to images that included me, surrounded by his family.

The best decision I'd ever made had been trusting Rune with my heart.

The second-best decision had been attending the Greedy Readers Book Club and getting drunk enough to confess my desire to Rune.

God bless book club.

Rune pulled me into his arms, pressing a kiss to my forehead. "You okay with this?"

I looked up at him, cupping his jaw. "Your family can be overwhelming, but this is good. I'm glad they're so excited."

"Don't let them railroad you."

I grinned. "Only your Nan can do that."

He chuckled. "I love you, Gabby."

"I love you too."

"You wanna act out that scene from The King's Horrible Bride, tonight?"

I laughed. "You mean the one that got me all hot the other night?"

"Mm," he ran hands down my back, cupping my ass. "There's something so fucking attractive about a woman who reads."

"Well, Mr. Librarian. Perhaps you should get me between the covers."

He chuckled. "Yes, Ma'am, right away."

Epilogue Two

Gabby

I tiptoed down the hall, pausing at the door to our daughter's room.

"And then the princess declared that she didn't need a prince to complete her, but that she loved him anyway, and so they lived happily ever after. The end."

I rolled my eyes, chuckling quietly to myself.

"Daddy?"

"Yes, baby girl?"

"When I grow up can I marry a princess?"

God love my husband; he didn't even pause.

"Of course, sweetie. You can marry whoever you want." He paused then, and I waited knowing a caveat was on its way. "Except a politician. I'm sorry, baby. No matter how much I love you I just can't allow that kind of negativity into our house."

"Okay, Daddy."

I heard him kiss her then walk across the floorboards to stand at the door. "Now, straight to sleep, munchkin."

"Love you times a million!"

"And I love you times a million. Night."

He switched off the light, softly pulling the door halfway closed, blocking the light from the hall.

"Hey," I whispered looking pointedly at my watch. "She was meant to be down a half hour ago."

"And you weren't meant to be home until ten."

"I skipped out early."

We met half-way, Rune wrapping arms around me, while I tucked my hands into the back of his jean pockets.

"Everything okay?" he asked, searching my face.

I nodded, breathing in his familiar scent. "Just missed you."

"Oh really?" He pressed into me, letting me feel the hard outline of his cock.

"And maybe that," I admitted, flushing.

This month's book club had been discussing Kresley Cole's Game Maker series. I *may* have gotten a little worked up talking about my favorite scene.

"Daddy? Can I have a water?"

Rune sighed, shaking his head. "She's your daughter."

He twisted, calling over his shoulder, "No. You already had a drink and went to the toilet and got a second story. Go to sleep, Tora!"

"Okay."

We both stood still for a long moment, trying to suppress our giggles. When we were sure she was down and staying that way, we crept back down the hall to the living room, Rune pulling me onto the couch then across his lap.

"Here?" I asked as he settled me over his erection.

"Anywhere," he grunted, hands sliding up my thighs to find my bare skin. "Jesus, Gabby. Where's your underwear?"

"I took them off when I got home. Complaining?"

"Fuck no."

Rune lifted up, turned, then gently placed me back on the couch before dropping to his knees and disappearing under my skirt.

"Quiet," he ordered against my core, his breath hot on my sensitive skin. "Don't wanna wake her up."

I bit the inside of my cheek as he pressed slow, druggy kisses to my thighs, my abdomen, my lips. He parted me, his fingers sliding through my slick wetness, teasing at first, then becoming faster, the pressure increasing as he fed my need, building up my climax.

"Rune…"

"Shh…" he admonished. "We don't want to wake Tora."

I reached for a throw pillow, pressing it against my face as he replaced his fingers with his mouth, his tongue finding my clit, tasting me, circling in the way that he knew was guaranteed to drive me crazy.

It came like a freight train, my body clenching, arching, grasping for more.

"In me," I ordered, throwing the pillow aside. "Now!"

Rune surged up, almost lifting my skirt over my head in his haste to cover my body with his, guiding his cock into me, thrusting hard and deep. I wrapped my legs around his waist, the angle causing us both to groan.

Even after all this time he constantly rocked my world.

"Quiet," he reminded me, one hand coming up to cover my lips. "Or I'll have to fill this filthy little mouth."

I moaned against his palm, remembering the last book club night when he'd done just that. Remembering how he'd tasted as he'd come down my throat.

My body clenched around him, my pussy milking his cock as that memory crashed into this moment, pushing me over the edge. I came, biting his palm as my world exploded, Rune buried deep in me.

"Fuck yes, Gabby. Come around my cock. That's it, milk me, honey."

I felt his thrusts increase in tempo, his cock pulsing as he came deep, hot cum warming my inside.

Rune collapsed on top of me, breathing heavily.

"Wow," I whispered some time later.

Rune chuckled. "You can say that again."

We got up, me moving to our bedroom to clean up, Rune moving to close down the house. We met on the bed.

I was rolling on my compression sock when he came in, standing at the end of the bed, clothed only in boxer briefs.

"Again?" I asked, eyeing his rapidly hardening cock.

"Mm, seems I can't get enough of you tonight."

This time was slow and sensual, hours of foreplay and touching, of kissing and tasting before Rune rolled over, his hands gripping my waist to support me as I rode him to completion.

"Love you, Gabby."

I snuggled into him, pressing a kiss to his heart. "Love you too, Rune."

We were quiet for a moment, the house silent around us.

"Gabby?"

"Mm?"

"The agent got back to me today. They want to option our comic."

I pushed up, leaning across the bed to stare at him. "Are you serious?"

He grinned, his teeth flashing in the dark. "Yeah."

Two years ago, Rune and I had worked on a comic book together. I'd been pregnant and terrified our baby would be born without a limb. Not because I was worried she wouldn't be loved – I had no fear on that end. No, I was worried that she wouldn't have good role models to look up to. No superheroes or comic characters that she could point to and say, "they're like me."

Rune, in his infinite wisdom, had suggested we write our own. I did the storyline; he did the images. We'd called it The Last Librarian, and it'd featured a woman who saved the world – and just happened to be a wheelchair user.

"This is amazing news! Think of all the kids that'll get to see Frankie." I pulled him close, kissing his beautiful lips. "Rune, this is…"

"I know." He gave me a tight squeeze.

"We make a pretty good team."

"No, babe. We make the best *family*."

My heart smiled.

Yeah, we do.

IV

Reality Check

Reality Check

Liv

Unemployed, homeless and pregnant - not how I intended to spend this Thanksgiving.

To be fair, I quit my job, and no one could have predicted the flood in my apartment.

The baby? Well, that's on me.

A tipsy hook-up at my brother's wedding, a failed condom, and suddenly I'm stuck with my nemesis, Ian Campbell.

The man is infuriating - he looks like a red-haired Big Foot, is built like a lumberjack, and acts like a refined laird of some crumbling castle.

He's confusing, irritating and... kissable?

No, no way. There is absolutely no possible universe in which I'm falling for the Sasquatch... right?

Ian

Liv 'The Harpy' Larsson is pregnant with my baby. How the good god did that happen?

I mean, I know how it happened. Those memories don't seem to want to quit.

But now she's in my house. And my car. And at my work. And we're going to pregnancy classes and buying diapers,

and she's suddenly not so much a harpy as happy.
Wait. No. Do I like Liv?
Is this... love?

Warning: This book is inspired by reality TV, strong scotch, and lumberjacks. So, get thee a man, a camera, and settle in — this read will have you questioning if hate is really such a bad thing.

Prologue

Liv

August 15

"And so," I said, holding up my glass and looking at the happy couple. "In summary, welcome to the family, Ella. Sorry you got stuck with my useless lump of a brother. But at least you get me."

Laughter exploded around the tent while Gunnar, the groom in question, rolled his eyes, subtly flipping me the bird.

"To Ella and Gunnar!"

"To Ella and Gunnar!" the room toasted, glasses clinking, laughter, and conversation swelling.

I sat down, lifting my glass to take a sip of the sparkling wine, heart aching with gladness, hope, love, and a little envy, that my brother had finally found his one.

My younger sister, Astrid, leaned over, laughter on her lips. "Great speech."

"Thanks, I thought you'd enjoy the roasting."

The wedding ceremony had taken place in Gunnar and Ella's yard, the altar positioned out to face the ocean. It had been beautiful, sentimental, and above all, them. My brother and his beautiful bride pledging to love one another forever under a beautiful sky.

The reception had kicked off immediately. A large tent covered in garlands and fairy lights provided some protection from the afternoon sun. Now that darkness had fallen, the long picnic tables that were covered in white fabric and pretty lights created a magical backdrop for this perfect night.

The caterers were food trucks, and guests were invited to help themselves. There were no assigned tables, no formal placemats, just good food, great music, and lots of laughs.

"Great wedding." A plate of food landed beside me with a thump, the accompanying body settling onto the bench seat taking up any available space.

"Really?" I asked, raising an eyebrow at the intruder as he squirmed in, his thigh pressed against mine. "You couldn't have found any other table?"

Ian Campbell grinned at me, his teeth flashing through the red hair of his unkempt beard. "Look around, love. There's not a space to be had."

I glanced around seeing the truth of his words. With gritted teeth I turned away, reaching for my wine glass.

He lifted a slider, managing to not drop a bite in his crazy beard.

"How's the junk TV going?" he asked a moment later, spearing a forkful of potato salad.

I arched an eyebrow. "Excuse me?"

Since when do you care?

"Ye're still doing those reality TV shows, yeah?"

I crossed my arms, bristling. "I didn't realize we were the

small talk kind of people."

"Settle down, Harpy." He lifted his beer, taking a sip. "I'm just being polite."

"Don't. It doesn't look good on you."

He chuckled, turning to give me his full attention.

"Are ye saying something else does?"

"Yes." I pushed to a stand, giving him my chilliest smile, the one I saved for misogynists. "Death looks great on you."

I turned, walking away, Ian's laughter following me.

I made it to the dance floor just as the singer cleared his throat, drawing attention to the small stage.

"And now, the first dance. If the bride and groom will take the floor?"

I watched my brother lead his bride to the dance floor, blinking back tears as they began to sway to a cover of 'Unconditional' by Freya Ridings.

"They're gorgeous," Astrid whispered beside me, wiping tears from her cheek.

"Yeah, they are." I leaned into her, wrapping my arms around her.

As the song wound up, we all clapped, laughing as Gunnar tipped Ella back in a graceful dip before pulling her back into his arms to kiss her.

We cheered and catcalled, Ian raising two fingers to his mouth to let out an ear splitting wolf-whistle.

With a smile a mile wide, Ella swept her arm out, inviting us to join them on the dance floor.

I looked around, catching sight of my father leading my mother onto the cleared space. My heart gave a little flop as he pulled Mom close, holding her tight.

Oh, to have a love like theirs.

Forty years on, they still looked at each other with hearts in their eyes.

The singer started back up, doing a slowed down, less country and more soulful rock cover of Kane Brown's 'Thunder in the Rain.'

"Come on." My brother, Erik, lifted Laura's hand, pressing a kiss to his fiancé's knuckles. "Let's dance."

On his other side, Gabby, my youngest sibling's fiancé, led him onto the dance floor, cajoling Rune with a shimmy of her shoulders, setting her breasts jiggling. With a sigh and a roll of his eyes, he pulled her into his arms, bending to kiss her.

Astrid leaned closer, sighing. "It sucks to be the single ones."

"Preach."

"I wanna dance too."

"Come on then," I told her, linking our fingers. "Let's dance."

Stepping out with a laugh, we slung arms around each other, swaying together in time to the music.

"This playlist is very country!" Astrid called as the singer transitioned into Sam Hunt's 'Body Like A Back Road.'

I nodded, laughing as Rune allowed Gabby to grind up against him, his body moving from side to side in what I could only call an awkward white guy shuffle. Beside him, the local Sheriff and his wife, Honey, ground together, their bodies pure magic as they performed a kind of flamenco-cross-country swing.

"Come on." A hand caught mine, skillfully spinning me away from Astrid and into the thick chest of a giant. "Let's give the good Sheriff a run for his money."

I'd later blame this moment on shock– really it was the only reasonable explanation for what happened next.

Ian and I danced. We moved around the dance floor in tandem, our bodies coming together in a way that felt intimate and sensual. We were in sync, perfectly so.

The world fell away as he guided me around the dance floor, his body pressed to mine.

"Just because you can dance doesn't mean I like you," I told him as Ian twirled me out and skillfully pulled me back in.

"Ye know I'd never presume that ye'd find me even the least bit palatable." He grinned, twisting me this way then that, his hands warm and confident on my hips. "Even I'm not that stupid."

And therein lay the problem. Ian Campbell wasn't stupid. Not even a fraction. Not even close. The man completed degrees in his spare time for goodness sake. And he did them for fun. Fun!

"Ye ready, lass?"

I blinked. "For?"

"The finale."

He dipped me, catching my neck and guiding me low. Around us, the crowd erupted, clapping and cheering as he gently lifted me back up, my body sliding along his.

"I hate you," I whispered, glaring at him even as my body gave a little shiver.

His eyes flashed, amusement, and something darker in their depths. "The feeling, I can assure ye, is entirely mutual."

With a fake laugh, I tossed my hair, stepping back from him clapping and joining in the festivities, throwing off the faint kick of attraction that had begun burning in my belly.

No way in hell am I attracted to Ian Campbell.

"Here." Astrid handed me a glass of water, grinning as she watched me suck it down.

"What?"

She gave a half-shoulder shrug. "Nothing."

"Bullshit."

She laughed, turning away. "You know what they say, hate and love are two sides of the same coin."

I rolled my eyes, watching as Ian claimed another partner, doing with her what he'd done with me.

Only, it really has to be said, far less impressively.

I shoved that thought aside, pressing the cool glass to my warm forehead.

It's just the wedding vibes getting to you. You're tougher than this, Liv.

Feeling suddenly overheated, I moved through the crowd, seeking the cool night air. Outside the tent, I blended into the shadows, following the twinkling fairy lights that led down a short walk onto Ella and Gunnar's private beach.

With a sigh, I made my way to the wooden boathouse, laughing when I found the inside similarly lit with lights and some bedding.

"Oh, Ella." I shook my head, knowing this had to be the work of my sister-in-law. It wouldn't surprise me to learn that she'd set this up, likely expecting that there would be at least one wedding guest who'd need to crash the night after consuming too much alcohol.

"Liv?"

I turned, finding Ian coming down the beach, his shoes in one hand, a bottle of wine in the other.

I sighed, plucking one of the blankets from the bed and wrapping it around my shoulders as I walked to meet him, the sand cool beneath my feet.

"Couldn't leave me alone for five minutes?"

His lips quirked one bushy eyebrow cocking. "I'd say it's the other way around, lass. Ye've found my bed."

I paused, suddenly registering the masculine scent coming from the blanket around my shoulders.

"Oh."

He grinned, gesturing towards the small dock. "Come sit with me?"

I'd never be quite sure why I followed him. Maybe because he asked rather than told. Maybe because I felt a little melancholy. Either way you looked at it, I ended up sitting beside Ian, sharing his wine.

"You ever feel lost?" I asked, finding myself suddenly morose as we stared at the moonlight shimmering on the waves.

I felt Ian turn, considering me in the dim light. "Depends."

"On?"

"If I want to be lost or not."

I laughed, turning to him. "You want to be lost?"

"Sure. The best adventures start when the trail ends."

"Are you a Hallmark card?"

He grinned, sipping from the wine bottle.

I processed his words, thinking it over.

"You know, sometimes you can be a decent human being."

"Sometimes?" He bumped me with his arm. "Hardly a recommendation."

"Aye," I said, trying to imitate his accent. "And ye'll do well to not push yer luck."

He laughed, lifting the wine to his lips and looking back out at the ocean. "Do ye want a family, Liv?"

325

I shrugged. "I haven't really thought about it."

Liar, liar, pants on fire.

"Why not? A pretty lass like you should be beating the men away."

I reached for the bottle, plucking it from his hands and sucking down a sip. "I've got a goal. I've worked hard to get where I am."

"As queen of reality shows?"

"Is that judgment I hear?"

He shrugged, taking back the bottle. "Always thought ye were better than that."

I bristled, part of me angry at his judgment, another annoyed that he echoed my own thoughts. "We all start somewhere. My plan isn't to be in reality forever. Well, not the entertainment reality anyway."

"No?"

"Mm. I wanna move into documentaries."

"Really?"

It was my turn to bump him. "Don't sound so surprised."

He caught my chin, turning me to face him, his gaze searching mine. "I'm not surprised, Liv. I'm pleased for ye. It's been a long time since ye sounded so excited."

I swallowed, pulling away from him and turning to look back out at the water, attempting to hide how much I wanted this.

"Yeah… well… it's gotta happen first. I should know in the next few months, once they go through all the interviews and whatnot."

"And I have no doubt ye'll make it so. If nothing else ye're persistent."

I laughed, moving to shove him but he shifted, catching

my hand and pulling me into him.

"W-w-what are you doing?" I asked as he bent his head.

"Kissing ye."

With that declaration, he bent, pressing a hot, rough, demanding kiss to my mouth. His tongue took advantage of my surprise, slipping between my lips and stroking mine with delicious intention.

For a moment I remained stiff, shock holding me rigid against him. Then he made a noise, a mix between a groan and a grunt, and I melted, kissing him back.

Oh, God. Why am I enjoying this? This is Ian. Ian! You hate Ian!

But I didn't need to like him to want to sleep with him.

"Fuck," he muttered, pulling back slightly to trail kisses down my neck. "Ye taste like the devil."

I huffed out a laugh, his beard rasping against my skin in a way I'd never have thought I'd find arousing. "You're one to talk."

He bit the seam of my shoulder, immediately licking away the sting. "Shall we do this, lass? Or am I to leave ye now?"

I glanced back at the boathouse and the cozy bed inside. "We can never tell another soul. One and done."

"Of course." He grinned. "No one'd believe us anyway. Ye hate my guts too much."

He stood, helping me up, pulling me into his arms and kissing me again.

"Gonna fuck ye into next week," he muttered against my lips. "Gotta get this outta our systems."

A deep ache began to pulse between my thighs, my body tightening at his words. "Then you better get this over with."

He boosted me up, my arms and legs automatically

wrapping around him, holding on as he walked us to the tiny cabin, his rigid cock a teasing heat between my legs.

I'd blame it on the wine. Or the ocean setting. Or perhaps the romance of a perfect wedding. I'd blame the next hour on anything but what it was– pure animal attraction.

In a fumble, we stripped each other, lips tasting newly revealed skin. I expected missionary, Ian pounding over me, and perhaps a small tingle of an orgasm if I were lucky.

I got an explosion.

He pushed me down, flipped me over, pulling my arms forward, and covering my back with his front.

"Gonna fuck ye dirty," he whispered against the shell of my ear. "Ye yell if it gets too much."

With that, he pulled back, one hand still holding mine in front of me, his other rolling on a condom.

"I don't have all night," I complained, my wet arousal coating my thighs.

Instead of answering, he slapped a palm against my butt, immediately cupping the area and rubbing the sting away. His teeth grazed my shoulder, nipping at the sensitive skin.

"For once in ye life, shut ye mouth and let me fucking work."

I opened my mouth again, a retort on the tip of my tongue but Ian beat me to the punch, sliding his cock into me, thrusting hard and fast, violently seating himself, possessing my body.

"Fuck!" I gasped, throwing my head back, my body clenching and clutching at his intrusion. "Fuck!"

"Good?" he asked, a dark chuckle on his lips.

"Shut up and keep moving."

He answered my demand with another spank, my pussy

clenching around his long member.

"Ah, I see ye like a little pain with ye pleasure."

He let go of my hands, lifting me up.

"What are you—" I broke off, my body bucking as sensations ratcheted through me, each building rapidly. He pulled my nipples, pinching my areolas with just the right amount of pain to send me spiraling.

"Ian!"

His body began to move, his cock thrusting in and out of me, hitting all the deliciously sensitive nerve endings.

Oh, God, how is this so good!?

Ian pulled back slightly, moving a little, changing his angle. My eyes rolled back into my head; a strangled moan ripped from my throat.

Holy God of thunder!

He answered me with a grunt, picking up his pace, his body rough and heavy, the weight and heat of him adding to the moment.

I felt like a peasant girl being ravaged by a conquering laird. My pleasure secondary to his release.

The thought tipped me over, my body spasming as wave after wave of hot, heated bliss crashed over me, every nerve in my body filled with liquid heat.

"Ian!"

"Fuck!"

He slapped my ass, sending me into another delicious spin.

"Fuck you," I grunted, pushing myself back against his cock. "Stop spanking me."

"Stop enjoying it."

Ian abandoned my nipples, one hand fisting in my hair, the other sliding down my body to find my clit.

"Ye're gonna come again, Liv. And this time, I'm coming too."

He pulled my head back, tipping my face until he could suck on my neck. His fingers circled, teasing then stroking even as his cock ground into me, the rough friction turning me into a whimpering mess.

As promised, I came in a wet, messy moment of utter perfection. Biting the inside of my cheek to keep from screaming, I arched back, offering myself to him in filthy submission.

Fuck you, Ian Campbell.

I hated him. I loathed his power over my body. I hated every minute of this.

So good. So goddamn good. Again, again, again!

I slipped forward, my body crushed by his as he came, dropping us both into the bed.

We lay for a moment, gasping for breath, his weight pressing me into the mattress, reality intruding.

Ah, reality check, Liv. You just fucked Ian. Ian who you hate. Ian who hates you. Ian fucking Campbell.

Shit.

He rolled off, giving my ass a little spank.

"Be right back, gotta take care of the condom."

He walked to the bathroom, closing the door.

For a moment I lay on the bed like one of those lambs that tip over when startled—still and silent, shocked by the pleasure still bouncing through my body, and the stark reality that I'd just had sex with Ian.

Well, shit.

I scrambled up, tossing my dress over my head and grabbing a blanket to wrap around myself and hide my braless state. In a mad dash, I found my shoes but couldn't locate my underwear—bra or panties.

I heard Ian flush the toilet, the faucet turning on as he washed his hands.

Go, go, go!

I left, heading back up to the reception, finding the majority of wedding guests were still dancing the night away.

Acting as if I hadn't just had the most mind-blowing sexual experience of my life.

I bypassed the tent, heading inside Gunnar's house to clean up and find some underwear. I met Astrid at the door.

"Hey, you okay? You disappeared."

"Mm, fine. Just needed to cool down."

Astrid laughed, slapping my shoulder. "You really burned up that dance floor. Pity you hate Ian so much. You guys looked amazing together."

With a gulp, I nodded, bearing my teeth in what I hoped was a sarcastic grin. "Yeah, such a pity."

Returning to the party, I found myself gliding around the dance floor with my father.

"One day this will be you, Livvy," he said, gesturing around the tent. "You and some dashing young man set to carry you away."

My gaze caught on the far side of the tent, Ian's red hair sticking out amongst the blonde, black, and brunette.

He stood leaning against a table, arms crossed, a small smile on his lips, his hair wild, beard crazy, his jacket discarded leaving him in black suit pants and a white collared shirt with the sleeves rolled up to his biceps.

Why is that so attractive?

Our gaze met, caught, held.

331

As Dad continued to get sentimental, I watched Ian, some foreign feeling taking up residence in my chest.

Finally, the song finished, Dad letting go of me to clap with the rest of the crowd. I did the same on autopilot, unable to break Ian's stare.

He inclined his head towards the entrance, one eyebrow arching in question. It was a blatant invitation, a request to join him once again.

With practiced determination I turned my back on him, drawing the last of my shredded dignity around me, putting space between us.

Back in your box, Ian. Back to the other side of the picket line.

"Another?" I asked my dad, lifting my arms in question.

"Always for my second favorite daughter."

With a laugh, I let him take the lead, whirling me around the dance floor, grinning at all his jokes.

When I next looked back, Ian was gone.

Chapter One

Liv

November 17

I sucked desperately on the ginger candy, willing the nausea that had plagued me for the last month to disappear. I didn't have time for whatever illness currently beleaguered me. I had a job offer to accept.

Thinking about this new opportunity sent my stomach into another spiral.

It's only the most important meeting of your life. Calm down.

I drew in a long breath, pressing the remains of the candy to the roof of my mouth, trying to suck at whatever tiny bit of ginger remained.

You can do this. You got this you glorious, badass, boss of a woman.

I checked my watch, noting it was ten minutes to the meeting.

Always be early.

I kicked off my flats, swapping them for heels. I shimmied a little, straightening the skirt of my corporate but fashionable navy dress.

You got this, Liv. Go crush it.

I exited my office, giving a nod to James, my assistant. "I'm just heading over to Bob's office. Do you need anything?"

"Nope, but good luck!" He flashed thumbs up at me. "Not that you need it."

With a sly grin, I nodded, setting off through the office heading for the elevator that would take me up to the C-suite.

I'd worked at Catch 22 Productions for over a decade now, clawing myself up the ranks, chipping away at the glass ceilings, carving out a niche in this male-dominated company. I'd started as a high school intern moving across the country to work summers in LA. Once I'd graduated, I'd studied at the American Film Institute, working at Catch 22 every evening and weekend, then graduated and taken on any job I could in an effort to cement my place in the company.

It'd worked. Five years ago, I'd been asked to build the reality TV branch of the company. I'm sure they expected a knock-off *Real Housewives*, or perhaps an equivalent of *Keeping up with the Kardashians* but instead, I'd built reality shows with heart. The shows we produced had integrity, honesty, and I'd built that arm to be one of our most successful products.

Shows like *The Queen of Clean*, where we helped people turn their lives around through organization and education. Or *Home Bound*, where we worked with a celebrity and the charity *Habitat for Humanity* to build homes for people who would otherwise never have the opportunity to own their own house. Or *Country Crush*, a dating show where we took eligible singles out to lonely farms across America all in hopes of them finding their one true love.

Proudly, *Country Crush* had resulted in three babies, eight marriages, and one town mayor writing to thank me for raising awareness of his town. Their tourism had doubled thanks to our show—allowing them to reopen some of the dying businesses and giving locals a much-needed economic boost.

But I wanted a new challenge. I wanted documentaries. I wanted to have an opportunity to go to the next level and produce series and shows that made people question what they knew. I wanted to sink my teeth into topics and explore. I'd pushed the boundaries with all of my shows, exploring issues like race, sexuality, gender, disability, and class in digestible but gentle ways. Documentaries would be an opportunity to push the envelope, to explore the meaty issues like why it was that that little town in rural America had a deficient of women and opportunity.

The elevator pinged softly, the doors sliding open to the C-Suite. With a bracing breath, I stepped into the plush suite, grinning at Jenny, Bob's executive assistant.

"He's just finishing up with Robbie Huynh," Jenny said with a grin. "He's such a nice boy." She lifted a hand fanning herself. "And ooh! Those arms? If I were twenty years younger…."

I grinned, giving her a wink. "I don't know, Jenny. I hear Aussies don't mind an older woman. Look at Hugh Jackman and Deborra-Lee Furness, there's like twelve years between them."

Jenny waved me off. "Oh, go on with you. That boy has more models and movie stars throwing themselves at him than a tomcat on a Saturday night."

I couldn't help but laugh at the analogy. Jenny was famous for strange examples.

"I thought Robbie was still in Australia?"

She shrugged. "Says he's got a proposal for Bob. Though goodness knows it's probably not going to be what he wants. Bob's set to keep him as the next big heartthrob. Wants to farm him out to some superhero movies. I think Robbie wants to explore his artistic side more."

I nodded, glancing at the door.

"Anyway, take a seat, Bob shouldn't be long. Can I get you something?"

I shook my head. "Nope, all good, thanks."

I settled on one of the comfortable chairs in his waiting area, listening to the rhythmic clicking of Jenny's keyboard while mentally going over my notes. My numbers were excellent, my ideas sound. In five years, I'd only needed to cancel two programs after the pilots had flopped. Both, I would point out, were ideas I'd inherited.

You've got this, Liv. There's no way he's saying no.

The door to Bob's office opened, Robbie stepping out.

"Thanks again," he said, shaking Bob's hand.

"I'll call you Thursday to discuss further." Bob clapped a hand on Robbie's shoulder. "And don't worry kid, we'll find the right fit for you."

"Yeah, thanks." Robbie turned away but not before I saw his jaw clench.

Bob watched him leave the suite, shaking his head before turning to me. "Liv, come on in."

"Good meeting?" I asked, following him into the room and closing the door behind us.

"You know how it is." He waved a hand around the room,

settling behind his giant wooden desk. "These kids come to Hollywood expecting to win an Oscar with some arty-farty indie shit. Sometimes you gotta be cruel to be kind. He'll come 'round."

I nodded, biting my tongue to keep from reminding Bob that Robbie's contract with us was up in March.

"Now, let's talk about you." He leaned back in his chair, knitting his hands over his solid belly. "You applied for the doco's job. Why?"

Excitement sizzled up my veins, those butterflies taking flight in my belly once more. I tried to ignore the accompanying nausea, swallowing hard.

"Well Bob, let's be honest. Documentaries has floundered in the last three years. We both know Jim wasn't that interested in the lead up to his retirement. We need fresh blood. Edgy content. New life. In the interview I gave to the panel last month I outlined—"

He stopped me with a dismissive wave of his hand. "This ain't an interview, Liv. I've already made a decision. I'm just wondering why you wanted to leave your position. You ain't docos, you're entertainment. And you're good at it."

I blinked, processing his words. "I'm sorry?"

"Your place is in entertainment, Hun. I'm sorry but I'm giving the job to Malone."

"Malone?" I repeated, shock rendering me incapable of further cognition.

"Yeah. The boy worked through documentaries in his undergrad."

I cleared my throat, feeling my chances at this job slipping away. "But, Bob, I worked two years in documentaries. I put in the hours through college. And shifting me from reality

337

makes more sense than moving him from—"

"Liv, my mind is made up."

"Bob," I leaned forward, desperation creeping into my tone. "I need this. My numbers are solid. My team is trained. Please. There's no reason for me to stay."

"Actually, those numbers are the exact reason we want you to stay." He sat forward, his rotund belly pressing against his desk. "Your productions are one of our biggest earners. We can't afford to lose that."

I floundered for a moment, my mouth opening and closing but no noise came out. I forcefully brought myself under control, yanking back my emotions and stuffing them into a little box.

"So, what you're saying, is that I'm too successful for you to lose?" I finally asked.

"Them the facts, Liv."

"And the board agreed to this?"

He nodded.

"And the selection panel?"

He sighed, running a hand over his face. "Look, you were always a shoo-in for it. But like I said, we can't afford to lose you."

I nodded, an eerie calm settling over me. "How long?"

"How long what?" he asked, a frown marring his forehead.

"How long do I stay in reality? How long before you let me move elsewhere?"

He shrugged. "I don't know. How long is a piece of string?"

I nodded. "And there's no option for Malone and I to share the documentary role?"

He laughed. "No, definitely not. That wouldn't be fair to the kid."

I nodded again. "What about allowing me to produce a few documentaries a year? Maybe one a quarter?"

"Liv, please. I need you to focus on reality. We both know that's where your talent lies."

I sucked in a breath, taking that gut punch.

"Okay, so just to clarify. I was the top candidate for the position but you and the board decided to give it to Malone because I'm too successful in my job. And you cannot foresee any possible scenario where I could produce a documentary at this time. Is that right?"

He nodded, grinning. "Yeah, that about sums it up."

I stood, smoothing down my skirt before holding a hand out for him to shake. He took it automatically, the smile on his lips turning into a frown.

"Bob, thank you. It's been an absolute privilege working for Catch 22. As per my contract, consider this my two weeks' notice. I'm meant to be on vacation as of tomorrow so I'll have my desk cleared out by lunch today." I dropped his hand, stepping back. "I'm happy to do handover with my replacement once they start. My suggestion would be to look at Caroline. She's got both the experience and creativity. But considering this company seems to still be a boy's club if you don't want Caroline, look at Omar. He's young but knows people. He'll do right by you."

I paused, considering if there was anything else I needed to say.

Nope. You're good.

With a final nod, I turned on my heel, reaching for the door. "Goodbye, Bob."

That galvanized my former boss into action. "Liv! Wait!"

I ripped the door open, striding through the suite.

"See ya later, Hun!" Jenny called from her desk.

"Bye, Jenny. And FYI, I just quit." Saying it aloud freed something in me, a weight lifting from my shoulders. "If you wanna catch up for coffee, let me know."

I stepped into the waiting elevator, hitting my floor. As the doors began to slide closed, Bob exited his office shouting my name while Jenny stared at me, her mouth open, eyes wide.

Back on my floor, I headed immediately for my office, beginning to throw all my personal items into a box.

"Um... Liv?"

I glanced up, finding James loitering at the door. "Come in, you can help me pack."

He entered, glancing at the box then at me. "Um, what's happening?"

"Oh, I quit. They refused to give me the job so I just... quit." I shrugged.

"What will you do?" he asked, opening up one of my drawers and beginning to automatically sort through the items.

"I don't know yet." I paused, tipping my head to the side as I considered my options. "Actually, I know exactly what I'm gonna do."

"Yeah?"

"Mmhm, start my own company."

James coughed, eyes wide, eyebrows lifted. "Seriously?"

"Uh-huh." I finished stuffing my things into the box then gestured at the awards hung around the room. "Can you hold these for me? I'll send someone to pick them and anything else up later this afternoon."

"Of course." He glanced around. "Is there anything else

you need?"

I thought for a minute. "Send me my personal contact list, not the one the company keeps on file. That's it."

I lifted the heavy box then paused. "James, if you want in on this, let me know. I'd love to have you once I get this process started."

He swallowed audibly. "Liv, you're the best boss I've ever had. But health insurance…."

I laughed, nodding. "I'll call you once it's all sorted. No harm no foul if it ends up not being for you."

With that, I shifted, placing the box on my hip, grabbed my tote then walked out. I could feel the glances and questions from the bullpen but I ignored it, secure in my decision.

You're too badass for this place.

Outside, I flagged a cab, settling into the back seat with a sigh.

"Bad day?" the cabby asked with a pointed look at my box of belongings.

"Nope, perfect day."

He took off from the sidewalk, leaving the headquarters of Catch 22 in the rear-view mirror.

My stomach, which had been playing ball up to this moment, rolled, moisture flooding my mouth.

"Pull over!"

I threw the door open, leaning out to vomit in the gutter, my body heaving as I emptied what little I'd consumed today into the street.

"Sorry," I whispered, pulling a tissue from my tote and wiping my mouth. "I think I've picked up a bug. Can't seem to shake it."

"Sure you aren't pregnant?" the cabby asked with a grin.

"Seems to be going around at the moment."

I froze, my heart racing as my mind went blank.

Oh shit. Ohhhhhh shit!

The symptoms checked out. The timing might be right too.

"Umm, can you stop by a pharmacy?"

The cabby glanced my way, one eyebrow cocked. "Sure."

Fuck.

Chapter Two

Liv

I stared at my landlord, my box of belongings in one arm, my tote holding the dreaded pregnancy test in the other.

"I'm sorry, did you say flooded?"

Warren nodded, grimacing. "Those fucking builders hit a water pipe. Sorry, doll, but your apartment and everyone else on your level is flooded. Whole building's gotta be evacuated until they can repair the damage. Electric is shot. Ain't safe to do much more than get some valuables and hightail it outta here."

I blinked, processing this news. "Are you saying I have to find a hotel?"

"More like a short-stay apartment. Gonna be weeks if not months before we can fix the damage. Motherfuckers," he swore, shaking his head.

Months!?

"Um, right." I stared at Mrs. Gelder, the old woman had her soaking wet Pekinese-cross tucked under one arm and was struggling to pull a roller suitcase behind her with the other. As I watched, her son arrived, lifting the bag easily

343

and walking her to his car.

"I better go see what I can salvage."

In my apartment, I stared in stunned dismay at the damage. Brown, smelly water squished underfoot and dripped like rain from the ceiling. Every item of clothing, furniture, or knickknack lay in soaked ruin. There was little to recover here.

"Well… fuck."

I shrugged off my jacket, using it to wipe water from my counter and place my box on the semi-dry spot.

"Okay, Liv, you've lived through worse than this moment. Let's prioritize, organize, and mobilize."

My stomach rumbled, reminding me that it'd been a while since I'd managed to keep anything down.

"And then food."

I pulled suitcases from my closet, lining them with garbage bags to keep the water from soaking into the lining. I wrung out my saturated clothing before tossing them into the bags and piling it all into the suitcases. My paintings were ruined, my photos completely destroyed. Any electrical items would need to be tossed, but I had everything backed up on the cloud so I wasn't worried.

In a surprisingly short amount of time, I'd packed up my life, searching the apartment for any small sentimental item I'd missed. There were none. This apartment in which I'd spent the last three years of my life was surprisingly devoid of personality.

Maybe this is for the best.

The thought popped into my head as I loaded myself into another cab, this time heading for a hotel near the airport.

You can start fresh, try out a new life. A new Liv, if you will.

In the hotel, I handed over my soggy clothing to the concierge, who assured me they'd put a rush on it. In my room, I called the airline getting my flight swapped to the first one out tomorrow and cancelling my return. I ordered room service, showered then, wrapped in a cozy robe, I stared at the pregnancy test, my bladder protesting its fullness.

"Okay, Liv. Let's do this."

I read the instructions twice just to ensure I understood completely.

It's just peeing on a stick. Who knew there was an art to this?

Mid-stream I stuck the stick in my pee, grimacing as some got on my hand.

I can't believe some women choose to do this.

Fully peed, I lay the stick on the bathroom sink and hit the timer on my phone pacing as I determinedly ignored looking at the test until the alarm went off.

Beep, beep, beep.

I sucked in a breath then flipped it over, my heart stuttering to a stop.

Two lines. Positive. I'm pregnant. I'm motherfucking pregnant.

"Oh shit." I dropped onto the toilet, cradling my head in my hands. "Homeless, jobless, pregnant. What am I gonna do now?"

Reality hit, horror dawning.

"Oh, God," I placed a shaky hand on my belly, staring down at my hand. "I'm pregnant with a sasquatch."

Chapter Three

Ian

I poured coffee into my mug, struggling against the haze of exhaustion that had settled on my shoulders.

It was still early enough that none of the guys had arrived at the Thor's Shipbuilding workshop for work yet but late enough that the first blush of dawn had begun to light the sky.

I watched the grey lighten to a soft pink and orange out the kitchenette window, sipping my coffee and thinking about nothing in particular.

I'd moved into the tiny apartment above the workshop last week. My rental had sold last month, and I'd decided to take the plunge and buy a property. Unfortunately, it wouldn't close until Monday, which had left me temporarily homeless. Thankfully, Erik had offered me the loft apartment and I'd happily accepted.

The tiny apartment had everything I needed—bed, small lounge area, and kitchenette with breakfast bar. When Erik had adopted his twin boys, he'd moved out of the apartment leaving it vacant. His sister, Astrid, occasionally stayed here over the college breaks, but the place remained empty for most of the year only occasionally serving as temporary accommodation for one of our staff.

I lifted the mug to my lips again, the sip getting caught in my throat as I caught sight of a woman wrangling with the lock on our front gate.

Or should I say *the* woman.

Coughing, I dropped the mug in the sink, a curse forming on my tongue as I headed for the stairs.

What the fuck is she doing here?

I didn't have time to pull on boots, instead slipping my socked feet into flip-flops before thundering down the stairs and out into the yard.

The Harpy had managed to get the gate open; her curses audible from across the yard as she struggled to pull a giant suitcase through the small gap she'd left herself.

"What are you doing?"

She froze, her body stiffening as her head twisted slowly in my direction.

"Oh no." She dropped the suitcase, turning fully to me, her hands coming up as if to ward me off. "No, no, no, no, no!"

"Oh, hush ye mouth," I barked, stopping just out of arm's reach from her. I'd learned my lesson, never be within slapping distance of Liv Larsson.

Except when you kiss her...

I shoved the thought away, crossing my arms over my chest, suddenly aware of the fact I wore only socks with flip-flops and a pair of navy boxer shorts.

"What are ye doing here, Liv?" I asked, brazening this out.

She crossed her arms, mimicking my stance. "I think the

347

better question is what are *you* doing here and dressed like—"
She waved her hand at me. "—that."

"Staying in the apartment. Not that it's any of ye business."

She blanched, her face paling. "Y-y-you're staying here?"

I frowned, suddenly uneasy. "Yeah. Ye got a problem with that?"

She dropped her arms, her hands fluttering for a moment before settling on her belly covering it in a pose that was all too familiar.

"Ah fuck." I shook my head. "Ye're pregnant."

Her eyes widened, her face paling further as she stared at me. "How… how did you…?"

I nodded at the possessive hands over her belly. "My sisters have had a parcel of kids between them. Ye think I don't recognize that pose?"

Her gaze dropped, staring for a beat at her hands as if they were foreign objects. She moved, both hands coming up to press against her cheeks.

"I'm gonna be sick."

I stepped back as she bent, her body heaving as she vomited onto the gravel lot.

"Well, shit. Can hardly be mad at ye now." I moved, laying my hands on her back and gently rubbing. "It'll be alright, lass. Let it up."

I continued to rub her back in what I hoped was a soothing pattern as anger sizzled my blood.

Where's the father? Bet it's some fancy Hollywood type with more money than sense whose abandoned her. I better call the Larssons and tell them to sharpen the pitchforks.

Liv interrupted my silent tirade, spitting on the ground then groaning as she straightened, my hands catching her

348

as she stumbled backwards.

"Thanks," she whispered, turning back to her piled luggage. "Let me just get some water and I'll go."

"Over my dead body," I told her, reaching for the giant suitcase. "I may not be the most chivalrous male on the planet, but I can at least offer ye a cup of tea while ye wait for ye family to arrive."

"I can't have—"

"Ginger tea," I interrupted, cutting off her protest. "Come on, I'll bring ye things in."

She stood, wringing her hands together as I easily lifted her luggage, leading the way across the yard.

Even pale and sweaty with greasy hair and vomit breath, Liv took my breath away. Beautiful didn't cut it. She'd always glowed, burning brighter than the rest of us. A lesser man may try to dim that light but I'd always found it her most attractive trait.

Pity it came attached to that mouth of hers.

Is it though? Ye liked that mouth on yer—

I killed that thought, mentally imaging Liv vomiting over it.

Pregnant. Needing help. Keep it in ye pants, Campbell.

Upstairs I discarded her luggage, then set about making tea. Liv stood awkwardly, her big coat wrapped tight around her, as if it were a shield protecting her from me.

"Take a seat before someone thinks ye're a coat rack." I gestured at the barstools, frowning when she didn't respond with a quick retort.

This isn't good.

The kettle boiled and I poured the water, watching as Liv slid onto one of the stools, slowly dragging her coat off and laying it across her lap. She slumped on her seat, staring at her hands as they rested on the kitchen counter.

"Here." I placed the mug before her, the steam billowing out and sending the strong scent of ginger into the air. "Now hit me with it. Tell Uncle Ian what's wrong."

Alarm bells rang in my ears when she didn't take the bait, just reached out a hand to pull the mug to her then wrapped both palms around the warm ceramic.

I waited, expecting Liv to speak. When she remained silent, those alarm bells turned into emergency warnings, loud and insistent.

I yanked the fridge open, removing two bottles of beer. Uncapping them both, I slid one across the counter to her nodding at it.

"Ye can't drink it, and I've to be at work in an hour. So, I'll allow ye to sniff it while ye tell me what's on ye mind."

She chuckled, the corners of her generous mouth lifting a few beats before dropping once more.

"I didn't get the documentary role. I wanted it, Ian. Badly."

That's what this is about? Not the babe?

"There'll be other roles."

"No." She shook her head. "Or at least not at Catch 22. Bob, my boss, made that clear. I'm too valuable doing infotainment, reality TV pays and they need me to keep it profitable." She pulled the beer to her face, taking a deep inhale.

"I quit my job."

I sucked in a breath. "But ye love working there."

She shrugged. "I thought I did. But now, looking back, I realize I had to fight for everything. Every idea, every new production, every budget." She looked up, pinning me with her baby blues. "They used to do business meetings at the local men's club. I'd have to get a read out of the minutes to find out what decisions had been made. It took me eighteen months to get that changed."

"What the fuck? Did we fall back into the 1940s and I missed it?"

She chuckled, the sound dry and humorless. "Yeah. I guess I stayed because I thought I could make a difference. I don't mind fighting, and I was winning, you know?" She blew out a sigh. "Or at least I thought I was."

I waited, rolling the beer bottle between my palms, comfortable with the silence as Liv searched for more words.

"I quit. I realized there was nothing for me there anymore. So, I just up and quit."

I nodded, encouraging her to continue.

She ran a hand over her face. "I'm starting my own company. From here, in the Cape. I'll move back home, hire a cheap workspace, and we'll operate out of there for a while." Her lips twisted up into a small grin, some of the sparkle that she'd been missing reigniting.

"What about ye apartment?"

She laughed, shaking her head. "I think the universe is transpiring against me. My apartment's flooded. Some builder hit the main water pipe. The place is a write-off."

I winced. "Ouch. What a week, huh?"

"Yeah."

She fiddled with the label on her beer bottle, the silence suddenly awkward.

"So ye don't need to be in LA for filming?"

She shook her head. "With documentaries they can be filmed anywhere. It'll probably be good to set up an LA office further down the track, but in the meantime the Cape will work. The local tax breaks are awesome, and I have a support network here for when the baby comes."

And there it is. The baby elephant in the room.

"Ah, the baby...." I sucked in a breath. "Are ye keeping it?"

Liv's face flushed but she nodded. "Are you angry?"

I shook my head. "Never, lass. Ye'll be a good mother. Great. I see how ye are with ye siblings. Bossing them about like a little mother hen. Ye'll love the little one fiercely."

She blew out a breath. "Thanks. What about you?"

"Me?" I blinked, eyebrows raising in surprise.

"Yeah. Will you love her or him?"

I scratched my chest, suddenly aware of the fact I still wasn't wearing a shirt. "Well... I guess. I mean, I love ye brother's kids like they're me own."

The pinched expression on her face relaxed slightly. "And visitation? We'll have to work that out."

"Visit—" I broke off, a deadly chill freezing the blood in my veins. "Liv... are... are ye saying ye're pregnant with my babe?"

She frowned. "I thought... yes. Who else did you think?"

Around me the world began to sparkle, black dots winking in my vision.

"But... we used a condom...." My protestation sounded weak and breathy, as if I'd run up the side of a mountain at full steam.

"I think it must have been a dud. Or, maybe you have super sperm? All I know is I haven't slept with anyone but you for over twelve months. Likely longer." She leaned forward, resting a hand on my arm. "Ian, you're the father."

And just like that my world blanked, my vision going

black.

"Ian!"

Chapter Four

Liv

Well, I hadn't planned for this scenario.

I stood over Ian, staring down at the sasquatch passed out on the kitchen floor. He'd crumbled slowly rather than fainting, so at least I didn't need to look for head injuries. I leaned over, giving his hand a hard squeeze.

"Ian, wake up. Ian?"

He moaned, his eyes flickering open for a moment before they settled on my waist then rolled back into his head, his body flopping back onto the floor once more.

Father of my child, ladies and gentlemen!

With a sigh, I found a pillow and blanket, propping his big head up and covering his half-naked form.

Now what?

This wasn't at all how I'd seen today going. The exhaustion I'd been fighting overtook me, the last of my adrenaline dissipating to leave behind a bone aching weariness.

I looked to Ian's bed with its crumbled sheets and messy comforter. It invited me to sit awhile and rest my weary head.

Maybe just for a moment. Just until Ian wakes.

With a groan I sank onto the soft mattress, Ian's scent enveloping me.

Stupid sasquatch.

I closed my eyes for a moment, finding the mixed scent of saw dust, cinnamon and clean laundry strangely comforting.

I'll close my eyes for a moment. Just a minute. Just... one... minute....

* * *

Ian

Why am I on the floor?

Not only was I on the floor, but I seemed to be laying in the kitchen covered by a blanket with a pillow under my head. It took a moment for the memory of Liv's announcement to return.

Ah, ye shithead. Ye've royally cocked that up.

Did one normally faint at the news of their impending fatherhood? I couldn't recall any of my siblings mentioning this occurrence but then they'd all been safely wedded before being bedded in a way that had resulted in progeny.

Fuck.

I pushed up from the floor, glancing at the clock above my bed only for my gaze to stutter and halt on the woman curled around my remaining pillow.

For a tall, statuesque woman she looked remarkably small and vulnerable in my bed, the dark circles around her eyes suddenly more pronounced in sleep.

On quiet feet, I gently pulled a blanket over her then shuffled around the apartment, dressing as quietly as I could. I scribbled a note on a scrap of paper, dropping it on the kitchen counter before heading down into the warehouse.

"Morning," Erik called when I walked in the office. "Coffee's on."

My boss flipped through the mail, opening bills and muttering to himself as I poured a cup.

"Erik?"

"Mm?"

I hesitated, knowing this wasn't going to end well. "Liv is upstairs in the apartment. Rocked up early this morning."

Erik looked up from his papers. "Liv? As in my sister Liv?"

"Aye."

Erik frowned. "I'm sorry, I think I misheard. My sister is upstairs? As in upstairs in your apartment?"

I nodded, shuffling from foot to foot. "Arrived early this morning. Thought the apartment would be empty."

"Ah," Erik nodded, leaning back in his seat. "Is she coming down?"

I shook my head. "Poor lass passed out on my bed." I took a sip of the pot coffee, grimacing at the cheap brew. "Brother, ye need to up yer coffee game. This isn't fit for human consumption."

He tossed a pen my way, the tip hitting my chest and bouncing to the floor. "Shut it, you bourgeois coffee snob."

"What can I say? Yer brother has ruined me for all time. The way he pours a cup of coffee…." I made a chef's kiss motion. "Bliss."

Erik laughed, shaking a finger in my direction. "I'll tell him you said that. I'm sure Gabby'll be pleased to know

356

you're competition for his affections."

"Whose affections?" Gabby asked, walking through the door.

"Ye husband-to-be. That man can make a cup of coffee like nobody's business."

Gabby paused, her hand on the coffee pot. "Did Erik make this."

I nodded glumly, holding my mug up. "Tastes like Satan's ass."

"Hey!" Erik shoved up from the desk. "I know how to make coffee, okay? I just happen to like mine strong."

"Strong enough a damned spoon could stand in it," I muttered, grimacing again at the taste.

"Changing subject," Erik drawled, shooting me the bird. "Why is Liv passed out on your bed."

Gabby's head shot up. "Excuse me? Liv as in our Liv?"

I nodded, my heart doing a weird tap dance as I attempted to skirt the issue.

"She caught the red eye. Doubt she meant to fall asleep, just sat down for a moment then passed out. Suspect she'll be out for a few hours."

Erik pulled his phone free, thumb scrolling across the screen. "She didn't post anything in family chat."

"Didn't call us either," Gabby said, adding creamer and three packets of sugar to her strong as sin coffee. "Normally we get a little advanced notice of when the whirlwind is arriving."

I cleared my throat, finding myself giving into the strangest sensation—a need to protect the mother of my child.

"Perhaps she wanted to surprise ye," I crossed my arms,

trying for a casual shrug. "It is nearly Thanksgiving after all."

Gabby and Erik exchanged a look then shrugged.

"Maybe," Erik said, looking back down at his paperwork. "Alright, let's get to it."

Gabby led the way out the door, her coffee in hand. I trailed, glancing up at the apartment above the workshop where Liv still slept.

I have no idea what we're doing but I'm not giving up my child without a fight.

With that decided, I got to work, trying to lose myself in the demanding physicality of the job I loved.

Chapter Five

Liv

I stared at myself in the mirror of Ian's bathroom.

Is that a bump?

I cupped hands around my belly, giving it a little jiggle.

"Oh, God, it's a bump."

I reached for my phone quickly googling *how many months before baby bump?*

Google, as always, had held the answers to my life's mysteries.

You'll likely notice the first signs of a bump early in the second trimester, between weeks 12 and 16.

I did the sums, counting back to Gunnar's wedding.

"Thirteen weeks. Thirteen goddamned weeks." I looked down at my stomach, the tiny little pooch staring right back at me. "Well, we can't say you're not prompt. You must get that from me."

I'd known about the baby for less than twenty-four hours and here I was assigning traits to her.

Or him. Shit. When can I find out the sex? Is it possible to raise a baby gender neutral? Oh, God!

I spent the next hour sitting in a towel on the edge of the bathtub googling baby and parenthood questions.

"Liv?" Ian's voice floated through the door, a gentle tap following. "Ye in here?"

I yanked the door open, staring at the man who'd done this to me.

"You!"

His eyebrows went up, eyes widening as he took in my towel-clad body. "Um, are ye—"

"You did this to me!"

The man's face flushed. "I'd say it took two."

"Do you have any idea what kind of person it takes to raise a child in this day and age? I didn't!" I held up my phone. "Google tells me that good parents raise children that will positively contribute to society. I'M NOT A GOOD PARENT! I CAN'T DO THIS!"

He reached out and I tried to dodge his hand but the tiny bathroom severely limited my ability to maneuver. Ian snagged my arm, gently but deliberately, pulling me into his chest. He wrapped me in a hug that felt all encompassing, cradling me in such a way that I felt surrounded without feeling suppressed.

"Ye'll be a great mamma," he told me, his big hand cupping the back of my hair and gently stroking. "Ye love ye little nephews fiercely. Ye'll do the same for this wee one, I've no doubt."

I nodded against his chest, my fingers clutching his plaid overshirt, the smell of woodchips, oil and soap both familiar and nostalgic. My father had smelled like Ian, my brothers, my grandfather. I'd grown up around men who smelled like hard work and clean living. And it felt comforting to be

360

embraced by someone who reminded me of all the men I loved in my life... even if I hated Ian with the fire of a billion suns.

"Ye good?" he asked after a long moment, his hand still gently caressing my hair.

"Yeah." I stepped back, hitching the towel which had fallen slightly. "I should get dressed. I need to eat, find a place to live, and announce to my family the baby situation."

Ian cleared his throat. "Ye're planning on keeping it then?"

My eyebrows rose, my temper flaring, any good will gone. "Of course I'm keeping it! It's our baby! Do you think I'm this conflicted about parenting because I'm planning to discard our child?"

He held hands up in a pacifying gesture. "Yer body, yer rules. I'm not here to judge, lass. I'm here to help no matter what option you choose. And thankfully, unlike some, ye do have options. And support. And a man who's willing to do whatever's necessary to support ye and the wee one."

That took some of the heat out of my temper.

Ian lifted his big hand, cupping my cheek. "So tell me what ye need right now."

"Pie."

He pulled back a little at the same time it hit me what I'd just asked for.

"Pie?"

I nodded, my stomach grumbling. "Yeah, actually. Pie."

The nausea that had hovered at the edges of my conscience for the past few months suddenly evaporated, my mouth actually watering as I thought about pie.

Pregnant.

No job.

No home.

This definitely called for pie.

"Pie. Right. What type? Pumpkin? Lime? Pecan?"

"Yes. And chocolate."

Ian cocked an eyebrow. "Sorry, did ye just want the chocolate?"

"No, bring me all of it."

Ian tilted his head in my direction as if he hadn't quite heard me. "All…?"

I nodded, rubbing my little bump. "And cherry. Oh, and blueberry if they have it? Actually, give me five minutes to get dressed and I'll come with you. We can hit up Cathy's Bakery."

I made a move to stand but Ian clapped a hand on my shoulder keeping me in place.

"Stay. I'll get ye pie. Just get decent and I'll be back."

He left, shutting the door, leaving me with a rumbling tummy and a baby bump.

Story of my fucking life.

Chapter Six

Ian

Liv wasn't kidding about the pies. The woman was hoovering them with the enthusiasm of a rabid labrador.

"Ye want to slow down?" I asked as she finished her second pie and began reaching for the third.

"Um, you want to shut your pie hole?" she retorted, pulling the bakery box to her and lifting the lid. "I have hardly eaten in months. This baby wants pie? This baby gets pie."

I shook my head, watching her scoop up a giant chunk of cherry filling. "Are ye really blaming our unborn baby for yer need to inhale pie?"

She paused, fork hovering just in front of her lips. "Is this really a conversation you want to be having, Ian?"

Sensing I was far out of my depth I kept my mouth shut.

"Good choice." She moaned as the cherry coated bite disappeared between her lips, her eyelids drifting close, her head tipping back to savor the taste.

Unbidden and unwelcome memories surfaced.

Liv bent over the bed. My hand fisted in her hair, drawing her head back, baring her neck for me to taste. Pressing hot, hungry

363

kisses along her throat. Nipping at her as my cock—

Pull it together man!

My cock didn't get the message. The traitor stiffened, pulsing in angry protest when I made no attempt to reach across the table and kiss Liv.

She's pregnant, ye filthy bugger. Settle down.

She may be pregnant, but she ain't dead... neither are you.

"Does Erik know you're up here?"

Liv pulled me from my thoughts.

"Aye."

"What did you tell him?"

I shrugged. "Just that I was taking a half-day. I've worked overtime the last few weeks on a project or two, and ye know we set our own times around here."

She nodded; her mouth full of cherry pie.

I bet she tastes delicious.

I shoved that away, locking it in a dungeon in the recesses of my mind.

Jesus, this is the Harpy, remember?

I remember the way her mouth felt when she—

"So when are we telling ye parents the news?" I asked, my gut pinching.

Liv stopped chewing, her nose wrinkling as she swallowed. "Ah, about that."

"I suspect it'll be hard to keep the bump hidden in another month or so."

She blew out a breath. "So, here's the thing... I've been thinking."

Uh-oh.

"We should probably tell them tonight. But if they suspect for even a moment that we're not in love, it's going to be hell."

I coughed, choking on air. "Sorry, did ye say in *love?*"

She nodded, forking another bite of cherry pie. "You know my parents, and Nan for that matter. They'll accept anything so long as it includes love."

"But… they all know we hate each other."

She cocked her eyebrow at me, her fork held at a jaunty angle. "I'd say this baby bump proves otherwise."

I swallowed, attempting to get moisture back into my mouth. "Ye want me to pretend."

She nodded. "At least until the baby's born. Then we can say that we parted amicably."

"And the wee one?"

She hesitated, chewing for a long moment. "That depends. How involved do you want to be?"

My gaze dropped to the tiny swell of her belly and I felt something I'd never experienced before. A strange mixture of fierce protection, abject fear, and a love so strong I knew I'd die with it burning in my gut.

"At a push? A hundred and ten percent."

She sighed, finally discarding the fork, one hand unconsciously resting on her stomach. "I thought so."

"Ye have an issue with that?"

She shook her head. "No, just complicates things. I'm prepared to raise our baby alone. You being in the picture makes this simultaneously harder and easier."

"Because of ye job?"

She nodded then shook her head. "Yes and no. If you're keen then I want our child to have even time with their parents. But shared parenting also means we need to be on the same page about their upbringing."

"Alright, let's work through it." I reached for a slice of cherry pie, noting Liv's eyes narrow as she watched me spoon it onto my plate.

Greedy wench.

"Do you have pen and paper?"

I waved a hand towards the kitchenette. "I'm sure somewhere in there."

"In that case I'll use my phone. That way I can email you a copy."

I hid a smile, amused that Liv thought a twenty-minute conversation followed by a no doubt well-crafted email could solve all our problems.

"Oh! Google has a questionnaire available." She looked up grinning. "You ready for us to work out how different we are?"

"Not sure we need a quiz to tell us that but go on."

"Okay, what religion should we raise the baby?"

My eyebrows lifted. "I didn't take ye for a God-fearing type."

"I'm not. But my family is... Lutheran? Pentecostal?" She shrugged. "Something like that. I'm sure Mom will want them to know that side."

I nodded. "We're Catholic, born and raised. But I have no particular ties to it." The palm of my hand gave an involuntary twitch, a reminder of school-boy punishments dished out by the head Nun.

"Let's say Christian, then."

"Works for me."

She made a note on her phone. "Oh, should we call your parents?"

A bitterness twisted in my gut. "We can announce after

we tell your family. Let's just see how that goes first."

Liv nodded, absently flicking a chunk of hair from her face. "I'll admit, I don't remember ever meeting your parents."

Good.

"Aye, it's rare they come out to America. Ye've met Mam, though it was a fleeting visit."

"How many siblings do you have?"

"Eight. Last I checked."

She laughed as if it were a joke. "Wow, your house must have been a riot growing up."

Not quite.

I nodded vaguely. "Next question?"

Liv looked down at her phone, reading, "Bottle or breast?"

"Uh, I suspect that's up to you, lass."

She shook her head, scrunching up her nose. "Bottle means you can take her overnight. Breast means she'll have to stay with me full time for the first few months."

"But what do ye want?" I asked softly, watching her face carefully.

A naked longing crossed her face before it was wiped clear. *Breast it is then.*

"Maybe... I mean... if you don't mind—"

"Pop breast down on ye list. We'll make it work."

"Are you sure?"

I nodded, watching as a small pleased blush colored her cheeks. "Next question?"

"Vaccinations?"

I blanched. "That bloody well better be a trick question."

She laughed, typing on the screen. "Pro-vaccines. Agreed. How about discipline?"

"I don't believe in hitting."

"Good, neither do I." She gave me an approving look. "Circumcision?"

My cock, which had remained at half-mast through this entire conversation, shriveled. "Not a fan of genital mutilation."

"Good, neither am I."

"Photos online?"

I crossed my arms, bracing for a battle. "No. No baby of mine is having a digital footprint before they can even walk."

"Um, agreed." Liv raised an eyebrow. "Why is this so easy?"

No idea.

"Raising the child?" She asked.

"Well that should be easy, we're both in the Cape for now. And when we get to a point that changes then we'll make decisions together."

Liv raised a hand, nibbling absently on her thumbnail. "Speaking of, I'm going to need to find a house. Or at least an apartment."

The words rolled off my tongue before I could think better of it. "No ye won't. Ye'll move in with me."

Silence dominated the room, Liv staring at me with her big blue eyes.

In the pause I took her in. She'd showered, her hair now slightly damp but clean, the blonde shiny and soft looking. She'd dressed casually, jeans and a navy-blue T-shirt, but still managed to look like a million dollars.

"Move in with you?" she repeated, her hand now rubbing her stomach. "Why would I do that?"

"I... I want the full experience."

God, it feels weird to admit that.

Liv's eyebrows, already lifted, surged a fraction higher.

"I'm sorry?"

"I want to see ye get round with our babe. I want to rub ye ankles when they're swollen and go with ye to the appointments. I wanna be there for ye, Liv. And when our babe is older and going through this themselves—if they choose to—then I want to have that point of reference. I want to be the man, the father, they'd expect me to be from the verra moment I knew of them."

My voice had grown thick, emotion clogging my throat.

"But you don't even like me," she pointed out, as if that changed anything.

"I like ye. Ye just niggle me the wrong way sometimes."

"I... what? No I don't."

"Aye, ye do." I pointed a forkful of pie in her direction. "Ye constantly hen pecking me, making me out to be some kind of neanderthal as if I've not a brain in my head."

"I know you have a brain. It's the rest of you that's the issue."

My eyebrows rose, surprise coloring my reaction. "Ye want to explain more?"

She waved a hand dismissively. "You know what you did."

"What *I* did?"

What the devil is she on about?

"Yeah, that first year."

I tried to remember, wracking my brains and coming up empty. "Ye're gonna have to enlighten me."

"Wait, you really don't remember?"

I shook my head, completely mystified by this turn of events.

"Ian." Liv's big blue eyes searched my face, her cheeks flushing with anger. "Please tell me you're joking."

Something lit in my gut, a rough kind of anticipation. "Tell me."

"You… you…." Liv slapped a hand on the table top, practically vibrating with rage. "You idiot! I got drunk one night and you happened to be in the bar. I was home for the holidays and blowing off steam. Remember that?"

A hazy memory came to me, Liv in a low-cut dress, her ass practically hanging out while her breasts bounced enticingly. She'd been young, wild, and carefree. I'd been young, wild, and far too randy.

"You freaking hauled me over your shoulder, took me out to the parking lot and spanked me! Spanked, Ian! Like I was two freaking years old. Then you called my brothers to come pick me up as if I were some naughty child and not an adult. You were completely out of line!"

A newer memory transferred itself, clinging greedily as I listened to Liv rage.

My cock fucking Liv with wild abandon. Liv under me, squirming, panting, desperate. The clench of her. The feel. Years of frustration, annoyance and attraction channeled into mind-fucking pleasure.

Liv pushed to her feet beginning to pace, her hands waving wildly in agitation.

My hand curved around her throat; my palm still hot from spanking her ass. Her resistance followed by her sweet submission.

My cock hardened pressing against my zipper.

Kiss her.

I pushed up, stalking across the small space to back Liv against the wall. She stared at me with wide eyes, any anger momentarily wiped from her expression.

"What are you doing?"

"What's it look like, ye daft lass? I'm kissing ye." I leaned down, my lips a bare whisper from hers when hands slapped into my chest, forcing me back a step.

"Uh-uh. No way, bucko. Thanks for the offer, but no thanks. The last time we kissed I ended up pregnant. This—" She gestured between us, "—it ain't happening."

Masculine sexual outrage lit my blood, the need to prove her wrong nearly overwhelming.

Ye're not that kind of man. Get a hold of yeself.

I pulled back, physically turning away from her, fighting with my control, reigning in the desire to imprint my body upon this woman's.

"I'm sorry," I said finally, turning back around to face her. "For then and now. I'm sorry I was a neanderthal and made ye feel less. Ye're not, Liv. Ye never have been. Yer a talented, beautiful woman. If anything, I wanted ye to be mine back then and was likely sloshed myself that night. And I'm sorry for now. For getting ye pregnant and for wanting to kiss ye. I'm not sorry for the babe, could never be, but I'm sorry for the complication I've added."

For a moment Liv just looked at me, her expression shuttered. A heartbeat passed and as I watched she crumpled, her body bowing in, her face falling as she began to sob as if her world were ending.

"Ooch, come here." I hauled her into my arms, and into a chair, slightly concerned at its ability to hold our combined weight as it groaned in protest under us.

"Y-y-you can't be nice to me one minute and a complete dickhead the next! It's not fair!" she wailed, one fist pounding at my chest. "Not when I'm unemployed, homeless

371

and pregnant! I've never been even *one* of those! This is really hard!"

She cried and I let her, listening and making soothing noises. She needed to let it out, purge herself of grief and stress.

It took a while but finally she quietened, the only sound little hitches of her breath and the occasional hiccup.

"We'll get through this," I promised, cupping her head and pressing a kiss to her crown.

"Yeah."

Her soft agreement warmed me, giving me hope.

Perhaps we can make this work.

Chapter Seven

Liv

I'd had an afternoon nap, my first since leaving the age of toddlerhood behind. I felt strangely refreshed and ready to take on the world.

Perhaps I should have napped more often in my life.

I'd rallied the troops, group texting the family to assemble for dinner at Erik's house. Gunnar and Ella would be video calling in as they were in Capricorn Cove spending the holidays with her family this year.

Good luck to them, they're gonna need it.

The Bronzes made my family look practically angelic.

I tugged at my dress sighing at the noticeable bump that stretched the material.

No hiding it. I'm definitely pregnant.

"Worried?" Ian asked from beside me in the cab of his truck.

"No. Just wanting to get it over with."

"And yer a hundred percent sure ye want to go through with this charade?" Ian asked as he turned onto my parents' street. "

I nodded, pressing damp palms to the material across my thighs. "It's the only option that doesn't leave my mother in tears of worry."

Ian parked the truck smoothly, twisting to look at me. "Ye forget, I know yer mother. The woman will worry no matter what."

My mother was both a warrior and a worrier, the combination making her a fierce protector of her family. I vowed to be just like her.

"Let's just get this over with."

We exited the truck, my arms full of pie, Ian carrying pizzas. It wasn't the most glamorous dinner, but considering I'd thrust myself upon Erik and Laura it was the least I could do.

We let ourselves in, Ian's big voice booming a welcome.

"Anyone home?" he called, leading the way.

Laura's head poked from around the hall door, a welcoming smile on her lips. "Hey, Ian. Oh, and Liv! Hi. Come on in, we're just in the kitchen."

My brother owned a large house on one of the canals. It suited him. A jetty out the back for whichever boat he'd designed for himself that month, a big house he and Laura would no doubt fill with children.

Perhaps one of the best decisions I'd ever made had been to sign Laura Sweep as my reality TV Queen of Clean. She'd not only helped me create a show with heart and soul, scoring us both an Emmy and a GLAAD, but through the show she'd also met my brother. Their romance had played out like a choreographed love story, the reality TV show host falling for the adorably clueless single dad of adopted twin boys.

Truly, I couldn't have written that any better.

"Liv! All this fuss for your homecoming." My mother approached, wrapping me in her arms, her familiar perfume reducing me to a five-year-old, clinging to her for reassurance.

"Mom," I greeted, closing my eyes and holding her just a little tighter, a little longer.

She let go, stepping back to cup my cheeks, searching my face. "What's wrong?"

"Is everyone here?"

"No, but Rune and Gabby are on their way," Erik replied, gently shifting Mom out of his way to give me a one-armed hug. "Hey, sis."

"Hey you." I embraced him, circling both him and the baby in his arm. "And you, Mister Ulf."

Ulf, my gorgeous nephew, chortled happily, his little hands clapping.

"You're so big!" I exclaimed, pressing exuberant kisses to his cheek, delighting in his baby laughter.

"Don't remind me, he's starting to cruise now. It's terrifying. We're in a mad dash to install baby gates," Laura said, Leif, my other nephew, balanced on her hip.

"Hey, babe." She leaned in, pressing a kiss to my cheek as we hugged.

"So where are Dad and Nan?" I asked, as we crowded around the kitchen island.

"You sister came home early from college. She's staying at the house and working at the bookstore." Mom shook her head. "There's something going on with that girl and she won't reveal a word."

"She's young," Erik dismissed, bustling around the kitchen to remove cups and place them on the counter. "She's probably just burned out from a hectic college year."

Mom shook her head, her blonde hair, now faded to a silvery grey, flying about. "Liv, she dyed her hair. Brown! It's a nice brown but still. When has your sister ever dyed her hair? It's like she's rebelling and I have no idea why."

I exchanged an amused look with Laura who dipped her head, hiding behind her own long brunette strands, her shoulders shaking as she struggled not to laugh. My whole family were blonde-headed, Viking giants. Tall, broad, we reflected Dad's Nordic heritage. Mom, while golden blonde, had the stature of a small Madonna, coming up only to my father's armpit. That she took Astrid's decision to change up her look as a personal rejection of the family didn't surprise me. Mom was nothing if not a little dramatic.

"Now Jemma," Ian tutted, shaking his shaggy head. "Ye know yer daughter well enough. She's not the kind of girl to brood in silence. She seems happy enough."

Mom nodded, patting Ian on the arm. "You're a treasure, Ian. But a mother always knows when something is bothering her children."

She sent me a side eye and I swallowed, nausea rising as my stomach began to roil with nerves.

"We're here!" Gabby, my youngest brother's fiancé, stepped through the door, a bottle of wine held in each hand. Gabby had to be one of my favorite people alive. Fierce, loving, unashamed, I'd never met a woman who was so simultaneously vulnerable and bold.

An aquamarine choker decorated her neck, matching the color of her new prosthetic leg.

"Hello!" she gushed, wrapping me in a hug, a bottle digging into my back. "Don't you look wonderful."

She smelled like saw dust, coconut and salt, the combination a result of her perfume and occupation.

"And hello to you, Ms. Former Apprentice." I greeted, pleased as punch for her. "I hope my brother gave you a pay rise to go with that shiny new title."

She cackled, shooting Erik, who also happened to be her boss, a wink. "A small one but we're still negotiating."

My brother's eyebrows lifted. "The fuck we are. You may be family but girl, you're not getting any preferential treatment."

Gabby's arms were replaced by Rune's solid form. He lifted me up, squeezing me tight, my youngest sibling the gentle (but massive) giant of the family.

"Rune, put me down." I laughed, squirming a little. He did, pressing a quick kiss to my forehead before trailing his fiancé through the house.

"Yer family loves hard and fierce," Ian commented, handing me a glass of something sparkling.

"And loud," I agreed, sniffing at the contents.

"Lemonade. For the… nerves," he said softly, glancing at the gathering group.

"Thanks."

Dad and Nan arrived a moment later, Nan seated like a queen in her wheelchair.

"Hello, darling." She kissed my cheek, patting my hair as I bent to hug her. "You've been missed."

Dad followed, though was so quickly distracted by Mom pestering him about opening the wine that his greeting was nothing more than a fleeting squeeze.

Astrid hovered in the doorway; her cheeks flushed as she stared at the family.

"Are you here for me?" she asked as I started towards her, her mouth a thin line.

"Nope, but nice hair. The color suits you." I pulled her into my arms, holding her tight. "You okay?"

She stood stiff in my arms for a moment, her body tense, stress written in every line. Slowly she melted, her arms squeezing me back. "Yeah. I'm just working things through, you know?"

I nodded, letting my hug do all the talking. Of my siblings Gunnar was the oldest, then came Erik, me, Astrid, and finally Rune. I'd always thought my sister would become a teacher. But instead she was in her final semester of a masters in Architecture, a field she'd never expressed an interest in before heading off to college to pursue. It hadn't made any sense then and didn't now but I wasn't one to question another's life choices.

Well, not unless I thought those life choices warranted interference.

"Dinner?" Ian asked the crowd as they mingled.

"Yes," Mom decided, picking up plates. "Sune, get the napkins, Rune, help Ian with the pizzas. Liv, can you bring Nan?"

"I can bring myself!" Nan yelled, pressing the joystick to send her chair into movement.

Astrid chuckled; one arm wrapped around my middle as we followed the rabble out to the back patio. Space heaters and a cheerfully crackling fire kept the cold night air at bay as we crowded around the table, serving up pizza and laughing at each other. Erik handed Ulf off to Ian, disappearing inside to return with a small laptop.

"Hi family!" Ella called, waving through the screen. My

378

eldest brother sat beside her, a beer in one hand, his other arm around his bride.

Possessive thy name is Gunnar.

As everyone settled, greeting Ella and Gunnar, or chatting as pizzas were eaten and drinks sipped, I swallowed against the nausea, staring at the single slice of pizza on my plate.

I want pie.

My mouth watered at the thought. Cherry, apple, chocolate, it didn't matter. I wanted pie, God damn it!

I felt eyes on me, lifting my gaze to see Ian staring at me across the table. He still looked like a sasquatch, with his explosion of red hair, and out of control beard. But I found myself looking past that exterior, seeing him through new eyes.

He still held Ulf who tugged at Ian's beard, Ian ignoring him to watch me. He'd greeted my family with the familiarity of a man invited to many of these events. He fit in, teasing Laura, niggling Gabby, helping Mom. Dad, Erik and he regularly shared a beer, raging about the local football team.

He fits.

I sucked in a breath, looking away from Ian's piercing gaze to the table. They'd quieted a little while eating, the dim the perfect time to raise my news. With a deep breath I stood, lifting my glass and holding it out.

"I have an announcement," I declared, determined to make this a good thing. "Actually, I have a few and I hope you'll celebrate with me."

Worried glances were exchanged around the table.

"Go on, Liv," Gunnar encouraged through the screen. "Tell us."

"I...." I swallowed, taking the easy out. "I quit my job. I'm moving back to the Cape and starting my own company. We're going to make documentaries."

The table exploded, congratulations, hugs, cheers, my family didn't question my decision, simply supported me a hundred percent.

I met Ian's gaze across the table, Ulf still in the crook of his arm, the toddler still fascinated with his beard.

"Thank you," I said as they began to settle down. "And I have another announcement."

"Two in one day? How exciting!" Mom called, giving me a thumbs up.

Oh, Mother, you sweet, innocent lady. I hope this doesn't destroy you.

Determined, I lifted my glass, bracing for the inevitable impact. "Ian and I are together and we're having a baby."

Silence.

Deathly, fucking silence.

My nephews picked up on the vibe, their little heads swirling to look around the table. Ulf stuck a fist in his mouth, urgently sucking while Leif began to fuss in Laura's arms, his tiny face screwing up, ready to begin screaming.

This does not bode well.

"I fucking knew it!" Ella exploded, her body bouncing up and down on the screen. "I told you! It happened at the wedding, didn't it? You got together at our wedding!"

"Umm... yes?"

She laughed, turning to punch Gunnar's arm. "I told you! I said there was something there. That dance." She fanned herself, shaking her head. "Phew! I nearly got pregnant just watching you two."

"Pregnant? Are you sure?" Erik asked, his expression

shell-shocked.

I rolled my eyes. "Do you think I'd look this bloated for fun?"

"But you hate each other," Erik said, beginning to slowly shake his head back and forth. "You do nothing but fight."

"Hate and love, the gap between both is narrow," Astrid offered, eyeing my belly. "Perhaps it wasn't so much hate as…."

"Foreplay?" Gabby offered with a laugh.

"Are you sure you're pregnant?" Mom asked, tears in her eyes. "Have you done the test? Seen a doctor?"

"Test yes, doctor no. But we're sure. I've all the signs and every test from the first to the twenty-first came back positive."

"Oh, Livvy!" Mom threw herself across the table, scrambling to come and wrap me in a hug. "My babies are having babies!"

Across the table I saw Dad offering Ian a handshake, clapping him enthusiastically on the back.

"To Liv and Ian!" Gunnar called, toasting.

"To Liv and Ian!" my family echoed laughing and clinking glasses.

Ian reached across the table, tapping his beer against my glass. "To our babe."

I drank, my eyes never leaving his as around us the questions began to fly thick and fast.

He toasted to our baby.

Well shit. Now I have to like him.

Chapter Eight

Ian

I rolled, trying not to wince as the tiny couch protested under my weight. The clock from the microwave blinked at me with its too bright digits.

1:00 a.m. and I had yet to catch a wink.

From the bed across the room, I heard Liv give a soft sigh, the bed clothes shifting as she turned in her sleep.

Whose idea was this again? Oh right, mine.

Dinner had gone well. Surprisingly so. We'd played the adoring couple, falling into an easy rhythm of give and take. Having called this temporary truce, Liv and I could apparently get along without niggling each other. The banter was still there, don't get me wrong. But it felt softer, less antagonizing and more... affectionate?

I frowned, replaying tonight in my head.

Yeah, affectionate seemed the right word. No one overly drilled us on our relationship, and we kept details vague but her family didn't mind, more interested in finding out what we'd need for the baby and what our plans were—Sune in particular had been very interested in understanding if I had any marriage-minded plans for his precious daughter.

Like she'd even say yes.

Jesus, Ian. What are ye thinking man? Marriage?

Sleep had obviously deserted me. With a sigh, I reached for my phone, searching for eBooks to read while waiting for dawn to arrive.

What to expect when you're expecting.

The Expectant Father.

Being a Dad is Weird.

The Feminist Guide to Daddy-ing.

I hit download, beginning to flick through them at random.

So, you wanna be a dad. Well brother, strap in. We're about to go on a hell of a journey.

"Ian?"

I blinked, looking up from my phone, pulled back from my reading haze by Liv. She stood before me, a cup of tea in one hand, a plate of toast in the other, holding them out to me. A quick glance at the clock showed hours had passed without my notice.

My mind swirled with all the facts and advice, an uncomfortable sense of overwhelm hitting me.

"Oh, morning." I dropped the phone, reaching for the crockery. "Is this for me?"

She laughed, nodding, her face still flushed from sleep. She wore a loose robe, the thick material protecting her from the cold.

"Yes, you look like you need it."

"Thanks." I took a long sip, finding she'd made my tea just how I liked it, strong with a dash of milk. "How'd ye know this is how I take it?"

She shrugged, returning to the fridge and beginning to rummage through the shelves. "I listen."

She poked her head out. "Do you know where the other pie is? All I can find is apple."

Shit.

"Ah, I might have eaten it."

She reared up, narrowing her eyes on me. "Excuse me?'"

I winced. "I got hungry."

"You got... Ian! What am I meant to do now?"

With a sigh, I pushed to my feet. "Eat the apple. I'll get dressed and go get you some more."

My back protested, reminding me that I couldn't do another night on the couch.

Monday can't come quick enough.

Liv smashed angrily around the kitchen, banging and clanging before shaking a giant can of whipped cream. Her gaze met mine, her eyes flashing with rage as she began to spray cream on the pastry.

One swirl, two, three.

"Do ye think ye have enough?" I asked, staring as she continued to hold the button down.

"No."

Frustration lit in me as I watched her add more cream. "Ye'll make yerself sick. Stop."

"I will not. Don't tell me what to do."

With a curse, I stalked across the kitchen, snatching for the can, Liv pulling back to avoid my reach. An arc of cream flew through the air covering the counter, me and the ceiling.

"Look what you did!"

"Me?" I roared. "Ye're the idiot with the cream fetish!"

"It's not a fetish! It's what the baby wants!"

"The baby isn't even old enough to know what it wants! She's only just getting taste buds!"

Liv froze, her eyes widening. "What?"

I paused, my anger banking. "Taste buds develop at around thirteen weeks. When she tastes the amniotic fluid, she'll get a wee sample of yer diet."

Liv's hands dropped to her stomach; the fight forgotten. "You keep calling it her."

As do ye.

I shrugged, all my anger dissipating. "I've no doubt ye're birthing another heathen woman to bring hellfire and brimstone down upon the heads of any man stupid enough to underestimate her. Now, stop with the cream and let me get ye another pie."

I turned, heading to the closet to get some clothes.

"Ian?"

"Yeah?"

"Just saying, if you'd tried again, I'd have let you kiss me just now."

I turned, grinning.

"Oh really?"

Liv's face had flushed, a small grin on her lips, one hand resting on her belly. She'd never looked more beautiful.

Stop before ye get feelings.

"Yeah. But you know…." She shrugged. "I still hate you." There was no heat in her tone.

I laughed, turning away from her, my heart lighter. "I know, now eat your pie."

Chapter Nine

Liv

I'd officially moved in with Ian. Ian and I were living together.

God that sounds weird.

The weekend had passed in a whirlwind of activity, Ian buying me pie, both of us googling a hundred different things about babies.

We'd briefly gone shopping to look at strollers, and baby carriers, and cradles—all the detritus that came with a newborn.

Things I now knew—tiny booties made me hyperventilate. And Ian was damned good at soothing me through a panic attack.

I stood staring at the room that Ian had given me, the bed we'd picked up today, my things I'd unpacked. It felt... strange. Wrong. Uncomfortable. As if I were a puzzle piece in the wrong box.

I should be sleeping with Ian.

"Ye ready?"

I jerked upright, twisting to find the man in question

standing in the doorway to my bedroom, jeans molded to his legs, shirt pulled tight across his chest.

I want to ride him like a pony.

"Liv?"

I snapped to, hyper aware of the fact my underwear felt damp, my body throbbing with desire.

A man buys me pie and moves me into his house and I'm ready to jump his bones.

"Yep, let's do this." I picked up my tote, allowing him to lead us out. We chatted as he drove us downtown to the doctor's office where I'd have my first scan.

At reception, I filled in the clipboard handing it back as butterflies began to take flight.

"Ye okay?"

I nodded, my hand finding his, linking our fingers. "Just nervous. I've never been a mom before."

He chuckled, nodding at the other pregnant women in the waiting room. "I suspect the doctor knows what she's doing."

"Ms. Larsson?"

I stood, Ian's hand still reassuringly gripping mine. "Here."

"Come on through." The nurse led us through the offices to a small room at the back. A woman of indeterminate age stood inside, a friendly grin on her face.

"Hi, Liv, I'm Dr. Kristen Lowe, take a seat."

We settled, Ian still allowing me to death grip his hand.

"Now, let me have a look at this file. This is your first, yes?"

I nodded, struck mute by the equipment in the room, and intimidated by this competent woman.

"They're always fun. Congratulations." She flicked

through the chart I'd filled out, reading the info. "Says here you think the date of conception is August 15? That's very specific."

I nodded, swallowing. "We're long-distance. It was the only opportunity."

She nodded. "Alright, and no blood test?"

I shook my head. "No, we didn't even think we were until last week."

"That's no problem. We'll do an ultrasound today just to confirm there is a baby but everything I'm seeing here is good so let's have a little peek and see what we have."

She helped me onto the bed, then asked me to lift my shirt and pull down my pants a little. I did so, shuffling around as she got the equipment ready.

"Okay, sorry, it'll feel cool and sticky for a little while thanks to the gel but let's see what we've got."

I reached out, clinging to Ian, fear pounding through me. *Oh, God, what if I'm wrong. What if there is no baby?*

She moved the sensor around, spreading the gel. For a moment nothing appeared on the screen then I saw it, a teeny tiny head.

Ian's hand jerked in mine, crushing my fingers.

"There we go, hello baby." Kristen said with a grin, moving the sensor around. "Now let me see if I can...." She touched some buttons and a thumping sound filtered through the speakers. "There. That's your baby's heartbeat. Congratulations."

Tears sprang to my eyes, sliding down my cheeks. Ian leaned in; his beard rough against my cheek.

"Congratulations, mummy."

I looked at him, our gazes meeting and holding, his eyes

glassy with tears.

"And to you, daddy."

He laughed, his teeth flashing, skin flushing with pleasure. "Now there's a thought. Me, a dad? Crazy."

I chuckled, turning back to watch the screen avidly, our baby beginning to move just a little at all the poking and prodding.

Ian cleared his throat. "Can ye print that out? I'd like a copy for our mantle. Our babe's first picture."

"Of course," Kristen replied grinning. "It's always nice when the partners are this invested."

I love Ian.

The thought hit me, unbidden and unwelcome, rejection immediate.

No, I don't.

It had to be the pregnancy hormones. I didn't just fall in love with a sasquatch over a weekend. No way no how.

"Definitely around that thirteen to fourteen-week mark, so your timing checks out. We're too early for sex if you wanted to know. But come back after the holidays and we'll do the twenty-week scan, make sure everything is as it should be and, if you want, we can find out the sex then."

"I want," I told her, looking up at Ian. "That okay?"

"Fine by me."

She took more measurements and scans, checking everything out before letting me clean up. I left with a referral for a blood test, some vitamins, a list of local prenatal and parenting classes, and a pamphlet as thick as my arm on birthing options.

And three little printouts of the scan. Baby's first picture.

"Should we call your parents now?" I asked, staring down

390

at the image of our little one as Ian drove us home.

"Uh…." He cleared his throat. "If ye wish."

Wait. What?

I twisted in my seat, giving him an eyebrow lift. "I'm sorry, if I wish? This coming from the man who asked for pictures of our unborn child? Alright buddy, spill. What the fuck?"

He ran a hand over his face, his shoulders slumping. "This calls for alcohol."

My eyebrows lifted. "Excuse me?"

"Let me get a beer and something to eat and we can talk."

I glanced at the dash clock; it was barely after eleven in the morning. "Ian—"

"Please, Liv."

I bit my tongue, struggling against my initial reaction to demand answers.

"Fine," I said finally. "The Literary Academy is open and Rune might be willing to part with a beer at this time of the day. If you're lucky."

With that decided he hit the indicator, navigating the streets towards Rune's establishment while I wondered what exactly I was getting myself into.

Chapter Ten

Ian

The Literary Academy had been around for more than twenty years. Passed down in the Larsson family, Rune had taken it over when Nan had gotten too old. The kid had revamped it, popping out one side of the building and taking over the adjacent warehouse. He'd turned one part into a café-by-day-tapas-bar-by-night deal, with the other the original bookstore. But he'd revamped that too, creating a wonderland with fantasy-inspired sculptures made entirely from old books, delighting readers and becoming a photography mecca for social media influencers.

That Rune got free publicity from the social media darlings hadn't gone unnoticed, the guy capitalized on that shit like nobody's business.

With a strange sense of foreboding, we entered the café finding it in the mid-morning, just before lunch, lull.

We found a small booth set off from the book tunnel, tucked away for privacy. Liv set her bag down, ordering a small hot chocolate, unwinding her scarf from around her neck and pulling off her mittens.

"Can I get a beer?" I asked, praying for luck.

The waiter blinked. "Um… no. Sorry. But Rune might be able to do an Irish coffee?"

"That'll do."

"Actually, do you have pie?" Liv asked, catching the waiter before he moved off.

"Yeah, we've got pumpkin, rhubarb and strawberry, custard, or peach."

"Um, yes, please." Liv moaned, licking her lips. "One slice of each, thanks."

The guy's eyebrows raised but to his credit he took the order, shuffling away.

"Alright, Campbell. Hit me."

I reached for a sugar packet, needing to do something with my hands. "Let's wait 'til ye pie arrives, I don't want to be interrupted.

Liv's lips pressed into a thin line, her blue eyes flashing with annoyance. But she did as asked, waiting until the pies and drinks were delivered.

She picked up a fork stabbing it viciously into one of the pies. "Now talk."

I took a hearty sip of the coffee, embracing the alcoholic kick.

Now or never.

"My father is both an alcoholic and an adulterer. I have eight siblings because most are stepsiblings. The man is still married to Mam, and she knows about the children but turns a blind eye, such is her love for the no-good son of a bitch."

Liv winced. "Damn. That sucks."

I nodded, running a tired hand over my face. "Aye, and

393

it gets worse. For many a year he took me along, using me as an excuse. Play dates with the local kids, he said while stepping out, taking advantage. By the time I realized, Mam had already found out and shrunk in on herself, deciding it weren't in her best interest to do anything about it."

I looked up, finding Liv's gaze on me. "I hate him, Liv. For what he did to her. For what he did to all the women. Telling them he loved them. Leading them on. Knocking them up. I'm the eldest and have eight direct siblings—and they're the ones we know about."

"He must pay child support, surely."

"Aye, that he does."

"God, that must ruin him."

And now for the shitty part.

I cleared my throat, scratching at my beard nervously. "Not quite. Ye see, we're... um... that is to say..."

Spit it out Campbell!

"My father is a laird. A duke. He's got a massive holding in Scotland. We're what you call well-heeled."

"A duke? You mean you're royalty?"

I shook my head. "Not to the Brits. Our bloodline is pure Scot. Well, it was 'til this little one." I nodded at her belly. "But we're aristocracy."

She sucked in a breath, putting two and two together, such a clever lass.

"It's why you were able to move to America at seventeen," she whispered, her face draining of color. "You had a fall back."

"Aye. Nan and Mam were sad to see me go, but they knew I couldn't stay. I couldn't sit back and watch Dad play her like that. Not again."

"And the degrees?" she asked, referring to my multiple university titles.

"Paid for from me trust fund. Thought I'd better put at least some of it to good use, even if it's only bailing drunk women out of jail."

The reminder of her drunken shenanigans at Ella's bachelorette party didn't even get a flicker.

She blinked, looking at me as if through new eyes. "How wealthy is wealthy?"

I shrugged.

"No, really. Are we talking wealthy enough to own Thor's Shipbuilding or wealthy enough to own your own country?"

I hesitated, wincing. "Aye, the latter."

She fell back in her chair, the pies forgotten. "Ian... are you saying you're the heir to a fortune?"

"Aye, and if it weren't for the fact I'm the only child of my Mam, I'd have long since bowed out of ever taking even a cent of the cursed lot."

"Your mother?"

I blew out a breath. "She's got her own money. And a lot of it. If she were to die before my father and I've left the family...."

"It'd all go to your father. I understand." Liv nodded.

"Do ye? 'Cause I don't. It's petty and I hate that I'm this kind of man."

"Ian." She reached across the table, linking our fingers. "It's okay. The man hurt you. Worse, he hurt someone you love. I do believe you're allowed to be petty sometimes."

I tried to summon a smile but suspected it looked more like a grimace. "I've not spoken to the man in over fifteen years, Liv. Not since leaving home."

"But you go back?"

"Aye. See my siblings and Mam. Nan's passed now, but Mam's still lively. Has her sisters and such over there. Tried to convince her to come here but she says there's nothing here for her." I glanced at Liv's stomach. "I'll admit to not being above using our wee bairn to tempt her."

Liv smiled, and I was struck once again by her beauty. "Bribe away. Who knows, maybe you'll be successful this time." She tilted her head to one side. "Did you know your accent gets strong when you talk about home?"

I shook my head.

"It does. It's... lovely. I hope our baby picks up a little of it."

"But not the red hair?" I asked, glad for the distraction.

She grinned, eyeing my beard. "Oh, I don't know. I think it's starting to grow on me."

I lifted her hand, pressing a kiss to her palm, watching as her big blue eyes grew round, focusing on where my lips met her soft skin.

"Thank ye, Liv. For listening and understanding. And for... well, carrying my baby and letting me be a part of this."

Her face softened, and I caught a glimpse of... something. Something naked and raw that had the power to devastate me.

"Right. Well." She shook me off, the look gone as quickly as it had appeared.

She settled back in her seat and reached for her fork once more. "That's done. Let me eat pie and then we'll call them from the car. Nice and brief. Keep it short. We'll go from there, shall we?"

That wouldn't happen, I needed more time to process but

I nodded, watching her begin to devour the pastries with a single-mindedness I couldn't help but admire.

As she ate, my mind replayed that look and I couldn't help but wonder, did Liv want more with me?

Chapter Eleven

Liv

"Ian? I'm home!" I called, stamping my feet at the door to his mud room.

"Down the hall!" he called back, his voice carrying.

"Fine, I'll get the groceries." I muttered, kicking off my boots. With a grunt, I hauled the bags up carrying them into the house. I dumped them in the kitchen, tossing the cold stuff in the fridge before heading off in search of Ian.

His house wasn't big for a man who could, apparently, afford castles. Just four bedrooms and two baths. A family home for a man who, until recently, hadn't even had a girlfriend.

Well, now he's got a live-in baby momma and rapidly approaching child.

I found him in the third bedroom, paint brush in hand.

"What do ye think?" he asked, gesturing at the wall.

"Oh, Ian."

My hands flew to my lips, my heart practically exploding as I took in the mural.

"Now don't be getting all sentimental," he warned, waggling the paint brush in my direction. "'Twasn't all me. Yer brother came over and helped. Rune's the one that came up with the idea, even drew all the lines. I just have to not fuck it up when painting."

The mural stretched along the wall where I'd planned to place the crib, a sky scene, hot air balloons filled with cute little animals bobbed merrily amongst the clouds.

"It's perfect," I whispered. "Absolutely perfect."

He turned, looping an arm over my shoulder and surveying his work. "Not bad, needs a few coats but she's coming along."

My body's reaction to his touch was fast becoming predictable.

Forgive me Father, for I am about to sin. Again. Only this time, I can't get pregnant.

I twisted, giving in to desire, tired of spending my nights alone and my days struggling against my growing need for Ian.

We'd been living together for just over a week and I'd never been hotter. My dreams the last few nights had centered entirely on that fucking boathouse and Ian fisting his cock. We'd explored positions I wasn't even sure existed outside of my dreams, and each day I'd woken hotter, wetter and more wrung out than the last.

Incoming!

I fisted his hair, yanking his head down until I could smash my lips to his.

He let out a startled yelp, the paint brush crashing to the ground as we both tripped backwards, stumbling as I threw him off balance.

"Liv, what are ye—"

"Speak now and say no, or fuck me. God, Ian. You're driving me crazy."

His mouth crashed down on mine, his tongue delving as he feasted. I felt his cock grow thick and rigid against my belly.

Yes!

"What took ye so long?" he asked, his fingers unsnapping each of the buttons of my coat.

"God knows," I answered with a laugh, nipping at his bottom lip. "But doesn't it feel good now?"

"Like I'm burning," he admitted, tossing off my coat, his hands dropping to the bottom of my sweater. "Ye're a saucy wench, my Liv. Now shut ye mouth and let me concentrate."

I tipped my head back, my eyelids drifting shut as he stripped me, his hot mouth pausing to taste each inch of revealed skin.

"Aye, I remember these," he whispered, his voice rough and heavy as he cupped my breasts, gently stroking thumbs over my erect nipples.

I whimpered, shocked at their sensitivity.

"Mm, let me take care of ye." He bent, laving one breast then the other, back and forth until my body screamed for release, a tight, wet heat boiling deep within me.

"Ian!"

"I think I told ye to hush," he said, pulling back. "Now ye want me to continue or…?"

I glared at him, wanting desperately to move back. Finding myself instead pushing forward, rocking my body against his, needy and searching for release.

"Good lass." His praise set something off in me, a bone deep ache tightening all the muscles in me.

I throbbed with need. My body nothing more than an extension of pleasure.

Touch me. Touch me. Touch me.

I silently pleaded, begged, bargained as Ian stepped back, leisurely stripping his paint splattered clothing from his body.

Oh, my.

In the light of day, he looked different to the night of the wedding. His body bigger, harder, heftier. Ian had no six pack, he was what they'd call fat strong, his body all thickness and bulk. I loved it.

With no alcohol in my system to blur my vision or memory, I took him in, watching as he stepped out of his pants, leaving him in the skin in which he was born.

Perfection.

He reached for my jeans, stripping me of pants and underwear. He dropped to his knees, helping me step free then reached for my socks pausing when I stilled him with a shake of my head.

"Sorry, not sexy, but my feet are ice."

He chuckled, cupping one ankle and pressing a kiss to the inside of my thigh. "Everything ye do is sexy, Liv. Ye should know that by now. From the first time I saw ye to this moment right now, ye've always been the most beautiful woman in the room."

Pleasure bloomed in me, curling out and filling all the little corners of my soul.

"Add to ye looks yer personality, yer love, yer spark—it's too much for a man to resist." He pressed a kiss to my inner thigh, his tongue gliding along the sensitive skin. "I've a mighty craving for ye, lass. Now let me taste."

He licked his way up my thighs, pausing as he came to their apex, his hot breath a tease as I waited in desperate anticipation.

Finally, he leaned in, his lips and tongue a welcome balm to my oversensitive skin.

"Yes!" I cried, my head falling back, hands gripping his shoulders. "Ian!"

He made soothing noises as he devoured me, his tongue an unrelenting pleasure.

My body coiled, my thighs quivering as he played with me, stroking me, his tongue laving my sensitive flesh before dancing away only to build me back again.

Now, now, now, now, now!

As if hearing my silent plea, he changed tack, sucking roughly on my clit, ripping me straight into orgasm, the intensity overwhelming as I crashed headfirst into pleasure.

He helped me down to the floor, gathering me in, petting me as if I needed comfort. Perhaps I did, but I needed him more.

I reached between us, snaking a hand out until I could grip his length, stroking him in a tight fist.

"Fuck!" he hissed, burying his head in my neck and nipping at the sensitive skin. "Ye filthy wench, harder."

Perhaps I should have been outraged with how he spoke to me, ordering me this way and that. But his tone, the gravel of need that threaded through his voice, it all worked together to drive me higher.

"Let me taste you."

He allowed it, guiding me down, holding his cock in one tight fist as I hovered my mouth for a moment before darting my tongue out to catch a salty drop of precum.

Yes....

His scent surrounded me, his unique mix of soap and saw dust, and the sharp bite of paint. I sucked him deep, my tongue dancing as I thrust forward and back, hollowing out my cheeks to fuck his cock with my mouth.

"Liv! Fuck!" Curses spilled from his mouth as he arched back, his head dropping, his body tight and focused.

Mine. All mine.

He allowed me to control him for but a few moments, my tongue and mouth overruling all of him. Then he hauled me up his body, positioning me just so and thrusting up and into me, filling me with his big cock, fucking me with wild, possessive need.

"Ian!"

"Take it, take me. All of me!" he barked, hands gripping my hips, holding me in place as his cock ravaged my tender flesh. "Gotta fuck ye. Gotta make ye see...."

I wanted to ask what I was meant to see but the thought was swept away in a tidal wave of pleasure as my second orgasm crashed over me, shaking my body, ripping a hoarse scream from my throat.

Into me, Ian emptied himself, his body heaving, praises and curses by equal measures falling from his lips and my body milked his, both of us dropping to the floor in a clash of limbs and secret lies.

You can't love with only your body, Liv. He needs to know.

It's been him. It's always been him. It is him. He's your one, Liv. And you have to tell him.

God help me.

Chapter Twelve

Ian

I straightened my collar, staring at myself in the mirror.

Tonight was Thanksgiving dinner with the Larssons. I'd just finished a shift at work, pulling an extra day to get a project over a line for a particularly VIP client. I was meeting Liv at dinner and was running a little late.

It wouldn't be the first nor the last time I'd be invited to these events, but it was certainly the first one I'd attended where I was in love with their daughter. I wanted to make a good impression.

You need to tell her, ye daft goat.

It'd been over a week since Liv and I had come together. Within the space of a few hours, she'd gone from roommate and mother of my child, to lover.

Hot as fuck lover.

Tell her!

We could barely keep our hands off each other, breaking in each room in the house, some multiple times over. I'd become addicted to her kisses, to her sweet little moans and harsh, needy screams. I craved the way she clutched me as

405

she came, her body staking a claim on mine, branding me in a way I knew I'd never escape.

Tell her!

With a curse I turned away from the mirror, palming the cell in my pocket.

There was only one thing preventing me from telling Liv I loved her, it was the same thing that plagued me each night as I fell asleep—what if I turned into my father?

We'd yet to call my mother with the good news, each time I'd put Liv off, making up some excuse about time zones or plans. In reality, I feared nothing more than my mother's affirmation that I'd be a terrible father.

With a deep breath I pulled the phone from my pocket, dialing the number. It rang three times before she picked up.

"Hello?"

"Mam, it's me, Ian."

My throat tightened as I heard her exclamation of surprise and delight.

"My prodigal son! I thought I'd never hear from ye! What is happening over there in the big US of A?"

"Mam, I have something to tell ye… Ye remember Liv?"

"Aye, the Larsson girl. The elder one, I believe?"

"Aye." I swallowed, my stomach clenching. "She's pregnant. It's mine."

I heard her breath catch, a little hiccup of emotion.

"Oh, Ian." Her voice broke, a sob coming down the line.

My eyes screwed shut, despair overtaking me.

It's true then. I'm just like him.

"Congratulations, a wee bairn. Oh, my son, oh my dear, dear boy." She sobbed down the phone but her tone and words broke through my cloud.

"Wait, congratulations?"

"Aye, congratulations! What? Ye expected me to curse ye?"

"I...," I stumbled, needing to purge my greatest fear. "I worried ye'd say I was like him."

Her breath caught; the phone line silent for a long moment.

"Oh, my darling.... I know ye don't understand ye father, or me for that matter. But no, Ian, ye're not like him. Ye never were and never will be. Ye're a good man. Ye love with all ye heart. And ye'll treat that wee bairn better than anyone ever could. Ye father is a complicated man, and yes, I know what he is. But I love him. I know ye'll never understand that but that's okay, Ian. It truly is. Because I know ye'll fight tooth and nail for ye woman. Ye'll treat her like a queen and make her the center of ye world."

Her voice caught, and for a moment I worried the line had dropped.

"I love ye, son. So much. I'm so proud of ye and what ye've become. Never forget that."

"I love ye too, Mam." I swallowed around the lump in my throat. "And perhaps, when the babe is born, ye might like to come over for a visit?"

"Och, ye canna stop me!"

We spoke for a little while, about life, Liv and love. I knew then I'd never understand my mother but I had to let go of the fear and hate that had held me back from living my life. As we hung up it struck me what a fool I'd been. For years I'd pushed Liv away, replacing my attraction with antagonism, all in an effort to avoid becoming the man I most feared.

This life, this love, this baby could have all been but a dream.

A sudden need to tell Liv drove me out of the bathroom, sending me running for my truck.

God, how could ye have been so stupid? Anyone could have swept her up.

Possession burned through me, raging until I couldn't tell passion from anger. I pulled up at the Larsson's, thundering up their walk to the front door. I threw it open with a crash, my gaze taking in the entry, ears strained for Liv's voice.

Her laughter came from the kitchen, and I headed in that direction at a fast clip, rounding the corner in time to see her lift a forkful of pie to her lips.

"Liv Jemma Larsson!" I boomed, stopping to point at her. "You need to stop what you're doing and listen to me."

Everyone in the room fell silent. I dimly registered that a young, good looking if vaguely familiar man sat beside Astrid at the dinner table, but my focus centered on Liv.

She considered me for a moment, her eyes flashing. Slowly, deliberately, she raised the fork to her lips, her gaze locked with mine, taking a bit of the pastry.

You saucy wench, I'm gonna spank you for that later.

I sucked in a breath. "Liv, I love ye. I've loved ye since the moment I set eyes on ye ten years ago. Ye were wearing a wee summer dress with a bikini underneath. We were picnicking on a boat, yer brother thinking he'd been a right clever one by taking me out on the ocean to test my sea legs."

"Hey!" Erik cried, crossing his arms. "It was a good idea!"

We both ignored him.

"I thought I'd died and gone to heaven, seeing such a pretty girl on that boat. Then ye gave me the bird and bomb dived into the ocean, sending sass my way. Ever since we've been locked in a battle of wills, you and me. And I love it. I love how ye keep me on my toes. I love how ye force me to be a better man. I love that ye're pregnant with our baby, and that I've no doubt the wee one will be just as sassy and sweet as her gorgeous mother." I crossed the room, hauling her into my arms, loving how she wrapped herself around me just as tight.

"Ye're gonna be an amazing mother, Liv. But I want more for ye too. I'm gonna help ye build yer empire. I'm gonna be there, supporting ye, giving ye whatever ye need to be the woman ye want to be. To set the example for all our children that they get to dream and succeed. Ye're more than I've ever thought I could have. Ye're more than my heart, my Liv. Ye're my soul. I love ye, and I want to marry ye. Tomorrow, if possible. But any day that works for ye, I'll be there."

I kissed her, not waiting for an answer as around the room her family watched.

I pulled back, Liv's eyelids fluttered open, her expression a little dazed.

"Liv?" her mother called. "Do you have something to add to this conversation?"

Liv's lips quirked as her gaze met mine, amusement dancing in their depths.

There's the sparkle I love.

"Ditto," she said with a laugh. "Only, you know, with you being a great dad."

The family collectively sighed, eyes rolling, heads shaking but it was enough for me.

"Ye love me, lass?" I asked, cupping her cheek, brushing her complex braid out of my way.

"Yes," she said softly, a soft flush tinting her face. "I suspect

I've loved you from the beginning as well. These last few years… Ian, you've been a constant for me. With your little judgmental smirk and knowing eye rolls."

I laughed, delighted with her sass.

She sobered, reaching out to capture one of my hands, placing it on the swell of her tiny baby bump. "I love you, Ian Campbell. This baby, how you've jumped in with both feet, the care you're showing me? All of it reads love. Maybe our way has been a little backward, but it's ours. And I love that. I love you."

My heart swelled and I feared my large body would split in two attempting to contain my happiness and delight in this woman.

"This calls for—shit! What can pregnant women drink in celebration?" Astrid asked the group. "Like… sparkling grape juice? Apple juice? Hardly seems worth the effort."

"Apple juice," her mother declared. "Sune, go run to the store and get some."

"I'm not bloody going to the stores to get juice. It's fucking Thanksgiving, it's either going to bare, closed or busier than a mosquito on a nudist beach."

"Sune!"

"Someone should probably call Gunnar and Ella, right?" Erik asked, bouncing a giggling Leif on one knee. "Or maybe not? They're with the Bronzes, right? That family is mental. Truly mental."

"Wait, *you guys* think they're crazy?" Gabby asked. "What did they do?"

"Don't you remember the wedding?" Laura asked, shuffling around the kitchen. "Ella's brothers did that crazy spontaneous speech…."

410

I pressed my forehead against Liv's, loving the chatter and laughter around us.

"You sure you want to join this mad house?" Liv asked softly.

"Lass, if ye haven't noticed, I already have."

She laughed, pressing a jubilant kiss to my mouth before rocking back. "Ring?"

"We'll get ye one when ye're not bloated."

"Good thinking. Wedding?"

"I'd marry ye at Thor's Shipbuilding in that tiny apartment while ye're wearing a robe if ye so wish. Honest to God, Livvy, wherever, whenever, however ye want ye can have it."

She eyed me, a teasing gleam in her eye. "And you're *how* rich exactly?"

I laughed, wrapping an arm around her, pulling her in for another kiss.

Epilogue One

Liv

"You motherfucker!" I screamed, bearing down as the contraction tore me apart. "You fucking motherfucker!"

"Breathe, love. Come on, remember what the coach said? One, two, three. One, two—"

"I'm gonna smash you in the face if you don't get me some drugs this instant!"

"Too late," Dr. Kristen said cheerfully from her position at my nether regions. "This little bubba is on its way. Now get ready, the next contraction will be here right about…."

We'd been out on the boat. The motherfucking boat. The boat Ian had made for me as a wedding gift. This kid hadn't been due for another week and I'd liked the idea of spending some alone time together.

An hour out and the contractions had started, no biggie. First baby, we had plenty of time.

Half an hour later I was screaming at Ian to turn the fucking boat around and get me to the hospital. He'd done so, and we'd been rushed straight through, the paramedics having told me I was nearly ready to start pushing.

No fucking way was I ready to start pushing.

No.

Fucking.

Way.

"Push!"

With a hoarse scream I pressed down, every single cell in my body clenching, pain turning everything into a haze of red and grey.

Dimly, I heard Ian's encouragement, the doctor and nurses' praise. But all my focus remained on getting this child of Satan from my body.

"One more!"

I pushed again, screaming as my baby finally slid from my body, entering the world.

"She's here!" Kristen crowed, checking her over. "And she's perfect, momma. Well done!"

With practice she laid the now crying infant on my chest, Ian crowding in beside me.

My body clenched, pushing out the afterbirth, but I barely felt it, such was my joy as I took in my precious daughter's tiny face.

"Hello, darling." Ian cooed beside me. "Go on, Mummy, what's her name?"

"Brenna," I decided, staring at our perfect bundle. "It means sword."

"Perfect," Ian agreed, pressing a kiss to my temple. "As perfect as her fierce mother."

I looked up at him, our daughter in my arms, tears in my eyes, love in my heart.

"Any regrets?"

"Only one," he admitted as the nurses and Kristen cleaned

413

me up.

"Really?"

"Mm." He leaned down; his lips close to mine. "Only that I waited so long before claiming ye. We could have had this wee precious girl a long time ago."

I laughed, tears streaking down my face. "I don't know, this seems pretty perfect to me."

"It does indeed. I love ye, Livvy."

I lifted my chin, kissing him, letting Ian feel my love.

Epilogue Two

Ian

My phone vibrated in my pocket. I stepped on the kill switch, the table saw slowing to a stop as I stepped back, pulling off my ear muffs and answering the call.

"Liv?"

"Ian, the school called. Your daughter staged a protest at lunch. She's refusing to eat the cafeteria food until they improve the offerings. She managed to get half her class to do the same. We've got a meeting with the school at three."

I hid a laugh behind a cough. "Liv, she's in first grade."

"I know! You think I don't know that? Ian, what have we created?"

"We? Ooch, love, I told ye from day one, any girl child of ours was gonna be hellfire and brimstone with a Mam like you."

Liv made a sound somewhere between a laugh, a cry and a sigh. "Thank God, Oili isn't as much of a handful."

Our second daughter took after me, sweet as pie.

"Ah, but we both know Shelby is just waiting for her chance to shine."

Our youngest had just turned two and hit it with a vengeance. A tiny dictator, she'd wrapped the entire family around her fearsome little pinky. She'd either change the world or destroy it.

"Let's pray this next one is sweet."

My heart skipped. "Next one?"

Liv paused, her voice catching. "I mean… I'm not pregnant but with the production company going so well, and me delegating more… I just thought… maybe… if you wanted to…."

"Woman, get home. Now."

I began to strip off my safety gear, my body hardening at the idea of impregnating my wife. Again. Liv in full bloom was a glorious sight to behold.

"Wait, right now? I have a meeting with a crew about that—"

"Now!"

"Pushy." She didn't sound displeased. But she'd be getting a little spank for the protesting anyway.

"Love ye, Liv."

"Love you too, Sasquatch."

"Ye on yer way?"

"I'll be there in ten. And you better bring that super sperm, I want to be pregnant by lunch tomorrow."

"I'll do my best."

"Mm, I can work with that."

V

The Christmas Contract

The Christmas Contract

Astrid

I forgot to tell my family I wrote a novel.

I didn't think it would be that big a deal. Then a big name movie star raved about it and suddenly my face is splashed across morning talk shows, and producers are offering me millions for film rights.

Enter Robert 'Robbie' Huynh — America's rom-com heart-throb. He's tall, dark, handsome, and Australian. He's like all my weaknesses rolled into one delicious package.

He's also the one who started this mess, and he wants my film rights. He wants them real bad.

So we strike a deal; I'll sign the contract if he gives me full creative license.

It seemed like a good idea at the time. Only this Christmas contract? It's got all the strings attached.

Robbie

I'm in a rut. An acting rut. Being typecast as the romantic lead is getting old real fast. I want action, adventure, mystery.

I want Astrid Larsson's film rights. And I'm not above using a little Aussie charm to get it.

Only Astrid's not at all what I expected. For a woman who writes crime thrillers, I expected someone hard, seasoned, rough. She's the exact opposite, and she's getting under my skin — big time.

I need to keep my head in the game. After all, this Christmas, all I really want is... Astrid?!

Warning: This book is inspired by Christmas movies, true crime podcasts, and a crisp Aussie accent. So, get thee a man, some mistletoe, and settle in — this read will have you jingling all the way to the bedroom.

Prologue

Robbie

I knocked urgently on the door, praying that behind it would hold the answer to my salvation. A woman tugged it open, her long brunette hair falling gently to one side, a ready grin on her face. It froze in place when she caught sight of me.

"Sorry to interrupt but—"

"Holy mother of God, you're Robbie fucking Huynh." The woman's gaze flicked to the guy behind me. "And... friend?"

I glanced back at Matt, my bodyguard, who stood just down the garden path, the wind battering both of us as he watched my back.

"That's Matt. Look, sorry to interrupt you, but I'm trying to find Liv Larsson. Her former assistant said she might be here?"

The young woman twisted slightly, yelling over her shoulder, "Liv! You have a visitor." She turned back to me. "Come on in. She's in the dining room."

I stepped through, Matt following, as we trailed the young woman. Even in my anxious state, I had to grin at her Thanksgiving-themed sweater. The mustard-colored monstrosity had a dancing cooked turkey wearing sunglasses on the back, with the words *Don't put me at the kids' table* written in a font made to resemble spilled gravy. It was hideous. Absolutely hideous.

I loved it.

"Liv, did you hear me?" the woman called again. "You have a visitor!"

"They better have pie!" came Liv's yelled response.

We followed a hall down and into a main living area, across the lounge, and around a corner, stepping into a comfortable dining room, the back of which had French doors that opened onto a patio that overlooked a canal.

Note to self, look into buying a beach house.

Holding court at the head of an old wooden table sat Liv Larsson, producer extraordinaire and the only woman who could help me.

God, I hope she can help me.

"Robbie? What the dickens are you doing here?" She rose, coming to wrap me in a hug and press a kiss to my cheek.

I returned it, introducing Matt then taking in the food-laden table, the two vacant high-chairs, and festive décor.

"Shit. I'm interrupting. Sorry, I'll just—"

"Nonsense!" An older woman, silver streaking her blonde hair, plonked a bowl of mashed potato on the table. "Sit! Both of you. The more the merrier." She gestured to the table with a rueful smile. "And it's not as if we don't have enough. I'm afraid we go overboard during the holidays."

"We eat leftovers for at least a month," the woman in the turkey sweater agreed.

"Jemma, he's Robbie freaking Huynh. No doubt he's got better places to be than having dinner with this clan." An older man, his salt and pepper beard trimmed close to his face, his eyes sharp but kind, sat down at the table. "I'm Sune, the father of this motley crew. And I apologize in advance for their craziness, they get it from their mother."

"Excuse me?"

"And that's Jemma, our mother," Liv said waving toward the older woman who now had her hands on her hips as she death-stared her husband. "Take a seat, guys. We can talk after dinner."

Matt and I were quickly added to the table, and I found myself seated beside Liv's sister, the woman wearing the turkey sweater.

She passed me a bowl of green beans. "It's self-serve around here. And you better get in before Rune and Erik make it to the table. My brothers will eat us out of house and home."

I grinned, accepting the offered bowl. "Thanks for the tip."

The men entered the room trailed by an entourage.

"What? We've already started?"

"That's Erik," the woman said in a hushed whisper, nodding towards the shorter of the two giants. "He's my second oldest brother. Gunnar, my eldest brother, lives down south with his wife."

"And the giant?" I asked, passing her a basket of fresh bread rolls.

"Rune. The baby of the family, if you can believe it. He owns the local bookstore. You should go, they do great food and coffee as well."

I filed that suggestion away.

"And you are?"

She laughed, giving me a saucy wink. "Astrid. But you can

call me girlfriend."

I grinned, enjoying her easy, no-strings attached teasing. "Astrid. Rune, Erik, Gunnar, Liv… I sense a Nordic theme."

She lifted one shoulder in a half shrug. "Dad and Mom are old school. They like to keep some traditions alive and Nordic names are one way they can do that."

She waved at the two women who were settling young children into high chairs. "Gabby is holding Ulf, and Laura is holding Leif. They're Erik's kids."

"I've met Laura."

She slapped her forehead, rolling her eyes at herself. "Of course! Sorry, I forgot about that. You guys work for the same production company."

Not for long, I hope.

Matt leaned over. "I just want to say, this food is fucking ace."

"Thanks. I did absolutely nothing but buy the drinks," Astrid said with a chuckle.

"Where's Nan?" Liv asked, cutting a huge chunk of pie for herself.

"Toilet. She'll be here in a moment. Where's Ian?" Jemma asked, settling at the table.

"On his way. Shouldn't be too far."

Laura set two bowls of mashed vegetables before the kids. "Let's see how long this—"

A spoonful of squash arched across the table slapping me in the cheek.

"Oh, God! Robbie! I'm so sorry!"

I laughed, reaching for a napkin. "Don't worry about it. Kids being kids, right?"

On either side of me, Matt and Astrid laughed heartily.

424

"As long as this doesn't end up on social media, I think we're good."

Astrid pursed her lips together, tipping her head to one side as her eyes danced with amusement.

"Definitely not." She gestured at her sweater. "This is far too fabulous to be appropriately captured on film and there's just not enough space at this table to take sneaky images without getting me in the shot."

I chuckled as the anxious tension that had been coiling in my gut loosened.

Don't get attached. She's Liv's sister. Even if she's not crazy (and the sweater really brings that into question), Liv is unlikely to be supportive of you dating her.

Oh, and you don't date. Remember?

"So, Robbie, Matt," Astrid propped her chin on her hands, shooting us an interested but amused look. "Tell me, do bodyguards have to follow you into the toilet when—"

A large burly, incredibly hairy man burst into the dining room, his wild eyes searching the room, zeroing in on Liv.

"Liv Jemma Larsson!" he bellowed, pointing a large finger directly at her. "Ye need to stop what ye're doing and listen to me."

The table fell silent and I exchanged a startled glance with Astrid.

"Don't worry," she whispered, leaning into me. "It's just Ian, Liv's boyfriend. We're all a little crazy around here."

She grinned and I couldn't stop the ache that settled in my gut. I tried to categorize it and failed. Perhaps it was regret, or maybe longing. Or perhaps some strange mixture of the two, but either way it left me melancholy and feeling as if I were an outsider looking in.

That's because you are.

"I'll keep that in mind," I whispered back, Astrid's perfume tickling my nose, the scent a mix of vanilla and something spicy.

Under the table her thigh pressed into mine for a moment before quickly sliding away. A thread of desire unfurled in me at the innocent touch. I shifted in my seat, my cock beginning to stand to attention.

What the hell, Robbie? You're never like this.

"Just so you know, we may be crazy but we do have a weakness."

"And that is?"

She leaned in, her grin wide, her eyes shimmering with barely contained amusement.

"Pie."

I laughed, turning back to watch the sasquatch declare his undying love for Liv. "I'll keep that in mind."

"Do. It's the only way to a Larsson woman's heart."

Chapter One

Robbie

I checked myself in the mirror a final time. Black jeans, black sweater, black overcoat. Black, black, black.

Good thing I look good in black.

Cape Hardgrave hardly seemed the place to be concerned with looks but I was determined that today would be *my* day. The day I landed the film rights to the book I wanted.

The last time I'd been in Cape Hardgrave had been a mere two weeks ago during Thanksgiving. I'd been chasing Liv Larsson, my producer and the only woman who could help me.

I wasn't one to celebrate Thanksgiving simply because it wasn't something I'd grown up with. I was Vietnamese-Australian. My father hailed originally from South Vietnam having migrated to Australia as a refugee during the war. My mother was a fourth-generation white Australian woman. I'd moved to the United States in my late teens to pursue acting.

At first, I'd been the token Asian kid, the quirky side character with the funny one lines. Then I'd managed to land the lead role in a high school comedy. From there I'd turned into leading man material, America's rom-com heartthrob.

It'd been my worst nightmare.

While other actors got meaty roles in indie films or superhero movies, I'd been stuck playing the romantic lead in movie after movie.

Don't get me wrong, the work was nice and the films did amazing at the box office, but to quote The Little Mermaid, 'I want more'.

Which led me to Thanksgiving dinner with Liv and her family. She'd quit the production company I'd signed with, Catch 22, and I knew her contract had an option in it– she could take with her any three clients that she'd brought into the business.

Liv had signed me back when she'd been working in the film division. We'd made a movie, it'd exceeded expectations, and then she'd been scuttled across to the failing reality show arm of the company while I'd been dumped into rom-com hell.

Now I needed out. Badly. And, to quote *Star Wars*, Liv was my only hope.

Over turkey and sides, we'd chatted through the options. It'd been slightly awkward, her partner, Ian, had just proposed, there was a baby involved and something about Astrid's hair? I didn't get it but Liv had been open to helping me escape my contract.

"I want five years," she'd said around a spoonful of gooseberry pie. "And I want you to choose your projects. I want you to find them, hunt them down, bring me stuff that gets you excited."

"Can you fund it?" I'd asked, a little niggle of concern growing.

Her new fiancé, Ian, had thrown an arm around her shoulder with a laugh, giving her a squeeze. "Aye, she can fund it. She'll have whatever she needs."

Over pie and cider, the sound of football in the background, we'd struck our deal.

It'd been the next morning that I'd found my first project.

In search of coffee and with time to kill before I needed to head to the airport; I'd taken Astrid's suggestion and stumbled into The Literary Academy, the town's local bookstore. While avoiding fans wanting selfies, I'd buried myself amongst the books, hiding between the shelves, getting lost in tiny hidey-holes and pleasant reading nooks. It'd been a wonderland, an escape of simple pleasure.

The book had been in the second-hand section. Shoved in a pile of romance novels and the occasional cookbook waiting to be reshelved, the cover had caught my attention. Plain black, a gun made from blood, *Shadow Lies* in a semi-transparent font that made it look almost as if it were hiding amongst the black, the author's name, A. N. Strid, in plain white.

I knew better than to judge a book by its cover, and this one wasn't fantastic. But there was something about it that called to me.

I'd picked it up, finding a small, hidden alcove with an armchair, Matt taking a seat not too far away. Sipping my coffee, I'd turned to the first page and immediately become engrossed in the story.

I decided to kill Ms. Avery on Tuesday at four o'clock.

Hours passed before I'd been forced to abandon my

reading to travel to the airport and catch my flight home.

I'd practically rushed to be seated on the plane just so I could dive back in, becoming captivated by the narrative, spellbound by the wicked web of deceit and terror the author had woven. The book had ignited something in me, burrowing it deep. I'd neared the climax as we'd gently landed, the plane bumping along the runway as we taxied towards the gate, me hurriedly devouring every sentence.

I'd stayed on board, the last person on the plane to leave in order to finish that final page.

So spellbound by the story, I'd spent that night imagining the screenplay—with me as the antagonist.

Evil walks among us. Ordinary. Friendly. Affable. It steps into the light with the sole intention of casting a shadow. And that shadow runs deep. It spreads until it blocks all light.

I live only to leave those dark places in my wake.

Around 3.00am I'd given up on sleep and spent the rest of the night scrolling the internet to find the mysterious A. N. Strid. Two days passed, then three, then a week. Despite my best efforts, there wasn't anything to find. The author had self-published. They didn't have a website or social pages, and their bio contained a scant three lines.

Fan of true crime podcasts.

Lover of pie and obscure facts.

Not a murderer.

So, I'd done what any sane person did these days– I asked the internet for help.

@TheOfficialRobbieHuynh: Hi internet! Need some help tracking down an author. Anyone have a contact for A. N. Strid? Loved Shadow Lies! Honestly hoping for a sequel. Any info appreciated.

I'd included a picture of me holding the book. While my inbox blew up, within hours a real lead slid into my DMs.

@TheEditbyJane: Hey! OMG! I just wanna start by saying I loved you in The Bro Prince! Anyways, I edited this book. I too thought it was brilliant. Bone-chilling but totally brilliant.

@TheOfficialRobbieHuynh: Which was your favorite part?

@TheEditbyJane: Megan at the end. Did you see that coming!? I didn't!

@TheOfficialRobbieHuynh: Holy shit! Right!? So you know the author?

@TheEditbyJane: Know? Dude, we're like best friends.

@TheOfficialRobbieHuynh: You are? Who is it? Can you give me their details? I need to contact them!

@TheEditbyJane: Sure! Her name is Astrid Larsson. We were roommates during college. She asked me to edit it about six months ago. I didn't realize she'd published it. Kept that one quiet lol!

@TheOfficialRobbieHuynh: Wait. As in Astrid Larsson who lives in Cape Hardgrave?

@TheEditbyJane: That's the one! Last I heard she'd moved back home.

@TheOfficialRobbieHuynh: I thought you were best friends?

@TheEditbyJane: We were but we lost touch after I graduated.

@TheOfficialRobbieHyunh: Do you know if she has socials? Or an email? A phone number even?

@TheEditbyJane: Sorry, no luck. Astrid hates all forms of social media. Shuns it. Probably why you can't find her online. Always said social media was how people found out enough to gain your trust then kill you. I think her cell number has changed but you could try Thor's Shipbuilding. It's her family's business.

One phone call to Thor's Shipbuilding later and I'd

discovered that Astrid Larsson was harder to track down than even the most diligent of A-list celebrities.

You could just call Liv. She'd be able to help.

I ignored that little voice, not wanting to bring my new boss in just yet. I wanted to go to her with a complete project. I wanted to impress her.

I needed to impress her.

Which led me to today, to this very moment.

I'm gonna get these film rights. I have to.

I checked myself in the mirror once again, studying my appearance with a critical eye. If I were to convince Astrid to sign over her creation then I needed to look the part.

And look the part I did. With a small smirk, I turned, heading towards the door, Matt falling in beside me.

A. N. Strid, I'm coming for you.

Chapter Two

Astrid

"This isn't the book I ordered."

The woman, dressed in a Christmas sweater complete with Rudolph with a flashing nose, glared at me holding the book out for me to take.

Would it be rude to ask where she got her sweater from?

Her foot began tapping as her arms crossed.

Uh-oh! Abort! Abort!

"Ah, sorry. Let me take care of this for you. Name?"

"Susan Dawson."

"Just a moment."

I began to type her name into the computer system searching for her order but Susan wasn't having it.

"No, I won't wait a moment. Do you have any idea how busy my day is? I have three other stores to get to in the next two hours. I have presents to buy. I have food to purchase. It's nearly the holidays. I will *not* wait a moment! I want my book now!"

I found her order checking the title with the book.

"Well, Susan, our records show this is the book you

ordered. But if you tell me which book you meant to order I'll—"

"Your records are wrong!" She screamed, her face taking on a red splotchy appearance. "I did *not* order this!"

I sucked in a breath trying to find some calm.

Why did I let Rune talk me into this? Was it money? Cause surely I don't need cash to live and eat and clothe my body this badly. I could become a nudist hermit who lives on the rays from the sun. Christmas in retail is the worst. I regret everything. Everything.

The little voice that I liked to call Evil Astrid, answered back.

You wouldn't be in this predicament if you just told your family about that one teeny weeny minor detail.

Shut your mouth, you whore.

Susan reached for the book, tossing it on the floor as her screaming kicked up a decibel.

I opened my mouth to interject when Rune, my younger brother, and owner of The Literary Academy, appeared at my elbow.

"Ms. Dawson," he greeted smoothly. "Which book were you after?"

I'm not sure if it was his size (well over six feet), his looks (devilishly Viking handsome), or his tone (calming but no-nonsense) but Ms. Dawson calmed the fuck down.

Huh. How do I learn that trick?

"Oh Rune, this woman—"

"My sister."

Ms. Dawson's eyes widened, her throat moving as she visibly gulped. The pulse in her neck jumped, the carotid artery bulging. Evil Astrid began whispering in my ear.

There's a pen knife on the counter. If you press it against the tender flesh at her neck, she might squeak.

"Do you know how long it takes to bleed out?" Your lips would graze the shell of her ear as you'd whisper the question. She'd shake her head, too terrified to speak.

"Let's find out, shall we?"

"Astrid!"

I snapped out of my daydream, blinking up to find Rune's unamused gaze had settled on me.

"Sorry?"

He pressed his lips together, crossing his arms. "I'd ask what you'd done to upset Ms. Dawson, but she's always like that."

I blew out a breath. "Sorry, I'm just a bit...."

"Distracted?"

I nodded, running a hand over my face.

"Astrid, is something wrong?"

You're gonna have to tell them sooner or later.

I looked up into the eyes of my little brother, finding only calm understanding and a lack of judgment.

I'm twenty-seven and currently living in an apartment above my older brother's workshop and temping at my younger brother's bookstore. I hate architecture and failed my final semester which means I have to go back and spend more time and money that I don't have to finish a degree I no longer want. I have an obsession with true crime podcasts that has resulted in me manifesting an Evil Astrid voice in my head. I wrote and self-published a novel that hasn't sold even one copy. I dyed my hair and Mom thinks that means I'm having an existential crisis and... I'm not sure she's wrong.

I pasted a smile on my face, forcing cheer I didn't feel.

435

"Nope, all good."

You little liar.

"Excuse me? Can someone help? I'm looking for a book."

I kept the fake smile glued to my face, turning to the older woman standing at the counter.

"Sure, I can help. What's the title?"

She squinted at me. "Do I know you?"

"Maybe, I'm Rune's sister."

She shook her head. "No, that's not it."

"Um, I've been working here for a week?"

"No, that's not it either."

I shrugged, my patience beginning to wear thin. "So, your book?"

"Yes, it has a red cover and white writing."

I waited for her to continue, mentally sighing when I realized that was all the info she was going to give me.

"Do you remember what it was about? An author or genre? Anything?"

The woman frowned, glancing around. "Where's Rune?"

My brother had vanished into thin air.

The bastard. Can you smother someone with a book? That seems like a way he'd love to die.

"Probably out back dealing with new deliveries." I gritted my teeth, attempting to maintain my smile. "Did you need him for something?"

"He always finds me the book I want."

I sucked in a deep breath holding it for a count of five then let it out slowly. "How about I go for a search? See if I can't find this book you were after. Did you see it in this store? Do you remember approximately where? Maybe we can retrace your steps to work it out."

436

The woman shoved her bifocals up her nose, narrowing her eyes on me. "You had blonde hair."

I raised an eyebrow. "Sorry?"

"In the news article. You had blonde hair."

Great. I'm dealing with a crazy person. Merry Christmas to me.

"News article?" I asked politely.

The woman reached into her massive handbag, rifling through, muttering to herself as she pulled things free, dumping packets of candies, a candle, three tissue packets, and a rather large tube of antacids on the counter.

"Where did I put that darn phone? Always moving about, not where I want it to be when I need it. Useless piece of – here!" She pulled the phone from her bag, holding it up in triumph.

I watched, bemused, as she slowly unlocked it, typing onto the touchscreen with one finger.

"Here we go. This is you, isn't it?"

I took the offered phone, my stomach bottoming out when I saw myself staring out from the screen.

That's my college ID. Shit, am I a missing person? Wait. Am I dead? Is this the bad place?

I scrolled down, reading the article, beginning to experience an out-of-body moment.

It looks like Hollywood heartthrob Robbie Huynh's search for the mysterious A. N. Strid is over – and in record time! Less than 24 hours after he first tweeted his search, an anonymous fan has come forward to reveal the author.

Astrid Larsson, 27, of Cape Hardgrave self-published the book online earlier this year. While it appears to have languished at the bottom of online rankings, reportedly selling less than a hundred

437

copies, it certainly managed to capture Robbie's attention.

"Less than a hundred? More like it didn't sell even one," I muttered.

Robbie reportedly purchased the paperback in the author's home town, becoming obsessed with the crime thriller. His one tweet now has the book rocketing up the rankings, and based on the heated debates on social media, it's likely Shadow Lies might just become the hottest read of the holiday season.

But why is Robbie so interested in tracking down the author? Well, word has it he's after the film rights. For a man who's known for his rom-coms, it's hard to imagine Robbie playing anything other than the hero. Is this his moment to pivot? Or will this gamble flop?

Stay tuned for more updates as they come to hand. Like, share, and subscribe below.

I handed the phone back to the woman in a daze.

"See? That's you, isn't it?"

"Um...."

Shock had rendered me speechless. I pulled my phone from my pocket, needing to verify if this were a joke.

4032 text notifications.

I stared at my screen for a moment, then quickly navigated to my book sales dashboard, unable to comprehend what I was seeing.

206, 509 books sold.

I gulped, my hands shaking as I tucked the phone back into my pocket.

How is this possible? How?

"Excuse me? Astrid?"

My head twisted, gaze landing on the man dressed in all black. The Australian accent, the gorgeous dark eyes, his small cheeky grin, Robbie fucking Huynh was looking at me like he wanted to eat me up.

"Robbie?" I squeaked, fumbling with my phone. "What are... what are you doing here?"

His gaze started at the reindeer antlers gently flashing on my head, dropped to my Christmas wreath earrings, paused on my cherry red lipstick, then continued to my ugly *Home Alone* inspired Christmas sweater before stopping on the candy cane leggings that I'd paired with red Chuck Taylors.

He finally looked up, a muscle jumping in his cheek as if he were fighting a grin. "You wrote *Shadow Lies*?"

I swallowed as Rune approached looking from me, to the old lady, who watched this entire exchange with unconcealed fascination, to Robbie, to Matt, Robbie's bodyguard who hovered in the background.

"I...." I swallowed again, my mouth a desert, my heart in my throat. "Yeah. I wrote it."

"*Shadow Lies?*" Rune asked.

"A book. I wrote a book."

Rune started, his eyebrows raising. "Sorry, did I hear correctly? You wrote a book?"

I nodded, panic beginning to overwhelm me.

"Wow, that's—"

Robbie interrupted Rune, stepping forward, capturing both of my hands in his.

"I need the film rights. Will you sell them to me?" His dark eyes bore into me, pinning me with their intensity.

I stared back, wide-eyed, and freaking out.

"You.... What?"

His face softened, a small grin appearing at the corner of his mouth. "Astrid, you wrote a book I want to make into a movie. What do you say?"

I looked from him to Rune, to the old lady, then back. "No."

Chapter Three

Robbie

Okay, today wasn't exactly going as planned.

For one, Astrid wore the most hideously blatant Christmas outfit I'd ever seen. She also looked tired, strung out, stressed. Dark circles bruised the soft skin under her eyes, her lipstick had been worried mostly away, a perpetual frown marred lines into her forehead, and the tension in her shoulders was evident.

I'd expected tortured artist or the sassy woman from Thanksgiving, not Santa's helper mid-breakdown.

"No?" I repeated.

Astrid withdrew her hands from mine, stepping back. "That's correct. *Shadow Lies* isn't for sale."

Frustration and desperation bubbled up in me, the combination dangerous.

Patience, Robert. You can do this.

"Astrid, let me apologize for the rude introduction. Let's start over." I held out a hand for her to shake. "I'm Robert Huynh."

She took my hand automatically, shaking it with a frown.

"Dude, do you not remember? You came to Thanksgiving."

Well, this is going well.

"I just meant… that is, I thought we could start over."

She made a dismissive gesture. "Look, it's fine. It's nice to see you but I have to get back to work."

"Oh, don't rush on my account." The old lady shoved her glasses up her nose, the bifocals making her eyes look huge. "I'm Maeve, by the way." She held a hand out to me.

I took her offered hand, staring at it awkwardly when she didn't shake but turned it so her knuckles were facing up, holding it as if she were the Queen.

"You're meant to kiss it," she directed with a little push of our joined hands my way.

"Maeve," Rune sighed. "Leave him alone. He's got enough to worry about without you forcing him to kiss you."

He turned to his sister, crossing his arms and giving her an eyebrow lift. "So, you wrote a book?"

She blushed, looking away. "Yeah."

"And you didn't tell me because…?"

"Because it's not great. It hasn't sold even a copy."

Rune, arms still crossed, moved his hand so his thumb pointed at me. "Um, this guy right here who's wanting to buy your film rights says that's a lie."

She coughed, shaking her head. "Sorry, I should say *hadn't*. Not until yesterday."

"And now?"

She pulled the phone out playing on the screen for a second before handing it over to Rune. He read it letting out a low whistle.

"Astie, this is… you're a bestseller. You're going to be famous."

442

She audibly swallowed, shaking her head. "I'm not. Honestly, I'm—" she broke off, spinning to look at me. "Wait. Where did you even get a copy?"

"Here. It was in the second-hand section."

Her eyes bugged out. "And you bought it?"

"Uh-huh. Read it in one day." I stepped forward, attempting to close what felt like a chasm between us. "Astrid, it's really good. Being told through the eyes of the antagonist? You think he's one thing and it turns out he's something else? It's like... Jekyll and Hyde for the modern-day."

She frowned. "I'm sorry. What?"

I pulled the copy from my backpack holding it out to her. "Can you sign it?"

Her eyes grew huge, their blue depths swimming. "Again, I'm sorry, what?"

I grinned. "I want it signed. It'll be a collector's item."

She took the offered book, Rune producing a pen. For a second she hesitated, her face taking on a sense of wonder. Then she wrote on the title page, signed it with a flourish, and handed it back.

"I didn't know you were selling these in my store," Rune commented to his sister.

"Um, I wasn't. The book has been out for over six months and no one wanted to read it. So, I traded in all my copies."

"How many?"

"Three. I could only afford to order three author copies originally."

"Did you keep any of them?"

She shook her head. "No. I needed the money... and I didn't want to see them."

"Fuck. Stay here." Rune disappeared into the shelves,

leaving me with Maeve and Astrid.

I opened the book reading her inscription.

Dear Robbie,

It feels surreal to write this but thank you for being my number one fan.

Granted, you're also my only fan but still, thank you.

Your girlfriend, A. N. Strid.

I laughed, amused she'd remembered our joke from Thanksgiving. "Thanks, girlfriend, but what's the N stand for?"

"Huh?"

I tapped the cover, pointing at the N. "A and Strid is Astrid, right?"

She laughed, nodding. "Yeah."

"And the N?"

"It's for my grandmother, Nan. She's a fellow true crime fan. We listen to podcasts together."

Maeve chose that moment to interrupt.

"Well, this is lovely, but if the boy isn't going to give me his number then I need to get going. Astrid, do you have that book I was after?"

"The one with the red cover and white writing?"

She nodded.

Astrid's face took on a pink color. "I'm not sure which... um... maybe I can—"

Rune reappeared, two books cradled in his arm, a third in his hand. He handed Maeve the red-covered book. She took one look at it and nodded.

"Yep, this is the one."

She slapped a few notes on the counter then toddled off toward the exit, calling a farewell over her shoulder. Rune handed Astrid the two other books.

"Here."

"Rune...." She took the copies of *Shadow Lies*, placing them on the counter. "At least let me pay for them."

"Nope. But I'll take you signing my first batch when it comes in."

The brother and sister smiled at each other; their love for each other clear.

That ache I only ever experienced around the Larssons returned like an unwanted and uninvited toothache.

You have everything you could ever want. Except for these film rights. Just pull it together, man!

"Now," Rune pulled back, waggling a finger at Astrid. "Get back to work, Ms. Author. Today is a madhouse."

Astrid rolled her eyes, catching sight of me still hovering. "You're still here?"

I nodded. "I'll be here all day until you let me pitch to you."

She shook her head, gesturing at the line of people. "You're gonna be waiting a while."

My resolve hardened. "Surely you'll have a lunch break at some point."

She considered me. "If you pay, I'll listen. I'm not promising anything though."

"Done." Triumph had me smiling. "I'll even pitch in and help. I did retail for a few years during my starving artist stage, you know."

She grimaced. "As much as I'd love the help, please don't. You'll cause a riot. Go hide in the shelves, I'll find you when I'm ready."

With that direction she turned, jumping back into the hectic craziness of holiday retail shopping leaving me with a weird sense of anticipation.

To quote Jerry Maguire, show me the money!

Chapter Four

Astrid

Christmas movies were nothing but lies. There was nothing good about this time of the year.

Well, not if you worked in retail. I'd once again bought into the lies, wearing the paraphernalia and thinking that this time of year was full of cookies, roasted chestnuts, Christmas trees, and goodwill to all men.

Lies. I called lies on the whole damned thing. There was nothing good about this time of the year, bah humbug!

"—which is why you're going to give me a discount!" The man finished screeching in my face. His core complaint seemed to be centered around a spelling mistake he'd found in a traditionally published book.

"Well, sir, as you would be aware, we are not the publishing company. I would be more than happy to give you a refund, however, we can't—"

"I want it fixed! Today! I can't gift this to someone with a mistake in it."

I gritted my teeth, attempting to paste a smile on my face. "Sir, please, as you can understand—"

"I said I want a new book! Corrected! Now!"

Spittle flew through the air landing on my cheek. We both stared at each other for a beat, his gaze dropping to the large wad on my skin.

"Dude… ew. Seriously, so uncool." I reached under the counter finding an antibacterial wipe and quickly cleaning my cheek. "I think you'd better leave."

"But what about my—"

My patience snapped. I suddenly understood why someone might commit murder.

"Sir, it's time to go. You can come back when you're ready to be calm."

"Excuse me, I—"

"Good day to you, sir." I snapped.

"But—"

"I said, good day!" I crossed my arms, glaring over the counter.

Behind him, the line of customers was a mix of eye-rolls, amusement, or sympathetic smiles as they watched me deal with this crazy man.

With a final bluster, he gathered his things and stormed from the counter, heading towards the door, brushing past Rune on his way out.

Rune's eyebrows raised and he shook his head, disappearing back into the shelves.

I should really try not to alienate all the customers in one day.

I managed to serve the rest of the line without incident, clearly a Christmas miracle with the way this day was going.

"You ready for lunch?" Ashley, my brother's assistant store manager, asked, her shock of red hair, bobbing dangerously as her Santa hat hair clip pulled the precarious mass to one side.

My stomach grumbled in response to her question. She laughed, waving me off, turning to serve a young woman searching for a book on tantric breathing for her anniversary.

Hmm, I wonder if there are books on how to suffocate people.

I forcefully shoved Evil Astrid into a dungeon, sending her to the naughty corner.

Hush you, we can think about that creepy shit when we're not in public.

I went searching through the shelves finding Robbie in one of the small alcoves, his bodyguard pretending to read a book nearby. The guy looked like a linebacker which meant his attempt at blending was failing, big time.

I crept up, leaning on the shelf beside him.

"Hey Matt, is he free?"

He nodded, holding out his hand to give it a firm shake. "You can go over, he's just rereading."

"Rereading?"

"Mm, your book. He's pretty obsessed. Highlights passages and everything."

I raised an eyebrow, glancing Robbie's way. Sure enough, he was engrossed in my book, the pages marked with post-it notes.

"He's serious?"

"Deadly."

Huh. There you go.

I glanced at Matt, raising an eyebrow. "Have you read it?"

He grinned, nodding. "Forced it on me. It's good. Real good. And I say that as someone who hates reading. That scene with the cops in the sewer?" He shuddered. "Stuff of goddamned nightmares."

Something warm lit in me, a weird fluttering of anxious pleasure.

They liked it. They really, really liked it.

At the same time, for some reason that made me almost panicked. I'd published hoping someone would read my story. Only two people had ever read *Shadow Lies* before I hit publish, that being me and my former roommate, Jane. She'd edited it in exchange for me cleaning the apartment for a month.

I hadn't expected anything special. Maybe one or two sales. But after six months of nothing but crickets, I'd slowly shelved any hope, focusing on my final semester.

Load of good that did me.

"Robbie?"

His head jerked up, his gaze focusing on me.

"Oh, hey. Is it lunchtime?"

God, that accent.

Evil Astrid agreed, letting out a contented purr.

"Um," I cleared my throat. "Yep. Shall we?"

The Literary Academy was split across two warehouses. One held the giant bookstore, the other, connected via a small walkway which Rune had turned into a book tunnel, held the café-slash-bar.

We walked through, Robbie staring up at the walls of the tunnel as Matt trailed us.

"Are these books all real?" He asked, running fingers along the spine.

"Of course. It took Rune over two months to build it. He made us all pitch in, even Liv. Though it would have taken half the time if she'd not accidentally destroyed a quarter of it."

"Your family seems close."

A knot formed in my stomach, guilt roiling in my gut. "We are."

"Must be nice."

I glanced his way, raising an eyebrow. "You're not?"

He shook his head. "I was a mistake, the only child of only children. My parents are great, don't get me wrong, but I wasn't in the plans. They did their best but never quite knew what to do with me."

"You moved to LA when you were young, right?"

He nodded, his face tilting back as we exited the tunnel, walking into the warmly lit café. "Yeah. Sixteen, seventeen. Something like that. They had a friend who was willing to put me up in his spare room."

"What about school?" I asked as we snagged an empty booth, the café hopping with holiday catch-ups.

"I did distance for a while. Graduated and tried to get into Juilliard but that fell over. So I did the poor waiter thing, working as a store clerk at night, going to auditions all day."

I handed him a menu while Matt took a seat at the bar. "And that worked out for you."

He laughed. "Yeah, I got lucky. Ran into Glenn, my agent. He took me on, found me a few small gigs and it grew from there."

"And now you're America's heartthrob."

His face twisted, something passing over it. "Yeah."

Uh-oh. There's a story there.

The waiter arrived, we ordered, then sat awkwardly while Matt watched discreetly from the bar.

"So—"

"Can I—"

We broke off, laughing.

"You first," I said, giving him a nod.

"Can I tell you what I loved the most?"

A blush crept up my neck, heat flushing my cheeks. "Um, sure."

He tapped the book cover, shaking his head. "Megan."

Ah, the protagonist.

"Every moment you were thinking she's nothing but a doe in a hunter's periscope. Then that shift at the end? Phwaww!" He laughed. "Took me by surprise. Took the killer by surprise as well."

A reluctant grin tugged at my lips. "She enjoyed toying with him."

"And you enjoyed toying with the reader."

Yeah, I did.

The entire book was premised on the idea that the narrator was stalking little Megan Somett from 11 Dresden Drive. The murderer, a man, was obsessed with killing her. He fantasized about it as he committed atrocities on others, but never quite got her in the right place to enact the deed.

In the closing chapters it finally happened, the stars aligned and the reader braced for him to finish Megan off... only for Megan to turn around and kill him. The hunter, it turned out, was really the prey.

The waiter returned with our lunch, handing over drinks, hesitating as she served up our plates.

"Um, I hope this isn't rude but... would you mind if I took a photo?"

I glanced at Robbie seeing him nod.

"Sure, go right ahead."

"Oh my God, thanks so much!"

She pulled a phone out of her pocket, crouching in front of the table as Robbie shifted, leaning over her shoulder and smiling. I pulled back, moving out of the shot only for the girl to frown, shaking her head.

"Astrid, aren't you going to be in it too? You're famous!"

"Oh... um... sure. I mean. Of course."

I leaned in, pasting a smile on my face, staring into the lens as she clicked a few.

"Thanks so much!" She squealed, cradling her phone. "No one was going to believe me otherwise. Enjoy your lunch!"

She bounced away, disappearing into the crush of diners.

"Does that happen often?" I asked, reaching for my latte.

"Yeah. Multiple times a day."

I shook my head. "I honestly can't imagine that. It seems so intrusive."

He shrugged, digging into his pulled pork sandwich. "Price of fame."

Sucky price.

I scooped up a spoonful of my soup, blowing softly. "You know, even if I wanted to give you the rights, which I don't because the books are always better, there's an issue."

He raised an eyebrow, still chewing.

"Liv." I gave a one-shouldered shrug. "Not that they're for sale but if they were, my sister forever and always gets first dibs."

Robbie scratched his chin. "So, I need to speak to Liv?"

I nodded then shook my head. "Yes. I mean no. It's not going to change anything."

"But I can try?"

I blew out a breath, rolling my eyes. "Look, you can but

453

could you wait? I mean, that is... I haven't actually told them about the book just yet."

"I'm sorry?"

I hesitated, using my spoon to stir my soup. "Umm... I mean... that is to say... um...." I cleared my throat. "I kind of didn't tell them."

"Like... at all?"

I nodded, cringing. "Yeah."

"Oh man," he sniggered. "You're dead meat."

He's not wrong.

"Yeah well, this is all your fault you know." I pointed my spoon at him. "If you'd just left me alone like a normal person—"

"Nope. Not gonna happen. I need those film rights."

"Then I guess we're in a standoff, cause, for the hundredth time, they're not for sale."

He took an aggressive bite of his sandwich frowning at me as he chewed.

"What?" I asked, the trill of my phone interrupting us. I pulled it free, frowning at the unknown number.

"Hello?"

"Is this A. N. Strid?"

"Yes?"

"Hold please."

I frowned as the phone went silent for a beat then a man's booming voice echoed down the line.

"Is this Ms. Strid?" He asked, his tone jolly.

"Um, yes. Who are you?"

"Bob Taylor, Catch 22 Productions. I want to buy your film rights for *Shadow*—"

I hung up on him, sliding the phone onto the table.

Robbie raised an eyebrow, swallowing his bite. "All good?"

I nodded, glancing at the number as my phone began to ring again.

Unknown number.

I blew out a breath, answering it.

"Hello?"

"Ms. Strid? It's Bob, looks like we were disconnected."

"Nope, I hung up. Don't want to talk to you. Please stop calling."

"Wait! Why? I'm offering you millions here!"

"Dude, I'm Astrid Larsson, my sister is Liv Larsson. You know, the woman you decided not to promote? I don't care how much you're offering me; you can get stuffed."

With that parting snap, I ended the call, slapping my phone back on the table with a huff.

"Was that... Bob?" Robbie asked, his eyes wide.

For an actor, he has zero poker face. He'd never be able to be a serial killer. A victim though....

I hushed Evil Astrid.

"Yeah. Hopefully, he took the hint."

"How much did he offer?"

I shrugged. "Supposedly millions. But nothing is worth my dignity. Or that of my sister."

Robbie finished his sandwich, chewing slowly as he wiped his hands clean on a napkin, considering me with a thoughtful expression.

"What?" I asked, lifting my spoon to my mouth. "You keep looking at me like that."

"If I call Liv right now and got her permission, would you sell me the rights?"

I hesitated for a moment, tempted to lie to him then shook

my head slowly. "Sorry, no."

"But why?"

Because I'm a failure. Because I know this wouldn't be a success.

"Because the movie is never as good as the book."

Chapter Five

Robbie

I found myself on an abandoned beach, staring into the distance like some discarded lover. The freezing wind whipped at my hair and cheeks but I ignored the chill, determined to clear my head. Even Matt had abandoned me, swearing softly a half hour ago and retreating into our car, watching me from inside the warmth.

On a day like this, even the most diehard of stalkers would be hard-pressed to get out of bed.

Unless you're me.

And therein lay the issue. Ms. Astrid Larsson had turned me into a stalker.

Wind whipped up damp sand tossing it in my face as the ocean crashed into the shore. My violent emotions appreciated the turbulence of the churning sea and bitter icy wind.

No.

Astrid's overt rejection echoed through my ears, hardening my resolve. I needed her to say yes. I needed her to trust me with this project.

The movie is never as good as the book.

Her reasoning dug into me, niggling, burrowing like a splinter, prodding me to consider the problem from all perspectives.

I need Liv.

Liv Larsson had to be one of the most brilliant producers I'd ever met. She had a mind that I envied, able connect dots to pull at heartstrings in a way few could rival.

It also didn't hurt that she was Astrid's sister.

I pulled my phone from my pocket hesitating on calling her.

This would be a mistake. Astrid asked me not to talk to Liv until she'd told the family about Shadow Lies. You can't break her trust—no matter how much you want those rights.

I sighed, beginning to shove the phone back in my pocket when it rang. I glanced at the screen, shaking my head when I saw Liv's name.

"Liv?"

"Robbie fucking Huynh, what's this I hear about you stalking my sister?"

Ah crap.

"Look, all I wanted was to get a contact. How was I to know her face would end up splashed across news sites?"

I'd woken to messages from my publicist advising that my search for Astrid had gone viral, her face plastered across news sites and bulletins as the image of me and her in the coffee shop with that waitress had appeared.

The confirmation that I'd not only met but was having lunch with the author I sought, had set the gossip mill atwitter with theories.

Liv made a noise, one I associated with pursed lips, raised

eyebrows, and heavy judgment.

Okay, this isn't going well.

I ran a hand over my face, grimacing as I rubbed sand into my skin. "Liv, I need this. You asked me to find a project. This is the one. I want *Shadow Lies.*"

There was a long pause. "Robbie, where are you? You sound like you're in a wind tunnel."

"I'm on a beach."

Another pause. "Exactly *which* beach?"

I glanced at the sign. "Coral?"

Liv huffed down the phone. "So it's true. You're in Cape Hardgrave?"

I winced at her tone. "Um, yes?"

Silence roared down the line, her judgment thick.

I squirmed, unsure of what I could say that wouldn't make this whole situation ten times worse.

Oh, and I find your sister delightful and am legitimately contemplating asking her for a date?

Eventually, Liv sighed. "Right, here's what we're going to do. You'll come to my parents' house for dinner tonight. Astrid is going to *finally* announce to the family she's written a novel. We're going to eat my mother's cooking and listen to my father bemoan the weather. You'll accept the wine my fiancé offers, and won't, I repeat, *won't* mention how I've popped in the last two weeks. Seriously, Robbie, I'm birthing a hippo."

I swallowed a laugh.

"After dinner, Astrid and I will retreat to the study where you will pitch your idea. We will then discuss it and work out if it is the right decision for her. I love you, Robbie. But my loyalty is forever and always with Astrid."

"That's what she said about you."

She chuckled, her voice warming incrementally. "So, you spoke to her first?"

"Yeah. Yesterday."

"And?"

"She turned me down."

Liv barked out a laugh. "Good girl."

"But you'll help me?"

She remained quiet for a long time. "Yes. But only because you sound desperate. Seriously, dude, it's not an attractive attribute. Do better."

I laughed, feeling lighter than I had in days. "Can you text me the address?"

"Will do. Be on time. And bring something. My mother likes flowers."

I hung up, pushing to a stand with a groan, cold muscles tight from disuse. I stretched for a moment then headed back up to the car where Matt waited, listening to a podcast.

"You done?" He asked as I slid into the passenger seat.

"Yep."

"Home?"

I glanced outside, watching as the first heavy drops of sleet begin to fall, dotting the window. Resolve stiffened my spine and I suffered an overwhelming need to see what weird and wacky cardigan Astrid wore that day.

"Actually, you want a coffee?"

Matt chuckled, putting the car in drive. "Is coffee what we're calling it now?"

"No comment."

Unfortunately Astrid wasn't working but at least the coffee was good.

460

CHAPTER FIVE

Chapter Six

Astrid

Ambushed. My family had ambushed me.

I'd had the day off and spent it avoiding calls, text and any form of news article.

My family, apparently, had not.

Around the table sat my Nan, Father, my brother Erik and his fiancé, Laura, Rune, and his fiancé, Gabby, Liv, and her fiancé, Ian, and Robbie, all of us sitting in deadly silence as I stared at the meatloaf that dominated the middle of the table. My unease grew as Mom placed dishes of boiled potatoes and green beans beside the lump of baked meat.

If you didn't already know you were in trouble...

Rune leaned in, his whisper barely audible. "You are *so* dead."

I barely resisted the urge to elbow my younger sibling. "Shut up. It could be they just want a healthy alternative."

"Meatloaf, Astrid? Really?"

Mom took her seat at the table reaching for her napkin. She flicked it with a sharp snap, laying it on her lap.

Uh-oh. No rolls. I am about to be slaughtered.

"Please." She gestured at our surprise guest for the evening. "Robbie, do start."

The table winced collectively as he reached for the meatloaf, slicing off a hunk.

"Am I missing something?" he asked in a low tone as he passed the plate to me.

I bit my lip, shooting Mom a glance. She ignored me, serving Nan three plain potatoes.

This is it. This is how I die. Over a plate of meatloaf and unseasoned vegetables.

My mother was a former gourmet chef. Her worst dish was meatloaf because she didn't believe in cooking something that came out looking like a rather large poo.

I leaned toward Robbie, about to give him a heads up when my mother dropped a platter on the table with a clang, staring across the table at me.

"Really, Astrid? Really? You couldn't have told us about this achievement? I had to hear about it from Martha Stanisbury who saw it on the news?"

I cringed at the hurt in her voice. "I'm sorry, Ma. But—"

"No buts," Dad interrupted, shaking his head. "You owe your family an apology."

My cheeks burned, my eyes beginning to sting. "I'm sorry for not telling you."

Are you going to admit why?

"Thank you for your apology," Mom said with a little sniff. "Now, why didn't you tell us before? It's fine to be private but this isn't a small thing, Astrid. This is life changing. Is this to do with your hair?"

I raised a hand, hovering it over my hair, a little part of me sighing in frustration.

463

I'd dyed my hair brown just before Thanksgiving. I'd been itchy, unsettled, and thought a new look might help. It hadn't but that didn't mean I didn't like the hair color.

"What's wrong with my hair?"

Mom waved me off. "That's not the true question here, Astrid. The question is why didn't you trust us?"

Because I'm a failure and didn't want to disappoint you.

The words stuck in my throat, shame swirling in my belly.

I sucked in a breath, the lie falling from my lips easily. "I didn't think it was that big a deal."

Mom pressed her lips together, her eyes flashing with annoyance. "And when it became a big deal?"

I looked at Robbie, my eyes pleading with him to help. He gave me an encouraging smile, his hand finding mine under the table but he didn't say anything, simply allowing me space to speak.

Ugh. Why is this so hard?

"I…." I swallowed, trying to conjure up a believable story.

A kernel of truth in a lie rings truer than a fabricated tale.

Thanks, Evil Astrid.

"I guess it was fear. And maybe a bit of doubt. Before Robbie read it and started tweeting, *Shadow Lies* was a certifiable flop. I guess I just thought… if I kept it to myself no one had to know it wasn't successful."

All heads swiveled from me to watch Mom weigh my words.

"And your degree?"

Fuck.

I stiffened, casting my gaze around the table, finding my siblings all with their heads down, studiously shoveling meat into their mouths. Only Robbie faced me, his hand still warm and reassuring in mine under the table.

Thanks, team. I appreciate the support.

Though, in all fairness, I'd have done the same had I been in their shoes. And I had, many times before.

"I...." I choked, unable to push out the words.

"You?" Mom asked, raising an eyebrow in question.

"Failed."

There was a collective sucking in of breath, all heads lifting to stare at me.

My already red face flushed hotter, humiliation churning my gut.

Failed. I'm a big fat failure.

"You.... Oh, Astrid." Any residual anger or hurt melted from my mother's face as she pushed to stand, immediately rounding the table. "Come here, my darling."

I shoved up, letting her pull me into a hug, savoring the feel of her arms around me, taking all the comfort she could give.

"You worked so hard," she whispered, her hand cupping my head. "I'm sorry, baby."

I swallowed, fighting the bitter tears that rose at her empathetic tone. "I'm sorry for failing."

"Did you do your best?"

I thought of all those nights working on my thesis, the extra study groups, the multiple meetings with my useless, sexist mentor.

We should have killed him with a stapler.

"Yes."

"Then you didn't fail. You just learned what to do differently next time." She cupped my cheek, tilting my head down until she could press a kiss to my forehead. "Now, eat

465

your dinner."

I watched her walk away, the table relaxing with Mom's blessing.

Not for long, Evil Astrid whispered. *It would have been easier if you'd laced the meatloaf with cyanide.*

I straightened my shoulders, determined to get this over and done with.

"Actually, I'm not going back."

The table froze, all heads whipping to me then across to Mom.

"Astrid?" She whispered her eyes wide. "What do you mean?"

"I'm not going back. I... I don't want to be an architect. I hate it. I've hated it for years but I didn't know what else to do. I thought I had to do... something. And it seemed as good as anything." My hands began to fly around as I tried to justify my decision. "I'm going to write novels. Don't worry, I'll pay you back for my schooling. Even if I have to—"

A thought occurred to me, an idea that might wipe the worried expression from my mother's face.

"Astrid?"

I looked at Robbie, the idea taking root, giddy excitement beginning to bubble in my chest. "Robbie and I are going to co-write *Shadow Lies*."

"We're going to—" Robbie bit off, forcing a smile on his face. "Yep. That's exactly what we're doing."

"But you've never written a script before," Liv pointed out. "Either of you."

Robbie cleared this throat. "Actually, I have. It just wasn't very good. But *Shadow Lies* is already amazing. I expect it

466

won't be too hard to work out how to translate it to the big screen."

I caught Dad's exasperated shake of his head.

"Dad, I'm sorry. But this is what I want to do. Even if it never gets made, *Shadow Lies* is selling well, thanks to Robbie."

"I wouldn't be surprised if it makes the bestseller lists this week," Rune commented as he forked a bland potato. "And Astie's self-published. More royalties for her. The book is also excellent. If she follows it up, she could make a lucrative career out of thriller novels."

My brother's praise which was so rarely delivered, felt doubly special as I knew he'd have read the book as soon as he found out about it.

"Thanks, bro."

He sent me a smile. "It's really good. Thank you for being an amazing author."

Erik slapped a hand on the table, drawing attention to him. "You'll need a lawyer. We're not having our sister get taken advantage of by some no-good actor."

Robbie flushed while Liv rolled her eyes.

"Ian?" She asked her fiancé, arching an eyebrow in his direction.

"I think I could handle it for ye." He said, swirling his wine gently in his glass. "But I'll be wanting a signed copy of ye book, Astrid. Or maybe two." He reached over, placing a large hand on Liv's gently rounding stomach. "We've got to support the tiny dictator once she arrives."

It was Erik's turn to roll his eyes. "As if you're hurting for money."

A trust fund child, Ian had more money than my entire

family combined – not that you'd ever know it. The man looked like a sasquatch, all red hair and crazy beard. His fashion sense also left something to be desired, but he made my sister blissfully happy so I didn't mind.

Laura chuckled, pushing Erik's face away. "Well, I for one think this is an amazing opportunity, Astrid. Let us know what we can do to help. Will you need blood removal suggestions? Cause I once had to assist with cleaning a crime scene and—"

Laura, the Queen of Clean, was off, describing in gruesome but fascinating detail how to remove brain matter from fabric wallpaper as we continued to eat Mom's offering.

"All right," Nan tapped her fork against her plate, interrupting Laura's explanation. "As fascinating as splattered brain matter and cleaning agents are, let's change the subject before I decide I can't eat pie for dessert."

"Pie?" Liv asked, perking up. "What kind of pie?"

"Pecan," Dad said, serving himself a second helping of green beans. "And yes, *I* made it."

"Sune's a brilliant baker," Gabby told Robbie with a grin. "I'm trying to talk him into making our wedding cake."

"My son wants a book stack wedding cake. I'm not making that shit," Sune grunted, shaking his head.

"I said I'd accept a single book," Rune replied with a shrug.

"You!" Nan brought the attention back to her, her gaze narrowed in on Robbie. "Movie star, pick a subject."

Robbie threw me a wide-eyed glance.

"What would you like to talk about?"

Nan shrugged. "Anything *but* brain matter would be a good start."

"Er…." He cast a glance around the room, his gaze focusing on my chest.

Well, hello Mr. Huynh.

My body clenched, awareness spiking between us as he met my gaze.

"Movies!" He declared, turning away, a slight flush heating his cheeks. "Christmas movies. Which is your favorite and why?"

Excuse me? Christmas movies? He looks at my chest and thinks Christmas movies? Oh, this man is about to—

I silenced Evil Astrid.

"Christmas movies… hmm…." Nan nodded at my sweater. "Well, we all know Astrid's favorite."

I looked down, suddenly feeling like an idiot as I took in the *Home Alone* inspired ugly sweater, one of six I owned.

He's a movie star you dolt. He's not going to be interested in some backwater failure of a woman.

And yet…

"Rune, you start," Nan directed.

"*A Christmas Carol.* Though I prefer the book."

The table collectively groaned, Erik throwing a bean in Rune's direction.

"Of course you do." Gabby patted her fiancé's hand. "Sune?"

"*The Grinch,*" Dad grunted. "There's something rather appealing about being alone for Christmas."

"Oh, hush." Mom laughed, slapping him lightly. "You all know mine."

Robbie shot me a raised eyebrow.

"*The Holiday.* Mom's a big romantic and loves a good Kate Winslet film."

469

"Well give me *Die Hard* any day," Nan declared raising her glass in a toast. "If I were forty years younger, I'd have married Bruce Willis and you'd all be movie royalty."

"If that's a Christmas movie then I'll eat my hat," Erik retorted, wrapping an arm around Laura's chair and snuggling her into him.

"Oh yeah? Then what's yours?" Laura asked him.

"*Love, Actually*. Emma Thompson is a queen and every time I watch it I want to dick punch Alan Rickman."

I chuckled, looking at Robbie.

"*Blinky Bill*. It's an Australian cartoon about a koala. There's a whole series but every year they'd trot out the Christmas special. While my parents were celebrating with friends that's the movie I'd be in my bedroom watching."

"Just you?"

He laughed, nodding. "My parents had me late in life. A little surprise for both of them, I'm afraid. Their friendship group weren't exactly kid-people, and those who had children, the kids were already grown by the time I came along."

My heart squeezed at the thought of this lonely little boy watching Christmas movies by himself.

"Well, mine is *Rudolph*," Gabby declared, bopping Rune on the nose. "I love an underdog story."

"You know, I always thought he could do better." I shrugged. "Just seemed like those so-called friends were royal dicks."

Beside me, Robbie sniggered as the table groaned.

"Thanks for ruining Gabby's Christmas," Gabby said with a laugh, flicking me the bird.

"Any time."

"What's yours then?" Robbie asked. "Is it *Home Alone?*"

"Contrary to popular belief, it's actually not. Mine's the same as Ian, after all, he introduced me to it two years ago."

Eyebrows collectively raised around the table.

"*Arthur Christmas,*" he said with a grin. "The grandfather cracks me up every time."

Liv rolled her eyes. "I should have known. You watched it three times last week."

"It's a good thing ye love me."

"Aye," she said in a terrible accent. "That it is."

They kissed as Mom stood. "Dessert! And a movie, I should think. How about *The Holiday?*"

With laughter we separated, clearing the table as pie was served, and coffee and tea handed out.

Liv caught me, gesturing to Robbie to follow, leading us into Dad's study.

She settled behind the desk, a giant slice of pie in front of her. She lifted her steaming cup of tea to her lips, blowing on it gently.

"This seems a bit redundant now, what with Astrid's dinner declaration. But go on, Robbie. Pitch your vision to us."

I settled on the settee, sipping my own tea as he turned away from us, offering his back. His shoulders hunched for a moment as if he were folding in on himself, then he sucked in an audible breath, straightened them, and spun back around his gaze terrifyingly blank.

"I decided to kill Ms. Avery on Tuesday at four o'clock."

Chills raced down my spine, goosebumps dimpling my skin, the hairs on the back of my neck rising at his tone. He'd done something to his voice, it was lower, softer

471

but so clear and horrifyingly devoid of inflection that you simultaneously revolted against him and inched closer to hear every horrific word utter from between his lips.

I lost myself in his monologue, his dead-eyed stare so perfectly capturing James that I could no longer conjure the image of the character I'd created. Now, there was only Robbie.

I've never been more attracted to someone in my life.

A phone rang, startling Liv and me. From his pocket, Robbie pulled the phone free, his blank expression still in place.

He slid his thumb across the face of the screen, his expression morphing into a charming mask that slid over his features with far too much ease.

"Ms. Avery? Yes, this is James. I've consulted my calendar, how does Tuesday at four sound?"

The switch from dead-eyed killer to charming guy-next-door was so abrupt, so jarring that Liv and I exchanged startled glances, our eyes wide and filled with questions.

He drew us back as he chatted with the fake caller, his expression animated up to the point he hit end, then the mask fell away, leaving death in its wake.

Perfection. He is utter perfection.

He lifted his head, his gaze meeting mine.

"I find I love the way they die."

He turned away from us, his body curving back into himself before he shook off the character, turning back around.

"Co-star?" Liv barked.

"Beatrix Bennett for Piper. The rest we'll need to audition for."

"Director?"

"Samuel Archer."

Liv nodded in approval. "Budget?"

"Twenty-five million."

"So low?"

He shrugged. "If we do it right, sure. This isn't a flash-bang blockbuster. This is quietly insidious. It's about the actors and the score. The cinematography. There are no explosions or car chases. Just a predator manipulating those around him."

Liv considered him for a moment as my stomach clenched at the casual way they discussed millions of dollars as if it were but a drop in an ever-expanding ocean.

"Alright. That makes sense to me, but we'll need a buffer of thirty-percent." She glanced my way. "Astrid?"

I swallowed, my heart hammering loud enough to drown out the television outside. "Yes?"

She arched an eyebrow, tilting her head in Robbie's direction. "It's your story, sis. You get to decide if he's going to bring this to life."

I looked at Robbie, his expression hopefully.

"I accept. On one condition."

"Anything."

"I want to write it. I want full creative control of the script, Robbie. I need to be involved in every aspect of its development."

He hesitated, glancing at Liv.

Please. I need this.

She sipped her tea, letting us work out the details.

"That's my one condition. Take it or leave it." I pressed my palms together in my lap, hating how damp they felt.

473

He nodded once then held out a hand, waiting for me to take it. I covertly wiped mine on my jean leg then accepted his brisk shake.

"Let's make a movie."

Chapter Seven

Robbie

This was a huge mistake.

I watched Astrid stare at the blank whiteboard, the marker turning over and over in her hand as she worried her lip, a frown marring her forehead.

We'd been at this for forty-minutes and not one word had been written, not one scene discussed. She'd arrived at the doorstep of my rental at the crack of dawn, whiteboard tucked under one arm, a bag overflowing with props and stationery thrown over the other.

I'd welcomed her into the condo with a smile, offering coffee and pastries. She'd accepted the coffee, waving off the breakfast sweets in order to get started.

Only, we'd hit a block. And that block was named Astrid Larsson.

At least she's a cute block. Would it be weird to tell her that?

She wore a red Christmas sweater today, the fabric so plush and soft that I wanted to reach out and compare its feel to that of Astrid's skin.

Wait. You want to what?

I frowned into my cooling coffee.

You're not into Astrid. You can't be. You're work colleagues now. Remember?

Besides, I'd been on a celibacy pledge for close to ten years, ever since I'd started getting decent parts. I didn't have time for romance, and hook-ups had never been my style.

And yet....

I shoved any thoughts of romance aside, downing the dregs of my cold coffee with a grimace.

"Okay, let's talk. What's the issue, Astrid?"

She glanced at me, a slight blush dusting her cheeks. "You'll laugh if I tell you."

I raised an eyebrow. "Try me."

She hesitated then handed me the whiteboard marker, digging through her prop bag to pull out a set of reindeer antlers.

"I need to wear these."

Don't laugh. Don't laugh. Don't laugh.

I nodded, swallowing my amusement and pasting what I hoped was a blank expression on my face. "Okay, sure. I've seen weirder things than that. Whatever you need."

She blew out a breath, a small grin beginning to tug at her lips. "You think I'm weird."

"No more... eccentric maybe? I mean you write gruesome thrillers and yet look like a kindergarten teacher. It's an amusing dichotomy."

"Great," she laughed, rolling her eyes as she settled the antlers on her head. "I'm weird."

I opened my mouth to defend eccentricity but hesitated, aware of the risk of revealing too much of myself. I'd long ago learnt that people often took that information and sold it to the highest bidder.

You have to trust someone.

I swallowed, deciding to take a chance.

"When I first started in the industry, I wore fake glasses."

Astrid laughed, her eyes twinkling. "Are you serious?"

"Completely." I leaned in, lowering my voice. "You can't tell anyone because I just brushed it off later as having reading glasses. But sometimes, when I'm particularly nervous about an audition or attending a gala or interview or whatever, I'll dig them out and wear them around."

"You didn't wear them yesterday."

I grinned, pushed up from the table, and went to the coat rack by the door. For a moment I dug through the pockets of my jacket before pulling the glasses free. I held them up, enjoying Astrid's surprised giggles.

"See? Even just having them on me is comforting."

She shook her head, the antlers swaying with her movement. "Why glasses?"

I shrugged, returning them to my pocket. "I don't know. Superman complex maybe? There's just something really reassuring about them. It's like I'm able to turn into someone else when I wear them. As if I'm marketing 'Robbie Huynh, America's sweetheart', and not 'Robert Huynh, the guy they called Bob back at school'."

"Bob?" Her eyebrows flew up.

I nodded, chuckling. "When I signed on with Catch 22 Productions, they made me change it. Said it didn't feel sexy enough."

"What do you prefer?"

"Robbie works."

Astrid wrinkled her nose. "I can't believe they made you

change your—" she cut herself off, her eyes losing focus for a moment.

"Uh, Astrid?"

"Shh." She held up a hand, staring off into the distance for a moment. "Marketing…. You said you turned into someone else and it was all just marketing."

She pushed to her feet, urgently popping the cap on a whiteboard marker as she began to scribble in the top left-hand corner.

Opening scene – James at a pitch meeting. He's charismatic, charming, and likable.

"Oh," I whispered, leaning closer to catch her small murmurs as she wrote on the board. "I like that."

"He's going to be in marketing in the movie. We can't have the slow build-up as we did in the book, it's a different medium. And we don't want them to learn he's a serial killer just yet. We want them to like him. To feel for him. To be cheering him on."

"Unreliable narrator. I love it." I stood, reaching for my own marker and began to draw opposite Astrid on the board. "Let me storyboard this."

While Astrid wrote dot points for each of the scenes, I built a set sketch, each of us bouncing ideas off the other.

"What if we don't know he's the killer until half-way? Like we build him up to be the hero, never showing the killer's face until there's a subtle reveal?"

"Ohh, that's evil." I lifted a hand for her to slap. "That's worthy of a coveted high-five."

She laughed, slapping my palm then turning back to make a note on the timeline she'd begun to build out. "This is surprisingly more fun than I anticipated."

I reached out, flicking her antler ears gently. "I'd say these certainly helped."

We got back to it, working out how her already incredible story could be adapted to the screen.

Matt wandered in a while later, scratching his chest. "Hey, you guys want some lunch? I was thinking about going and getting a sandwich from that café you like, Robbie."

I blinked, glancing up at the clock, startled to see that four hours had passed since we'd started.

"Um, yeah, that'd be great. Astrid?"

"Hm?" she was staring at her computer screen, having finished at the whiteboard.

"Lunch?"

"Sure. A coke, please."

I shared a grin with Matt.

"Just grab us whatever is on special. You need cash?"

Matt shook his head, tapping his pocket. "I'm good. You cool to stay here?"

"Yep."

He shot me a thumbs up before heading out, leaving Astrid and me to our work.

I studied her as she frowned at her screen, viciously backspacing.

"You okay?" I asked, pushing my sketchbook aside.

Astrid came back to herself slowly, blinking a few times as she disconnected from the laptop.

"Sorry... did you say something?"

I grinned, rising from my seat. "Come on, let's go for a walk."

"Walk?" Astrid asked.

"Uh-huh."

I grabbed our coats then led her from the room toward the back of the house.

"Where are we going?"

"Not far."

I paused at the door, helping her into her coat. For a moment her body grazed up against mine, her silky hair brushing against the back of my hands.

Kiss her.

Astrid pulled away turning around to face me.

"Outside? It's freezing."

"Yeah, but we need to clear our heads. We can only flow for so long."

I pulled my own jacket on then opened the back doors leading Astrid out onto the deck.

"It's windy!" She yelled; her words snatched by the gale.

"It's perfect! Come on!" I clutched her hands, pulling her down the short staircase and onto the private beach.

"What are we doing?" Astrid yelled, her hair whipping wildly about her.

"Screaming!" I tipped my head back, raised our joined hands, and let out a belly-deep roar, all the tension draining from me.

Astrid laughed, squeezing my hands. "You're crazy."

"Give it a go. It works. Promise!"

She sent me a laughing look then tilted her head back, closed her eyes, and let out a holler that would have made her Viking ancestors proud.

"Better?" I asked as she dropped our hands.

"Actually yeah."

Her cheeks were flushed, her nose beginning to redden, but her grin reached her eyes, their twinkle igniting an answering spark in me.

I grinned. "Again?"

"Let's do it."

With that, we tilted our heads back, raised our hands, and screamed our stresses to the dark winter sky.

If only my overwhelming attraction could be so easily dispersed.

Chapter Eight

Astrid

It had taken me less than three days to brush off any hero-worship I might have held for Robbie. Over the past two weeks, I'd come to learn that he was a funny, charming but absolutely human individual.

He didn't like when his pencils weren't sharp. He hated all types of Jack cheese and green peppers (though he called them capsicum). He declared that his favorite movie ever was *The Princess Bride* and he'd fight anyone who called it a chick-flick. He loved dogs and felt neutral towards cats. He was allergic to papaya and loved to hum pop music under his breath when he concentrated.

And somehow, knowing all this made me like him even more. These facts, these simple quirks that made up the complex being that was Robbie, had turned me from an admirer into a friend.

And yet you hope for more.

I sighed as I scanned yet another book into the system for yet another customer who was too frazzled by Christmas to be interested in maintaining a modicum of politeness.

I want to kiss the living daylights out of him.

I both loved and hated that I wanted to kiss Robbie. He was a Good Guy (capitals included). He made me laugh, talked me through writer's block and had become a fixture at our family dinners. He helped Mom in the kitchen, chatted about true crime podcasts with Nan, bemoaned politics with Dad, played with my nephews, teased Liv, discussed books with Rune, asked Gabby and Erik for sailing tips, and shared wine suggestions with Ian. He'd even met Gunnar and Ella via a video call. Ella– predictably—had flipped out.

It was as if he had been the missing piece in our jigsaw of a family. He fit. Perfectly.

And yet...

I wasn't sure if we had chemistry. Oh, sure, sometimes he'd look at me and there'd be a spark, a little flash of possibility.

And then it'd be gone. Vanishing so quickly I had to wonder if I imagined it.

"Here you go." I handed the bag to the customer offering him a smile. "Happy Holidays!"

He snatched the bag, ticking off something on his list before pivoting to leave, not even acknowledging my existence.

"Bah humbug," I muttered, rolling my eyes.

"I'd believe you if it weren't for that monstrosity of a cardigan."

I twisted, smiling in delight at Robbie. "What are you doing here?"

He pushed off the shelf he'd been leaning on, a coffee in each hand. "Waiting for you to be free. I wanted to run something past you."

He handed me the to-go cup and I inhaled gratefully, enjoying the soothing scent of vanilla and rich dark blend.

"How did you know I'd need this? Are you a hero in disguise?"

He laughed, nodding. "Yep, call me Coffee Man. Here to deliver beans to those in need."

I couldn't help but appreciate his smile, his easy laugh, and his good humor.

God, just kill him already. Anything is better than this weird purgatory between love, lust, and the friendzone.

I shushed Evil Astrid, taking a long sip.

"So about tonight. I was thinking we could storyboard—"

I groaned, pressing a hand to my face and shaking my head. "Robbie, no. Not tonight. I'm wrecked. It's two days before Christmas. I need a break."

"Well… okay. What did you have in mind?"

I peeked at him from between my fingers. "You want to hang out with me?"

He frowned. "Sure. I mean, only if you want me to. I guess Matt and I could organize a movie or—"

"No!" I yelped, leaning forward to squeeze his bicep.

Jesus. He is built!

I cleared my throat. "Let's go to the Christmas markets. I can get some last-minute Christmas gifts, we can watch the tree lighting, listen to carolers, and eat like kings."

His lips curled into a half-smile. "I guess I could do that."

"Guess?" I tilted my head to the side. "Can't muster any excitement?"

"Oh, I'd say I'm pretty thrilled to be spending time with my girlfriend."

I froze, then laughed, forcing myself to relax even as a little pang of hurt speared my insides. "Ah yes, the old girlfriend schtick. We should really kill that before someone thinks

484

we mean it for real."

Robbie watched me for a moment, his gaze turning thoughtful. "Astrid, what if—"

"Excuse me? Do you work here?"

I sighed, stepping back from Robbie and turning to the waiting customer. "I do. How can I help?"

Out of the corner of my eye, I caught Robbie watching me, a strange expression on his face.

Seriously. Just kill him. The man is obviously clueless and we don't need that kind of negativity in our life.

I took another sip of coffee then put him from my mind, focusing entirely on the customer and their search for the perfect book.

* * *

"Okay, I concede," Robbie said, laughing as he took a bite of flammkuchen. "This is delicious."

"I told you!" I bumped my hip into his, grinning as I lifted my own slice of the delightful flatbread pizza-not-pizza to my lips. "Best part of Christmas is the food."

"Hor-ry schit!" Robbie yelped around a mouthful of meat and cheese. "Cuprul gumpers!"

I choked on my bite, snorting as I tried to swallow. "What did you say?"

Robbie caught my hand, dragging me across the square. "Couples jumpers!"

Jumpers?

I caught sight of the ugly sweaters displayed in the stall, laughing. "Really?"

"Yep." He began to peruse the options on hand as he held

the remaining flammkuchen out for me to take. "You want the last piece?"

"Sure." I chewed, amused by his clear delight as he pulled sweater after sweater free, considering it then discarding it with a sigh.

"What are you looking for?" I asked, discarding our garbage in a nearby trash can.

"Something we can wear to Christmas with your family."

"What?"

He held up a sweater pursing his lips together in a ridiculously attractive pout before discarding it. "Your mum invited me."

I love the way he says Mom.

"I've never had a big family Christmas. She said to wear an ugly sweater so I figured I should embrace a couple's theme." He glanced my way looking pointedly at my sweater which read *I'm sexy and I snow it* with a snowman waving.

I giggled, coming up beside him to begin flicking through the rack. "Oh, what about this set?"

The two sweaters read, *I'm naughty* and *I'm nice*, each in either green or red.

"Nope, not special enough." He pulled a shirt combo free holding it out to me. "Thoughts?"

"Star Wars Christmas? Amateur. We can totally do better."

We both turned back to the rack, our hands brushing as we reached for the same sweater set. For a moment our gaze caught, our hands hovering in place, the heat from his skin warming mine.

Behind us Matt coughed, breaking the moment. With an awkward shift I moved back, giving Robbie space.

"What on earth…?" Robbie pulled the sweater free and we

both erupted into laughter, catching each other's eye and laughing harder.

As we settled down, Robbie glanced Matt's way. "There are three options here. Do you think...?"

I doubled over, my laughter returning with a vengeance as tears streamed down my face. "Oh my God, yes! A hundred percent yes!"

The stall owner, sensing a sale, rushed over. "We can personalize them in less than thirty minutes."

"Sold!" Robbie declared, reaching for his wallet. "One of these two, and this one with both on it, please." He nodded towards Matt who stood outside the stall watching the crowded marketplace closely. "The extra one is for him."

"I just need your sizes and a photo of your face and I'll have it all ready in a short while."

We took each other's photo, giggling so hard that we barely managed to take the image.

"He's going to hate you," I commented as we stumbled out of the stall and down the street.

"Oh, I know." Robbie rubbed his hands together gleefully. "I can't wait."

My sweater featured an elf with Robbie's face hanging a stocking above a fireplace framed by the words, *Well Hung.* Robbie's shirt was likewise my face would be transposed on Mrs. Claus as she pole danced around a candy cane with the words, *Santa's Favorite Ho* floating about it.

Matt's shirt featured both our faces dressed as Christmas elves hugging each other and the words *When I think about you, I touch my elf.*

Honestly, the best!

"Should we get some cider while we wait?" Robbie asked,

glancing around.

"No, let's go ice skating." I shot him a grin. "You *do* ice skate, right?"

He shook his head. "Nope. But I'll give it a try."

We rented skates, Matt declining to join us.

"You kids have fun. I'll be fine here with my unbruised ass and hot cider."

"Grinch!" I teased, lacing up my skate. "Ready?"

Robbie wobbled awkwardly as he followed me the few steps across to the ice rink.

"It's simple. Just push and glide!" I threw my arms out, gliding across the ice.

"Simple, sure." He muttered, clutching at the sideboard.

"Come on." I held out my hands, wiggling my fingers with a cheeky grin. "I won't let you fall."

"Promises, promises, Astie. And to think I was going to buy you pie."

My heart skipped at the use of my nickname; the flash of desire now as familiar to me as his smile.

"Pie?"

"Mm, you said it was the quickest way to a Larsson woman's heart."

For a moment we stared at each other, something strange and exciting shimmering between us.

"So I did," I murmured, wanting to prolong the moment.

With a deep breath, Robbie let go of the sideboard, pushing away to wobble across to me.

I laughed at his awkward attempt, capturing his hand and holding him steady. "Just hold on to me, I'll pull you around while you get a feel for it."

I'd skated for years, playing hockey during winter. I'd

been the woman's league's top goalie three years in a row. The ice rink didn't scare me.

Robbie death gripped me, his face a wreath of frown lines as he watched my feet slide across the ice.

"I think I got it," he murmured as we rounded the rink a second time.

"Alright, ready? On three. One... two...." I let him go, watching as he pushed his skate against the ice, mimicking my movement. "That's it! Well—"

He slipped, falling heavily with a slap on the ice.

"—done." I winced in sympathy. "Oh, dear."

I couldn't stop giggling as I skated to his side, assisting him to get up.

He groaned, leaning heavily on me. "This is harder than the time I had to learn Romeo and Juliet in a week. Do you know how many freaking thou and dost that includes?"

I snorted, supporting him as he scrambled to his feet, his skates splaying to each side as he tried to brace himself. "Strong core, stand upright, find your balance, and then just... glide." I pushed off, lifting a leg and showing off a little as I glided away from him.

He watched, his face beginning to soften into an amused grin even as his arms shot wide to steady his wobbly balance. "You can totally do one of those spinning things, can't you? Maybe a jump?"

"You mean like this?"

I picked up some speed racing down towards the empty end of the rink, I pushed off the ice leaping into a graceful arch before landing and immediately throwing myself into a fast twist. I finished with a flourish, one hand pointed down behind me, the other raised in the air above my head with a sassy flick of my fingers, shooting him a wink.

Robbie clapped and nearly slipped over again, laughing as his arms windmilled, his legs locking as he shook his head, desperately trying to maintain his balance. "This was a terrible idea!"

"You wanted to do it!" I called as I skated back his way. Out of the corner of my eye I caught sight of a young group of girls staring at us, their gazes narrowed in on Robbie.

Uh-oh. Evil Astrid senses trouble.

Robbie shuffled across to the sideboard, one hand clinging to it as he tried to find his footing.

"I think you have a fan club," I said, tilting my head in the girls' direction.

Robbie slowly raised his head, glancing their way then swearing when they saw him look, their phones immediately coming out to snap pictures.

"Fuck. Astrid, sorry, but... we gotta go."

"What? Why?"

Matt appeared on the other side of the sideboard. "Robbie, we—"

"I saw. Let's motor."

"Wait. What's happening?"

Robbie quickly shuffled off the ice, Matt supporting him back to the bench where we'd stored our shoes.

"What's happening?" I asked as I plonked down on the bench beside him, beginning to unlace my boots. "What did I miss?"

"They're coming." Matt hissed; his gaze trained on the girls now hurrying around the rink. "Hurry!"

"Make sure Astrid's safe," Robbie barked, tugging on his boots. "You get me, Matt? They can't touch her."

"Are they fans?" I asked, utterly bewildered. "Why do we need to—"

"OH MY GOD! IT'S ROBBIE HUYNH!"

My head snapped up, my eyes widening as I saw the cluster of girls now scrambling through the crowd to get to us.

I managed to pull my boots on just as Matt hauled us both up, shoving us in the opposite direction to the oncoming cluster. The festive mood of the crowd shifted as people began to look our way, their eyes widening, their expressions turning into something like adoration mixed with selfish desire.

Shit. Was I like that the first time I met Robbie?

"Fuck. Go!" Matt hissed, shoving us deeper into the crowd. "Hurry."

We scrambled, pushing our way through the crowd and back into the main market.

"Robbie! Robbie!" The girls screaming had drawn attention and as people registered that a world-famous movie star was in their midst, they turned rabid.

"Oh my God!"

"Wait! I want a selfie!"

Word spread faster than we could move, the crowd now snatching at him as we tried to leave.

Holy shit. This is how people die. This is how I could die. Oh my God!

I began to throw my elbows as Matt attempted to bodily plow us through the crowd, his expression deadly.

"We gotta get out of here!" Robbie yelled. "Astrid's gonna get hurt."

"You're gonna get fucking hurt," Matt barked, his gaze scanning for options. "There! Head for the toilets. We'll loop around the back and out to the main street."

I caught a flash of a familiar blond head towering far above the crowd.

"Wait! It's Rune!" I snatched Robbie's hand, pulling him along behind me, Matt swearing but following as we headed towards my giant of a brother "Rune! Wait! Rune!"

My brother, his arm slung snuggly around Gabby, her arm around his waist, turned to stare at us as we emerged from the crowd.

"Astie? What are you guys—"

"No time! Can we borrow your car?"

"Why—"

"There he is! Over there!" A shrill female voice squealed followed by a cacophony of screaming.

"Quick!" I bounced on my toes, panic, and no small amount of fear injecting adrenaline in my veins.

Rune fumbled in his pocket holding the keys out. "We're parked at the store."

"Go!" Matt bellowed behind us. "Run!"

Hand-in-hand Robbie and I sprinted through the market, dodging shoppers and couples, nearly taking out a family with triplets.

"They're gaining!" I panted, chancing a glance over my shoulder.

"Down here!" Robbie pulled me into a small alley, Matt at our back. We dashed down it, squeezing through the tiny gap between the buildings, my hand clasped tightly in Robbie's.

"Go!" Matt called. "I'll slow them!"

The alley spewed us out onto the main street, the crowds sparse compared to that at the market.

"Which way?" Robbie asked, glancing this way and that.

"Towards the store, this way!"

Hand-in-hand we sprinted down the street, rounding a corner and making a mad dash toward the safety of The Literary Academy.

As we got close, I spied Ashley, the assistant store manager, closing up.

"Ash!" I yelled, my lungs burning. "Ashley! Open it!"

She turned; her eyes wide as she stared at us barreling down on her.

Without a word she stepped aside, holding the door open for us to rush through then closing it behind us with a click.

"You got keys?" She yelled through the thick door as she locked it from the other side.

"Yes," I replied, my voice sounding more like an asthmatic wheeze than a reply.

"Okay! You kids have a good night." We heard her move, her footsteps crunching on the gravel outside leaving us in the dark bookstore.

Robbie bent over, bracing his hands on his knees as he sucked in a breath. "Fuck."

I huffed out a laugh, bracing my hands on my hips and tipping my head back to suck in air. "What the fuck, Robbie?"

"I know."

He groaned, pushing to a stand, somehow his breathing settling into a normal rhythm. The man didn't even look sweaty. Bastard.

"It's unfortunately not that uncommon."

"We lost Matt."

He huffed out a laugh. "You might have missed it, but the man sacrificed himself for us. He likely bodily blocked those

493

girls at the alley to allow us time to get away."

I shook my head. "Your life is insane."

"I know."

His phone chirped and he pulled it out checking the message.

"Matt's safe. Said to stay put. The girls are roaming the streets. He'll come by in an hour or so when it's all clear."

I shivered, wrapping arms around myself. "What do you think they'd have done if they got you?"

He shrugged off his coat, tossing it over a chair then rolled back the arm of one sleeve baring his bicep.

Oh Lordy, I'm turning into a desperado. Has a bicep ever invoked such lust? I feel like I should be bearing an ankle in return. Shit, am I in a period drama?

He raised a finger tapping a faint scar on his bicep. "Last year I got caught in an airport toilet." He dropped his hands reaching for his shirt and lifting it to just below his nipples. He twisted slightly, showing me a thick welt on his right side.

"Three months ago, I tried to see a movie like a normal person. Big mistake. I lost two fistfuls of hair and ended the night with three stitches."

Unbidden, my hand lifted, my fingers reaching out to trail just below the healing wound.

Robbie sucked in a breath stilling under my hand.

For a moment neither of us spoke, just watched as my fingers moved across his dark skin.

"Astrid…." My name sounded like a plea on his lips.

I raised my head, my eyes meeting his. Our gazes clashed, desire erupting between us. Our bodies shifted and in less than a heartbeat he had me clasped to him, his hands fisted in my hair, his mouth a breath from mine.

"Astrid... I...."

I pressed forward unable to stand being separate from him. I needed his taste on my lips and his breath in my lungs.

I needed him.

Moisture pooled between my legs, my body instinctively responding to his.

He murmured my name then bent, boosting me up and stepping forward until my back hit the bookshelf behind me.

Oh, this boy is trouble.

Chapter Nine

Robbie

I'd wanted Astrid since the moment I'd seen her all those weeks ago at Thanksgiving. I could admit that now as I tasted her mouth, committing this moment to memory.

I forced myself to pull back, my hands to drop to the edge of her sweater.

"Can I….?"

She nodded, her lips swollen from our kiss, her eyes glazed with desire. My cock throbbed, desperate to feel her wet heat around me.

I pushed her coat off letting it pool on the ground. With deliberate slowness I tortured us both, gently lifting her cardigan to reveal soft creamy skin. Up and up, I pulled the material, her arms raising to allow me to pull it off and toss it aside. Before I'd even fully removed it, my lips found hers, desperate for another taste. Another kiss. Another stolen moment.

Perfection.

With a groan I pulled back, taking her in. Her full breasts were encased in black lace, her abundant curves making my mouth water as she kicked her boots off.

I ripped my shirt free then dropped my hands to her fly, fumbling with the zipper as her hands reached out to clasp my hips, holding us steady.

"You okay?" I whispered as I began to push her jeans down, wiggling the material over her hips and thighs, crouching to pull it down her legs and clear of her feet.

"Oh, I'm getting there."

I chuckled, the sound like gravel as I sucked in a breath, catching her scent.

God have mercy.

I slipped her jeans free, cupping her socked feet, smiling at the reindeer faces on the toes. "You want these on or off?"

"On. I don't want to kill you with my cold feet."

I grinned, sliding fingers slowly up her legs until I found the bottom of her boyshort underwear. "What about these?"

She bit her lip, her body flushed with desire.

"Off."

Heat sizzled my blood as my fingers turned clumsy, fumbling with the material. I finally tugged her underwear free, the material gratifyingly soaked with her need.

Astrid stepped free and I brought the fabric to my face breathing deep.

"Robbie what—"

I caught her startled gaze, knowing mine was fierce. "You smell divine."

She shuddered, her hips undulating towards me.

I lifted up to press kisses across her hip bones, pausing above her mound, her curls tickling my chin. "You okay if I taste you?"

"You going to ask me every time you want to touch me?"

She asked, her eyelids closed, her head tipped back as a cute smile touched her lips.

"Consent is sexy."

"Mm… well, I consent to anything and everything you want to do."

Thank God.

I dipped my head, my fingers parting her, revealing her tender flesh to my gaze.

"Fucking gorgeous."

I leaned in, breathing over the sensitive skin, grinning when her hands dropped to my shoulders, her nails leaving crescent shaped marks in my flesh.

I flicked out my tongue, closing my eyes as I savored the first glorious taste of her.

"Fucking fuck, Astie. You taste fucking amazing."

"Don't stop," she cried, her hands fisting my hair to pull me back to her. "Keep going!"

"Stop?" I chuckled, allowing her to press me back to her core. "Never."

Not even a million orcs could distract me from this moment.

I teased her with tongue and lips, carefully grazing my teeth across her sensitive skin, loving her breathy moans and startled gasps.

I dropped one hand, unzipping my jeans and shoving them down my hips far enough to pull my cock free, fisting myself roughly as I ate Astrid out.

I focused in on her clit, learning what made her sigh and whimper, what had her clenching and clutching at me, her sweet begging sending my own need soaring.

I found a rhythm, my tongue worshipping her clit. I lifted my spare hand to press a finger against her, filling her greedy body.

With a cry, Astrid arched, riding my face with wild abandon. No longer in control, I gave over, loving how she used me to reach for her pleasure, loving how she came in a hot, wet clench of lusty need.

"Robbie!"

I grinned, surging to my feet, immediately unbuckling her bra, replacing the cups with my hands.

"You come so prettily, Astie." I leaned down to blow air across her nipples. "Could you come just from me playing with these pretty breasts?"

She whimpered, her eyes wide as she watched me close the gap, my mouth suckling. My shaft pressed against her, trapped in the cradle of her thighs, throbbing with the need to fill her.

Patience.

I lifted my head, replacing my tongue with my fingers as I turned to her other breast, giving it the same dedicated attention.

Her head fell back against the bookshelf, books falling around us.

"I want to taste you," she murmured, her hips grinding against me. "Please, Robbie."

"Mm?" I lifted my head, capturing her lips, my tongue tangling with hers.

We kissed, hard and desperate, my thumbs raking over her nipples as we ravished each other's mouth.

Don't come. Don't come. Don't fucking come.

I pulled her into my arms, hauling us across the space and down into the maze of bookshelves, the dark of the store enveloping us.

"Robbie!"

I found a small study nook, complete with a desk.

Perfect.

With one last stagger, I stumbled us across to the desk, boosting Astrid onto it and positioning her until I was cradled between her legs, her breasts pressed deliciously against me.

She leaned in, her teeth nipping at my collarbone and I cursed, shoving my jeans down my legs, my cock jutting proudly as she squeezed me with her thighs.

She shifted, licking her way down to my nipples, nipping at the sensitive flesh, a hard groan ripping from my throat.

"You little minx." I fisted her hair, tilting her head back to ravish her mouth. She squirmed against me, her hands snaking between us to clasp my cock.

Danger, Will Robinson, danger!

I continued to kiss her, loathed to pull back as her fingers curled around my thick erection, her hands pumping my cock slow and tight, precum beading at the tip. Her thumb flicked out, capturing the moisture and using it to ease her glide.

My body arched closer, my cock throbbing at her ministrations.

I reached down, capturing her hand, pulling back just enough to caution her.

"Not yet. Keep going and it'll be over far too soon."

Her eyes flashed but she withdrew her hand. With deliberate provocation, she drew her fingers to her lips, licking away any remaining precum.

Holy fucking Christ. This woman is....

I swore, pulling her back into me, forcing my tongue

between her lips, fucking her mouth.

A strangled moan escaped Astrid and I swallowed it, letting it feed me.

"Your fucking mouth," I whispered, beginning to pepper kisses along her cheeks, down her throat, across her collarbone.

I love this woman. Fuck, I love her.

The revelation didn't startle me. The feeling had been building for weeks. Oh, I knew it was far too soon. Knew people would say it couldn't possibly be love.

But I knew the truth. Deep in my soul, the knowledge took root, immediately flowering.

Astrid was everything I'd ever wanted. Cheeky and kind. Fun and serious. Desirable and delightful. I wanted to spend every moment with her. Every part of her fit every part of me.

I love her.

"Robbie…." Her needy little moan set me off.

I fisted my cock, guiding it to her core, arching back slightly to watch as the head of my cock bridged her sex, beginning to stretch her as I eased inside.

"Oh, God. Oh, fuck. Oh, my fucking God!"

Her cries fueled the fire in me, her liquid heat and tight, clutching pussy now defined paradise.

I thrust, my eyes practically rolling back in my head as her muscles stretched, working to accommodate my width. I may not have been the longest guy in the world, but I had most beat on thickness.

"So big, so big, so big," Astrid's chant had me chuckling.

"Just for you," I whispered against the shell of her ear. "You okay there, Astie?"

"I…." her voice lost power while her hands roamed my skin as if unsure of where to land.

"Hold on, minx. I got you."

She linked her arms around my neck, and arched her hips, a gasp tearing free as I fed her more of my cock.

"That's it. Take me, Astie."

I stroked deeper inside her, groaning as her body clutched at my cock.

"More, more, more, more!"

"More? Such a greedy girl," I praised.

I pulled back then thrust in hard, loving how her body bowed against me, her head falling back, her sweet little cunt holding me tight.

Reality fell away, any memory of the close shave from early disappeared as I gave myself over to Astrid.

I want to brand her. Mark her. Prove to the world that she's mine.

My cock throbbed, my balls drawing up as my climax began to bear down on me.

Don't come. Don't come. Don't come.

Astrid screamed, her body breaking, her little cunt spasming as her orgasm shattered her into a million pieces.

Yes!

I erupted, fucking her into the desk, my cock pounding into her clutching flesh.

I had a mind to pull out a fraction before I came, cum coating her curvy belly and generous tits.

Fuck yes!

Without thinking, giving in to some mindless, primal instinct, I scoped a finger of cum then reached down, rubbing it against her clit, playing with her sensitive flesh.

502

"Robbie!"

With a dark huff, I continued to stroke her body until Astrid came in a screaming, begging, panting wet mess, collapsing back on the desk, her hand reaching down to still my fingers.

"Good?" I asked, pressing light kisses to her skin.

"I think you killed me."

I chuckled, the raging desire subsiding. "But what a way to die, hm?"

She opened one eyelid giving me a droll glare. "That's not going in the script."

"Oh, I never doubted it."

We smiled, our passion cooling, our bodies completely sated. I found this, this moment where I took care of her and we giggled and cuddled after amazing sex, this is what I wanted for the rest of my life.

Sex was great but Astrid? She was what made each moment magnificent. I'd forever choose this woman above all others.

Thank God you don't have to choose.

I opened my mouth, about to declare my undying love when she snapped up to a seat, her eyes wide.

"Oh no! Robbie! Our sweaters!"

I chuckled, rolling my eyes as she pushed past me, scrambling for her clothes.

"I see ugly sweaters get more attention than me."

She rolled her eyes, pulling on her bra. "You did great. I am thoroughly, and I mean this, satisfied. But ugly Christmas sweaters are a Larsson tradition. And it's your first Christmas with us. We *need* to get yours."

I paused one leg half in my jeans. "Sorry, did you say, *first*

Christmas?"

She froze her arms in her sweater. "Um... is that too presumptuous?"

I dropped my jeans, closing the distance between us to cup her head, staring into her gorgeous eyes.

"Presume away. I'm definitely not going anywhere. This?" I pressed into her. "You are too amazing by half. I'm not letting you get away."

She melted, her body sinking into mine, her hand coming up to lay over my heart.

"Robbie."

I bent, kissing her, loving the way my name tasted on her lips.

As Jerry McGuire said, she completes me.

Chapter Ten

Astrid

I pulled the ribbon on the gift box tight, repositioning the tag until it sat just-so then slid it under the tree.

"Ready?" Mom asked, placing a plate of cookies on the coffee table.

"Yep."

She leaned over, brushing a stray hair from my cheek before sitting down beside me, leaning into my side. "Astie, I owe you an apology."

I started, my head swiveling to stare at my mother. "Sorry?"

She smiled, her expression melancholy. "You're my baby. Oh, not in age but we all know Rune was never a child. That boy came out a forty-year-old man. You though? You were my sweet baby girl, the one I never had to worry about—unlike your siblings."

She sighed, reaching out to cup my face. "And then you returned from college a strange being. Secretive, changing your appearance, no longer my bright, shiny daughter. I worried." Her thumb grazed my cheek, a gentle smile touching her lips. "And now I see what happened. You tried to please us instead of following your own path. My beautiful girl, this life you're making? It's exactly who you were always meant to be. Brown hair or blonde, you are finally living. And it delights me that your shine is back."

Tears blurred my vision. "Ma…."

"I love you, my dearest Astrid. We're so proud of you."

She leaned forward pressing a kiss to my forehead.

"I love you, Ma."

She smiled. "Good. And now, tell me about your Robbie. Is it serious?"

I bit my lip, a flush heating my cheeks as I nodded.

"Mm, a mother always knows. Don't be afraid. If he makes you happy, don't wait."

"We've only known each other a short time."

"You know my feelings about time." She squeezed my hand. "Your soul knows when it has found its other half. Don't question it. Embrace."

My parents had married less than three hours after meeting, they'd just known. And five kids, and nearly fifty years later they still had the most beautiful love.

I nodded, reaching out to wrap my arms around her, hugging her tight.

"Oh, sorry."

We both twisted from our seat on the carpet, catching sight of Robbie as he retreated from the room.

"Nonsense!" Ma called, stopping him with a wave. "Come in, come in!" She pushed up with a heavy groan, throwing me a laughing eye-roll. "These old bones ain't what they used to be."

As I pulled myself together, Ma greeted Robbie, patting

him on the cheek and giving him a motherly hug.

"Go on in, our little Astie has something for you."

I watched him stroll across the lounge, his body loose and relaxed, his chest clad in the sweater that matched mine.

I made love to that man last night. And the day before. And the day before that.

In fact, I'd made love to Robbie every day and night since we'd lost control on the desk in The Literary Academy. Surrounded by books and quiet, that moment would forever be etched on my soul.

I love him. Completely. Crazily. Irrationally. I. Love. Him.

He eased down onto the carpet, crossing his legs and offering me a lopsided grin. "Well, hello, gorgeous." He leaned across, pressing a lingering kiss to my lips.

"Hey yourself." My stomach fluttered even as the pleasure of being in his space relaxed me. "I have something for you."

"Oh really? Is it a knife?"

I grinned, shooting him a wink. "Maybe. Open it."

"Uh-uh." He shook his head, shrugging a backpack off and pulling it around to unzip it. "You first."

From its depth, he withdrew a soft, flat package handing it over.

"Is this another sweater?" I laughed as I took the package.

"Open it and see."

I ripped into it finding two sweaters, both with the same writing. I lifted the soft fabric free of the wrapping, reading the cursive on the front.

Our First Christmas as Mr. and Mrs.

Under the writing were pictures of pies.

I stared at the fabric, desperately trying not to put two and two together and come up with a marriage proposal.

"Sorry, what?"

He huffed out a nervous laugh. "You said pies were the way to a Larsson woman's heart so…." He cleared his throat, his gaze serious and intense. "Will you marry me, Astrid?"

I gapped at him, shock rendering me completely dumb. A moment of silence followed his declaration.

"It doesn't have to be today," he rushed to add, filling the silence I'd left. "Fuck. It's too soon, right? Shit. Look, it doesn't have to be a proposal or anything… I mean… unless you want it to be. That is to say… um… I just…" He ran a hand through his hair, the strands sticking up at odd angles.

"You just?" I asked, my heart in my throat, giddy joy unfurling.

"I just think you're wonderful, Astrid. Completely amazing. Honestly, you're everything. You delight me, frighten me, your mind is a freaking scary-wonderful place. I love listening to you laugh. I love holding you. I love kissing you. I love you. I know it's way too fast and this is completely irrational but—"

I threw myself at him, knocking us both backward and into the coffee table.

"Oof! What are you—"

I covered his mouth with mine putting all my passion and feeling into our kiss.

His mouth opened, our tongues tangling, hands urgently tugging at each other's clothing.

"Yes!" I cried against him as I pulled back, rocking up to rip his sweater from his body. "A million times, yes!"

"Yes? What are you—Oh! Astrid! Robbie! What are you doing?" My mother's startled cry had us freezing, our heads twisting to stare at her in shock.

Oh, that's right. It's Christmas Day, you're at your parents' house, you just got engaged to a freaking movie star, and your mother just walked in on you trying to strip your fiancé naked.

Shit, I need a distraction!

"Robbie and I are getting married!" I squeaked.

My mother's face morphed from horrified to ecstatic in less than a heartbeat.

"Oh my God! He said yes!"

She surged forward dropping to her knees to wrap us both in a hug.

Under me, I could feel Robbie's thick erection immediately droop, the poor guy looked mortified as my mother practically strangled him.

"What's going on?" my father asked from the doorway.

"Sune! They're getting married!"

Robbie shot me a startled look and I laughed, leaning in to kiss him.

Behind us the family began celebrating as the news moved through the house, cries of delight coming from the kitchen and dining room.

"I love you."

"So, it's a definite yes?" he asked his adorable grin in place.

"Sure," I leaned back giving him a saucy wink. "But I look forward to seeing the terms of the contract first."

He threw back his head, laughter spilling free.

My phone dinged and I pulled it free, laughing when I saw the notification for family chat.

Liv added Robbie to group chat.

Ella: Oh! I take it they're serious?

Gunnar: Should someone warn him?

Erik: Nah. He got the craziest one of us all. I think he'll be fine.

I lifted the phone, snapping a selfie of us then sending it through. "Welcome to the family. You're official now."

He smiled, pressing his forehead against mine. "There's honestly nowhere I'd rather be."

It wasn't until later that night that I finally got to hand Robbie my gift.

With bated breath, I watched from the end of the bed as he untied the ribbon and lifted the lid on the box. The silk pooled across his chest, giving me all sorts of naughty ideas.

Is a ribbon strong enough to use as a handcuff?

"Astrid…." He lifted the bound screenplay free from the box, running a finger along the cover. "This is…."

"For you." I reached out, capturing his hand, tangling our fingers. "And for me. Writing this has given me the greatest pleasure of my life. This is the path I want to take. And I want to share it with you. Open it."

I let go of his hand watching as he opened the cover to the first page.

Dear Robbie,

How about we make this official?

Marry me?

Astrid

He looked up, his gaze electric.

"I know I'm late," I gave him a lopsided grin. "But it's nice to know we're on the same page."

He surged up, the screenplay forgotten as he wrapped arms around me, pushing me back down on the bed, his body covering mine. "I fucking love you."

"To quote Han Solo," I grinned, running my thumb across his lips. "I know."

And we spent the rest of the night consummating that love.

Epilogue One

Robbie

I looped an arm over Astrid's chair, gratified when she leaned into me, needing the reassurance only she could offer.

"Nervous?" She asked in a whisper.

"Fucking terrified," I admitted with a laugh, my spare hand digging into my jacket pocket to thumb the glasses tucked safely inside.

She cupped my cheek, pressing a kiss to my chin. "You've got this, Robert Huynh. This is your moment."

On the stage above us, the actress smiled prettily as the cameras zoomed in.

"These five actors have awarded moviegoers with truly magnificent stories. They touched our hearts, ravished our minds, and thrilled our souls. Tonight's nominees for best actor are," the famous actress paused for dramatic effect before rattling off the names of my fellow actors, leaving me to last.

Astrid's hand found mine, giving me a squeeze.

"And Robert Huynh, *Shadow Lies.*"

The audience applauded as the highlight reel played, a

hush falling as it ended.

"And the Oscar goes to…." The actress opened the envelope. "Robert Huynh, *Shadow Lies!*"

Astrid shrieked, throwing herself on me, pressing a frantic kiss to my lips.

"Go!" She ordered, dropping back in her seat. "Go accept your award!"

In stunned disbelief I walked up the aisle, accepting handshakes and back slaps before hopping up the three stairs to the stage.

The actress shook my hand, kissing my cheek before handing me the award and stepping back.

I turned, seeing a standing ovation as cameras flashed and people shouted praise.

"Wow," I said into the microphone looking down at the award glittering in my hand. "Who would have thought it, hey? Winning an Oscar for killing people."

There was laughter and cheering from the audience.

I looked up, searching the crowd, finding Astrid. "There are so many people to thank for this amazing award. Firstly, thank you to the academy for this privilege."

I looked around, finding my agent, my director, and my producer in the crowd.

"To Liv Larsson-Campbell from Freya Productions, thanks for taking a chance on me and this script. I know it was a risk but I think we can both agree it paid off."

Liv laughed, blowing me a kiss, Ian standing proudly beside her.

"To Glenn, my agent, and his entire crew. Thank you for your support over the years. I wouldn't be here if you hadn't taken on a punk-ass kid from Australia."

Glenn grinned, shooting me a thumbs up.

"To all the cast and crew who worked on *Shadow Lies* this film wouldn't have been half as amazing without you. To Beatrix Bennett, my amazing colleague, and partner in crime, who brought this phenomenal story to life, and Samuel Archer, who took the script and our vision and directed the shit out of it, and to everyone who worked on *Shadow Lies*, this award is as much yours as it is mine."

Applause and more cheers. My co-star giving a little bow in my direction.

"To everyone who has helped on this journey; my family, my friends, my teachers, and colleagues, and a million other people. Thank you for keeping me humble and lifting me up. For telling me that I could do this even when I thought it wasn't possible."

I sucked in a breath, meeting Astrid's gaze, smiling at the tears sliding unashamedly down her cheeks.

"And to the woman who made this all possible, Astrid Larsson, my gorgeous wife. Thank you for saying no a hundred-and-five times before finally trusting me with this story. It just made me work a hundred-and-six times harder to ensure this was the best movie it could be."

There was laughter at that, Astrid blowing me an air kiss. I held up the Oscar, holding it out towards her.

"This is yours, Astie. The script you wrote, the chance you took, the love and terror you built into each and every scene, you are phenomenal, you are brilliant, and you terrify me and delight me each and every day. We said dream big, we said we were aiming for the best, we said we wanted nothing but perfection." I placed one hand over my heart. "Well, we did it, Astie. *You* did it. I love you," I paused dramatically.

"And I just want everyone watching to know that if I ever go missing don't bother looking—my wife knows how to hide a body."

Another round of laughter and applause as I looked back at the audience. "Thank you, and good night."

I stepped away from the podium, following the ushers as they led me from the stage.

"Can someone get my wife, please? I want to share this with her."

One of them scurried off as they took me through to the green room, a makeup artist hurrying over to do a final touch up before I headed into the press area.

Questions were thrown thick and fast, cameras popping until all I could see were squiggles of light.

Questions done, my publicist ushered me through to a small room where Astrid stood waiting, her own Oscar clutched in her hand.

"You won!" She squealed, throwing herself at me.

"I can't believe it. *Shadow Lies* is cleaning up."

"We have to hurry; they're announcing Best Motion Picture."

We scurried outside, thankful for the slight break in commercial filming.

Shadow Lies had won multiple awards prior to tonight, raking in BAFTAs, Golden Globes, and Film Critic awards. But tonight we were cleaning up, Best Director, Best Actor, Best Screenplay. We'd missed out on Best Actress and I honestly felt that Beatrix had been robbed. There was only Best Motion Picture to go.

Shadow Lies had rocked the box office, cashing in staggering figures its first weekend and every weekend after.

We were a runaway hit, and Astrid deserved every piece of praise.

We hurried to our seats, accepting congratulations along the way, shooting friends and family air high-fives and kisses across the room.

"And the nominees are...."

I gripped her hand, clutching Astrid close.

"It's okay, we're still amazing even if we don't win," Astrid whispered, her fingers squeezing mine. "I'll still love you tomorrow."

I chuckled, pressing a kiss to her temple. "But perhaps a little less?"

She grinned, teasing me. "Only a fraction. But there's always next time."

Our attention was drawn back to the stage.

"And the Oscar goes to...."

Epilogue Two

Astrid

I pushed back from my desk, tossing the antlers next to my laptop and standing with a groan, my hands immediately dropping to press into my lower back.

"Hey, you okay?"

Robbie's hands gently brushed my own away, his thumbs digging into the tight muscles of my lower back as he massaged the stubborn knots. He pushed me forward slowly until I was bent at my hips, my hands braced on the desk, giving him ready access to my back.

"Mm, I am now." I muttered.

He chuckled, leaning forward to press a kiss to my neck as his fingers continued to work my tight back.

"It's done," I said, my eyes drifting closed as I turned into putty under his hands. "Needs some spit and polish but it's done."

His fingers halted, his body freezing. "What?"

I twisted my neck, looking at him over my shoulder. "*Turn Around*. It's done. You want to read it?"

He swallowed; I could see the indecision on his face.

With a soft huff of amusement, I pushed away from the desk, patting him on the shoulder. "Go on. I'll have a nap while you read."

"I love you!" He called as he took my abandoned seat.

"Oh, I know. That's why you're totally taking me out for dinner tonight."

"Your wish, my command."

I woke hours later, feeling refreshed and less like a woman on a deadline.

I stepped into the shower, determined to rid myself of the swamp monster feel on my skin. Robbie entered his naked body immediately embraced by the steam and water.

"Mm, hello," I whispered, my hands coming up to run over his muscular chest. "I didn't think you'd be joining me, Mr. Huynh."

"Well, Mrs. Larsson-Huynh, it appears that I'm in the mood for some nookie." He nuzzled my neck, his lips grazing the sensitive skin. "And I just finished."

I braced, ready to take on his feedback. "Go on then, what did you think?"

"Three words – Best Motion Picture."

I laughed, tossing my wet hair away. "You're still chasing that award?"

"Ah, reality check, Astie. You deserve a clean sweep. You were robbed last time. You deserved to get Best Motion Picture. This movie? It's gonna be the one that has you crossing off every award on the list—I'm telling you, Best Actress, Best Screenplay, Motion Picture, Actor, Director, all of them. I can *feel* it."

His hands drifted down, cupping my gently rounding stomach. "But we'll wait till after this one comes."

I laughed, leaning against him, letting Robbie hold me as water ran over our skin, heating us. "Do you ever worry that he'll be some kind of psychopath? What with you being an actor and me having the brain of a serial killer?"

"She." He corrected, both of us still locked in a battle of wills. "And babe, you wear holiday-themed underwear year-round. Last Christmas you dressed as an elf for three days. Our daughter never had a chance."

With that, he kissed me, deliciously, toe-curlingly, deep and slow.

"Mm," he murmured against my lips. "Love you, Astie."

"Love you too, Robbie."

"Bed or desk?"

"Both?"

He chuckled, his hands running down my back to cup my ass. "Perfect."

Dear Greedy Reader

I hope you fell in love with the Larsson siblings.

This family started with Gunnar (who also starts the
Capricorn Cove series), and before I knew it Erik was
demanding his story, then Rune, and… you get the idea.
I delighted in telling their stories and falling in love
alongside them.
I really hope you did as well!

Be sure to sign up to my newsletter, follow my Facebook
page, or check out my website for updates on future books.

Thank you, Greedy Reader, for allowing me the privilege of
writing books you want to read.

Until next book!

Cheers,
Evie Mitchell

Connect with Evie Mitchell

Website
www.EvieMitchell.com

Newsletter
https://www.subscribepage.com/z2p2x3

Amazon
https://www.amazon.com/author/eviemitchell

Bookbub, Instagram and Facebook
@EvieMitchellAuthor

Facebook Group
Evie Mitchell's Greedy Reader Book Club

Books by Evie Mitchell

Capricorn Cove Series
Thunder Thighs
Double the D
Muffin Top
The Mrs. Clause
New Year Knew You
The Shake-Up
Double Breasted
As You Wish
Beach Party
You Sleigh Me
Resolution Revolution
Meat Load
Trunk Junk

Archer Series
Just Joshing
He wants Candy
Leave Me Bea
Pride and Joy
Tom and Jeremey

Thor's Shipbuilding Series
Clean Sweep

The X-list
Reality Check
The Christmas Contract

Nameless Souls MC Series
Runner
Wrath
Ghost

Elliot Security Series
Rough Edge
Bleeding Edge
Knife Edge

Other books
Reign Anthology - The Marriage Contract
Puppy Love
Pier Pressure
Bad English

CPSIA information can be obtained
at www.ICGtesting.com
Printed in the USA
BVHW081401120421
604733BV00001B/27